MAPS FOR A MORTAL MOON

MAPS FOR A MORTAL MOON

ESSAYS AND ENTERTAINMENTS

Selected Prose by Adil Jussawalla

Edited and Introduced by
Jerry Pinto

ALEPH

ALEPH BOOK COMPANY
An independent publishing firm
promoted by **Rupa Publications India**

Published in 2014 by
Aleph Book Company
7/16 Ansari Road, Daryaganj
New Delhi 110 002

Copyright © Adil Jussawalla 2014
Introduction Copyright © Jerry Pinto 2014

All rights reserved

No part of this publication may be reproduced,
transmitted, or stored in a retrieval system, in any
form or by any means, without permission in writing
from Aleph Book Company.

ISBN: 978-93-82277-67-5

1 3 5 7 9 10 8 6 4 2

Typeset in Bembo Roman by SÜRYA, New Delhi

Printed and bound in India by Replika Press Pvt. Ltd.

This book is sold subject to the condition that it shall not, by way of trade or otherwise, be lent, resold, hired out, or otherwise circulated without the publisher's prior consent in any form of binding or cover other than that in which it is published and without a similar condition including this condition being imposed on the subsequent purchaser.

CONTENTS

INTRODUCTION   ix
*The Boy Who Wept Because a Bird Did
and Other Adil Jussawallas*

WRITERS

Six Authors in Search of a Reader	3
Introduction to *Fair Tree of the Void* by Vilas Sarang	10
Salman and the Sea of Paper	15
The Civilized Malcontent	18
Aubrey Menen: A Space of His Own	24
Notes towards a Portrait of Nissim Ezekiel	29
With Daya Pawar in Paris	33
Remembering Raman	35
Remembering Sudhir	38

WRITING

The Joy of Sensuous Writing	45
What's This? A New Two-nation Theory?	46
Between Vikram and the Vacuum	49
The Ant in Publishing	52
Who Reads Us?	54
The Book Should Be the Thing	56

READING

C is for Comics	65
Library Memories	67
Who Is My Neighbour?	70
Who Needs Novels?	74

AT HOME

A Glass Too Many	79
Maps for a Mortal Moon	82
In Praise of Straggling	84
The Cuffe Link	86
A Stranger in the Village	90
Dead Man with Butterfly	93
Show Me the Way to Go Home	96
Starting from Scratch	98

TRAVELLING

Sandstorm at Sea	103
Geography Lessons	106
Memories of a Book Fair	108
Letter from Venice	112
Let Sleeping Passports Lie	113
On Fire	116
Toni Morrison, Paris and Me	118
Patterns of Domicile	121
Out of Place	124
A Grave in the Hills	126

BEING HUMAN

Republic of Victims	135
The Heart of Standing Is	137
Part of an Education	139
A Balancing Act	144
The Worst Thing about Being Human	146
Humanist Fires	148

Who Are You Calling Mad?	151
Uprooted	154
Boycott	156
Visibility Zero	158
Incident in Paris	163

PEOPLE

Conversation with an Invisible Man	171
Two Sisters	176
The Gambler	184
The Librarian and the Labyrinth	187
The Many Murders of Datta Samant	192

THE ARTS

Lalitha Lajmi and the Family	197
Souza: A Bitter Parting	199
Naipaul's Fiction and Rembrandt's Goose	202
Candour and Secrecy	204
Make Mine Movies	213
The Showgirl and the Baby	219

MEDIA

The Joys of Xerox	229
The New India, the New Media and Literature	231
Radio Days	241
Death of a Journalist	243
The Folds of an Origami Lotus	245

LANGUAGE

Rainbow of Languages	251

Getting on in English	253
Being There: Aspects of an Indian Crisis	255

POETRY

Preface to *3 Poets*: Silgardo, d'Gama Rose, Rodrigues	269
Small Beginnings	271
Readings with Parrots and Angels	272
Poems after Ayodhya	275
Shut Up, Memory	277

AUTOBIOGRAPHICAL

A Destination of the Heart	283
A Life Presumed Lost	285
A Place in the Sun	294
Black Moon Rising	302
When Earth Rose Up To Get Me	304
Take Me in the Sky of Your Hands	308

JOKES APART

Portrait of a Lady	315
The None O'Clock News	319
Discoveries of India	331
No Reply	334
Acknowledgements	336
Sources	337

INTRODUCTION

The Boy Who Wept Because a Bird Did and Other Adil Jussawallas

'Do you remember that housing development named for Lawrence Bantleman?' Adil Jussawalla asked me one cool morning in November 2012. I felt a twinge of guilt. Jussawalla had once given me a fat file on the almost-forgotten poet of Anglo-Indian origin who wrote for an early influential magazine called *The Century* and P. Lal's literary magazine *Miscellany*. When Bantleman emigrated to Canada, he dropped off the literary map in India, despite having written four books of poetry. In Vancouver, Bantleman reinvented himself as an activist for the rights of the homeless; hence the housing development named for him. I think Jussawalla had hoped I might resurrect Bantleman in some unspecified way, perhaps with a long non-fiction piece. I hadn't.

'I just heard they've changed the name of the housing development. One more erasure,' he said and smiled, waving his large spade-like hands in the air, perhaps dismissing the shade of Bantleman from the room; perhaps trying to forgive me for ignoring that file. Yes, he smiled but of a sort as if he mock'd himself and scorn'd his spirit that could be moved to smile at such a thing.

For Adil Jussawalla seems to have spent the better part of his life battling amnesia, a condition that we wish upon ourselves in India.

'I just read a column in *The Asian Age* in which a writer called D. K. Bose said that he went to *Jam-e-Jamshed* and asked them if he might document them and they refused in a single word: No,' he said on that same morning. 'The oldest paper in the city, if not the country, the *Mumbai Samachar*? Someone told me it doesn't even have an archive.'

Perhaps as a response, his flat on the eighteenth floor of a Cuffe Parade high-rise has become a treasure trove of memory. Many anthologists—Jeet Thayil, Eunice de Souza and Bhisham Bherwani come to mind—owe some of the poems they have used to the collection of books and magazines and clippings that Jussawalla has collected and preserved over the years. If there's an unpublished poem from a major Indian writer in English, it will turn up in Jussawalla's paper-lined flat on Cuffe Parade. (The unpublished Dom Moraes poem in Thayil's *The Bloodaxe Book of Contemporary Indian Poets* [London; 2008]; and the unpublished Nissim Ezekiel poem in *Nissim Ezekiel Remembered* [New Delhi; Sahitya Akademi, 2008] edited by Havovi Anklesaria are cases in point.)

It is difficult to underestimate the impact Jussawalla has had on the intellectual life of those who care about the intellect. He has edited some of the most exciting books pages we have seen; it was in his tenure at the *Indian Express* that Arvind Krishna Mehrotra was given two broadsheet pages for a book review. When Jussawalla was editor of *Debonair*, he got Nissim Ezekiel interviewed to explain why he supported the ban on Salman Rushdie's *The Satanic Verses* while a signed-up member of PEN, whose basic credo is freedom of speech. Fellow poets have found in him a painstaking publisher, a supportive critic and a somewhat acerbic friend. Others remember him as the dynamic young teacher of literature who introduced them to 'Dangerous Animals', a series of readings of poetry at St. Xavier's College in the 1970s; he resurrected this model in Loquations in the late 1990s, where each Tuesday for several years, he read poetry on a theme, introducing us to poets such as William Snodgrass and Li Po, contextualizing them with vignettes, lending books to those who asked for them.

One day, in June 2010, he gestured to a blue Rexine bag and said that he had the entire Clearing House correspondence in it. I smiled and said, 'But surely you don't have your own letters.'

Jussawalla is known among his friends for his intense loyalty, his gift for intellectual companionship and his thin skin. His voice went soft as it does when he wants to growl.

'Of course, I do. It was a business venture and in a business venture, you have to keep a record of what is said and what is not. So I kept copies of my own letters too.'

For those who came in late: Clearing House was a poets' cooperative set up by Arvind Krishna Mehrotra, Gieve Patel, Arun Kolatkar and Jussawalla himself in the mid-1970s. The publishing house was meant to act as a clearing house for the many manuscripts that were lying around unpublished. It is here that we see the workings of history and geography in the realm of poetry and memory. This was the 1970s. There were no mobile phones. Telephony was a government monopoly and in order to talk to someone in another city, one had to book a trunk call in advance and then hang around near a telephone, waiting. There was no internet and so everyone had to write letters.

Next: two of the four founder members did not live in Bombay. Mehrotra was beginning a life-time of teaching in Allahabad. Gieve Patel spent some time in Gujarat, practising medicine in a village. Finally: it had been decided that all decisions would be unanimous. This meant that Jussawalla spent a good deal of his time writing to Mehrotra, keeping him abreast of what had been discussed in Bombay.

And since Jussawalla was a good poet and a good manager and a good archivist, he kept all those letters, the ones he wrote and the ones he received, filing many of them. Thus a single blue Rexine bag would have a picture of Indian poetry's finest, talking, arguing, and challenging each other as they brought out books, several of which were to be major events in the nation's literary history. That was just one of the many boxes, files, collections of papers and magazines, notebooks, scrapbooks that fill Jussawalla's world with paper.

'It's usual to say,' Jussawalla writes in a piece from 2002 that we could not include here for want of space, 'that writing is a way of making sense of the shrapnel of data.' In that sense, when I offered to edit his prose writing, I was looking at nearly fifty years of shrapnel. Some of the earliest pieces in this collection date back to the 1960s. Many of the shorter pieces were written for Yogi Aggarwal's Associated News Features, as a fortnightly syndicated column from 1991 to 2002. The last piece, on his mother, was datelined April 2012.

~

Over the many years that I have known Jussawalla, I have rarely seen him without a stubby-pointed pencil, the kind he celebrates in 'The Joy of Sensuous Writing' (see Page 45), and a notebook. This could be a student's exercise book or it could be one of those miniature books that the dhobis all over the city use to note down the number of babyfrocks, housecoats and pyjamas given for washing and ironing. He did not fetishise his tools, nor would he bother about the utilitarian value of the notes he was making, the scribbles that might become poems or prose. That did not matter. What did, it seemed, was the act of taking down, of committing to words, of turning the madness of civilisation into something that can be handled.

Or something that might earn him some money.

There is some belief that Jussawalla was born to affluence because he lives on the eighteenth floor of a building in a rather posh area of the island city of Bombay. There may be something to that belief, I don't know. But as long as I have known him, he has been a working stiff, trying to make his way on some offensive salaries. (Don't get me started on what newspapers and magazines and the editors thereof think is okay to pay freelance journalists.) It embarrassed me terribly to know that I was earning more than he was at the *Times of India*, where he was the Books Review Editor. It was part-time work but he took it seriously, turning up almost every other day, looking solemnly at every book that came in.

'Surely you won't send that out for review?' I said once when I saw him looking at a book called *Oil Presses of India*.

'No,' he said with a hint of regret. 'They don't give me enough space. But Arun [Kolatkar] might like it.'

Journalism was Adil's day job because in his time, as now, poetry earns you a place in anthologies but no money in the bank. When he left Cathedral School, Bombay, in 1956, he decided to study architecture in London, because he felt trapped in the city of his birth.

'I did not feel I had a choice,' he said to me. Architecture, 'not because I had a great passion for it. It had become quite clear that I was good at art and not very good at the sciences. So I suppose the reasoning was that architecture represented the intersection of the arts and the sciences. And it was a career,' he told me. This sounded familiar; a career is the Holy Grail of the middle-class Indian parent.

But England was not the promised land. 'The getaway place turned out to be formidable and dark and Satanic, like [William] Blake's mills,' he told me on another occasion. 'But London was also exciting; it made me a writer. Though I had begun to take poetry seriously in Bombay, I had no literary ambitions. I had kept a diary in school but I had no idea I wanted to be a writer or that I could be one. My ambition to be a writer burst out in London. I didn't have time to keep a diary since we kept long hours at the School of Architecture. Suppressing the little writing I did, denying myself my own words, I had a breakdown. New kinds of poems—new for me—came out of that. Poetry was a kind of release; having literary ambitions was something hopeful. It gave shape to one's days.'

He stopped studying architecture to write a play. His father was appalled at this—the theatre could be a hobby, it often was for Parsis in Bombay at the time, but it was not a career—and tried to intervene. Dr Jehangir Jussawalla thought E. M. Forster might be able to talk some sense into his son and got one of his patients to arrange a meeting between the two. Jussawalla remembers his own outrage.

'I got right to the point and said I didn't see why he [Forster] should have been asked to intervene,' he said. 'And he agreed. But he was very kind. He agreed to read the play I was working on.'

That would have been *Jian*, completed in 1958. Once again, space did not permit us to use a section of *Jian* or of *Floodwaters*, a second play, written in 1959; nor the short stories, nor yet a section of the novel he abandoned. The second play was written at Felsham, at a private school, where the young Jussawalla was sent to prepare for entry to Oxbridge. (Some of those moments, those landscapes are evoked in poems in the section 'Fieldwork' in his third book of poems, *Trying to Say Goodbye*.) He was admitted to University College, Oxford, to read English language and literature in 1960.

The poems began to form themselves into a book. *Land's End* came out with Writers Workshop in 1962. This means that Jussawalla paid to get it into print; there simply was no other way to get a book of poems out at the time. But even P. Lal (about whom you will find more on Page 3 in 'Six Authors in Search of a Reader') knew that he was on to something special. He had read some of the young poet's work and asked Nissim Ezekiel to tell Jussawalla to send him some poems for his literary journal, *Miscellany*. Jussawalla remembers that Lal came personally to Bombay with a rush order of the books so that he could take them back with him to England.

Jussawalla would consider the possibility of staying on in London as so many of the other Indians did. At the International Language Centre where he was teaching English as a foreign language, he met Veronik Joannides, a French woman who had separated from her husband. But he was also beginning to work on what would become one of the most important anthologies of Indian writing. This was *New Writing in India* (London: Penguin, 1974) and it still makes for a searing read. Many of the writers in it are now canonical; at that time, readers in English were barely aware of them. This is because Jussawalla was not afraid of the work entailed in identifying the writers, finding the translations and in some case, working on those translations to put together his book. There is a hoarse shouting of Indian voices here; that it has not been reprinted in India is a matter of shame.

What brought him back to India is not clear though 'A Destination of the Heart' on Page 283 may have some clues. That sets the emotional record as straight as humanly possible. The chronological record shows that he and Veronik and Veronik's daughter, Katia, came to Bombay in 1970, 'the sort of provincial place where I am happy' as he said to literary journalist Sunil Sethi in an interview for *India Today*. Jussawalla and Joannides got married and he began to teach English at St Xavier's College where he was greatly loved by his students. In 1975 he took a year-long sabbatical to write a novel. He never did complete it and at the time blamed Clearing House for aborting 'my poor novel, my monster, my child' (as he put it to Arvind Krishna Mehrotra in a letter in 1976). Today he believes he was equally to blame for its death: 'What went wrong with my short stories as well as my novel, is that my journalistic self kept taking over my imaginative self. I can't hold anyone responsible for the death of my novel but myself.'

In 1977, Jussawalla went to America, an Honorary Fellow at the International Writing Program in Iowa. When he returned, he worked at a number of jobs. S. V. Vasudev, the art critic, given the chance to edit *For You*, a short-lived general interest magazine, asked him to be Book Reviews editor. When *For You* folded up, Dom Moraes offered him the same job at *Sunday Standard*, as the Sunday edition of the *Indian Express* was then called. A lock-out followed and he lost his job there; traces of this story are to be found in 'The Many Murders of Datta Samant' (Page 192).

He worked as copy editor for the magazine *Science Age*, into whose pages he inserted the occasional dose of poetry. He then went to *Debonair*, writing to Arvind Krishna Mehrotra that he needed the money since the fate of *Science Age* seemed forever in the balance. He was the literary editor of India's first girlie magazine, editor for an even shorter while and then went back to being its literary editor, all this between 1988 and 1991.

That was where I met him.

I had gone to submit the first of a column that I had been asked to write, a column on male style. What qualified me? Nothing. Why was I asked? I don't know. I just knew that I had to find a way out of the obscurity of *The Free Press Journal*—the only newspaper that seemed to have any space for me at the time—and this might be a route. I went with my first column—this was the time before email and so you wrote a draft, you typed it up with a carbon copy for safety, and if you were in the same city, you carried it to the magazine or newspaper where you hoped it would appear. *Debonair* had offices in the basement of a state-run five star hotel in North Bombay.

Jussawalla was lurking in the office and suggested that we go out for a drink. We did and he commissioned two more stories, enough to make him any freelance journalist's friend for life. In the course of that conversation, I mentioned how much I admired the Clearing House experiment.

'Oh God,' he said, half-moan, half-sigh. 'That.'

'It must have been wonderful,' I said.

'I got myself into a position that I didn't really enjoy. It became a responsibility which I couldn't pull out of. The whole thing would have collapsed if I had. There were always problems about raising money and then there was the secretarial work, the running around, the avoidable and unavoidable delays ... Much as Clearing House has been responsible for producing my book and other books, I won't like to go through that experience again.'

I pointed out that he had. He was a publisher for XAL-Praxis which brought out two books of poems—Eunice de Souza's *Women in Dutch Painting*, Manohar Shetty's *Borrowed Time*—and a play, Gieve Patel's *Mister Behram*, all in 1988. In 1990, Jussawalla followed this up with Menka Shivdasani's poetry book *Nirvana at Ten Rupees* and in 1991, with Cyrus Mistry's play *Doongaji House*.

'Why do that to yourself again?' I asked him.

'I got paid,' he said.

~

I knew, of course, that Jussawalla had done an enormous amount of writing. I knew that he would have kept all of it, or as much as it was humanly possible to preserve, as part of his commitment to memory. I knew that it would mean a lot of reading but when you're dealing with someone who is so obviously a master prose stylist, that doesn't mean much pain.

What I was not prepared for was the range of Jussawalla's interests and the connections he could make between seemingly disparate events, odd moments. (He seems to be the poet of the synapse, the prose stylist at the fissure.) Organising these into subheads has proved a bit of a nightmare, but then that's because every writer knows that one's interests leak. The film you saw illuminates the book you read. The moment in the park twenty years ago can be used to talk about the decline of a city. We do this all the time, all of us, but few so effectively as Jussawalla. He places the dead man against the butterfly, a poem by Nissim Ezekiel against the cheerful crackle of sparrow song.

Jussawalla walked the city, swam through it sometimes when it was raining, encountered xenophobia and arrogance. It seems as if Jussawalla was not the missing person of his most famous poem; he was the alien observer whose gaze was always disconcerting the object. In England, he could pass, he tells us, as any number of nationalities. In India, he's often mistaken for a 'foreigner', even when he speaks Hindi or Gujarati. In Mumbai, taxi drivers with glassy eyes demand certification. And the Zoroastrian is often mistaken for a Muslim, a contested identity in a city of uncertain alliances, uneasy peace and a jerry-built sense of community. This gives him a unique position from which to observe; he is always on the periphery of what is happening, the outsider looking in. And this, in turn, gives his prose a piquancy and a bitterness, and an undertone of longing. He is a compassionate and engaged writer, but he is also the outsider who would never join a group that would have him as a member.

To observe, to give witness, to hold in the memory. The bereaved cow, the boy who has come to deliver the groceries, the poet in transit, the little boy who wet his pants laughing and wept because a bird died, all these pass under the Jussawalla scanner, all these are transformed by the act of writing. Jussawalla's fight against the Indian predilection for amnesia is relentless. He will not let you forget. He wrote thirty articles about Rushdie and the fatwa—I am sorry that I could only include one, the magnificent 'Salman and the Sea of Paper'. He mentions Victor Anant's *The Revolving Man* several times, a book that has dropped off our horizons but which was one of the first to deal with racism in the East-West encounter. He gave us back several poets: Gopal Honnalgere, G. S. Sharat Chandra. He wrote scores of book reviews of which only one appears here.

That has been the heartbreak of editing this book: how much has had to be dropped. My first selection came up to 300,000 words. My second, after a month of ruthless chopping, weighed in at 280,000. Finally, I had to submit it to Jussawalla the surgeon, and he helped. We've got it down to this size. In writing this introduction, I've had to keep checking back. Did we keep that piece about the fire in the Calcutta Book Fair which ends with the resounding 'Words cannot be burnt'? No. Did we keep an essay called 'View of Artists Warming their Arses on the Edge of a Volcano'? Of course, I know we didn't. Jussawalla said he had changed many of his views about art and modern art since the time he wrote that as an angry young man. I just thought I'd put that name of the piece in so you'll know that it wasn't the dull pieces that got cut. There were no dull pieces. I just wanted you to get a sense of how many registers there were, how many variant Adils have walked, stalked through my head over this year. In this sea of photocopies, there have been lovely surprises: a manuscript of an interview with the reclusive genius architect Nari Gandhi—again excluded, as were classic interviews with figures as diverse as the painter Jehangir Sabavala, the novelist Angus Wilson, the film critic Marie Seton, all for want of space—annotated in Nari Gandhi's own handwriting: 'He has made too much of this Nari Gandhi. Can't we drop these two words and then print it? I should like that.'

Right. He would.

Now Adil is concentrating on his poems. This is good for all of us. *Trying to Say Goodbye* (Almost Island Books: 2011) has joined *Land's End* (Writers Workshop; 1962) and *Missing Person* (Clearing House; 1976). *The Right Kind of Dog* (Duckbill; 2013), poems for younger readers, is also out. And there are more poems in that paper-lined flat, in those dhobi notebooks, poems being built studiously and with infinite care, poems that are flying or falling apart, poems in transition. Over them looms an image of a knife-grinder, sparks flying, as he hones the blades he will camouflage in the silk of words.

'I can spend hours with a poem now,' Jussawalla said in March 2013. 'I don't want to do much else.'

But it's also a bit sad that we've lost Jussawalla the prose writer. Like James Baldwin, Jussawalla also seems to have striven to be 'an honest man and a good writer'. That kind is rare; the world of poetry may be richer for it but there's one less voice of reason and beauty in the world of prose.

Mumbai   JERRY PINTO
October 2013

PUBLISHER'S NOTE

The essays in this collection were written over forty-seven years: the earliest piece included here is an unpublished work from 1965, and the most recent appeared in the April 2012 issue of *Parsiana*. To fully appreciate the essays that refer to specific events, personalities or trends, refer to the dates in 'Sources' on Page 337.

'Hey, waiter, a packet of Charminar and a mini-book!'

WRITERS

SIX AUTHORS IN SEARCH OF A READER

When Penguin Books asked me to edit *New Writing in India* in 1968, it led to my corresponding with several Indian writers, a few of whom I knew personally. The correspondence grew and with some, continues to grow. Looking at it now, one clear fact emerges: how very much writers who are in their thirties or forties have had to depend on themselves and on one another to get their work published. Professional publishers didn't seem to have been around from the very time they started.

The situation now, in 1981, is much worse. The writers—novelists, playwrights, poets—have continued to write. New writers have emerged. But new publishers haven't. No publisher, that is, who has been willing to keep pace with the quality and quantity of the work. It's the writers themselves who've had to take this risk, venturing into a field about which they know nothing but must, of necessity, learn.

Is this the pattern that has been set for the future? If it is, it's a unique situation. Indian writers will have to continue to be responsible for publishing their own and one another's work. Publishers will continue irresponsibly to ignore them, preferring to drug the reader with whatever he's got used to. The reader will remain in the dark.

But the missing reader exists. Without him, the writer can't. Trying to find him may be a job but it's one some writers have taken up themselves. Referring to their letters, and writings published in inaccessible little magazines, I've put together some of the evidence of their common search.

~

Eighteen years ago, at the end of his first year at Bombay University, Vilas Sarang wrote a story. It's about a man who keeps a close watch on flies, mutilates, and kills them. He called the story 'Flies'.

He wrote the story in English—the one time he has done so—then translated it into Marathi. Both versions had to wait five years before they were published—the Marathi in the hardy *Abhiruchi*, the English in *Blunt*, a little magazine that didn't get beyond the first issue.

'Flies' was meant to appear in *New Writing in India*, but the publishers found it oppressive. So I used Sarang's 'Rabbit'. 'Flies' will soon appear in *London Magazine* which has very few readers in India. Sarang can truthfully claim that for eighteen years, the English version of his first story has found no new readers in India.

An older writer like 'Mowni', seventy-four, who writes in Tamil, might choose to live with the fact. 'A story is not just produced by waving a magic wand,' he writes in a letter. 'The author gives his life and creates his work but leaves it to loiter like a forlorn child with a responsibility to its imaginative-sympathetic chance reader who can adopt it.' Sarang, not yet forty, takes a different approach. He hasn't let his stories 'loiter'. On the contrary, he has placed both his Marathi originals and their English versions with assiduous care in the best literary journals here and abroad. This approach he shares with many of his contemporaries. It couldn't have been otherwise. He has, along with them, the experience of living politically free and in a shrunk world. Between their sensibilities and those of writers of an older generation, there is the fact of an altered earth, a vast gap.

'The young Indian writer is now more complexed than ever. Seldom has he come across such a wide range of works in translation and otherwise from all over and seldom before has he been made so aware as a consequence of his deep ignorance.'

So felt Arvind Krishna Mehrotra, writing at twenty-four, in

Iowa City, acutely aware of being a young Indian writer and living abroad. His situation connects with Sarang's in more ways than one. He has placed his poems in English in the best literary journals abroad as carefully and as craftily as Sarang has his stories. He also shared with Sarang, though for a briefer time, a strong sense of dislocation from India, a fear of losing it.

'The life in Bombay is getting vaguer and vaguer in my mind,' writes Sarang in a letter in March 1973. 'I have written literally nothing for over a year. I don't know if this has to do with lack of time or living abroad. I have a feeling it might be better for me to be back in Bombay.'

And Mehrotra, a month and a half later, from Iowa City: 'Two weeks ago I was so tired of America and travelling that I wanted to fly straight to Delhi and forget about all the in-between . . . we'll be in Bombay, homesick, forlorn, tired, eager by the third week of September.'

Like the publishing of his stories, Sarang's return took a much longer time than he expected. After three years at the University of Indiana, he taught English at the University of Basra for five. The last two years in Bombay have been productive. He has completed a novel, 200 pages of which he wrote in Basra, and a short play. He is now translating the novel into English. After that he will start another novel in Marathi.

But in two years his disappointments have grown sizeably too. He finds it as difficult getting the English versions of his stories published here as when he started. 'How can the Indo-Anglians have a literature when they don't even have a journal?' His attitude towards the Indo-English literary scene has hardened, he feels separated from it. He may soon take no interest in it at all.

Mehrotra returned in 1973, not to Bombay or Delhi, but to his hometown, Allahabad.

Once a year, when the university he teaches at is on vacation, he comes to Bombay and two occasions on recent visits have been invigorating. The first was getting a Bhabha fellowship to work on his poems and on translating Nirala. The second was a meeting with a poet.

They ran into each other in a business section of Bombay, each carrying material for his new book of poems, which each will be bringing out on his own. The poet was Manohar Shetty.

For Mehrotra, thirty-four, the production of books, both his own and other writers', is an activity which has continued with interruptions, for the last fourteen years. For Shetty, twenty-seven, it's the result of acknowledging a new situation: that the publishing activities of Mehrotra and other writers have altered his situation; that in the absence of even one respectable commercial outlet for poetry in English, he must publish his own. Before the book finds its readers, there must be evidence of a book.

The Bengali writer Sandipan Chattopadhyay writes in a letter from Calcutta:

> 'On 30th April, 1971, I sat on [sic] before a publishing house with a placard all alone and quietly reading: 'I'm a writer. This house published one book by me. The book has been sold out. They have refused me my royalties. So here I am.' I was there for four hours sitting on the pavements on sheets of newspaper. In the beginning I was alone. No one knew before. It was my decision. Then people and young writers began to collect—the latter came from the nearby coffee house. Students came from the University. At 9.30 p.m. the publisher apologized and gave me my honour back. Meanwhile photographers arrived, and I fled.'

Chattopadhyay's search for readers for his own and other writers' work took ingenious forms. In December 1969, he published his short story '*Biblap-o-Rajmohan*' (Revolution and Rajmohan) as a minibook, its size a mere 4' x 3¼'. A letter from Chattopadhyay brings back the occasion vividly:

'2200 copies were sold in all. About 1,200 copies ... with signature on 500 ... were sold within a week ... and that too from a single paan-shop at a Calcutta coffee house on College Street. Students and customers used to exclaim, 'Hey waiter! A pack of CHARMINAR and one MINI-BOOK' ... that is how it all started. I avoided bookstalls and took to paan-and-cigarette shops. The slogan was and still is, 'CHARMINAR or MINI-BOOK,' the price of both being the same ... Then on 28.12.1969, the rest of the copies were literally 'looted' to the last as the morning papers came out with PTI [Press Trust of India] news about it. The radio also broadcast the news at 7.30a.m. that day about the MINI-BOOK being 'the first of its kind in India,' as they put it.'

Chattopadhyay brought out three other mini-books, two in an impression of 3,300 copies, one of 8,800 copies. Except for the last, they all sold out within three to thirteen days.

On 10 May this year about a hundred people took out a procession in a street in Bombay 'to promote literary tastes and activities.' According to a report, children carried placards which said: 'One should live to read and read to live.' Passers-by were told of the importance of reading books and of buying books to encourage writers. The procession ended at Sahitya Sahavas, a writers' colony where on 28 December 1980, a far more dramatic event took place—Dilip Chitre began a hunger strike on the premises of the building which he had to vacate. As a long-standing member of the society that runs the colony, he was entitled to alternative accommodation—which wasn't forthcoming.

In about twenty years in Bombay, Chitre has had to find alternative accommodation as many times. He has been luckier with places to stay abroad. In Addis Ababa where he taught for three years, in Iowa City where he stayed for two, and in Russia, Hungary, Germany and France, where he and two other writers were officially invited recently.

Chitre is as 'complexed' a writer, in the sense Mehrotra uses the term, as any, and shares with him and Sarang the experience of living and travelling outside India. He fully realises the importance of the printed word, yet he sees his own written work from a medieval distance, with himself as reciter, keeper of the spoken word, rather than as author of printed books. However idiosyncratic this view may appear to other poets, Chitre has been consistent in finding the audience that meets his needs. Recent conversations with him suggest that he may believe his true audience to be outside Bombay in the smaller towns of Maharashtra. His readings there have drawn a response he has ceased to expect in the busy air of the metropolis.

In hostile, anti-literary, anti-intellectual surroundings, a writer may succumb to despair or exaggerate the futility of his best efforts, if only to force himself to continue, to try harder. 'It is my agony and the agony of all those who have been suddenly exposed to the mind's endless subtleties,' wrote Mehrotra in 1972, 'those who have strayed into its labyrinthine passages without knowing how to get back or across, if only to tell the world that the journey was better not taken . . . In the white light I see clearly what must happen. Indian literature will imperceptibly shift into the chilliness of the ivory tower. The step from birth, from spring to defoliation is a quick, painless one.'

In a recent issue of the Hindi journal *Sahitya*, Vishnu Khare predicts a similar extinction, though he reserves it for the Indo-English only. Those of us who write in English write solely for 'export', he believes, and are the first and last generation of such writers in India.

Such an opinion doesn't or perhaps refuses to take into account the phenomenon of young poets like Shetty who writes for readers here and is making efforts to publish himself locally. Or of Cyrus Mistry, who wrote a play *Doongaji House* for local audiences in 1977 and who with luck, will see it performed this year. It doesn't explain the attitude of older writers like Gieve Patel, who has recently completed his second play in English, who plans to translate both the plays into Gujarati. Or Arun Kolatkar, who, while still at work on *Balwant Bua*, a sequence of poems in Marathi, is working on an equally ambitious sequence, on another subject, in English.

All the same, extinction strikes in unexpected ways. The poem, feeling secondary to the poet's life, threatens to 'diminish bitterly,' leaving the poet 'dumb as a wall.' That is what Manohar Shetty's poem 'Secret' says. Silence may proceed from stasis or status, two of India's deadliest snakes. And there's always the inviting ivory tower. Unable to cope with the political reality of his country, the writer may take the reality for a dream. Or even take it to be a dream within a dream. The returning student in Sarang's story 'Return' does just that. Having had a dream of being back in his room in Bombay when he is about to return to the city from New York, he believes he has fallen asleep on the plane and that the events happening to him on his arrival in Bombay are merely a continuation of the earlier dream. In fact he is under detention and still thinking he's dreaming, is led away to be tortured.

Sarang's protagonist turned a larger reality into a dream into a fact. It's been dreamt in many minds and over a long period of time. Mehrotra speaks of it on May 19, 1974: 'If no financer comes our way we ought to think in terms of setting up a co-operative of sorts . . . A way out of this mess . . . And, believe me, Arun's *Jejuri* is the best sequence of poems in at least two generations.

'I keep thinking of starting another journal; the Civil and Military, and after a while, Civil and Military Publishers. But then I am impossibly behind things and whole weeks pass when all I've done is perfect my knowledge of Elizabethan low life or explored Pound's relationship with Joyce or cleaned a line or two of my own . . . Tell me what you think of C & M as a name. I am serious. Printing can be done very cheaply from here; the difficulty lies with paper. It must be 2 a.m. and the publishing dream is better continued in bed.'

What dreams lay behind the setting up of the successfully-run writers' co-operative in Kerala or, for that matter, Writers Workshop in Calcutta, I can't mention, simply because I don't know. Instead, I've used the evidence of letters and work published in inaccessible magazines to build up a patchwork the missing reader may be curious to examine since it chiefly concerns him. His continued absence from the Indian literary scene makes it a far more primitive one than it appears to be. It properly belongs to a very dark age. In its fearful context, the question 'Who do you write for?' if put to the writers I've mentioned, is far too sophisticated for the context. Its hostile emptiness drives them to write for the most basic and primitive of reasons: to stave off their own extinction.

'How much good talent this country destroys,' says Gieve Patel in a conversation recently. 'I pound at the typewriter only to keep fear out,' writes Dilip Chitre.

INTRODUCTION TO *FAIR TREE OF THE VOID*, STORIES BY VILAS SARANG

The presiding deity in Vilas Sarang's room at the University of Bombay, where he is head of the Department of English, is Kafka. A photograph of his hangs on a wall behind Sarang's desk. On the occasion I visited the room, the poets Ernesto Cardenal from Nicaragua, Miroslav Holub from Czechoslovakia, and Ferenc Juhasz from Hungary, were attempting to communicate in English with members of Sarang's department and invited guests. Holub spoke English confidently, the others needed interpreters; Cardenal seemed uncomfortable with his. This interpreter, I was later to find out, was the Nicaraguan consul-general in Bombay and he shadowed the Santa Claus-like Cardenal constantly, like an executioner with cannibalistic intent. As the university canteen's tea boys shuffled in and out of the crowded room with bottles of cold beverages and bottle-openers, as though no momentous event were taking place, the consul-general seemed to distend, until his presence almost filled the room. Holub's voice continued to sound clear and undisturbed, as though he were quite used to such a phenomenon. The room became stifling. Kafka had struck again.

I mention Kafka at the beginning of this piece only to get him out of the way as early as possible. Readers will be quick to see that the stories in this collection are Kafkaesque but unless at the same time they see the many ways in which they are not, the term diminishes Sarang. Beckett too is Kafkaesque; so are Borges and Camus. Yet, in India, the originality freely granted these writers is denied Sarang whose achievement in the twenty-five short stories he has written so far (only twenty are included in this collection) is comparable to theirs.

Outside India too, given the general ignorance about contemporary Indian writing and the Indian literary situation, it would be fair to expect non-Indian writers, coming across these stories in the British, American and French journals in which they were first published, not to look beyond Kafka to spot Sarang. However, there is a piece of evidence that indicates that this might not be so. In his introduction to *Le Terroriste*, the French edition of this collection, Alain Nadaud, who met Sarang when they were both teaching at the University of Basra, acknowledges that it was through reading Sarang's English translations of his stories that he 'first became aware of the inherent resources of the short story', and seeing what original use Sarang made of the unpromising environment they shared, began to write himself. He says: 'I translated these stories into French, then, not so much to repay a debt of recognition my own writing appears to owe to that of Sarang, as to make up for not having written them myself . . .' He also says, 'In translating these tales, I did not find myself in any sense disoriented—in fact I was in familiar territory, for I discovered in more than one story the influence of those writers (Kafka, Camus, Beckett and Borges) whose work I cherished, constituting that country's four geographic poles.'

A Marathi writer meets a Frenchman in a land that both are not citizens of, and sets the Frenchman writing. In his own land, Sarang reports that he sees no literary successor. In an unpublished interview he claims that there are only three Marathi writers who can truly be called modernist—Dilip Chitre, Arun Kolatkar and himself—and that while their achievement is recognized by the public and sometimes rewarded by the State, they are an island to themselves—isolated by other writers, ignored by the mainstream.

One reason for this may be that Sarang himself ignores the mainstream. His stories reject certain Indian, more specifically Hindu values and ideals cherished by the more popular Marathi writers and their readers. Unimpressed by the sanctity of ritual, for example, cremation rites in 'Bajrang—the Great Indian Bustard', or the idealized goddess-woman so central to Hindu male perception which he literally snaps in two in 'Interview With M. Chakko', or respect for one's elders, again a central tenet of Hindu society at which he looks askance in 'The Excursion', Sarang's response to such established signifiers of Indian culture is vehement, violent and nihilistic. He breaks open the glass case in which the precious icon is housed, and, like Dostoyevsky's nihilist in *The Possessed*, substitutes it with a mouse. Disquieting as the effect is in English I am told by those familiar with the original stories that it is even more so in Marathi; his aggressive use of it can be repellent. Can it be that he both requires and rejects his readers just as his many exceptionally lonely characters (in 'History is on Our Side' and 'Letters from Nikhil', for example) require and reject human companionship?

Even if that is the case, it would be a gross misunderstanding of the stories to deduce, with the hint provided by the title of this collection, that because of certain nihilistic impulses in them, that they are nihilistic. I believe instead that they are a profound tribute to human steadfastness. All the five interconnected characters in 'Musk Deer', for example, physically and morally brutalized as they are, have this quality of steadfastness and it would be a mistake to allow the many senselessly cruel acts (performed both on human beings and on other varieties of creation) with which the stories abound to detract from this quality since Sarang invests all his characters with it. I believe this vision of human steadfastness is crucial to Sarang's moral position as a writer, and has larger implications.

Consider Sarang's protagonists. They are almost invariably 'one-room-one-man' people, that is, they and the room they live in form a bond which, in the eyes of the reader, they cannot escape. We tend to see them and their rooms jointly just as we tend to see the two individuals that constitute a long-lasting couple, however far apart they may be, jointly. At the same time, his characters are solitaries. They do mundane jobs and are prone to wander off into the city or, as in the case of Kalluri in 'Kalluri's Radio', into open country, by themselves. They dream a lot and though, on occasion, their wanderings are part of an attempt to find a missing link between their past and present selves (both in states of past and present dreams and past and present reality) as in 'The Terrorist' and 'The Return', they are not questing people. Nor are they the questioning kind. The few questions they ask themselves about their sterile existence they invariably counter-question in their own minds so as to restore stasis, the present condition of existence as was and is forever meant to be.

The astonishing thing is that these people, perennially oppressed though they are, live with full knowledge of themselves and rarely seek to escape those selves or their fate. Nor do they complain about it. In 'The Metamorphosis of Anil Rao' the protagonist accepts his overnight transformation into a penis with the same equanimity as the other characters in other stories accept their impotent lives. Whether it is the beggar who propels himself on his back in 'Musk Deer', the schoolteacher who 'never left the schoolyard', having got a job in the very school he went to as a student in 'On the Stone Steps', or the tiny Manu carrying out his telephonic duties without a murmur of complaint in 'The Life and Death of Manu', each does his duty to the best of his ability, expecting neither reward nor recompense. When, despite his diligence, Manu's masters allow him to die, we care. Sarang wants us to. From the way he structures the final moments of the story, it is clear that neither cynicism nor nihilism informs Sarang's attitude to the human condition, but profound compassion.

I am not over-anxious to emphasize the 'Indianness' of Sarang's stories as Nadaud does, for example, by relating their 'fundamental circularity' to 'a tradition and state of mind specifically Indian', but it is hard to think of a set of protagonists, both in short fiction and the novel, who so faithfully follow their dharma—that hard-to-define Sanskrit word in which meanings of natural law and the performing of individual duty, yours and none other's, intersect. Seen in that light, while the man in 'Flies', who spends his time killing or maiming the creatures, or the man who persecutes a spider in the clock in the story with the same name, operate outside the 'normal' moral codes of decency and fair play, they at the same time operate within a larger moral framework, a universe whose dharmic law they accept even if they understand it very partially or not at all.

My unfamiliarity with Marathi prevents me from going into Sarang's readings in that language to discover how its literature shaped him as a writer. He has told me that the fiction of B.S. Mardhekar, particularly his detailed description of low life, absorbed him and that if he had not avidly read Gangadhar Gadgil, Vyankatesh Madgulkar and Arvind Gokhale in his youth, he would have found it difficult to write. The youngest of six brothers, the one immediately elder to him wrote humorous pieces which impressed Sarang and also made him want to write. Maupassant's books (in English translation) which 'lay around brother's house' were also a source of influence.

However, there were two pieces of information he provided which startled me into looking at his stories afresh. First, he read a Borges story for the first time in an English translation in *The Illustrated Weekly of India* in 1963, when he was twenty. Second, until 1958, his school-leaving year, apart from selected texts in his English class, he read only Marathi. Among those texts was *The Man-Eating Leopard of Rudraprayag* by Jim Corbett. So impressed was he by the story that he read all of Corbett's available work and, for some time, made a point of rereading all his work every year.

The information is revealing because it points to yet another transcultural episode in the shaping of Sarang—the inter-crossing of Marathi and English sources at formative stages of his life—and places him firmly among those Indian writers for whom colonialism, (which chiefly made such inter-crossings possible) was an inescapable fact.

SALMAN AND THE SEA OF PAPER

There's a boy who lives somewhere in the side streets of Bombay's Bori Bunder, one of the city's busiest hubs. The only thing that covers him is a piece of paper, half the size of this page. He occasionally darts out from the side streets into the lines of cars temporarily stalled at the traffic lights. He begs furtively and quickly, unlike his more persistent streetmates, his face contorted into a make-believe grin, the tendons of his neck stretched. A few months ago, his smile was more natural, his body less emaciated. He may well die as you read this, which would be a pity. This page alone would have provided him with two new sets of clothes. We have ways of treating our wolf-boys, our Mowglis, when they aren't the subjects of fiction.

And even when they are. That other wolf boy, that outcast Salman Rushdie, has been the subject of one of the grossest pieces of fiction in history. In the minds of those who believe in carrying out the fatwa against him, he is an entirely invented creature, a Satan without parallel, and neither his public statements to prove the contrary nor his conversion to Islam has made the slightest difference to them. Both they and those who defend Rushdie have written so many pages on him that if cut out and put end to end, they would more than cover him, they would probably enwrap the globe several times over, an enfolding sea or a giant mockery of an awareness quilt, the kind that's made by stitching together different panels on subjects like Vietnam, AIDS and communal harmony. Are we at all aware that a tiny bit of inattention on the part of those responsible for Rushdie's safety, could turn that quilt of paper into his shroud? What would all our words mean then, even if they were written in defence of Rushdie? As he enters the sixth year of his death sentence (passed on February 14, 1989), we are forced to realise that all our good words have been unable to get that sentence lifted.

The question may arise: why should the Indian citizen do anything about Rushdie? He left the country when he was a child and is now a British citizen. Our government was the first to ban his book but had nothing to do with the fatwa. Do we have a special responsibility towards him?

I believe we do, for at least three reasons. The first is Rushdie's fiction which is concerned almost exclusively with the subcontinent. Add to that his articles, essays and papers on various Indian subjects (collected in *Imaginary Homelands*) and you have a writer who has never divorced himself from India and who longs to be back.

That leads to the second reason. The ban on *The Satanic Verses* and the fatwa have physically separated Rushdie from a reality which is central to his existence and one of our responsibilities is to recreate the conditions which allow him the freedom to get back to it. In a recent interview Rushdie complained that his Indian friends weren't doing anything to get the ban lifted. It's true nothing came of an attempt to take the matter to the Supreme Court. But it's also true that communal tensions following the Babri Masjid destruction have grown to such proportions that the government will not consider lifting the ban for the present. The fatwa is a different matter altogether. And that's where our special responsibility comes in.

The third reason for that responsibility will surprise many. It already exists. A vast number of Indians sympathises with Rushdie and are ready to support him. Not many know that when the International Committee for the Defence of Salman Rushdie invited letters of support from all over the world, the greatest number came from the Soviet Union and India. That was five years ago. But the sympathy has not evaporated. It just has to be reactivated.

One of the most fruitful ways in which this could be done would be to follow Rushdie's example. In his recent meetings with different heads of state—Clinton, Major, Kohl—he has earned a measure of support which should put him on the agenda of any international dealings with Iran. The message expected to be given out is: revoke the fatwa or there's no deal. Our prime minister must be persuaded to send out the same message. For obvious reasons, Rushdie can't meet him personally to persuade him. We must do that for him. It's our special responsibility.

If this year is no different, not just for myself, but for those who care for Rushdie and continue doing nothing about it, then we may as well give this page away to the Mowgli of Bori Bunder who will make creative use of it. It will serve no other useful purpose, unless it be to hide our own nakedness. Sometimes, it doesn't take the wisdom of a condemned writer, a Mowgli or a child to point out that it is we who have no clothes.

THE CIVILIZED MALCONTENT

The man swung out of the gate I was heading towards, visibly irritated. He was blond—from northern France or Germany, I thought. Crossing the road, I had felt physically checked. Not by his blondness, the obvious look of irritation, but by his height. A giant, I thought. He strode past, and I noticed that he wasn't that much taller than me, just under six feet, the average height of a man for his part of the world.

It was something I'd forgotten—the physical upset of a first encounter with someone of another race, the discomfiture that has only marginally to do with colour. Mixed with the slightly sick excitement of being in a new country, at the start of a new adventure, was the feeling you had stepping off the ship at Tilbury, or years later, the plane at Heathrow, of being smaller than you were. Here, in the blue of porters' uniforms, or in dark suits, or in the white shirts and trousers of immigration and customs officers, were hundreds of pink beings, all taller than you. The customs officer had to do nothing to intimidate—just lower his eyes from his great height.

It is something that V. S. Naipaul won't let us forget—that the suspicion between different races, different tribes, has to do with the total physique, not colour alone. I saw the foreigner as though I had never seen one before. I had been reading Naipaul's new novel, *A Bend in the River*. It is set in Africa, a favoured hunting ground for some of this century's leading novelists: Conrad, Hemingway, Greene, Bellow, and of late, Updike. Naipaul's Africa makes theirs seem cloudy. Every detail in the novel stands out sharply, as though seen in the light of a depolluted rain-washed day. We see Africa as though we had never seen it before. Everything has its proper scale, its shape and size, every person in the novel is seen whole. It is a triumph of the middle vision, of a writer who, like his narrator Salim, has always sought to occupy 'the middle ground, between absorption in life and soaring above the cares of the earth'.

If this makes Naipaul's achievement seem smaller than it is, consider the temptation of his material: The Dark Continent, the Great River, Primitive Africa, Tribe vs Tribe, Civilization vs Barbarism, The Heart of Darkness, the Ruins of Time—the poetry of imperialist concepts handed down to us in its most banal forms—on the pages of newspapers and on the lips of politicians. If Naipaul challenges comparison with Conrad, who used similar material, it is to show up the difference between the two writers. Not many British and American critics will agree.

The British poet and critic Anthony Thwaite, reviewing the novel in *The Observer* (September 23, 1979) smothers Naipaul under his gift of Conrad's mantle. Naipaul can't be pleased. His near-brahminical distaste for a bit of someone else's old clothing must quite correctly extend to a literary distaste too. Conrad too used to be irritated by his British reviewers' well-meaning attempts to link him with writers as diverse as Kipling, Coleridge, Stevenson, Stephen Crane and Victor Hugo. It is a symptom of the professional reviewer's distress when dealing with a foreign original—any old pillar in the sand to throw your grapple on to. As long as you get a grip.

In an essay published in the *Times Literary Supplement* fifteen years ago, Naipaul refers to his reading Dickens as a schoolboy in Trinidad. He has this to say: 'Very little of what I read was of help . . . The vision was alien, it diminished my own and did not give me courage to do a simple thing like mentioning the name of a Port of Spain street.'

A House for Mr Biswas was published three years before Naipaul disowned Dickens, perhaps to get rid of the ghost the reviewers conjured. A big novel like *A House for Mr Biswas*, teeming with characters, with scenes of high social comedy, just had to be 'Dickensian'. So now, *A Bend in the River*, set by the river Conrad made memorable, and filled with long passages of meditative narrative, must be 'Conradian'.

Perhaps few reviewers know of Naipaul's lecture on Conrad

which he delivered, if I'm not mistaken, at one of the newer British universities in the early seventies. (It is reproduced in a book brought out by an American publisher. The title of the book, like the book itself, has escaped me.) If I remember the lecture right, Naipaul approaches Conrad cautiously, coolly, the older writer being the great forbidden river to Naipaul's more delicate, almost fragile craft; this craft being the sensibility by which Naipaul will traverse the man thoroughly, completely, the journey ending in a putting away of the old river, the older writer. He must continue to see and navigate for himself. It is his way with great writers. In an interview conducted by Elizabeth Hardwick for *The New York Times Book Review* (May 1979), Naipaul is hard on most of them. He claims he has no models. I see no arrogance in the statement. It is true. And the truth it contains is the truth of colonial loneliness, of not being seen, except in the distortion of false historical mirrors.

Naipaul is concerned with civilization and its lies. Or rather civilizations and their lies. An old civilization like India's has lived out its truth and lived off a hoard of lies. Newer and stronger ones, like the British and European, are being sucked dry. Nazruddin, a displaced Indian in Africa, like the narrator Salim, sees the Arabs 'pumping the oil into Europe only to suck the money out. Pumping the oil in to keep the system going, sucking the money out to send it crashing down.'

He has a terrible vision. 'All over the world money is in flight. People have scraped the world clean, as clean as an African scrapes his yard. And now they want to run from the dreadful places where they've made their money and find some nice safe country.'

From the unnamed country on the east coast (we imagine Zanzibar-Kenya), to the unnamed country in central Africa (we imagine Zaire) to Uganda to Canada and finally to Gloucester Road, London—that is the nature of Nazruddin's flight. Naipaul indicates defeat. Nazruddin is sixty. He has found 'in the half-mile or so of the Gloucester Road, between the underground railway station and the park, the perfect retirement resort'. London, the colonial magnet, once the centre of a great Empire. It is where Indar, Salim's dynamic school friend from East Africa, ends up—all his complicated brilliance, his flashy ambition, crumbled to a simple idea: to go 'home' to India.

Europe has taught both Salim and Indar to see the world and its real achievements. As a boy, Salim sees the picture of a dhow on a postage stamp. It helps him to see a real dhow for the first time. He develops the habit of 'looking, detaching myself from a familiar scene and trying to consider it from a distance.'

Ordinary subjects of European art are also responsible for Indar's illumination. After his stint at an unnamed university (we imagine Oxford), after the fiasco of his trying to get into the Indian Foreign Service, a scene of comic rage and frustration in London's India House, he walks by the Thames. He sees the dolphins on the lamp standards on the Embankment. He sees that the metal supports of the pavement benches are shaped as camels. And, 'I understood that London wasn't simply a place that was there as people say of mountains, but that it had been made by men, that men had given attention to details as minute as those camels . . . For someone like me there was only one civilization and one place—London, or a place like it.'

London? The one civilization? Fifteen years later, the Arabs are sucking it dry. And Indar, in it, has become nothing.

Against that civilization, and every other, Time. Naipaul deals with this grand subject with the greatest of restraint, with journalistic care. Using the sparest of details and the coolest of styles, he stirs us to the immense sadness of Time passing, of empires in decay, to a note of melancholy and pain new to his work. Despite the terror, the comedy and the violence of his material, we are left with a surviving tenderness.

Reading the first part of the novel, dealing with Salim's

arrival to the small town, the growth of the town, and then the advancing shadow of its destruction, I was struck by a quality of vision which Naipaul has tended to suppress before and which I can only call poetic. Two bits of Latin, a garbled line from Virgil at the base of a ruined monument only sixty years old and the motto of the Belgian missionary school, become an artistic palimpsest: the surviving poetry of old and dead powers layering the ghastly obliteration of the new. It is done with the utmost tact. We think of the Emperor Bokassa in his Central African Empire at the same time as we think of the gigantic empty pedestal of Shelley's 'Ozymandias'.

A Bend in the River is about civilizations, their ruins, their lies. It is also a narrative about Asian displacement in the context of African rage. Nazruddin, Indar, finally Salim, all take to flight. The beautiful couple of Mahesh and Shobha, staying on, shut themselves into a life of physical decay. Metty, Salim's family servant, a half-caste of African and Asian descent, is left to fend for himself in a town once again seething with insurrection, at the mercy of the Africans he dreads.

Threatening them all, the periodic African rage: 'They were not a sturdy people. They were small and slightly built. Yet, as though to make up for their puniness in that immensity of river and forest, they liked to wound with their hands.'

It is these small hands that try to strike the town flat for a second time too. Here is Naipaul's clear look at the aftermath: 'At the beginning of the causeway old cast-iron lamp standards from Europe had been placed as a decorative feature—old lamps at a site of new power. A pretty idea: but the lamp standards had also received a battering, and again attempts had been made to file away the lettering—the name of the nineteenth-century makers in Paris.

'It was the rage that made an impression—the rage of simple men tearing at metal with their hands.'

After the rebellion, the collection of African masks painstakingly built up by a Belgian missionary is allowed to rot.

A young American has it shipped to the US, 'No doubt to be the nucleus of the gallery of primitive art he often spoke of starting'.

About a month and a half before *A Bend in the River* was published in America, Naipaul published an article in *The New York Review of Books* (March 22, 1979) on Indian art—a marvelously fresh piece of writing on a subject staled by many dead minds. He writes on books dealing with several aspects of Indian painting and mediaeval sculpture, and on *A Historical Atlas of South Asia*. The last, published by Oxford University Press, New York, is priced at $150. Naipaul ends his article:

> 'Though the shutters go down on intellectual inquiry in so many countries that have emerged or come to wealth, and though revivalism and political simplicities always threaten to close up the world again, it is a kind of Golden Age that we live in, after all: books like Lope's (on Indian medieval sculpture) and this Atlas—inconceivable at any other period and in any other civilization—testify to it.'

The Golden Age? In today's America? The world's wealthiest and most powerful nation, where the paintings of India and the masks of Africa go—our one civilized peak after all? The optimism is uncharacteristic. We should perhaps be glad that this most restless and inquiring of writers has found something in one civilization to praise—and praise unstintingly. But we should also be right to suspect that the richness of his own sensibility, his own extraordinary gifts, will find, in America, no permanent home. He has shed too many of the simpler hopes by which colonials live, seen too many beliefs in simple political systems come crashing down. Nothing about him will let him reduce America to a simple idea. His edgy inquiring eye will deny him that gift. He is surviving Civilized Man, the civilized malcontent, uniquely alone in the literatures of the world; and in the civilized world itself, uniquely homeless.

AUBREY MENEN: A SPACE OF HIS OWN

Aubrey Menen has lived in more places than any other writer I know of. London, Bombay, a jungle in Gujarat, Amalfi, Rome, and Trivandrum. Except for the jungle, he lived in each place for several years at a time, and it's possible there were places I know nothing about. Superficially, he gives the impression of having been a restless writer, or at least one who could not stay in one place for any great length of time. Superficially too, that very restlessness could be seen to be the cause of his seeking out its opposite—the still centre or the space within the heart which he describes in his autobiographical book, *The Space within the Heart & It is All Right* (Penguin India). At a deeper level, this view just doesn't hold.

Menen himself is responsible for the more superficial view of himself, and his book is an attempt at owning up to that responsibility. At a crucial point in his life he realises he doesn't know who he is. His social self which required him to play a social role has been built on glib responses, accepted answers, the question being 'Who am I?' Quite early in his life he realises he has a problem. It isn't his homosexuality—he comes to terms with it very happily—but a zealous regard for his own privacy. He will not open his heart even to his most intimate friends lest they invade it. The problem was compounded by the fact that one particular anxiety he had, about incest—his mother was physically obsessed by him—did not find sympathetic listeners, even among the gracious liberals of Bloomsbury. He soon turned against them.

Very early on in the book we know that Menen knows that though he is a reasonably gregarious person he is also a very private one. Both these aspects come into play during his travels, and are responsible for where he chose to live, as we shall see. This isn't the traditional restlessness of the travel writer or of one commissioned to write a piece for a travel magazine, though, in fact, Menen did do some of his best writing on commission—for the magazine *Holiday*. It is rather the passage of a man caught 'between the twin hells of solitude and society'—to use Angus Wilson's phrase. Here hell is regarded as a state of being, not another place, as Menen came to realise. At one stage in his life he didn't think so.

He was a Roman Catholic. At his mother's funeral, for which he was present as he had been for his father's a year before, he wrote a message on the wreath, 'When you see him, tell Dada I love him.' He goes on to say, 'Although I did not know it at the time, I was subscribing to one of the myths that had built Western civilisation. But I had a long thinking road to traverse before I could see that.' The road that led him to abandon the myth—of an afterlife in which loved ones and friends meet up in Paradise, though hell could be an unprepared-for eventuality—lasted till Trivandrum, to the end of his life. It's part of the journey down that road, which the first section of *The Space within the Heart* describes. It was an inner journey, which made him discover who he was. His other journeys made him famous.

Menen has produced some of the best travel-writing there is. I was fortunate to lay my hands on some of it, borrowed from private libraries many years ago. But it has remained out of print and its excellence can only be guessed at by some passages in *The Space within the Heart*. That writing and those passages are fascinating for another reason too. They make a pattern not only of Menen's life and death, but that of persons like him—those who seem to go places on a hidden impulse, who will suddenly leave good company to go off into the desert of jungle or some remote spot without telling anyone.

'When I was forty,' Menen writes, 'I settled down in a house in Amalfi, not, as I told people, because it was a delectable spot on the Italian Riviera, but because it was near Pompeii. Whenever the world got too much for me and people too demanding, I could go to this empty city. I went so often I know every street and alley in it. I have seen it on a bitter January morning, under snow, and totally deserted. I do not know that I have ever seen anything so much after my own private heart.'

I first read the passage in an earlier Indian edition of the book (in 1973, I think) and have since read it again and again. It evokes for me similar wintry scenes in Europe and an envy that I never saw Pompeii the way he describes it or ever saw it at all. Above all, for want of going to such places now, it evokes the stillness of death, the solitude in which, one day, we face death alone. It is oddly reassuring.

He cherished what he thought was entirely his own space, 'an absorption with the remote past' that he didn't have to share with people. That's why he chose to live in Amalfi and later in Rome. Since the Romans had no love for their monuments, he could 'go among the ruins and never say or hear a word about them'.

Still later, he locked himself up in the Thieves' Quarter of that city to study what might have become another ruin, himself, if he didn't find out who he was. To do this, he set up a system that ensured privacy and enabled him to follow a rigorous intellectual discipline that wasn't so much based on the Upanishads as woven round them. He didn't 'practise meditation' as the accepted phrase goes but submitted himself to 'an intellectual process, like learning a foreign language'. It's interesting he uses those words since part of his problem was that one part of him was always a foreign language to the other. His Indian side and his Irish side sometimes faced each other as strangers, aggressively baffled by what each saw in the other. It was the wrong place to look, as Menen discovered. He had to seek out and find the space within the heart.

The language it taught him was one he had known in other forms: it was Silence. But this was not the silence of wintry Pompeii or of a hill in Rome. To find out who he was he had to go through a process of not that, not that, the peeling of the layers of an onion until, as the Upanishads claim, you come to an initially terrifying space, the space within the heart. The 'I' of that space, the Tranquil Eye as Menen came to call it, is itself and itself alone, not dependent on others' perception of that self and not needing its own perception of others to define itself.

Above all, as Menen puts it, 'Our true self is not superior to other people; it is not inferior either. It is not touched by other people at all. It does not wish other people to be better, or to be worse; it neither punishes nor praises. It can be totally indifferent to the world, as if sleeping; or it can awake and observe, but with the same indifference.' After the experience of peace which comes with or follows such knowledge, an experience which some would call mystical but which Menen scrupulously avoids defining as such, could a person go out into the world again and not lose that hard-won space, the 'new-found quiet of my spirit', as he calls it? His last testament 'It is All Right', included in this edition and written shortly before he died three years ago, indicates that it stayed with him to the end of his life. If he ever lost it, he found it again.

The testament is about facing death and the impossibility of fearing it. The young man in Pompeii who felt it in the air is now an older man in Trivandrum, dying of cancer of the mouth. When he wrote the testament after months of radiation therapy, he thought he was cured of it. Aware that it could recur, he followed his mother's example.

When she learned she had cancer, she called him over from Rome to help her kill herself. She was living alone in Kent. The son flew over and had to promise he would not come in her way if she chose that way out. Menen, in Trivandrum, had to extract the same promise of his friend Graham Hall.

Hall did make a promise but in the event, as with Menen in the case of his mother, didn't have to keep it. If he had he would have done what all good friends were supposed to do in Menen's beloved Rome once upon a time; hold the sword for a friend to fall upon.

That may seem an insensitive thing to say, especially to Hall who had to find the courage to tell his friend that he had little time to live. But the point about *It is All Right* is that it is all right. (The words are taken from Stonewall Jackson, 'Very good,' he said, 'very good' when told to prepare for death. 'It is all right.') Menen was indifferent to death, an indifference he acquired in the Thieves' Quarter in Rome more than twenty years previously. What he was not indifferent to was pain and the thought of living like a vegetable. He felt this applied to everyone; no one ever feared death. The supposed deterrent of the most painful killings and summary executions through the ages has not stopped militants, terrorists and soldiers from taking up arms. Without referring to the famous passage in the *Mahabharata*, Menen's position is very similar to Yudhisthir's, who, when questioned by a disguised Dharma as to what he thought was the greatest wonder in the world, replied, 'Each day death strikes and we live as though we were immortal'. Menen is also the young Nachiketas of the Upanishads, now closer to death than ever before because of his cancer, confronting it with similarly awkward questions. The boy he got to understand in the Upanishads in Rome stayed with him to the last.

Except that neither Nachiketas nor Yama has anything to say to him now. When asked by the boy what happens after death, Yama's answers are so evasive, Menen says he would have a great career if he went into Indian politics.

This is typical of Menen. Just as he discarded Bloomsbury's high-minded intellectuals once upon a time, he discarded the Upanishads towards the end of his life. They had nothing more to offer him. The last chapter shows him in some agitation, dredging up writer after writer he had read in the past— Western writers who had sustained him through difficulties before. He seeks Augustine (his favourite saint), Dante, Gibbon's Letters, Gray's 'Elegy' and quite appropriately for a much-travelled man, *Gulliver's Travels*. They eased him but didn't change him.

Menen's approach to himself and others was often cold. He embraced his mother coldly, even when she was wasted and dying. She noticed and said so. That was one of the reasons he tried to discover himself in Rome. Why had he been so cold? In his introduction to the book, Hall says he remained consistent. Close to the end, he 'shrugged as much as the hospital apparatus plugged into him allowed and then told me not to be emotional'. Death, the Great Friend, embraced him with more warmth than he ever embraced his mother.

NOTES TOWARDS A PORTRAIT OF NISSIM EZEKIEL

The house: ochre. Trees behind it and along its side: deep green, lemon-yellow, Vandyke brown. Grass leading to door: bushy, leaf green, undersides of leaves lined with kohl.

The door: blue-grey. Wrong door. We are told to enter by the side. Grill covering entrance: rust-brown with a lock on it.

A woman comes down from the floor above to let us in. We are R. Raj Rao, Cyrus Mistry and myself. Or so we think. We have come to visit Nissim Ezekiel.

Passing rooms with several people in them, we are taken to his.

It's past four in the afternoon, a day in December and the day's drawing in, making the room darker than it was during my two previous visits. Nissim is roused from bed by Malti, one of the women who look after him. He looks at us in wonder, his hand outstretched.

We have filed into the room awkwardly, Raj the tallest, entering last. We fumble with the courtesies, we fumble with the order in which we're to sit. We finally settle on a settee, me meant to be nearest Nissim, if only we knew where he would settle. He prefers sitting on the edge of his bed; Malti insists he sit on a chair.

A figure taller than Raj flits into the room, a giant bat. He shares the room with Nissim. He clearly enjoys going in and out of the room. His helper doesn't. She blocks the doorway with her stout frame, her eyes patient but tired. She asks him to go to his bed, softly.

In the meantime, my left foot has developed an itch. I calm it, but drawing hand back from foot, my elbow jogs Cyrus' side. He lets out a grunt, his left knee jumping reflexively. It narrowly misses Raj's face, since, just a moment before, Raj has decided to bend down to tie his bootlace. I sigh. I think it's going to be one of those afternoons. A projected portrait of Nissim turning into a visit by the Three Stooges.

But no. He's suddenly there, right in front of me, sitting on a chair, his hands folded on his lap. Hair: close-cropped, grey-brown. Eyes: spectacled, greyish. Smile: gentle; when broad: with a black hole punched in it. Shirt: blue-grey, like the wrong door.

He asks: 'Are all of you together?'

The three stooges: 'YES!'

He asks: 'You are all from the same place?'

The three stooges look at one another and in a hesitant tone say, 'Yes.'

He looks at the book of poems I have brought him. It's *Crossing the Border* by Tenzin Tsundue. He puts the book on his bed, folds his hands on his lap and talks:

'I will read the book by and by. There's a lot to read. After I read them, the books are taken away. Otherwise there'd be no space. There's an institution next door. There's something happening there all the time. I was there before you came. There's something going on all the time. If you go there now, you might hear a discussion. I think they'll be stopping soon.

'Are the three of you from the same place?'

The same place?

                        What are these?
So wither'd, and so wild in their attire,

> That they look not like th'inhabitants of th'earth
> And yet are on it?
>   You seem to understand me
> By each at once her choppy finger laying
> Upon her skinny lips. You should be women
> And yet your beards forbid me to interpret
> That you are so.

'I've been here a year as you know. My son visits me. He has been very busy. He looks after things in my absence. I don't write too much but there's always something to do. Are you sure you won't go next door? They may be stopping soon. Then everyone gets up and goes home suddenly. Before you know it, things are over. Suddenly.'

> *His love and how it hurt the girl, despair*
> *Absurdly at the core of hope, the tree*
> *Of life uprooted by a sudden storm . . .*

Suddenly a visitor.

'Suddenly there are many people. People come for advice, for this and that. They have very interesting programmes next door. Don't you want to have a look?

'You're sure you want to be with me?'

> *The other day I was visited*
> *By one absorbed in himself—*
> *I prefer the company of spiders*

'I had a good lunch. I eat regularly. I take whatever medicines they give me. It's routine.'

Nissim's tall room-mate, who has been listening from his bed, gets up. Nissim gets up too and goes to him. 'Are you all right?' he asks. 'Is everything all right?'

He comes back to his chair to sit for his portrait again.

'What else has been happening? I have been here for a year as you know.'

> *Three times the crow has cawed.*

'I will read the poetry book by and by. I always have something to read. Then they take it away.'

> Three times the crow has cawed
> At the window, baleful eyes fixed
> On mine . . .
>
> The ordinariness of most events.
>
> I prefer the company of spiders.
>
> All day I waited as befits
> The folk belief that following
> The crow a visitor would come,
> An angel in disguise perhaps . . .

'There's an institution next door. It's just round the corner. There's something going on there now. Every day, there's something. It's a good institution.'

> I see how wrong I was
> Not to foresee precisely this:
> Outside the miracles of mind,
> The figure in the carpet blazing,
> Ebb-flow of sex and the seasons,
> The ordinariness of most events

'Are you sure you don't want to go and see?'

We go and see. His shirt is blue-grey, his eyes greyish. Mustn't forget. Exit the Weird Sisters. Outside the house the grass is leaf green, each leaf etched in its curve of kohl. I look up towards the buildings opposite. Cyrus looks in another direction. Raj, Nissim's biographer, one knee on the grass, has his face down. He busies himself with a bootlace.

The kohl starts running, the buildings start breaking up.

Editor's note: All the lines quoted are from the poetry of Nissim Ezekiel, except of course for the lines ('*What are these?* . . .') from Shakespeare.

WITH DAYA PAWAR IN PARIS

'When I said autumn, autumn broke'
Elizabeth Jennings

There's a time in Europe when people instinctively know that a particular season has set in. That October evening in Paris, walking with Daya Pawar down a busy street, the old Opera House behind us, I got that feeling: autumn is truly here. The air was smokey with the fires of chestnut vendors. They drew attention to themselves with cries of 'Roasted chestnuts'. Daya and I walked down the busy street and talked of his autobiography, *Baluta*, written in Marathi.

He had shown me extracts of a French translation. I had shown it to a French publisher. That was almost exactly ten years ago.

I'd first met him in Frankfurt about a fortnight earlier. We were part of the contingent invited to an India-focused book fair, he as a writer, I as a publisher. The writers were staying in a hotel. I had been offered lodgings in the flat of a banker who preferred to be away from it. Urvashi Butalia of Kali for Women was the other guest.

The writers and publishers rarely met even at the fairgrounds. I don't think many writers were present even when P. V. Narasimha Rao did his march-around in the hall in which we displayed our books. He was then human resources development minister and in his opening speech, which many found impressive, asked 'Indian and German writers to join in a common endeavour to create a better world through literature.'

Easier said than done. One day I found myself in the company of several writers on the way to their hotel. If I remember right, most of us landed up in Daya's room. There was an argument between Daya and Madhu Kishwar, editor of *Manushi*, on the causes of the anti-Dalit riots which had erupted in Bombay during that year. I was impressed by Daya's calm and measured reasoning, especially when set against Madhu's petulance. Also, it seemed he spoke out of experience, Madhu more out of theory.

I didn't see much of Daya at Frankfurt after that meeting but before leaving the city he told me he'd be in Paris later in the month. I gave him my wife's telephone number and asked him to call just in case we were there at the time.

He called on 16 October and we were. He said he was living in a hotel near Charles de Gaulle airport. It sounded horribly expensive. Veronik, my wife, suggested we look for a cheaper one closer to where we were staying. The next day we met him at a railway station and took him home. A new hotel was found and we spent a lot of the next three days with him.

All that time I was struck by Daya's reticence, his near-legendary modesty. It wasn't just that he was diffident about his English—he and I conversed mostly in Hindi—it was part of his way of observing things—being there, warm, affable, almost always smiling, but observing things. Daya and I went for long walks, Veronik took him to the cinema. They saw Carlos Saura's *Blood Wedding* which Veronik liked but which Daya slept through for a while. They went to *The Colour Purple* which Veronik hated and which he loved. At no point did he try to impose his views on us, nor ever try to project himself as a Dalit, nor aggressively promote the idea of Dalit literature. I think we understood each other, despite our different backgrounds.

Back in Bombay, those different backgrounds kept us apart. If writers meet, they normally live or work in the same neighbourhood. Or they meet formally, at infrequent seminars or multilingual readings, very few of which have been successful. In the city we have to get on with the business of living, which can be killing.

I believe it killed Daya, though he died far from home, in a city he barely knew. Collapsing in the middle of a seminar in

Delhi isn't the best way to go, though it does convey an extreme reaction to seminars. I just wish it hadn't been Daya to show us what it's like—to be humble to the point of self-effacement and to go without fuss.

Strange that as I write this far from Paris, there should be a touch of autumn in the air, the smell of roasted chestnuts, and the presence of a warm smiling human being.

Just one more thing. I'll never know why Daya never told me that even as I took his work to a French publisher, he had already signed up with another French publisher to bring it out. Was it a misunderstanding on my part? Or just another example of the extreme reticence which can cause problems for others? Maybe one day I'll get to know.

REMEMBERING RAMAN

Polymath is not a word A. K. Ramanujan would have liked to hear used about himself. It's an ugly word, more suited to a bird than a poet and though Raman, as his friends used to call him, was a rare bird, he was an even rarer poet. The arch of his learning—in folklore, anthropology and linguistics, to mention three of his subjects—tends to overshadow his work as a poet, but it is to that work and the poetic sensibility behind it to which we must return if we are to come anywhere near understanding the man.

In a sense it isn't hard to understand him because Ramanujan is Everyman, the harried householder who has to work for a living and commute in one or the other of the planet's infernal cities. His poems consist of householder anxieties, little lists and prescriptions one can imagine him making in the morning to soothe his nerves. Take a bit of this and a bit of that and the children will stop howling, the nagging wife will go away; perhaps the boss too will be kind.

I can't speak of his poems in Kannada but in his English

work, Ramanujan is predominantly a domestic poet, unfreed by his sense of history or the past. The present holds his gaze, literally binds him—'living among relations/ binds the feet' as the memorable epigraph in his second book of poems, *Relations*, tells us. Escape is impossible, any attempt at it only leading to another bonding, another relation, another binding. The poem 'Snakes and Ladders' is concerned with just this kind of movement:

> *Losing every time I win, climbing*
> > *ladders, falling to the bottom with snakes,*
> *I make scenes:*
>
> *In my anger, I smash all transparent*
> > *things, crystal, glass panes, one-way mirrors*
> *and my glasses,*
>
> *blinding myself, I hit my head on white*
> > *walls, shut myself up in the bathroom,*
> *toying with razors . . .*

The poem begins with a descent to the bathroom where 'sick to the stomach' the poet wakes 'hugging the white toilet bowl,/my cool porcelain sister'.

Comic? Yes, but barely. That sister in the poet's delirium is not just a newfound relation; she's also the sister of sickness, the cool nurse in the hospital. The razor and the scalpel, never far away from Ramanujan's verse, stayed with him to the last. He died under anaesthesia, just before being operated on in a hospital in Chicago.

I first met Ramanujan when he was passing through London. I remember the foyer of a hotel in the Strand where he and his family had gathered in a state of disarray—Raman, his wife Molly and their son and daughter.

I also remember the poet R. Parthasarthy and Girish Karnad being there. They were far from being in a state of disarray. On the contrary, from the very start of the evening, they adopted the pillar-like postures of commissars of south Indian writing from which position they refused to be moved. The Ramanujans, on the other hand, were moving all over the place.

The hotel receptionist insisted that they hadn't booked rooms in advance; the hotel staff were rude; racist rejection hung in the air like the hotel's dull drapes. Finally, an attic room, a long corridor-like affair, was found. Molly and the children were ensconced there, while Raman, the pillars and I went to the dining room. I was at the time working on an anthology of new Indian writing. Raman gave useful advice. The pillars froze.

I met him several times since then, in various places. I stayed with him in Chicago in 1977. My second book of poems had been out the previous year and to my horror and trepidation, one evening he invited some of his university colleagues over to listen to me read from the book.

'You see, I told you it would go down well,' he said after the evening was over. I wasn't sure. He had found certain things wrong with the book and also told me, 'I wish you'd sent me your manuscript to read. I'd have given it a thorough look. I'm rather good at that.'

Anyone who's had his or her work scrutinized by Raman knows this to be true. I'm told he was always clear-sighted, zooming in quickly on a poem's weak spots. Though he had a wicked sense of humour, I'm told his criticism was free of malice. That he could keep several projects going at the same time was common knowledge among his friends and colleagues. Saul Bellow was one of them. I'd like to think that Dr Lal, one of the characters in *Mr Sammler's Planet*, is based at least a little on Raman.

On one occasion in the novel, when a pipe bursts, Sammler and his daughter watch helplessly. It's Lal who comes to the rescue, dashing up the stairs, his fists bunched against his fragile body. Perhaps there's a crueller portrait in Molly Ramanujan's novel *The Salt Doll* which she wrote under the name Shourie

Daniels. But that novel, published by Vikas, is out of print and hard to find.

Because of his several accomplishments and the highly sought-after American honour of a MacArthur Fellowship, we may believe that Ramanujan would have had no problem finding a publisher in the US. That wasn't the case. Though Oxford University Press, New York, published his three books of poems, his *Selected Poems* were published by that press from Delhi. Britain's Penguin, which published *Speaking of Siva*—his translations of Kannada bhakti poems—refused to reprint it. As every scholar and translator of South Asian writing knows, most major publishing houses abroad, including the academic ones, are still reluctant to touch such writing.

Whatever happens to such writing in the future, Ramanujan's reputation in this area is secure. He has inspired a band of translators at the University of Chicago where he taught for thirty-one years. His colleagues and students will miss him greatly. To them he was a polymath. Ugly as the word is, we return to it to mourn the flight of a rare bird and an even rarer poet.

REMEMBERING SUDHIR

The hibiscus plant has to be repotted. Its small red flowers glint in the morning sun. I think: he won't be around to see them. The phone rings. I think: it won't be him on the line. The newspaper announcement of Sudhir Sonalkar's death was brief and to the point. He died of cardiac arrest; it mentioned the papers and journals he wrote for. Anyone who had anything to do with his writing, whether as editor or colleague must feel a sense of absence now. Working with Sudhir, being with him, hearing him talk with passion about the subjects that oppressed him most—subjects like racism, communalism, injustice and poverty—was to work with, be with and hear more than a living presence.

It was this passion which got him into trouble with others, many of them his friends like me who would have liked him to step back from his concerns from time to time, to not make them obsessions which could dominate his life to the point of destruction. It was a vain hope. Once Sudhir got hold of an idea he would never let go of it but try it out on friend and foe, sometimes at odd hours of the day and night, via the phone. Useless to tell Sudhir that 3 a.m. wasn't the best of times to discuss the dialectics of madness or the Bharatiya Janata Party's position on cows. After a point, you just yelled into the receiver and slammed it down. It would be hard to find another person who was more yelled at and slammed down upon than Sudhir. When asked to explain why he didn't choose a more reasonable hour to make calls, he'd plead that he was lonely and needed someone to talk to. He felt he had no one to talk to in Pune for which he left Bombay a few years ago.

What he didn't say was what all drinkers know but dare not say. That if you've had more than one too many, you lose sense of time; the cocoon of drink produces a myriad bright lights, earth-shattering butterflies; you think, you feel, an urgent need to communicate. God knows I've felt that way too. But it's a one-way alley of communication that tolerates no rebuff, no dead-end. That's what made it worse for Sudhir.

Once when I was editor of *Debonair* he called me at my parents', at a reasonable hour, and asked to be given a job on the magazine again; he had been its assistant editor previously. He said he'd find himself a place in Bombay. I wasn't to worry. I turned him down as gently as I could. 'Then fuck off!' he snapped and disconnected. Just as well. If the conversation continued I wouldn't have been able to tell him why I'd turned him down; that I sometimes overdid my drinks too, that I had recently taken on the magazine a writer who turned out to have a drinking problem greater than any I'd seen, that taking Sudhir on board would have meant capsizing the raft altogether. When I had the opportunity to explain this to him personally, he understood. The interruptions in our friendship never lasted long.

I was touched when I heard from someone that he considered me his oldest friend. Strange then that though I know the awful day he died, I don't know when he was born. He must have been two or three years younger than me; we first met when I was about twenty and he was a student at the Elphinstone College. He wrote poetry then and we must have met at a poetry reading. I remember him showing me his poems with that serious intent gaze which was to stay with him to the end of his life. The poetry reading circle included people like R. Parthasarathy and Kumar Shahani and I know that with Kumar he struck a rapport that was to continue till long after Kumar had made a name for himself in cinema.

I had to go back to England in 1962 and I'm not sure how often I met Sudhir on a subsequent visit to India but we did meet in London when he joined his father who was posted there as head of a bank for a few years. Sudhir took a job with a newspaper, wrote articles, poems and short stories and grew increasingly disenchanted with what he saw around him. We edged closer to black politics in Britain, we were gripped by the American presence in Vietnam, we joined hands with several thousand others on a historic protest march that demanded the Americans quit. That was in 1968. Sudhir's hoarse chanting of slogans outdid the professionals.

It was perhaps inevitable that when he returned to India, his politics would take a radical turn. Naxalbari, the CPM-L, Marxist-Leninist thought itself inspired him to think and write more and more about a possible revolution in India. This belief, deeply aggravated by the inhuman conditions of living which he witnessed in the country, sometimes brought him close to megalomania and self-delusion. Not only close. I believe their poisonous colours tinged him more than once. Madness—not just the subject but the thing itself—fascinated him. It should come as no surprise, in retrospect, that when he decided to kick his drinking habit, he first visited the mental ward of Yerawada Hospital—a place most people of his class would shun. Bravely, but quite typically, he wrote about his experience.

That piece he wrote will survive him as will many others, including the one about his feelings of being a father for the first time. After his marriage broke up, his daughter became the centre of his life but his in-laws were given custody of her and his accounts of his attempts to visit her, almost always unsuccessful, were both pathetic and, in their sorrow, intolerable to listen to.

His wife was a dedicated Gandhian and in the break-up of their marriage and her subsequent death, lay a basic incompatibility of vision, of commitment. Sudhir greatly admired Gandhi—he was, perhaps, the main subject of most of our conversations—but he was also a lover of art, literature and sensual pleasure in a way that Gandhi was not. This inevitably led to disagreements between him and his wife over their daughter's upbringing.

Unlike many Marxists, Sudhir thought deeply about religion and recognised its importance in his own life. Oppressed by the casteist aspects of Hinduism, he was drawn to Christianity and sometimes spoke of the need for a Christian revolution in the country. More recently he said he wanted to convert to Islam since that was the only way he could find out what Muslims in the country felt. By being one of them.

I am told that in the last few weeks of his life he had stopped eating. The phone had been cut off because he couldn't pay the bills. Could he have felt, in his last few days, that the isolation he dreaded and which he tried to break out of so often had become a reality one last time? Did he try to reach out, make a final call at the end? I am told that though his body was wracked, his mind was sound. I am told he donated his body to the hospital he died in.

'A strange old-fashioned pleasure'

WRITING

THE JOY OF SENSUOUS WRITING

The other day, while writing the address of a friend on an envelope, I experienced a strange old-fashioned pleasure. The envelope was plump with the letter I'd fed it and the fine tip of the pen I was using sank into it as it formed the letters of his name, smoothening each curve and stroke, transmitting its message of silk to the tips of my fingers. That message had its origins in the first days of writing at school, when, learning the alphabet, you discovered that some days the letters turned out well, and some days so perfect that you thrilled to the prospect of writing forever, of forever taking pleasure in forming words and later sentences that took on an aesthetic life of their own, regardless of their meaning. The perfectly formed sentence, the perfectly straight margin and finally the block of a paragraph, chunky and sensuous as though made of marshmallow.

Those were the days when you discovered the various consistencies of graphite, the hard leads which almost incised the papers you wrote on, the softer leads which caressed it. The lead point submitted to your will, your pressure, eroding itself precisely to the contours of what you and other people came to regard as your handwriting. If a section of the page did not look good, if too much or too little space was left between words or lines you simply rubbed it out. There were good erasers which barely left a mark and bad erasers which smudged. There was pleasure in sharpening a pencil to the point of your desire and tears when the pencil fell to the floor and the point shattered, leaving crumbs of its head around it.

Later, when you were old enough to use a fountain pen, the process was repeated. There were broad nibs and fine nibs,

nibs that you fell in love with because they suited your fingers well, gave great pleasure to their tips, until the pens too nose-dived off the school-desk, their smooth platypus beaks as they went off the edge crooking on impact into those of vultures. A favourite pen destroyed, a favourite pen stolen and you learned what it meant to grow up. It meant a favourite pleasure gone and you had to live with it.

Graduating to the typewriter, though not yet to the word processor, has produced a different kind of pleasure, but typewriters aren't suited to a certain kind of writing, the sensuous kind, where the pleasure of what you write is supplemented, perhaps even shaped, by the texture of the paper you write on, the pen or pencil you hold in your hand.

I don't mean the pleasure of calligraphy, the words you write may be intelligible only to yourself. I mean writing with a pen or pencil evokes a whole set of feelings quite different from that conjured up by keyboards.

Try it. Revive an old pleasure as I am doing now. It beats most others in the book.

WHAT'S THIS?
A NEW TWO-NATION THEORY?

There's a strong rumour about, so strong that some of us are beginning to believe it. It was started by Bill Buford, editor of *Granta*, who is supposed to have said in a *New Yorker* issue on India that most Indians who write in English don't live in India. Significantly more than those who live in India, Mr Buford? Well, he might say, there's that group photograph of them in London to prove it. It appeared in the *New Yorker*. Not having seen the photograph, I must guess the number of 'gone-away' writers it frames. Ten, at most fifteen? In fifty years of independence, is that the sum total of almost all Indian writers in English?

It takes me back thirty-seven years, to my first year in Oxford when I tried to convince a fellow undergraduate, a white South African, that there was much more to Indian literature than the works of Tagore. He was sceptical. 'Why don't you believe me?' I asked him. 'Because,' he replied gravely, 'if there was much more, we'd have heard about it.' 'We in South Africa or we in Great Britain?' I should have asked Jeremy. But I was speechless.

The blindness was staggering, and going by Buford's supposed remark, the blindness continues. Paradoxically, it's a blindness linked to vision, or one vision. Believe only what you see is how that particular vision goes. What you don't see, doesn't exist. So when I was an undergraduate in England, if someone who wasn't an Indian had told me that Tagore was the most visible of Indian writers, I'd have agreed. Similarly, if Buford had only said that Indian writers who live outside India, particularly in Britain, the US and Canada, are the most visible writers, we'd have had little to argue with him about.

Can an editor of Buford's stature seriously expect to judge a nation's literature almost solely by the writing being done outside that nation? Would he have taken that attitude to the literatures of Africa or Ireland? Both those parts of the world have seen many of their writers go away and live in other parts of the world. Plain common sense should tell us that despite such a situation, a great many poems, plays, novels and short stories are still being written in Africa and Ireland. And if common sense doesn't tell us that, any good anthology of writing from those parts of the world will.

But, as usual, when it comes to India, common sense gives way to nonsense, insight to ignorance. For some, Indian writers living abroad have become beacons of light, those who live in India, with every few exceptions, will remain unlit and unlightable, each in an area of darkness.

Is there a new two-nation theory in the making—one language, two nations? Preparing for the eventual Partition, should we already start calling the nations Home and Abroad?

Praise is a new phenomenon, as anyone who has followed the West's critical indifference to Indian writing in English knows. It's only post-1981, post-*Midnight's Children* that the critics—some critics—started sitting up and taking notice. From 'Indian's can't write in English' we became 'the best writers of English prose'. From 'Indians lack a sense of humour' we became 'the people who write the best comic prose in English today'. (I read this or words to that effect in an issue of *The Times Literary Supplement* two years ago.) The shift of attitude was so sudden, it seemed it happened overnight.

Naturally there's been a backlash. Some British writers and critics feel we should be put in our place. That is, we should write only about the place we come from. We shouldn't mess with things British. We don't know enough about those things or the deep traditions they spring from. Like Chinese take-aways in Birmingham, I suppose. And beautiful laundrettes. But the backlash will pass, as will the present euphoria. One notable point: even before the dawn of our fiftieth anniversary of independence or our latest stroke of midnight ('stroke' having come to mean that we have the symptoms of never having recovered from one), nine collections of Indian writing and of writing on India are out. They come from London and New York—special issues of *Granta*, *Ambit*, *Acumen*, *Lines Review*, *The Financial Times*, *Times Literary Magazine*, *London Magazine*, *New Yorker*, and, of course, the notorious anthology edited by Rushdie and Elizabeth West. Given our celebratory year you mightn't think this unusual, but it is. Publishers and editors of literary journals in Britain and America almost always follow a simple rule. Get interested in the literature of a foreign country only if democracy in that country is under threat or when writers in that country work under conditions of extreme censorship. So the Pasternak affair led to an interest in Russian 'dissident' writing, Cuban writing got special treatment soon after Castro's takeover, the interest in Central and East European writing was at its height when those countries were under Communist rule.

I think this must be the first time in the last fifty years, perhaps in this century, that publishers on both sides of the Atlantic have joined hands to mark a foreign country's celebration of democracy and not its threatened or real extinction. That's something to think about.

One more thought before the last one. I worked on an anthology of Indian writing for more than five years. It was published by Penguin in 1974 and was called *New Writing in India*. Unlike Rushdie's and West's anthology, it contains a large amount of work by Indian language writers translated into English. Having some knowledge of that field, I found Rushdie's statement—that the editors found little of worth in Indian-language writing to include in their opus—to be hasty and ill-informed.

And the last thought: soon it'll be Sri Lanka's turn to celebrate fifty years of independence. I propose that the year 2000 see at least one anthology of writing from South Asia, not just Sri Lanka, consisting only of work translated into English or originally in English, done by writers who haven't gone away. If that happens, some people on both sides of the Atlantic might be very surprised.

BETWEEN VIKRAM AND THE VACUUM

Once upon a time there was a good boy called Vikram. He used to write poems which no one read. One day he decided to write a novel in verse. When it was published everyone wanted to read it. He was still a good boy. Then, for eight long years he worked on another novel. A British publisher offered him £250,000 for it. Now he is a bad boy.

Once upon a time there was a good boy called Salman. He wrote a novel no one read. Then he wrote a novel everyone tried to read but couldn't. Let's skip the bits in between—we know why he's a bad boy now, a very, very bad boy. In case anyone's forgotten, it's not just that he offended a number of Muslims. He became bad the moment we knew that a publisher had offered him a great deal of money for a novel.

Strange that other kinds of people, offered similar sums of money for other kinds of work, don't go bad on us overnight. Who grudges our filmstars and cricketers their lakhs? And if someone in the telecommunications business invented a phone that worked in every conceivable adverse condition in this country, day and night, we wouldn't grudge him the moon if he wanted it. But authors aren't supposed to want, oh no. Most of all, they aren't supposed to want money.

That's not the theme of my song today, however—an old and boring one for writers anyway. Rather, I'd like to talk about that interesting person in their lives who helps them make money, a person from a species that hasn't even started breeding in this country yet: the literary agent.

Seth's agent is Giles Gordon, a person who has written novels himself, and a report in the *Indian Express* tells us that while Seth himself stood 'under a window', it was Gordon who was on the line making the right deals for Seth.

I've forgotten the name of Rushdie's agent but I do recollect Rushdie saying somewhere that so appalled was he at the meagre sums of money that Anita Desai got for her work, that he took her under his wing and to his agent. Her fortunes have improved considerably since then even if the sales of her novels haven't. (All this talk of a market for Indian writing abroad fails to take into account that very few novelists, Indian or British or American, sell more than 5,000 copies of a book. As for poets, a recent article by the British poet Andrew Motion states that sales of even the best-known like Ted Hughes and Seamus Heaney, still hover around the 2,000-copies mark. In Bombay recently, Seth himself said: 'Most of my poetry is a joke. I can't earn anything on it.')

Practically every literary agent stipulates that he or she will accept manuscripts of novels only, not manuscripts of poems or even short stories. Once they accept an author they'll do their best to get the best deal from publishers—it's in their interest after all; they get a cut. In their exertions to drive hard bargains, they can drive and have driven many publishers up the wall. Most of the publishers I've met made no secret of their disliking literary agents. At the same time they concede that they do serve as a useful buffer between them and authors. Authors are generally illiterate about the many processes that go into publishing a book and in their obdurate illiteracy have been known to drive publishers not just up the wall but mad.

Larger firms of literary agents deal with not just an author's literary rights but his television and film rights too. It isn't often appreciated in this country that the much despised medium of television has saved many contemporary writers' lives, providing them with the cash to get on with their writing.

Though Joyce's *Ulysses* and *Finnegan's Wake* have grown to be legends, I'd have preferred their author to have been spared his legendary penury while writing them. It is too terrible to think of what he went through in Zurich, giving the occasional private tuition or reading proofs. He had no literary agent but friends, often as poor as he was, who acted on his behalf, encouraging him, trying to place his work with publishers. Had he been alive today, a professional literary agent would have got him a better deal. If Forster had been living today, I doubt if he'd be so squeamish about getting his novels filmed. In inflationary Britain, with practically everyone feeling the pinch, he might have needed the cash.

Of course what I've said is silly, since writers exist in only one time and place and, like everyone else, are products of their times. 'Iffing' never got anyone anywhere. At the same time, wouldn't it be fair to say that if this country had even two or three good literary agents, Indian authors would flounder less in the (sometimes treacherous) waters of publishing?

A good literary agent has to be both swimming coach and salesperson. He or she is part of the crucial chain which links writer and reader. A literary agent generally has more time or should have more time than a publisher to advise a writer about his manuscript, where it needs cutting, where it goes wrong or right. Seth is not the kind of writer who would normally feel that he writes in a vacuum—though some vacuous critics make it a point of insisting that all those who write in English do—but if, during the long period of eight years when he was writing *A Suitable Boy* he ever felt he was, there was a literary agent, though far away in London, to remind him he was not. Between Vikram and the vacuum fell his shadow, and we're all better off for that.

THE ANT IN PUBLISHING

An academic at the Massachusetts Institute of Technology is paid $1.4 million to write a textbook. The author of *A Suitable Boy* becomes the subject of *A Suitable Boy*, a television film on his life. The United Kingdom bans the poster of *Disclosure*, the film based on Michael Crichton's book, on the grounds that it's too explicit.

Money, Fame, Sex. If you go by the news these days, the literary world's got it all. Forgotten are the pen-pushers, the menials of literature, the proof-readers and the typesetters, including their keyboard counterparts, whose eyes burn out long before they should owing to the nature of their work. Forgotten are the paper manufacturers, the page makers and book binders. These days the book is its author. Yet it's the others who make the book 'happen', those the media have reduced to fine print if they are mentioned at all, the ants of the book trade. Consider their ways and be wise.

I don't know if there's a bachelor's degree in proofreading anywhere in the world, but countries which have set high standards in publishing certainly have courses in proofreading. As there are courses in publishing. As far as I know there are no such courses in India (in English at least) though trainee journalists learn some of the rudiments of proofreading. Most of us have to learn on the job.

Further complications arise when proofreaders are ill at ease with the language they're proofing. This is inevitably the case with English in India. There can only be a handful of professional proofreaders in the country who can spot an error in the language which their senior editors have overlooked. We are the third largest publisher of books in English in the world. Textbooks on various subjects predominate. Multiply the errors in one textbook publishing house by several hundreds and you can see what goes into the heads of our students.

It's true that errors in maths, physics and chemistry textbooks, for example, are not always language related. Such subjects require another kind of professional proofreader. Where do our publishers find him or her?

All the same, the ants are busy at work even now, and ill-paid and overworked as they are, there's little point in crushing them further. The solution is to make the publishing profession attract professionals and to make it accountable to the public. This has already happened in magazine publishing but textbook publishing has a long way to go. It would seem we're more concerned with producing glossies than providing our children with accurate textbooks. And just in case our business and industrial houses didn't know, there's money in the textbook business. The American publisher who pays an author $1.4 million for a textbook knows that. Our publishers knew that all along. The textbook sells best. Carried on the backs of ants.

WHO READS US?

The Daily contacts about a hundred women, to find out if they've read Shobha De's *Surviving Men*. The answer is an overwhelming 'No'. Yet booksellers say it's doing well.

So who reads Shobha De?

Vilas Sarang sends me a text from Safat, Kuwait. It's an extract from a new history of modern literature. Its author states that novelists not of British origin should not write on British matters. They aren't in the 'tradition' of pucca British fiction. Salman Rushdie and Hanif Kureishi are two of many recent culprits. A month ago Sarang mentions V. S. Naipaul. In a despairing letter he says Naipaul now claims that his books haven't sold well in Britain. So, is the history man right? We shouldn't write about Britishers because they only read their own?

So who reads Naipaul? In Mumbai, an audience of a hundred at a poetry reading is considered good going (there have been audiences of three). Books of poetry are among the first to be remaindered and when publishers strike poetry off their lists, poets publish themselves. You must be mad to publish poetry, they say, let alone write it.

Who reads us?

There are answers in the murk, genuine diamonds for the intrepid miner, but first of all, why the murk? Largely because the relationship between publisher, author and reader is a murky area. A publisher can only tell an author that so many copies have sold, he can't tell him how many of those copies are read or who reads them. I find this disquieting. I find myself wanting my readers to stand up and be counted.

No one steps forward. In the end it's others who do the counting for you, the bookseller, the publisher. The bookseller tells me so many copies sold or didn't sell this month, the publisher tells me so many copies sold or didn't sell this year. Can anyone tell me who bought them? The answer's a resounding 'No!' Then comes a voice on the phone: 'I did. I picked up a copy of your anthology from the pavement. It's the best.' Time stops. Am I hearing things? Am I in heaven?

Hearing things is perhaps the only way a writer discovers who reads him or her. In other words, it isn't through statistics but by old-fashioned word of mouth. It's also one way of finding an answer to my three questions, not a scientific way, but the only one at my disposal.

Who reads Shobha De?

Word of mouth tells me they're not the kind of people she writes about. Word of mouth tells me those who read her are students, secretaries, long-distance travellers and some from among the long-wintering tribes—Swedes, Finlanders, Alaskans and the like. She helps them melt, she's easy on the eyes and ears, she's global pop. Word of mouth may have told her something else. In which case she can correct me.

Who reads V. S. Naipaul?

Not the Brits, we always suspected that. Not us, not Pakistanis, not Trinidadians either. Word of mouth tells me his readers are again from the long-wintering tribes—of North America specially—the French, the Italians, the Spanish and some in Latin America. Word of mouth doesn't tell me but I suspect more copies of translations of his books have sold than the originals in their British editions.

Finally, who reads us?

Wait for it, you haven't guessed. If, by 'us', you thought I mean Indian writers based in India, especially poets, you'd be right. But if you thought we only read one another you'd be wrong. In fact, you'd be amazed (I often am) how studiously some of us avoid reading one another.

In 1976, the small press Clearing House published four books of poems. It was a mail-order outfit and slightly under half the total print run of 3,000 copies was ordered by mail. For once, we could tell who ordered the books and where the orders came from. Most of the orders were from Mumbai and

Delhi but there were several from smaller cities and small towns and those who ordered the books weren't fellow-poets and teachers and students of English literature; they were simply people who wanted to read new poetry. By word of mouth I got to know that several of them recommended the books, by word of mouth, to others.

Several of my friends have told me that I must read Arundhati Roy. Hang the statistics of seven thousand copies of *The God of Small Things* sold in a week. Because my friends said so, I will. I still get orders for the Clearing House books, long out of print. Is it possible that the books have changed hands several times before they've finally landed up on the pavement or fallen apart? Is it possible that we have more readers than we think we do?

Word of mouth makes me think perhaps we do.

THE BOOK SHOULD BE THE THING

When the *Oxford India Anthology of Twelve Modern Indian Poets* turned up at various newspaper and magazine offices recently, sighs of dismay swept the country. Editors responsible for commissioning book reviews saw that, in one stroke, they had lost thirteen potential reviewers of the book—the twelve poets it represented and its editor Arvind Krishna Mehrotra. How and where were they going to find other reviewers?

To the uninitiated it would seem to be a simple task. After all, there are hundreds of functioning departments of English in colleges and universities throughout the country and, of late, there has been a growing interest in Indian writing in English in some of them. Some offer their students special papers on the subject. Surely there's no dearth of bright young academics to review the book. If there is, surely there's no dearth of journalists. I agree there's no shortage of talent in both fields. Then why is it, that in more than thirty years of reading book reviews and, of late, commissioning them, I've found that the most perceptive reviewers of books of poetry are poets? Other readers of poetry must have asked themselves the same question, even when not necessarily agreeing with the point of view of the reviewers.

Part of the answer may lie along the bumpy historical route of a new literature. If we go back to the days of Henry Derozio, Michael Madhusudan Dutt and the Dutt sisters, the history of writing in English in this country reveals more strategies of defence than attacks, more bark than teeth. With some notable exceptions, like P. Lal's manifesto-filled anthology, the iconoclastic journals *ezra* and *fakir* which Mehrotra once edited, and the briefly efflorescent journal *Dionysus*, the attacks have always been launched by the poet's perceived enemy, the philistines—a heartless, artless establishment—and its press.

By and large, the press hasn't accepted the reality of Indian poetry in English. 'A clobbering for every slobbering' used to be the motto in the good old days and much clobbering have some of our macho editors done in their time. Poets remember this and it's this memory perhaps that gives their reviews a particular edge, an attitude, that those not in the business are not obliged to have. Empathy for another isn't exactly what I mean, but it comes close to it. Needless to say, this 'empathy' doesn't prevent a poet from reviewing another poet critically or even stupidly. But poets are aware that when they review books of poetry for the press, they're writing for a long-standing enemy. They are also aware, when they review such books for specialist journals like this one, that most readers have no interest in the art they're writing about. So they aim their reviews at those readers who do. Among such readers, inevitably, are a number of poets. So the circle of poets gets tighter and tighter, threatening to constrict the person at its centre—the editor of book reviews. To him or to her the situation seems hopelessly askew. Not only does the public believe that poets these days only write their books for one another, they must now be seen to review one another's books too. Since, to my mind, it's the situation itself which presents the public with a false view of the poetry being written today and unfairly limits its scope, it's best we get out of the situation as soon as possible. How do we do it?

When the Oxford anthology arrived at my desk, I tried to get out of the situation by sending it to a young Reader in English Literature who used to teach at the University of Poona. The results, for me, were very happy. They haven't always been so. In sending out books for review (and not those of poetry only), I've sometimes not suspected the depth of animosity between the reviewer and the author or editor of a book. Sometimes I haven't realised that they belong to two mutually exclusive schools of thought. The results are unsatisfactory reviews, even though, as fireworks, they have occasionally been entertaining.

I'm not asking for that much-admired but virtually non-existent touchstone—objectivity. What I ask for in a reviewer of books is that he should know what a book is about and what a book review is about. A book may be on an abstruse, even unpopular subject; but a book review has to try and lead every potential reader to it. Though I've dwelt on books of poetry at some length, I've used them only as an example which applies, with varying degrees, to every other kind of book and to the general task of finding suitable reviewers for them. The most suitable reviewer may not get the book because he or she lives too far away for me to ensure that a deadline will be met. So I may have to compromise and choose a reviewer closer at hand. But the principle behind my selection should remain the same. The reviewer should know what books are about and what a book review is about. Questions of bias are secondary.

I mention this because, going by the letters published in *Indian Review of Books*, many of the readers are concerned with such questions. So is the editorial staff of the Books Section of the *The Sunday Times*, London. As an item in the July issue of

IRB indicated, that section has formulated four questions in an attempt to minimise bias amongst its reviewers. The reviewers to whom the questions are addressed are supposed to answer them honestly. If the questions had been put to me, I doubt if I could have. Or if I had, I'd have been disqualified as a reviewer. All the questions are based on relationships—between authors, between authors and publishers, between reviewers and authors whose books have been brought out by the same publishing house. Relationships—friendly or inimical—in any of these areas, automatically disqualify a reviewer.

Since the very fabric of a literary culture is woven with these relationships, what the Books Section of *The Sunday Times*, London, is trying to do is impossible. Or if it succeeds, it will run the fabric threadbare. I can't look forward to a time when Seamus Heaney, say, will be kept off a book by Ted Hughes simply because they've been published by the same house, any more than I can look forward to the time when Agha Shahid Ali won't be allowed to write on a book by Jayanta Mahapatra for the same reason.

What editors can ensure is that books published by a certain house should not be sent for review to someone who works for that house, even if the person had nothing to do with the book. It follows that they should also ensure that if the groups their papers or journals belong to also publish books (like the group that brings out *IRB* does) then the books shouldn't be reviewed in those papers or journals. While the first rule can be easily enforced, the second can't be. Remember the furore a few years ago when it was discovered that *The New York Review of Books* carried a disproportionate number of reviews of books published by Random House? The journal was connected, I'm not sure exactly how, to Random House. That house was faced with the choice of sending all its books to the journal or none at all. A cut-back was morally impossible. How can any publishing house discriminate against some of its authors by not sending out their books for review? I don't know what Random House did. The question couldn't have bothered them much anyway. There was someone in the editor's chair at the journal who had to resolve it.

That chair is the best place from which to resolve questions of bias, if any, arise. Without imposing Draconian conditions to qualify as a reviewer, as *The Sunday Times*, London, has done, editors can disqualify reviewers if their reviews show signs of gross bias, vindictiveness, plagiarism or worse. I really do think that's the better option, considering that it's neither humanly possible nor desirable to eliminate bias. Bias doesn't necessarily imply prejudice, but it does, at its best, imply a point of view. And without a point of view, a review had better not be written at all.

The point of view may hurt an author. If it does, he has the right to reply. It's generally believed that he shouldn't, that he should 'take it on the chin', as Bill Aitken gallantly indicates in his letter in the August issue of *IRB*, and maintain a stoic silence. I believe that too. But editors must allow aggrieved authors their say if their reviewers get their facts wrong.

Reviews are sometimes used as an opportunity to settle old, even unsuspected scores. Nabokov was deeply offended when Edmund Wilson criticised his translation of *Eugene Onegin*. Nabokov had considered Wilson a friend. Wilson had thought so too. The harsh public exchanges that followed indicated a baffled hurt on both sides, an unexpected betrayal of trust. Clearly there was something more going on in the review than both friends had bargained for. The public, eventually, benefited. I wouldn't have missed following that exchange for anything in the world.

I suppose that's what happens when giants fight and I believe it would do us reviewers a great deal of good if we realised we're not giants; some of the authors we review are. Criticism may well be the prime discursive activity, as some critics believe, but it takes a good deal more than posturing as David against Goliath to be a prime critic. We are all prone to such posturings and when we are, there is no contest. At such times the giant, if he is one, will always win. Older writers will always be subject to the slings and arrows of outrageous Davids.

At times no posturing is intended. It just may be that a young reviewer is deeply disappointed in the latest work of an admired older writer and says so. But the climate of the estate he and I belong to, the press, is so charged with scepticism that the motive behind every critical review of his is bound to be questioned; and he is not likely to be given the benefit of the doubt. The press, like every other estate, also creates its own victims. It will report every bit of hype that heralds Vikram Seth's as yet unpublished book, say, only to report every bit of savaging when the book is finally published. That's news, we say, but we know the knives are already out.

An editor of book reviews can't do without the news and the knives, but the book reviewer he chooses must certainly have the ability to keep them at a distance. Even as he hears the sounds of gang warfare, even as both ignorant and knowledgeable armies clash by night, for him the book should be the thing.

If that sounds old-fashioned, if it reminds you of what used to be said in the practical criticism classes of our student days, it doesn't matter. I mean it. I'm all for practical criticism classes and practical criticism workshops. At least one part of book reviewing is an exercise in practical criticism; the text has to be its focus. How far such attention can take us is well illustrated by *Interpretations*, a book of essays on individual poems edited by John Wain. In my student days, it took me very far, right into the heart of poems I thought I knew everything about. It showed me I didn't. It took a masterly interpretation to open one more door.

However much we may be against interpretation (pace Susan Sontag) or over-interpretation (pace Umberto Eco), if we are given a book to review, we have to interpret it. If its blurb did that for us, there'd be no need to review it. To review a book, we have almost literally to taste it, to eat another person's words and say what they felt like. It may be a health hazard. As time has shown us again and again, after having eaten other people's words, we may have to eat our own.

That chomping sound you hear is the press eating its own words. May it chomp its way to greater glory through its book reviews.

'Unread. And dead.'

READING

C IS FOR COMICS

Many of us suffer, in one way or the other, from the 'A is for Apple' syndrome. Having begun our mastery of the alphabet with that glorious phrase, we learnt, in later life, that it has an inglorious colonial history. How many of us had seen a real apple in our ancient, kindergarten past?

Those who had were the lucky ones. There were others who hadn't and who still had to begin learning English with that mighty phrase. It soon stood for everything that was evil and wicked about imperialism and though this fact isn't widely known, it was this phrase that we most used to chant against our former masters when we decided to overthrow them. (It rang in our heads mostly, maybe that's why no one ever heard it.) We marched towards freedom shouting 'A is for Apple'.

The phrase had other effects. The apple that stood next to 'A' on the alphabet chart was of a primary red so intense that all of us who were students of that chart have spent the rest of our lives looking for just such a real apple. None of us has found it yet. Does that mean such a wondrous apple doesn't exist? Have we been victims of a hoax? Cruel fate! To have shown us such an apple in our childhood and kept the real thing hidden from our sight forever.

My point is that the learning process that leads to literacy has always had a visual component. Think of all the illustrated books we read before we got to the book with printed words only. In the beginning it seemed lifeless, an aberration. Riffle the pages time and again and not a single picture to be found. Getting used to the pictureless book was like getting used to trousers after the freedom of shorts. It was a sign of growing up. You had to take yourself more seriously.

Unfortunately, that is about the time when the adult world starts taking you seriously too and frowns when it sees you with comics. Despite the success of the *Superman* movies, *Flash Gordon*, *Batman* and, of late, *Dick Tracy*, the comics in which the original characters appeared are still frowned upon. There's much they can be criticised for, especially for their reinforcing stereotypes of race, gender and class. The ideology of popular comics—and these include the Asterix and Tintin series—has to be ultra-conservative.

But the educated adult world I grew up in wasn't really the right one to make that criticism. Considering what the comics said, the 'virtues' they enforced, the adult world should have praised them. The comics we read were out to make good citizens of all of us, heroes in our own eyes. If the adult world censored them, it wasn't because it knew what they contained; it was out of snobbery. Children should neither be seen nor heard with comic books in their hands.

There was an exception: The Classics Illustrated series where you got potted versions of *Lorna Doone*, *Ivanhoe*, *Kidnapped* and so on. But they lacked the impact of that primary-red apple, the use of vivid colour and exaggerated perspectives which the 'low brow' stuff we thrived on had. Their figures had the pallor of etiolated plants, the ringlets of their women's hair drooped like wet tendrils. We had eyes for Wonder Woman only and went back to her.

I'm not out to defend pop culture. It's too late in the day to do so and given its overwhelming power now, it's time to attack it. It suffers from over-interpretation more than its highbrow cousin which the interpreters are neglecting quite a bit because that is the culturally correct thing to do.

Millions of words are written saying that the written word is getting obsolete and that the visual arts, music and the performing arts, preferably leaning towards pop, are taking over. A few more million words are written on these arts telling us why they should be taken seriously.

I add a few more words only to say that comics are like any other books, except that the pictures speak louder than the words. As in even the most perfect marriage, this marriage of pictures and words which is the comic book will have one partner talking more loudly than the other.

If a great many human marriages, unlike the comic book marriage, break up, could it be that a great many of us males have Superman printed not on our chests (which would be an interesting dress code) but in our minds, and that the comics, especially the American ones which we read in our childhood, were a bad influence? If Time will tell, I don't want to hear what it says.

LIBRARY MEMORIES

One of the favorite haunts of the Marathi poet Sadanand Rege was the David Sassoon Library at Bombay's Kala Ghoda. A small, delicate-looking building, it has a garden at the back in which Sadanand would receive visitors. Opposite the library, on the first floor of the Jehangir Art Gallery, is a room full of books on art. The books once belonged to Dr Homi Bhabha and are now available for reference to anyone who pays a small annual fee.

One person who was frequently found there was Pandit Rochak, bent over some notes he was forever making. (You aren't allowed to do your own work in the library, only make notes from the books you read.) Next to that library is the Max Mueller Bhavan library, not known to harbour a permanent resident yet, but a haven for lonely students. And slightly further afield is the Asiatic Library whose members have so aged with it that they seem to have blended with the furniture.

The other day, visiting the J. N. Petit Library on Bombay's

busy Dadabhai Naoroji Road, I was surprised to find how many members had fallen asleep, slumped in their chairs in ominous postures that suggested death, but for their heavy breathing. The scene brought back memories of other libraries abroad where, in our younger days, we sought shelter from dark winter evenings and the bitter cold. London's public libraries used to be free and browsing through the books inside, you could forget your troubles for a while. Of course, bookshops could be used for the same purpose but they were noisier places. In libraries you felt the mind and body go quiet, it felt good to sleep there, perhaps even die there, among books. The French director, Alain Resnais, who called his film on the Bibliothèque Nationale (the National Library) in Paris *All the Memory of the World* had the right idea.

The sight of books on racks in libraries evokes other books, read in distant places, on cold, wet railway platforms, or in the firelit lounges of hotels. The books evoke memories of the places we first bought them or read them. My paperback copy of Alistair MacLean's *The Golden Gate* always makes me recall the train to Pune on which I first read it. I can recall the passenger sitting next to me, his brown safari suit and, not surprisingly, the ugly punch-up between two passengers over a vacant seat.

If one gets hold of a second-hand book one can conjure up memories one doesn't even have. My second-hand copy of Shelley's poetical works indicates that I bought it in Windermere in 1959. I remember Windermere, the mountains, my mother sitting by the lake. But the book had at least one other owner. Calligraphy on the contents page indicates that it was presented to Lily Bridson by her brother Edward on 9 January 1860. I can see him presenting it to her, though I'm not sure if I've got his clothes right. Though he's wearing something brown, it's definitely not a safari suit. She is definitely wearing a gown with blue flowers on it. It's part of my imagined memory of another person's memory. It's part of all the memory of the world.

Around 300 BC there existed a great library in Alexandria. According to Carl Sagan, it was there that humans first collected, seriously and systematically, the knowledge of the world. When that library was destroyed, there was nothing to fill its place, just as there was nothing to fill the place of the precious Arabic manuscripts destroyed by Spanish Christians during their conquest of Granada. Before the age of printing, when only a handful of manuscripts of an original work existed, the loss could never be made good. But even in this age, not everything that is written is printed. Under our very noses, old documents in the State Archives are crumbling to bits. This is happening in the state-run Elphinstone College, just next to the David Sassoon Library.

It is said that Bombay has some excellent libraries in certain specialised fields, like the library at the Tata Institute of Fundamental Research and the Tata Institute of Social Science. But it has no general library to match its cultural complexity and intellectual aspirations. English-speaking students have constantly to depend on the British Council and the American Center to read the latest books, only a tiny fraction of which are bought by their libraries. Things aren't necessarily better in our smaller cities; often they are a good deal worse. In many of the so-called Commonwealth countries, particularly in Africa, libraries are so poorly stocked and maintained that at a literary conference in Singapore in 1986, a delegate found it necessary to publicly deplore the wasteful expense of literary conferences and urged, instead, that the money be used to save the Commonwealth's sick libraries. There are too many on the critical list now and as they perish, one by one, so one by one, will the memories of the world.

WHO IS MY NEIGHBOUR?

Three writers who live in Bombay aged significantly this year. This had nothing to do with riots, bomb blasts or the aftermath of shock and disillusion. They just turned a year older in the normal course of time. But for the press it was a godsend. The Marathi poet Vinda Karandikar turned seventy-five. So did the Marathi playwright P. L. Deshpande. And the Urdu poet Ali Sardar Jafri turned eighty. We were duly informed about their achievements, significance etc.

What did I do about it? What could I do? Precisely nothing. I know Vindaji and Jafrisaab personally, and I could have rung them up to wish them. If I didn't it was because I didn't know whether they liked being reminded of their birthdays—there are some people who positively hate it—and probably because I felt I'd have to explain why I hadn't met them for years. The second thing I could have done is to have gone out and bought their books. But if I had I wouldn't have been able to read them.

I'm not sure how and when I lost my ability to read Urdu (it was one of the languages we were taught in Standard I, now Standard III) but somewhere along the way I did. Marathi poses another kind of problem. I can read the script but can hardly understand poems in it. And if someone were to read me a poem in Urdu and the same poem in Marathi, I would experience the Urdu version more completely.

There you have me: a reader in one of India's largest cities whose ears register about five languages every day (Bombay English, Bombay Hindi, Marathi, Parsi Gujarati and French) who can broadly understand poems in a language he can't read (Urdu) and not the poems in a language he can (Marathi). Multiply me by several million (awful thought) and you'll see my clones in every Indian city and town. Throw in Tamil, take out Urdu, add Bengali here, take out Assamese there and you have a composite picture of the Indian reader basically, and I mean basically, made from pieces of a linguistic jigsaw in which shades of one language invariably lock in with the colours of another—a leucodermic Barbie doll or crazy colour-charted harlequin not spotted (as yet) in any other part of the world.

This last statement is probably an exaggeration. We tend to pride ourselves on our uniqueness, forgetting that there are other multilingual and cross-cultured people in the world. But let it stand. What's important is to highlight the sense in which we feel unique. The sense which was sharply brought into focus during a poetry reading held in Bombay recently.

The occasion was Ithaca, the annual literary festival of the Department of English at St. Xavier's College and the reader was Gujarati poet Sitanshu Yashashchandra. After a reading of English translations of some of his poems and the poems themselves, he spoke on Gujarati poetry.

Borrowing one of U. R. Ananthamurthy's insights, he said there were two kinds of languages: mother languages and father languages. Gujarati was a mother language. So was Marathi. English and Hindi were father languages. There may have been one or two aberrations in the past but today's Gujarati poets had no intention of being national poets, of being mahakavis. They wrote as though they were speaking to their neighbours, to the persons next door.

This is admirable if true. It shows a healthy disregard for nationalist posturing and points to the more intimate meanings of good poetry, so often lost on public platforms. But who is Sitanshu's neighbour? Who is Vindaji's? Who is mine?

The question becomes more cogent if one considers something else the poet said after the reading. Referring to Chinua Achebe, he said the writer used to admonish young Nigerians by telling them that before they spoke of avenging their grandfathers, they should understand their fathers better. In other words, before getting into the rhetoric of anti-colonial and anti-slave attitudes, read me. Should they? Perhaps they should. But will they? It seems unlikely. I'm reminded of James Baldwin's memorable response to the older Richard Wright's annoyance at the fact that he didn't appear to be as important to Baldwin's writing as Hemingway was. Junior blacks owed senior blacks. Else how build up a tradition? Baldwin's response, hurtful as it must have been to Wright, was: 'We choose our ancestors.'

Young Nigerians—whether writers or not, it wasn't very clear from what Sitanshu said—may well respond to Achebe's admonition in the same way. He isn't one of their ancestors. They've chosen others. But can they choose their neighbours? Can anyone?

Technically of course we can't, but linguistically we always do. And it's in its linguistic sense that we must consider Sitanshu's use of the word 'neighbour' if we are to get the essence of his meaning. What's implied in that use in his context is that a shared language makes for good neighbours and a shared language of poetry makes for the best neighbours of all.

I know I share Sitanshu's language of poetry even if it has mainly come to me in a language not his. I also know that many who speak his language don't share his language of poetry. They would prefer simpler stuff, or no poetry at all. They are his immediate neighbours. I live twenty kilometres away. Who is my neighbour? Sitanshu. He'll continue to be one when he returns to Baroda where he teaches. If he decides to live abroad he'll still be my neighbour. We once had a common neighbour in A. K. Ramanujan who lived in Chicago. Distance has never defined our neighbourhood—the one Sitanshu said Gujarati poets write their poems for.

So, we can choose our neighours and we do. Dilip Chitre wrote on two of his in *The Sunday Observer*: poet Daniel Weissbort and Kazuko Shiraishi. The first teaches in Iowa City, the second lives in Tokyo. If Dilip's English translations of Tukaram have reached both cities, I'm sure some of their readers have chosen Dilip as a neighbour too. Dilip as neighbour and Tukaram as ancestor? In the USA and Japan?! It's quite normal in poetry. It's just that myopic forms of nationalism prevent us from seeing it. Some British poets chose Petrarch as their ancestor and the Italian poets of their time as their neighbours. The difference, of course, is that while there's a direct connection between Latin and English, there's little of that between Marathi and English or, for that matter, between Marathi and Japanese.

I myself am optimistic about the power of translations to forge such direct links and while it may not be as easy for translators to open new routes as it is for airlines, I believe we're already living in a time when an atlas of translations from one language into another and the transcontinental lines that have emerged as a result are beginning to resemble an atlas of international air routes. If we look at the map more closely, we'll probably find more translation lines, both international and national, than those of airlines. On the map of world literature, translations have been going on for a very long time.

Which is why I was a little uneasy when, after his reading, Sitanshu said that translations of his poems within the same family of languages pleased him more than those that went outside the family. In other words, he was more satisfied by Gujarati into Marathi than by Gujarati into English. If so, he must miss the pleasure of imagining his poems in Icelandic and Kikuyu. He might also discourage hypothetical translators outside the family by saying he prefers those in it. Well, it's an honest preference but I can't honestly say I like it. Under the preference lies the subtext: my poems can never be properly translated outside the family.

Neighbours are one thing, family another. I may be happy or unhappy with both for different reasons. I'm happy his talk led me to write about neighbours in poetry. Family we'll have to keep for another time.

WHO NEEDS NOVELS?

Daniel Defoe, the author of *Robinson Crusoe*, is generally considered to be the father of the English novel. He couldn't have known what he was fathering or that his progeny would go forth and multiply in the farthest colonies. *Crusoe* was published in 1719 CE and since then novels have come to hold a dominant position in Anglophone culture. Their critics have turned them inside out, gutted them, burned them and banned them, but they continue to hold their own, fiction flying in the face of fact, a notable fact being that they only play at being dead, formidable death certificates notwithstanding.

Why do so many people say the novel is dead? Why do so many people want it dead?

One answer to the first question is that there are many people around who persist in believing that what's unread is dead. I don't mean the illiterate. Persons who can't read or write are generally too conscious of their disadvantage to hold such an arrogant position. I mean those who speak on their behalf, those who do read and write but who find the purpose of fiction and hence the intentions of the novelist to be dangerously frivolous. Not the over-pious. I mean some of the most hallowed philosophers, artists and leaders in history— people like Plato, Chaucer, Tolstoy and Mahatma Gandhi.

Plato wanted poets, the storytellers or 'novelists' of his time, to be banished from his ideal republic; they had an unsettling effect on the people. Both Chaucer and Tolstoy, the former as much a 'novelist' in his *Canterbury Tales* as Defoe, turned against their art in their later years and wanted it destroyed. As for Gandhi, it's difficult to describe in a few words, to anyone who didn't grow up in the 1950s, the stultifying effect of his views on literature. Though Mulk Raj Anand repeatedly testifies that Gandhi liberated him, many young people in the 1950s wanted a more complex, more entertaining fiction than Gandhi's high moral purpose would allow. Scepticism about the quality of Gandhi's thinking and prose (as well as Nehru's and Radhakrishnan's) quickly led to irreverence. We could fight like them if the occasion arose but certainly not write like them. We were young India and free. There was no need to be solemn about it.

We didn't foresee the opposition. It often came from stalwart newspaper editors whose prose could only rise above the 'dead' body of the novel since, in the 1950s, there were so few novels to rise above. The prose of our editors appeared to be 'towering' when it was not; there was so little competition from other sources. Apart from the work of Mulk Raj Anand, R. K. Narayan, Raja Rao and K. A. Abbas, what novels were there to read? In its protracted absence, the Indian novel came not to be missed. The Indian journalist ruled supreme, sole arbiter of literary taste, surrogate mother of Indian prose because it seemed to readers that no other fertile being was around. Not at that time anyway.

Now that there's competition, now that Indian novelists are coming into their own, has the situation changed? One question leads to another, a previous one, before I can attempt an answer: once again, with so much life in the novel, why do so many people want it dead? One simple answer, to use a phrase of D. H. Lawrence's, is that such people are anti-life, but that sounds too pompous. I would hazard another guess.

The novelist, in his creation of different worlds is, like Shakespeare's Prospero, something of a sorcerer; there's magic in his craft. The magician tricks and fools us; so does the novelist. We're suspicious of such fellows. There's something disreputable about the profession, especially if it's practiced by persons of great talent or genius who show no signs of letting up. It's true . . . we like to believe that you can't fool all the people all the time but is that man at centre stage listening, did Dickens and Tolstoy listen, are Rushdie and Marquez listening? They went on, they go on producing novel after novel out of their deceptive hats as though possessed by the devil. We only asked for a rabbit or two but what's this, they're producing a whole menagerie. Think they're God? It's a parody of the holy creation, burn them at the stake.

The logic of this argument, even if it's not put forward in quite so totalitarian a way, hounds most novelists, especially if they have long and fertile careers. It is, I believe, one of the reasons that literary critics and sometimes the public suddenly turn against a novelist they've admired, especially if they feel they are being asked to read one more 'major' work.

In less tolerant times and societies, the argument has been, is and will continue to be put forward with its full totalitarian force. Puritans considered sorcery to be the work of the devil and sorcerers were burned at the stake.

Now that there are many more Indian novelists than there were in the 1950s, do we need their kind of magic? My guess is most of us would be indifferent to the question or say no. We have learned to do without novelists for too long. At best we find them irrelevant, at worst so relevant that they have to be banned, sorcerers on the edge of outer darkness. Unread. And dead.

'Is it such a small world, after all?'

AT HOME

A GLASS TOO MANY

I had gone to meet Anil Dharker at the *Mid-Day* office. The office was in a building that looked as though it had been made of a number of tatty filing cabinets stacked one on top of the other. It was the sort of building that looked as if a finger pushed at it would bring it tumbling down. I pushed a finger—at the lift button but the building didn't come tumbling down. I soared into the *Mid-Day* office.

The office was like a bloated midriff, its intestines lined with glass. I followed one loop of the intestine and found Dharker sitting behind glass. He beckoned to me. I pushed at what looked like a door. He beckoned again. I pushed again. The door didn't yield an inch.

Perhaps it was meant to be pulled. I looked for a handle and found none. A little frantic now, I began pressing the glass panel all over with my palms, hoping I'd find the one miraculous electronically sensitized patch that would unlock it. I saw Dharker rise and come towards me. I heard his voice.

I discovered he was standing behind me, unable to hide his smile. In my mind's eye, I saw several *Mid-Day* employees unable to hide their smiles. What I'd been trying to get to was Dharker's reflection. His cabin was directly behind me, the whole caboodle being reflected in obstinately unyielding glass.

That wasn't the first time that I stumbled upon the open treachery of glass, its transparent insolence. Nor the first time I questioned the motives, not to mention the depravity of architects who use the material freely. I've got into trouble with glass more often than I can remember. I've slammed into it when I thought I was walking through space and baulked at space, usually at airports, railway stations and congested public buildings where there was no glass, leading to human traffic snarls and bodily collisions behind me.

I've been deeply traumatized by glass, though not so severely, perhaps, as a highly-strung colleague of mine who, eager to leave a dentist's chair after having had two broken teeth fixed, smacked his head into glass and broke his nose.

When did our contemporary obsession with glass begin? You see it everywhere in Bombay. Old buildings are no longer pulled down. Instead they are draped in acres of cloth behind which ragged construction workers flit. They are the city's newest and worst paid plastic surgeons, giving its structures a facelift. Three to six months later the buildings emerge from their chrysalises, shimmering butterflies, most of them glass-fronted.

There's a liberal use of granite too, both on the buildings' surfaces and inside them, so liberal that even as you admire your reflection in some glassy sheen you can feel your feet slipping, you're about to fall, help! and there's nothing to hold on to for miles.

Come the monsoon, smooth polished granite will become slippery polished granite. Come the monsoon, bosses and stenos, peons and executives will slip on smooth polished granite. Come to think of it, nothing is so great a leveller, not death, not sex, not travelling on a cart behind diarrhoea-hit bullocks—it happened to me once—as smooth, polished granite.

Why do our architects and designers not think of it? What country do they think we're living in? As a student of architecture in London, I learnt about curtain-walling. That meant some buildings had outer walls which were not structural but were like curtains, mostly of glass. New office blocks had them, new department stores had them. They were among the worst buildings in Britain.

That was in 1957. Haven't chrome, glass, steel and granite,

used as liberally as we do in our new and renovated buildings, really had their day long ago? We know slippery surfaces make for a fall and as for glass, apart from its treacherous quality, with so much pent-up fury in us, well, glass is just a stone's throw away.

I'll tell you one more story about glass. It happened yesterday and the glass was in the shape of a bottle. Some bars serve liquor in quarter bottles and as I was halfway through mine before having to leave for an appointment, I asked the waiter to fill the bottle up with soda. He did. He was about to put the bottle into a brown paper bag when I thought, hang the bag, I have one made of cloth, it'll do, and then again I thought, let him put the bottle in the brown paper bag.

I dumped the wrapped bottle into the cloth bag and caught a taxi. Halfway to the five-star hotel where I had my appointment, the bottle exploded. Whisky and soda bled through the cloth bag, my lap was soaked with its injuries. It didn't make for a respectable entry into the hotel.

But the point of the story is this: the brown bag contained the explosion, no glass pierced it. I had taken the bottle along with the idea of having a swig in the taxi. It would have been out of its brown paper bag then. I can see the headlines still: Bottle Explodes in Columnist's Face . . . Piece of Glass Pierces Taxi Driver's Neck . . . Taxi Goes Off Road . . . Pavement Dwellers Crushed to Death.

And the two morals of the story are: One: never take anything fizzy along with you during a heat wave, with the temperature well above 35° Celsius. Two: you can never see through glass, you only think you can. Though openly treacherous, its motives are well hidden. In this cruel world, there's always one glass too many.

MAPS FOR A MORTAL MOON

Around three o'clock that day, four grey-haired men discuss, among other things, the Sumerian script. They sit on spacious sofas which are situated behind and above Sir Jagannath Sunkersett's statue in Mumbai's Asiatic Library, once the city's town hall. The Asiatic, as it's generally called, is a neo-classical structure, built in 1830, meant to awe as the Parthenon in Athens was once meant to, I suppose, except that it's like the Parthenon with its front end squashed, a Cinemascoped Parthenon if you like.

At 3.15 the four men come out of the building and descend its Eisensteinian steps, without, to my relief, imitating the Eisensteinian pram. To my relief, since I am one of the four men and if anyone was destined to follow in the wheels of Eisenstein's pram, forever rolling down the steps, it was going to be me.

At 3.18 the four men can be seen dodging traffic in a street which is being dug up for the city's new gas lines, the afternoon sun lighting up the hair, intensely white, of the poet Arun Kolatkar, who leads, then a scholar's hair, then the near-bald head of a bibliophile and finally I suppose whatever hair's left on mine. I can't see it, so I suppose. An unexpected ricochet from another film makes me stop in my tracks—this line of men twisting, turning to one another, dancing—it's Bergman's dance of death at the end of *The Seventh Seal*, isn't it? But no, we're too loud for that, thank God, we can hear ourselves above the pneumatic drills. Bergman's dance was silent.

Over coffee and potato chips in a vegetarian restaurant—we're now in a building that's much much younger than the Asiatic—only about seventy years old, I think—the argument continues. Who's a good poet, who not? We're well into real time, today's writing, the Sumerian script forgotten.

Around 4.00 we go our separate ways. Walking up Mahatma Gandhi Road, I find myself in another movie, not one of Eisenstein's or Bergman's but more like Shantaram's *Jhanak*

Jhanak Payal Baaje, technicoloured: very bright green scarves, woollen, on a group of very dark men who wear earrings. They are breakaways from the World Social Forum that's taking place in North Mumbai. They trawl Gandhi's road for Chinese goods.

At Kala Ghoda, as I half expected, I land smack in the middle of a film set. But it's not a film set, it's a deserted parking lot tinged by men in khaki, and large orange flags. The flags go up part of the length of Gandhi's road, mostly fixed on a railing in the middle of the road, and also congregate to one side of the entrance to Jehangir Art Gallery.

Inside, as several banners indicate, the Shiv Sena's Executive President Uddhav Thackeray is showing his aerial photographs of Maharashtra's forts. It's a preview. Tough-looking men in civilian clothes stand across the doors which lead to the photographs. The doors are closed.

How many time zones have I crossed and re-crossed in the last hour, I wonder, how many centuries? The line of four, the dance of death, returns. So does a line of poetry: 'The mortal moon hath her eclipse endured'. I see why I'm haunted. It's been only a few days since we lost one of ours—Nissim Ezekiel.

In an upstairs gallery, Zarina Hashmi, who lives in New York but who was born in Aligarh (in 1974, the catalogue tells me, though, again according to the catalogue, she graduated from the Aligarh Muslim University in 1958—all things are possible, some New Age people tell me) shows her prints: cities, countries, borders. They are maps of nine cities which have suffered violent change, some wiped out. The cities are Grozny, Sarajevo, Srebrenica, Beirut, Jenin, Baghdad, Kabul, Ahmedabad and New York. A small world. Considering the past hour, I live in a small world, I think. The writing on the maps is in the Arabic script. The writing on the banners advertising Thackeray's show is in Devanagari.

Mortal moon, tell me, if you're watching me make my own maps, these, is it such a small world after all?

IN PRAISE OF STRAGGLING

Worried about being late? Anxious that you've missed the bus yet again? Don't worry. Let others do that. There's pleasure to be had in crawling out of the clockwork, in taking things slow.

This evening's no exception. As I amble at my favoured pace of thirty centimetres per second, moving towards a garden by the sea, the sun about to set, the light dimming faster than I can lift my feet, I hear the tall spires of Ashoka trees ring with multitudinous bells—sparrows hidden behind the long leaves, only one or two darting out and back again, never seeming to make an effort to get past the foliage and stay there.

Are those two stragglers, or are they wardens of sparrow dormitories, making sure everyone's in, one eye on the lookout for an Ashwathama from the sky, startling predator of those who sleep?

I think they are stragglers, my preferred form of life. To this day, I don't understand the fuss people made after my first public school race when I allowed my fellow competitors to cross the finishing line before I made a start. It seems perfectly natural to me not to go along with the herd, to have the whole field to oneself, and, then too not to race across it as though pursued by an enraged housemaster, but to amble along, as I'm doing now, slowly enough to appreciate a line of Ashoka trees at Vespers, trying to distinguish the sound of one carillon from the next, thinking.

Oops, sorry! There goes Mrs Moolchandani, half-sprawling on the pavement after a collision—a minor collision—as I ambled along paying little heed.

If you're a bird and in two minds about migrating, better not straggle. Take off with the flock, the last flock if you must, but take off. Otherwise you'll be left to winter in the mercy of human kindness, which can be quite cruel, I can assure you, with a human insistence on treating you like a poor man's angel (spoon-fed with vitamins and muscle-building foods in an animal hospice) which you definitely are not.

If you're a deer, don't dawdle as you ogle her-with-the-antelope-eyes. Stay with the herd. That way the lion will breakfast on cowslips rather than you and choke to death.

If you're a man, well, there goes Mrs Moolchandani, or rather there went Mrs Moolchandani who I'm afraid I was unable to placate.

Still, despite the hazards, I'd say there's more pleasure to be had in straggling than hurrying. It all came back to me when someone I'd written a poem for asked me what 'straggler' meant. I'd used the word in the poem. I explained, but didn't tell him about the pleasures of straggling. It all came back...

There was the time I was invited to a radio interview in Honolulu and I arrived a month late. I was delighted to see how polite hosts could be when stressed. They still had to put me up free.

There was a time when the later it grew in London, the more I dawdled after dark. A policeman once stopped me and asked me if I shouldn't have been home at that hour. I replied, 'And you?' It was pleasant not to have been arrested but might have been more pleasant if I had been. I wanted someone to talk to, and it could have been him.

Once, setting out late to hitch-hike from Switzerland to France, I dawdled and lost out on opportunities to get a ride. Until a driver stopped. Instead of taking me close to the border which he'd agreed to do, he took me to a police station.

He was the police.

In his room at the station he pressed and continued to press lumps at the bottom of my duffel bag as though he were trying to milk a cow. He thought the lumps were dope. Several old socks and crumpled shirts later, all disgorged on his dairy-clean desk, he found they were rolls of film. What pleasure to see a face as round as a box of cream cheese grow as long as a Swiss army knife. And almost as red. What joy in not straggling now, thrusting my belongings back in the duffel bag in swift swoops and flouncing out.

Just three of the joys of straggling from my past.

As for those to come—there's one I particularly look forward to.

They used to say: 'He'll be late for his own funeral.'

I will.

THE CUFFE LINK

The earth is red and raised like a welt. Next to it stands a cigarette stall. Hafiz used to run the stall, but he grew thin and wasted with smack. A younger cousin runs it now. The nerves and arteries of Cuffe Parade run under his stall—telephone and electric cables which are constantly being laid or repaired. He knows every scar on the scraggy pavement before him, and how it was made. From his seat in the stall he watches men with pneumatic drills at work on the road. The drills spring to life in a burst of staccato thunderclaps. The noise will continue through the day and into the night.

Three rows of cars wait at the traffic lights on the junction of G.D. Somani Marg and Captain Pethe Marg (Cuffe Parade). They are about to sweep onto the main road during the peak traffic hour in the morning. As the engines tick over, two young men, in adjacent Marutis, swear loudly at each other. Each insults the other's mother at the top of his voice, then bangs the top of the other's car with his hand. It turns out to be a show of affection. Friends, they have seen each other after a long time. Still exchanging oaths, their hands on their steering wheels now, they are swept onto the main road, side by side, in a river of sputtering metal.

Will they return late at night, side by side again, their cars racing down the main road now, taking the turn into Somani Marg at high speed, their tyres squealing? Racing Marutis down the road is the fashion these days. One day the car won't take the turn but ram the lamppost on the corner, bits of the car and the driver going past it. The driver, if he survives, is too young to know that others have died at that very spot. We've lost count of the number of accidents we've witnessed in the twenty-one years we've been at Cuffe Parade. There's at least one each week, mostly at the junction.

In the first two or three years, when the high-rises were coming up, the victims were mostly construction workers, uncertain about how and when to cross the road. Relays of trucks carrying earth for the reclamation that went ahead at great speed those days, went up and down the road by the minute. I live on the eighteenth floor of a building that overlooks the main road and when the first accidents happened, I felt drawn to the scene, to take the lift and go down. But if you live in a high-rise for even a year, you soon realise that help moves in a straight line, mostly horizontally. The men who rush to the spot of the accident, after the initial pause of shock, are inevitably the newspaperwallas and cigarette-storewallas on the corner—men like Hafiz's cousin. I soon stopped taking the lift down, stood on the balcony, and watched. Freezing at the sound of screaming brakes and the expected thud, or crash of metal and glass, we now quickly move out to the balcony and watch. For some years now, the sound of those brakes has that effect on me that I'm told the sound of a siren has on those who survived in cities which were continually bombed. It's a kind of trauma, a gift, I suppose, from one of the city's posh areas. I associate most of Cuffe Parade's gifts with noise. Unlike help, it doesn't travel horizontally but in every direction. The flat I live in seems to be a node for all the noises in the area—from the murmurous hum of a throng of people haggling over the early morning catch on a quay in Sassoon Docks (a pleasant sound) to the most ghastly sounds of gargling. No conversation is possible in the living room during peak-hour traffic. Guests who come in the afternoon with a cheery 'What a lovely view!' are reduced to shouting at us between 6.30 and 7 in the evening. They can barely hear a word we say.

The sound of peak-hour traffic, in a flat on the eighteenth floor of a building in Cuffe Parade, must surely be a form of vengeance from down below, a fitting reply from those who live closer to the ground in the old buildings opposite the high-rises and whose view of the open sea we have forever blocked. It's quieter down there. I know. There are trees which muffle the sounds.

There weren't always trees but now I think Cuffe Parade has been more successfully greened than many other areas in Bombay. What used to be a municipal dump just below the building where I stay has been converted into a lush garden. At the bottom of the area are the Colaba Woods, a joggers' patch, where, in the morning, aggressive styles of walking are warning preludes to a bad day at the office. When you count the number of buildings in Cuffe Parade, and the number of flats in each, you think, with so many neighbours in the area, who needs friends? But then, neighbours only need neighbours, not friends.

Neighbourly relations in a high-rise building are a fragile affair, a tissue that tears very easily. Go up or down or across to a neighbour to borrow an egg and you know you're walking on eggshells. The proverbial 'openness' of Indian households has been replaced perhaps inevitably, considering the number of people crowded into one building, by a wary watchfulness.

Nevertheless the buildings do enshrine an ancient Indian principle which their builders have found very useful: there's always someone below you whom you crush, so crush him. The facilities in most of the high-rises, some of which rise to twenty-five storeys, are the same as those in four- or five-storey buildings in Bombay. Which is like equipping a Jumbo jet with the same facilities as a turboprop. I suppose no builder thought that by not allowing for spacious service lifts in the buildings, large piece of furniture would have to be carried up flight after flight of stairs on human backs. Well, what are certain human backs for? Our cupboards came that way—all the way up eighteen floors. Most of the buildings have no separate staircase to use in case of fire. In this posh area of escalating heights and prices, many buildings are serviced by water tankers.

Water mercifully comes in other forms too and we have seen some spectacular outbreaks of it during the monsoon. It's then that black clouds from the southwest almost touch the horizon, the sky cracks open over our heads and the river Cuffe begins its turgid journey below. Two or three times each monsoon, it moves into top gear, in full spate, trapping cars, taxis, scooters and the occasional bus. Occasionally too, a boat launched from the fishing colony down the road will pass to pick up passengers or pedestrians stranded in various stages of distress in waist-deep water. Help moves horizontally again, with postmen and porters and the boys on the corner extending their hands to help the residents on its banks cross the river. Just as I was once helped to get up and walk on dry land nearby, when I fell on some flinty stones and burst my mouth.

Of course I've been conned too, as perhaps every resident of Cuffe Parade has been—by the occasional taxi driver, electrician and carpenter. It teaches you nothing more than what you could learn as easily in any other part of the city: get conned again. I've also learned that if a certain kind of crowding of people as at Cuffe Parade is a breeding ground for suspicion, even hostility, it's also a breeding ground for birds. Friendship in Cuffe Parade is strictly for the birds. Forgetting for a moment the crows and pigeons, there's Meena and Jeevan, two mynahs who nested in an airconditioner in the building opposite. They are now joined by a yet unnamed third. A bird's-eye view of birds is what the eighteenth floor provides and it's a joy to watch a mynah's spotted wings extend as it pulls out of a dive. There's Mehmed and Mustapha and

Shireen—Brahminy kites who appear only during the monsoon, white heads and bodies soaring on brick-coloured wings. You could watch them forever.

Sometimes they make it seem worthwhile to live near the top of a high-rise. Like half the people who do, I'm wary of heights and lifts. But on certain evenings, one feels like joining the birds, taking to the air.

On a Sunday in Cuffe Parade, you can do worse than watch birds in flight.

A STRANGER IN THE VILLAGE

It's a twenty-minute walk from the Marine Drive side of Mumbai's Nariman Point to where I live but not when it's dark, not when it's raining. On Thursday, the day before I write this, the walk was an ordeal. The streets were flooded, there was no taxi in sight, and I was refused pao bhaji at a wayside stall.

Whenever a certain kind of person refuses to serve me or is rude to my face, I think it's because of my beard; I imagine that he or she has taken me to be a Muslim. It needn't be that but after the riots in 1993, it's got to me, this particular Mumbai syndrome. The city has changed not only its name but its character. Its precincts have become enclosures, its chawls and mohallas fortresses where most strangers are regarded as trespassers.

So I was touched when, the other day, a total stranger whom I'd met in a bar, took me home to meet his wife and family. I was nothing to him so why did he do it? He said he'd seen me drinking by myself and felt I needed the shelter of a home and family.

I wasn't touched by hostile presences during my Thursday walk, which was no walk; it was almost a swim upriver. But that's a story I'd like to get back to later.

It must have been during the Holi of 1962 when a writer friend and I were invited aboard a fishing trawler, moored on Versova beach, to share drinks and food with the fishermen. The drink was unadulterated country, and the smile on the face of the fisherman who invited us on board was unadulterated joy. The food was fried fish. It was a feast day, a festival day, and his gesture was a kind of sharing of joy with strangers. Again, as with the person who took me to see his family, we meant nothing to him.

The fisherman's gesture seems unlikely if not impossible now. 'They' have their problems. 'We' have ours. Attempts to cross barriers are nothing short of trespass. Didn't you read the sign: 'Keep out. There's a mad dog on the premises and it's called Suspicion?'

We can never have enough talk about Indian hospitality, can we? When foreigners join the chorus of praise I'm more than a little surprised. Some of them may not have lived to tell the tale.

Travelling around India to gather material for an anthology, my wife and I came across an Australian couple in Jaipur. Holi was over and it had been violent. Some of the woman's hair had been torn out by the roots. At Dharamshala, my wife, who happens to be French, was struck on the back of her skull by a heavy ball of wool. None of the Buddhists there seemed to mind. Only the woman who threw the ball did. She enjoyed every minute of the concussion which had to be treated with strong painkillers. She's mad after all, the impassive Buddhists seemed to say.

On Vypin Island, Cochin, children threw stones at us because they thought we were hippies. This was counteracted by a true act of Indian hospitality—a Catholic family took us into their home. When a neighbour's child, barely a toddler, was brought in to be shown off, she made much of Veronik, my wife. The child's mother proudly announced, in the presence of several members of the family and myself, that this was only natural because my wife was white. 'So fair,' I think, is the phrase she used.

I've spent a fantastic Mahashivratri on the beach with a writer friend without the revellers showing us any signs of hostility. I've waded far into the sea with a woman, following Ganapatis to their doom, and nobody touched us. Were we lucky? I don't think so. Mumbai is still a relatively safe place for strangers and foreigners, even at night, but its arteries have hardened, its taboos are in danger of becoming sacrosanct.

Who hasn't seen families with small children being refused rides by taxi drivers, even when they're stranded in the rain, just because the taxi drivers aren't going their way, or because the families want to go a short distance when, for the drivers, nothing less than ten kilometres will do?

What happened that day was this. The rain came down in torrents and wouldn't stop. Strong winds ripped down the streets and within minutes the ribs of my umbrella snapped. I found myself walking through knee-deep water which rushed dementedly towards some godforsaken drain or open manhole. I hoped I wouldn't fall through an open manhole myself. I fell, but on my knees. I felt the driving rain soak through the cloth bag I was carrying; its contents would soon be pulp. Then I saw the wayside stall, the bread neatly laid out and asked for pao bhaji. I was refused, the men around the stall grew hostile.

It was then that my guide arrived, like an amanuensis to take a blind man home. He said he knew of a place where I could eat. I guessed he was about fourteen years old. He guided me through what had become an underworld of water, flooded streets, driving rain and tunnels of darkness where the street lights had failed. He took me to the fishing village near where I live. One of its resident dogs snarled but it wasn't called Suspicion. I had a kheema pao at the stall the boy had taken me to. I settled down, the dog settled down. I felt the fishermen's concern for this stranger in their midst. I must have looked a sight. My knees began to hurt.

I paid and made my way home through more water, now

followed by a small boy who wanted nothing less than ten rupees. I could only give him five. The rest of the notes in my wallet were soaked through.

So that's the story of my Thursday walk, almost a swim, when I was touched again, in more senses than one. Back home, a knee began to bleed. For a while, my heart did too.

DEAD MAN WITH BUTTERFLY

October, and butterflies are out—the lemon yellows, the black-and-whites, the orange-and-blacks. So many others do their turns in the garden where I sometimes walk. But I'm not in the garden today. Today, my heart is heavy as I take a roundabout route to the post office. In my path is a dead man and it's orange-and-black's turn to flit about him. Let's call the flitter something, I think, as I pass the corpse. Call her Saraswati, goddess of learning, who can always be light if we choose to make her so.

It's one o'clock and school's out too—young girls with orange flowers in their hair and in dark school uniforms, young boys in white shirts and khaki shorts. They don't seem unduly oppressed by their school bags, they chatter and speak with their hands as they make their way home. Whatever they've learnt today seems to sit on them lightly. So many schoolchildren, excited, voluble, as I make my way to the post office. There are corpses in their path too.

After the first death, there are two others. They're on the private road that leads to the post office. The road is short but broad, a trespassers-will-be-prosecuted space between old, partly abandoned buildings. Citizens of the area choose this space as their rite of passage—to get to the other side, to pee in, to love in, and sometimes to die in. I pass my third corpse, crumpled like a foetus, one shoe off, and move towards their source of death.

Step out of the gate that is permanently ajar and it's there—St Mary's Bar, the country liquor I last had there about ten years ago still stored in my belly perhaps—it's strong and doesn't let go. I confront dingy curtains, the mark of every country liquor bar and think, 'No! Go to the post office with your sad sad letter. Go.'

I don't pass by. Instead, I part the curtains, membraneous walls of a vagina, and enter.

It's dark but not too dark. I think I recognise some faces. I know the ritual of the place. Go up to a window as you do at the post office, ask for what you want and cough up. You get your stamp—your chhota peg or your burra peg—immediately.

'Suntra?' I ask.

He nods.

'What else?'

'Coffee,' he says, 'nothing else.' He gives me a pitying look. Didn't I know there is never anything else? I've been away too long.

Suntra and soda in hand, I think I should toss it back standing. After the third, I sit on a bench, next to a drowsy Nepali, afraid that my presence may provoke him out of imminent slumber.

At the table opposite, men in regulation haircuts, looking more army than navy, though we're close to Navy Nagar, talk in Punjabi. Or try to talk. They are very high. The Maharashtrian with them, dressed in blue, sporting a Tanaji moustache, speaks to them in Hindi. He is clearly the boss. The talk revolves around women. Could he be a pimp? One of the Punjabis, open-mouthed, vacuous, is being ribbed. 'Stupid,' they call him, 'stupid.' Other tables begin to stir. A solitary young man, Muslim, black, handsome, curses the armyman with a smile. A strangely shaped man, blacker than him, enters the bar and drinks at a table, standing. 'Look,' says an armyman, 'drunk already.'

'No, no,' says one of his companions, 'it is only his posture.'

'Posture?'

'Only his posture.'

Posture, tribal in appearance, sits down and begins to talk to the man next to him. They talk shady business. Or so it seems to me. The handsome young man goes on cursing the assembly with a smile, then bursts into an ominous shair. Everyone seems to know everyone here, I think. Have I stumbled into a den of thugs, a gang of hitmen? Avoid eye contact.

It's difficult to. The armyman who was being ribbed has gone missing. 'Where's the fucker? Where is he?' his companions ask, increasingly agitated. He bursts back into the bar, parting the curtains violently. There's a knife in his hand, its sharp point aimed at Tanaji's moustache. A frozen second later I see it's not a knife. It's the tip of a paper-cone packed with channa. The man swivels aggressively towards the bartender's help, a scrawny man who wipes the tops of tables and, if ordered to, brings customers their drink. God-fearing shaayar orders rudely, with venom. Outside the bar a woman starts screaming.

She screams abuse at someone inside, one of the armymen as it turns out. Exasperated, he leaves the bar, there are sounds of a violent quarrel. I look at the God-fearer quizzically and make as though I'm going to get out and intervene. But he raises a finger to his lips—chhup—and motions me to sit down. Obedient boy, I do. I notice that the words 'Pepsi Cola', in large letters, adorn the blue wall in front of me, above the remaining armymen's heads. They look morose. The sounds of battle continue outside. Their afternoon's wrecked.

I get up and retrace my steps. It's been two hours since I re-entered the womb. The three dead men, previous receivers of St Mary's blessings, must have got up and left too, perhaps to face other women's wrath. They are nowhere to be seen. The butterflies, lemon yellows, black-and-white, orange-black, bounce along on their wheels of air. I don't go to the post office with my letter, addressed to someone I love and who I think I'll never see again.

SHOW ME THE WAY TO GO HOME

Badiruddin the breadman has just returned after spending three months in his village near Gorakhpur.

'Where were you?' I ask him.

'Gaon,' he says, running a hand down his face as though he were stroking a beard. He has no beard, only stubble. He is noticeably thinner, his face gaunt. To him gaon and gaunt go together. That's what his gesture was trying to tell me.

Raju the liftman has returned from his village in Bihar. He too is noticeably thinner. Housewives are pleased to say that when their servants return from their villages after a couple of months' leave, everyone can see that they have lost weight. We feed them well here. In their villages, there just isn't enough to eat.

Those same housewives will say the city is getting impossibly overcrowded (which it is) and no more migrants should be allowed into it. Let the government concentrate on rural development, then 'those people' will stay home.

To our eternal shame, none of the governments we have elected has concentrated on 'rural development'. 'Those people' can't stay home. For a great many of them, for many years, perhaps to the end of their working lives, the city will be their home away from home.

I have a poor sense of home. This may have to do with the numerous 'digs' I had to live in abroad—moving from room to room in what I took to be hostile cities—but that isn't all. I know I'm not alone in feeling this way. I know quite a few people who, having acquired the security of a home, want to chuck it up and move on. To take up jobs in other parts of the world, to travel endlessly, even to be a pilgrim or a fakir, divested of the burden of property.

Most of it is imaginary, practically speaking; it can't be done, we say; but it's a powerful source of discontent. It's this discontent with home, and its built-in concept of perpetual domesticity, which could explain some seemingly irrational disruptions and divorces: the man who walks out on his 'happy' family, the woman who takes fright on her wedding day and doesn't turn up, the adolescent who goes missing and never writes back.

The most pathetic cases are those of the old, who, having raised two generations under one roof, are made to feel neglected, a burden, who deliberately walk away to another kind of home or an ashram, defeated by circumstance, their original idea of home in tatters. There's no safety anywhere. There may be safe houses for terrorists and fugitives alike. There's no such thing as a safe home.

It amazes me, given this fact, how much time and trouble some people take to get their flats endlessly repainted, to rearrange the furniture every few months, to compulsively acquire antiques or decorative items until their homes begin to resemble museums. Could it be another form of domestic discontent, the syndrome of 'If you can't move out, move in?' I think so. The idea seems to be, if you can't move out, make every day in your home appear as though you're in a slightly different place, and after a while—when a white wall has been painted mauve, when the printed curtains have been changed for plain, when grandfather's antique table has been replaced by a glass top with silver bowlegs— a totally different one. It doesn't work. Before she knows it, husband and children have left.

There are no safe homes but if I leave my flat even for a couple of months, I do get homesick.

'I'm homesick,' cousin D said over the phone to her younger sister the other day. She lives in Karachi.

'Homesick?' her sister asked. 'What home do you mean? Pune? Mississauga?'

D wants to visit Mumbai, which she hardly knows. Her husband is dead, her children have emigrated.

Without a safe home, without a sense of direction, we get homesick. Perhaps we're all migrants on this planet, confused, like birds, on the eve of a big migration. Do we really know where home is? Do we really know where we are going? D is on the verge of migration to Mississauga and is uncertain if that can ever be her new home. She's probably terrified. If we look hard at ourselves, sometimes restless, sometimes scared, sometimes plain fed up, aren't we always asking someone, something, 'Where's home?' And if there is such a place, what's the way to get to it?

STARTING FROM SCRATCH

The child can't be more than two. The iron gate he seems to want to pull down can't be more than ten. The hotel the gate belongs to is a little less than thirty. The land the hotel's built on is about thirty-four. Before that it was sea. That's also true of the land the building I live in is built on. It's close to the hotel. The building's thirty-three.

Never mind the age of the Earth, the age of Mumbai's oldest structure, the city's hoarier parts. The part I live in is relatively new, a developing zone. That links it to other developing zones, some to the north of the city, some, like Navi Mumbai, across the harbour. When the lights of Navi Mumbai blink across the waters, it's hard not to see a glint of recognition in them, hard not to hear a collective whisper in the lights, a message from the citizens of Navi Mumbai to the citizens of Cuffe Parade, where I live. The message goes: 'We have so much in common. Those who live in developing zones are almost clones.'

What's it like, living in an area while it's starting from scratch? Ask any clone in a developing zone. Ask me. Yesterday, on one of my walks, a smell from a patch of earth which was being watered by a gardener brought back memories of the same smell from the same earth thirty-three years ago, when it was treeless, plantless. Then as now, its wet odour was mixed with dry, as though it had brought some of its original bareness along with it, which it has transported from drier lands in or by the city to take its place in, on and by the sea. That earth is now covered with vegetation, so much so that in parts of Cuffe Parade, the vegetation has begun to squeeze pedestrians off pavements. All the same, one of the first experiences of us clones when we come to occupy our respective zones is that the zones are treeless.

Isn't that wonderful? Perhaps those who haven't had that experience can't begin to understand the joy I feel. Because of that experience I am one with the citizens of not only Navi Mumbai, but of Milton Keynes, Chandigarh, Brasilia and Shenzhen. However long we've lived in our respective zones, if our lives there began when the zones did, they began on a treeless plain. In every place I've mentioned, our first cries have sounded as desolate and as familiar as the cries of the newly born: 'Why no trees? Where are the trees? Why no trees?' Those cries respond to the blessings of starting from scratch.

'Blessings?' ask those who live in older parts of the city, in older places like Old Delhi or very old places like Varanasi. 'Where's your History?'

To them I say, like single-cell organisms beginning to evolve, like the first footprint on the moon, like the eggman who has rung my doorbell 12,046 times expecting me to buy eggs every single day of the year beginning with the day I came to be where I am, history is what we make.

As for our child, the putative Samson who tried to bring down one of the President Hotel's newer gates . . . he and his parents are going towards the road that passes in front of the hotel. That road is a little less or a little more than hundred years old. It was part of a seafront project which was completed in 1905. As the family approaches the road, for a moment three of its feet are on land that's thirty-four years old (my side) and three on land that's about hundred. One more step and they step into History. Then they vanish.

'The sea is like love'

TRAVELLING

SANDSTORM AT SEA ... AND OTHER EXPERIENCES

It's the time of year when windows fly about the city and people get hurt. But despite the high winds, old cobwebs remain. The mind's gone stagnant.

'Travel,' they say and with clouds settling on the hills it seems a good idea. But for several reasons I can't. Best, perhaps, to while away the time, groping for places in lost memory, get some satisfaction from the fact that landlocked as I may be at present, I've seen some strange sights in different parts of the world and heard the weirdest sounds.

There was that sandstorm at sea, for example—3 July 1957. I was seventeen and on my way to London to study architecture. The ship was waiting to dock at Aden and this is an account of what happened:

> I went to the topmost deck with Pounde, and looking towards the horizon—I couldn't believe my eyes! It seemed as if a devastating fire had broken out in some oil refinery and was sweeping over the land, the smoke having congested half the sky with dense cotton-wool clouds of dirty browns and greys, each merging into the other to form a vast blanket, arching over the sky. The other side of the horizon was perfectly clear except for a slight brownish haze over the mountains.
>
> 'What is it?' I asked Pounde in astonishment.
>
> 'Yeah, what is it, I say?' he asked in turn.
>
> 'What on earth is it?' I asked, my astonishment rising.
>
> 'I can't make out, I say, what is it?' he asked again, bewildered.
>
> A tug was standing out prominently against this unearthly

background, looking like a paper cut-out. I grabbed my camera, and to my dismay, I found I had only one shot left in it.

'I wish I had colour film,' I moaned. 'I don't know what to take.'

'Is it fog or something?' Pounde asked.

'It looks like some fire to me but I can't see any flames, and the smoke seems to be remaining in one place.'

And truly it seemed to have frozen there, like some awesome storm cloud, waiting to break over us at the right moment. The light seemed to grow dimmer every moment and I rushed to the ship's stern to see if there was anything better to photograph. A couple of sailors were hoisting a flag, staring intently at the cloud. A crowd of shirtless sailors from the tanker alongside were waving their hands and shouting at us.

'It looks like a sandstorm coming up,' one of the sailors hoisting the flag said.

A sandstorm? Of course. 'Look at the edges,' I shouted to Pounde. For the edge of the cloud was speeding over the horizon like a whirlwind, blotting out the sky more and more, as though trying to enclose us in before breaking over us. Unnoticed, the top of the cloud of dust had arched almost directly above our heads and it looked ominously black as we looked up. The atmosphere was very still, though more and more ships were being blotted out by the haze.

'May I have your attention please? There is a sandstorm approaching,' said a voice from the loudspeaker. 'Please shut all doors and windows.'

We could hear people banging things shut downstairs and the commotion of voices and pattering feet. The storm was coming over. I couldn't wait anymore and took a chance shot. It was coming over . . . The wind suddenly hit us and pushed us sideways driving us down the stairs. People were running into shuttered rooms, but thinking another good subject might crop up during or after the storm, I rushed to my cabin and feverishly loaded a new roll of film. Coming upstairs once again, I managed to escape on to the deck through one of the doors and found the dust swirling around me in a murky darkness. There were many others out on the deck with handkerchiefs wrapped around their noses, some trying to open the locked doors of the lounge to take shelter, some trying to wipe away the dust that was settling on them. Many had been taken completely by surprise, because, as we found out later, not even the ship's officers had thought the storm would strike us so quickly. We stood in the gritty atmosphere for a few more minutes until there was a lull in the breeze and it began clearing up . . .

That was from a diary I kept at the time. Teenage stuff and awkward English with expected grammatical glitches. But the experience itself was one of the strangest I've had.

Then there was the hailstorm on top of St Paul's Cathedral, London 'like a shower of wet mothballs clattering down before us.' I had never seen hail before and a friend and I had to make our way through it but not before I tried to take a shot of London under hail, with friend shielding the camera with his mackintosh:

> After a while, seeing that the downpour wasn't likely to abate, we rushed out, sharing the mackintosh over our heads but the pellets still stung like mad. A small boy was running before us, screaming as though we were chasing him and the three of us reached the stairs, dripping, where a group of people looked at us amazed, as though we had come down with the hail.

Then there was the pea-soup fog which hit while I was on my way to my digs in North London. It was like walking blind, touching the fences of a row of houses for guidance. Strangely, it wasn't a frightening experience. What was frightening was my one and only LSD trip, when it seemed all London's streets had changed direction and that I would never find my way home.

Finding myself in another kind of darkness—the one in the school of architecture's dark room—was another strange experience. Not just because we used the darkroom only to print and enlarge photographs, never to develop film, but also because the photographs being printed and enlarged came from a camera that was back in India. The customs at Tilbury wanted me to pay a duty of £75 on it. I couldn't, no student could have. After months of correspondence which stressed that I needed the camera for my professional work, the customs didn't relent. The camera was sent back to India. I felt I had lost a limb. A kind cousin provided me with another—his own camera.

So much for some of the sights of my first year abroad. And the sounds? Before the year was out, I heard one of the weirdest, in a club called 2i's in Soho. In it a man gyrated and pelvised like Elvis. Strange sounds came from his mouth and guitar. He looked familiarly Anglo-Indian.

About two years later my camera came back but I took it around with me more for moral support than to take photographs. My self-confidence had been shattered. I had left the school of architecture, I went downhill, while the singer I'd heard in the club, Cliff Richard, rose step by step, to become, as we all know, Sir Cliff.

GEOGRAPHY LESSONS

Invited to Lahore in 1993, I booked a flight through an agency called The Great Escape. There was some irony, entirely unintentional, in my choice of agency, as my trip wasn't meant to be a great escape at all. I was going on business, as one of the three judges who had to select two books for The Commonwealth Writers' Prize. Choosing two books out of more than fifty is a lot of business.

As it turned out the trip was sheer pleasure. At one stage we found ourselves in the mountains beyond Murree, looking out over a valley through which a line of water ran. The line twisted in its tracks like a trapped snake, bright silver in the mornings, an exhausted grey by evening. The mountains held us and the line in thrall. 'We shall not be moved,' they seemed to say. 'Do your worst. We're here to stay.'

Living among mountains, even for a little while, you begin to learn why they engender so many myths and why they are the objects of so much worship. Their faces blacken as clouds pass over them, they blaze white hot under snow, they shield you from fierce suns. They have moods which they let you know of in no uncertain terms.

We had been taken to Nathya Galli, a hilltown close to Pakistan's border with Kashmir. There was our host, the novelist Bapsi Sidhwa, Lyn Innes of the University of Canterbury, England, and myself. From that hilltown we ranged the world in our reading. The novels took us to the American West of the last century, to New Zealand and to the Andaman Islands. They took us into the minds of the very young and the very old, through worlds radiantly whole or hopelessly disconnected.

We journeyed without maps, occasionally losing our way, but however far we travelled we came back to the mound under our feet, its rocks and slopes. We came back, in fact, to a map, its security, and what we had learned at school: how to draw maps with mapping pen and Indian ink, rivers' names in italics, borders in broken line, big cities' names in caps.

An atlas may not be literature but learning to read it at school was like getting to know a masterpiece. What work went into the making of those wonderful maps, what wealth of detail, gathered from millions of cubic meters of earth, air, water and sky, was finally reduced in scale to a few square centimetres so that it was possible for even the most timid of schoolchildren to look earth in the face and say: you don't scare me so much now. Below our feet in Nathya Galli were the ever-widening contour lines our geography teachers had taught us to draw.

Since maps stabilise an unstable world, however temporarily, those teachers made the world a safe place to live in. But the world didn't turn out to be a safe place for them. All the geography teachers who taught me in Bombay left India for places where they led cramped and impoverished lives. All of them are dead. They conjured up foreign lands for us but found them inhospitable when they got there. It's as though they were tricked by their own profession, the maps that forever hovered in front of their eyes.

Perhaps history taught them what geography couldn't—that the world is a dangerous place, after all, that it's flat, and that if you travel too far along its surface, you can slip off it into a monster's jaws. Perhaps they should have spent their years of retirement in India, travelling abroad only through the atlases they once taught us to read and which brought the world to our doorsteps.

One of those teachers, Alan Glynne-Howell, lost sight in one eye in his late years. All the same, he managed to finish writing a novel set is India. No British publisher touched it so he sent the novel to Bombay through one of his ex-students, hoping it would be published in India. It couldn't be. I'd like to think that words from an atlas came back to him during his final years, that on certain evenings, the walls of a room in a small English town heard strange sounds being repeated.

'We're crossing the Jhelum.' Bapsi said on a flight to Rawalpindi. The words came back to me in slow motion: 'Jhelum, Chenab, Ravi, Beas, Sutlej.'

Mr. Howell stood by his desk in the Geography Room opening and shutting his mouth. It was his voice I heard.

MEMORIES OF A BOOK FAIR

Book fairs attract bookworms and the maidans of at least three cities are carpeted with the worms for a few days at the beginning of the year. Winter is the traditional time for book fairs in Delhi and Calcutta, while Bombay has its own more modest book fair in March. The Frankfurt Book Fair, reputedly the biggest of them all, is normally held in October and I once landed up there as a participant, probably due to oversight.

At a press conference held at the Max Mueller Bhavan, Bombay on 11 December 1985, I asked Peter Weidhaas, the director of the book fair, who was scouting around for publishers in India, whether he had met the right publishers. There were small publishers, I told him, like Ashok Shahane of Pras Prakashan, who were doing valuable work and who could be contacted at the restaurant just across the road at three o'clock any Thursday. I don't know if Weidhaas ever crossed that road and met Shahane but I soon found myself crossing continents to meet Weidhaas. I'd been invited to the fair to represent Clearing House, which had published eight books of poetry. By drawing attention to Ashok Shahane I had probably drawn attention to myself. The theme of the fair, the thirty-eighth, was 'India: Change in Continuity'. A number of writers, including Arun Kolatkar and Dilip Chitre, who were also very much part of Clearing House, had been invited. So we were going to be out in force.

The fair was opened by P. V. Narasimha Rao, our current prime minister, who looked gloomier than he does today. In 1986, the year of the fair, he was minister of human resource development and perhaps human resources were even scarcer that year than they are now. We scurried like mice between the Congress Hall, where he delivered his address, to Hall 7, where our stalls were, to be there when he began the tour of the hall.

On the previous evening there had been an altercation. A tipsy Indian publisher had insisted that he needed German assistance to put up his stall. The organisers had politely but firmly declined. It wasn't in the rules; they clearly said we had to put up our own stalls. His protests had grown louder and louder but the organisers had paid no attention and had walked off.

He finally did succeed in putting up his stall with the shelves at wild angles, the heavy art books on them threatening to fall off. It was a sad sight but the publisher was beyond reason. Perhaps it was his stall which caught P. V. Narasimha Rao's eye first during the tour of inspection, since he marched past every stall looking straight ahead, without a glance at our pretty handiwork. He looked like a man who was urgently seeking the exit door and by the time he and his security guards got to it, they seemed to be running. The fairgoers who followed were in less of a hurry but they soon came to realise that many of the books were closed to them. A book is a book is a book after all, unless it can be read, and the Germans, fluent in English but unfamiliar with our many languages and scripts, couldn't make sense of many of the books at all. What was the point of displaying them then—just to prove to the Germans that Indians could read? That we have a great publishing industry that can produce the finest books in the world as well as the most tatty? The questions aren't mine but were the kind being asked in sections of the German media—both print and TV—hostile to Weidhaas. They claimed that his special focus on Orwell, two years before the Indian idea, had been a flop. You could stretch Orwell only that far in Germany and he had already been stretched a lot. German publishers wanted to deal with foreign publishers who brought them money. Now, as if one empty-handed author weren't enough, there were a whole lot of them—authors and publishers who spoke funny languages and wrote books in funny scripts. Empty-handed all of them, to be sent back empty-handed.

Which is what happened. In terms of the commercial deals struck between Indian and German publishers, the thirty-eighth Frankfurt Book Fair couldn't have been a success. A knowledgeable German publisher, with a deep interest in India, was pained by the indifference to Indian writing in his country, and lamented the great difficulty of selling translations of contemporary writing there. A couple of German universities with departments of South Asian studies were delighted to get their hands on some of the books but the publishers had other business to attend to. The last day set us scurrying like mice again. We had stalls to dismantle and books to buy: even the most reputed publishers were selling at throwaway prices. (Sales aren't allowed during the days of the fair itself.)

'It's too big to go around,' R. K. Narayan, one of the invited authors had told a German journalist. But some of us raced round the fair at a speed that would normally have compelled the security guards with which the fairground was littered to give chase. By the last day they had got used to us.

We had probably taken some getting used to. Apart from the incident of the wild shelves, there'd been the curry incident. An Indian restaurateur from Dusseldorf had taken it upon himself to dish out Indian food in a makeshift canteen in Hall 7. Long queues formed on the first couple of days since the canteen was within easy reach, but it soon became apparent that we were being grossly overcharged. Besides, the food was indifferent and the restaurateur positively rude. One day a group of publishers threatened to pour the curry he was serving them over his head. Dressed in brown and grey suits they had gathered in a threatening semicircle around him. The security guards, unsettled by the quarrel which was being conducted in Hindi, edged closer. Fortunately, the restaurateur backed down and apologized. The next day he fled.

No security guards were present during the second curry incident which took place in the house of a distinguished German professor who was hosting a party for some of the visiting writers. A large saucepan of curry got upset at the top of the stairs leading to the dining room with the professor sliding down behind the cascade. Or did he ride it? My memory of the reported incident is blurred.

Günter Grass had warned us when he was in Bombay that a visit to the Frankfurt Book Fair would put us off books forever. It didn't do that to him and it couldn't have done that to anyone who was there in 1986. I hope Peter Weidhaas continues to be director of the fair despite the flak he received that year. It takes courage to put on a non-commercial show in a city of bankers and very hard-nosed publishers.

LETTER FROM VENICE

Living in a stranger's house, drinking tea from a cup decorated with strawberries, while the saucer, with its intricate blue rim, clearly comes from another set, I wonder if I should step out; it's a sunny day.

Much of yesterday was cold and wet but the hour-long passage down the Grand Canal, from the railway station to the Lido where we're staying, was spectacular, as expected, the eye unable to rest on any one building for long, however stunning its facade. Perspectives on the Grand Canal change fast as the vaporetto moves from station to station down its snaking curves.

Yesterday was history and its sloppy passages through water. Today the present and the accumulations of domicile. The owner of the house I'm living in is a designer; her good taste shows. It's clear that every little detail has been thought out, perhaps jointly with her son who is also a designer: the gilded cherub hung at the parting of two long white drapes that hide a wardrobe, a poncho spread out on a wall like an item of clothing a Mexican Christ might have left behind while being taken down from the cross, the photograph of a native American woman on the flap of a 1995 calendar hanging from a diya, part of an ornamental piece from Bastar.

The house is at two levels; I'm having my tea at the upper level. Below, there are cast-iron butterflies, wooden chimes and a lampshade that looks like a common shopping bag, but stylishly perforated. There are three wooden tortoises at the turning of the steps.

I believe I've turned into a tortoise too—slow, unable to get out of my shell. I could at least step out of the house this bright day, if not to visit places with literary associations (I've lost my taste for places with literary associations), then at least to wander in the city's crooked lanes. This is only my second time in Venice, the first was in 1966. I spent a lot of time looking at paintings during the Biennale which was on then. I don't remember much else—not even the Grand Canal. In Corsica, less than a week ago, I saw 'Amnesia' written on a ship and a hotel. Perhaps they were places of rest for people with Alzheimer's, I don't know. Have I been on that ship? Is the house I'm in called 'Amnesia'?

I forget. Rather than step out it does me good to itemize the house I'm in: there's that strawberry cup on its ill-matched saucer, there's a transistor called 'Cube Mate' in the shape of a black cube, there's an empty box of Ilford HPS film (ISO 400), and above the tortoises at the turning of the steps, a small striped kurta-like shirt, this time, one that might have belonged to a baby Christ, crucified on the wall.

I'm going to Rome. I've just discovered, next to me, a red bookmark (almost the colour of the small shirt), which shows Keats, a Grecian urn as drawn by him, and his house in Rome. In one of my bags I have *Abba Abba*, a novel about Keats' last days in Rome. He wrote wonderful letters. I'm going to Rome.

LET SLEEPING PASSPORTS LIE

It was a mistake to have dug them out, the seven passports I clutch but still don't believe I hold. Old passports should be allowed to live or die undisturbed, like a nest of mice in some dark, self-privileged corner. Touch them and they feel as dry as death. Turn their pages and sticky little feet will patter all over you. The photographs show us in a flash, a face gone from youth to age. Computer graphics can wrinkle a face in a second, old passports can do that just as quickly.

The reason I dug them out is that I wanted to write about spring. Bombay's spring has truly gone with the fresh leaves on the lime tree on the balcony almost fully grown and a dead red-and-black bug impaled on one of its thorns. Red-and-black must have eaten lime tree leaves all of Bombay's brief winter. Pierced by a thorn, it must have hissed and died in a mist of lime scent. I thought of the springs I'd experienced in other countries and wanted to check exactly when I'd been in those countries. I thought my old passports would give me a clue.

Instead my first passport showed me the date it was issued: 16 August 1956. It showed me the photograph of an angry, acne-less sixteen-year-old, ready to take on the world.

The photograph is a lie; I know I had acne then. But some dates don't lie. I now know exactly when I was in Paris around Christmas 1959—from 19 December to 31 December. The Paris I experienced then has never been repeated for me. To be nineteen and alone in the most sinful city in the world is an experience which can't be forgotten, especially when all I did was mope, wander about the city with my hands in my pockets, see the French make pigs of themselves over their food and drink, get my first taste of real mayonnaise in a bench-and-table workers' dining hall (I'll never forget the taste) and eye a hooker in Pigalle for hours. I returned to London a virgin but with an embarrassment of stowaway pubic lice which had boarded me not through any person but by way of the unchanged bedsheets of the dirtiest youth hostel in the world.

The passport gave up another date: 8 July 1957. I'm at Port Said, 'Allowed To Visit City During Staying Hours of Ship' according to a rubber stamp. The ship is the P&O *Strathmore* and the first one to have gone down the Suez Canal after the Suez War. It's night and Port Said is thirsty. It has seen no liner for almost two years. It's been a long drought.

The drought breaks as some of us step on shore. Port Said flings everything it has at us—leather belts, slippers, wallets, watches, stick-daggers. Port Said is also tense. Ship steward Michael who's fallen in with us Indians falls out with an Egyptian. The Egyptian is angry about Suez. Michael tells the owner of the café where we're at to tell the man to leave us alone. Arguing volubly, the owner pushes the man away. 'Nasser is next to god to the people,' a shopkeeper later tells Michael.

No, it's not my memory. I got that from a diary I used to keep. But what's the point of talking about it? Old passports, old diaries are terrible reminders of places you visited, the incidents you went through that can never come back. Without seeing any more dates, I know what the other passports contain. Distant lands and incidents pressed between their pages like leaves, passports and ferns hand you back both your past and a desiccated version of it.

There is the boiling sea off The Hague as I saw it. But it's very long ago. The water boiling in the kitchen in a stainless steel handi has grown more real. There is a woman I went to meet in Switzerland. I can see her smiling still but the foetid woman of the streets, the one who curses me every time I pass her, has grown more real.

Or am I mistaken? Sometimes memory plays such tricks, lends itself to such total recall, that you feel you were born yesterday, lying in a maternity ward, eyes still wet and shut, but ready to open them, ready to take on the world.

Passports play strange tricks too. If a passport were part of a pack of cards, it would be the joker in the pack. An Indian with an Indian passport is an Indian national. An Indian with a British passport is a British national. In London as students, and later as professionals, some of us agonised for years over our passports. Should we give up our Indian and get the British? If we did, that would mean that from then on we'd be British not Indian.

On the other hand, Indian passports were among the worst in the world. They generally got you nowhere and when they did, it was only after you overcame a series of bureaucratic obstacles that made you never want to travel again. Now most of the Indians I knew in Britain thirty years ago have British passports. Travel's much easier for them though not life necessarily. As far as I'm concerned they're Indians but with wings on their feet instead of padlocks.

Now that my seven passports are with me again, I start flying. I'm in a small town in France, a couple of policemen on the scene. Some boys from the boys' youth hostel have tried to break into the girls' youth hostel and the warden is enraged.

Now I'm in New York, in the middle of a blizzard. Taxis don't move down the street, they rotate like toys. A friend who was supposed to put me up has gone away without leaving a word. It's going to be a cold night.

But spring in Britain's another story, a tale told by an idiot, full of sound and bother. The sound came from stereos, the bother from the neighbourhood. I can see him standing there still, the policeman at the door, saying he received a complaint from the neighbours. But I had no sound system, it must be the neighbours themselves.

'May I see your papers, sir?' he asked.

I showed him my passport, the first, the one with the angry acne-less photograph. He took one look at the photograph, one look at my acne and grinned. I grinned back.

I was ready to take on the world.

ON FIRE

A glow appears on the hill to the right of Vesuvius. It grows more intense as the train moves away from it—a glow like that of a steel furnace—orange, with tinges of white. It fades away as the train goes out of the reflecting range of the glass that causes it—no single window pane it seems, but a whole wall of panes, so large is the area of light. Whatever it is, it catches the evening sun and flashes it to the train heading for Naples' main station.

If there'd been glass on the hill to the right of Vesuvius, 1,921 years ago—and we know there couldn't have been—it would have reflected the eruption as intensely as it does the sun now. No glass but the sea, the sea! Pompeii's harbour, loud with people, reflects a mountain on fire, the sea, with lava streaming into it, itself on fire.

The gutter of a house opposite Hotel delle Nazzione has a channel that looks as though it had been cut through pumice and ash, part of a recent dig. It runs by the side of a roof which has more than four hundred watches in the windows below it. It's part of a street that sells electronic goods.

The electronic items on sale in La Bourboule are displayed more discreetly. Formed by eruptions too, like the hills around Naples, its long-dead volcanoes are silent. Even the clocks made from its cooled rocks—agate, onyx, malachite—don't tick. Quartz, their companion, led to a profusion of hammerless clocks. Time passes silently in La Bourboule's shop windows as they wait for the shop to shut, the town to shut. While trees make their statements of fire more and more intensely, by the minute, by the hour, as autumn rises.

Autumn rising. And on a bridge above the Dordogne that runs through the town, I hear the Buddha's sermon: 'Bhikku, the tongue is on fire, the heart is on fire, the hair . . .' and so on. I open a notebook to put something down and a packet of Doctor Ciccarelli's corn pads, bought in Florence, falls out. Dear God, I forgot. My feet are on fire!

Waving an arm over the river Arno, writer Steven Grieco makes the bridges over it crumble like cake. Florence burns under German command. Smoke pours out of the city. 'They spared only the Ponte Vecchio, the old bridge. They blew up the others and some buildings on the banks.'

My toes are contused, red from walking. I must get them amputated.

It's a hard climb up Vesuvius. Its open mouth is toothless, a silenced gargle of rocks and sand, a deception, a cover-up biding its time.

Fuel, what they the call mazou, is piped into a tank outside a children's home. It goes to the heart of the home, a modern-day furnace. When the children come next year, it will fill the pipes with hot water. I'm shown the children's rooms, the four beds in each. The woods are on fire.

To catch a bus to Bastia, go to Porto Vecchio in a taxi. Setting out from Bonifacio, the driver says, 'Whole forests have been burnt. The trees were hundred years old. How does it serve the cause?' The cause is a Corsica free of France.

The house will be alive next year. The taps and showers will run with hot water. I'm shown where the children eat. An open window is shut but just before it closes one of its panes shows flames—an image of the wood opposite. Against dark green, swirls of orange and red. I'm shown the rooms under the roof of the house. I'm shown where the children sleep. I'm shown the fire escape.

TONI MORRISON, PARIS AND ME

Her hands fluttered expressively and her face took on a vacant look. The television was on in the living room, especially put on for news of Toni Morrison. It was the day after she had won the Nobel Prize but there was no news of Toni Morrison.

'They think the afternoon news is for housewives who spend their time in the kitchen,' said the temporarily agitated lady. 'Are they supposed to have an interest in literature? No!'

It wasn't the first time we heard French television being criticised in France, nor was it the last. For me too no news of Ms Morrison was bad news. The missing Ms Morrison—

missing on French television at least—meant I'd have to put together a picture of her from the opinions of those who'd read her. And I knew no one who had.

I called on Vijay Singh who writes for *Le Monde* and he gave me an article from the paper. It didn't say very much apart from the usual 'giving a black voice to American blacks'. Being a novelist himself, he had a great deal more to say: 'She writes from the heart, from the spleen, and we need such writing. People are tired of well-crafted novels about small adulteries and about the goings on in the fashionable districts of Paris. Her importance for me lies also in the fact that she uses English in her own way, not as part of the main Anglo-American stream.'

At Village Voice, the Anglo-American bookshop in Paris, a neat display in one of the show windows indicated Morrison's presence. There were copies of *The Song of Solomon*, *Beloved* and an audio cassette of her readings from *Tar Baby*. Inside the shop they talked dinosaurs. (Village Voice is something of a magnet for the English-speaking population of Paris, residents and visitors; those drawn to the bookshop at any particular time may talk about everything but books.)

This time, an over-earnest Englishwoman was advising her American friends—almost ordering them—to choose the book she preferred. 'Oh!' she cried, spotting *Jurassic Park* on display. 'You must read the book before you see the film. It's so much better.' The Americans, doubtless friends of Spielberg, responded with a frozen silence. 'Er . . . would you know anything about Toni Morrison?' I asked one of them by way of breaking the ice.

'No,' he said politely.

I may be wrong but it seems to me Wole Soyinka had it better in Paris. (Better than Toni Morrison, that is, not me). That time too, in 1986, I was in the city when the prize was announced and I distinctly remember the papers being full of him. Perhaps it's just because he may have been more widely translated into French than Morrison and, unlike her, had been in prison. The French adore writers who've been in prison, especially those they themselves have jailed, like the poet Villon and writer Jean Genet.

Genet is very much in the news in France and I was lucky to see Bernard Rapp's literary programme *'Jamais sans mon livre'* ('Never without my book') in which the American writer Edmund White was interviewed on his biography of Genet which was just out in France.

One of the most interesting bits of the programme was when he quoted Genet on language. According to Genet, Céline, the French novelist, being bourgeois, could write in argot. He himself being socially disadvantaged, wanted to write like a master.

Poetry is never in the news in France. That sort of thing seems to have stopped mid-century. Everyone tells me they don't read it. Odile Hellier who runs Village Voice wonders why she stocks it.

She's sorry but she can't tell me how many copies of the books published by the small presses I've been associated with have sold. Two years ago, she and her assistants packed the unsold poetry into cartons and fed it to cattle. (What she really said was they sent it away.)

All the same the attractive Forum, a commercial-cum-cultural centre in Paris has a 'Maison de la Poesie' (House of Poetry) where the poets of our time read. There's also a government-sponsored effort which encourages cities and towns all over France to organise literary programmes of their choice this time of year.

In the small library of La Bourboule, where my wife's and stepdaughter's families live, there was an afternoon of poetry quizzes with handwritten poems stuck on the walls and a display of poetry books.

Among them were translations of Tagore. And quite near them, on a separate shelf with a note of welcome lying across two pages 'Approaching Santa Cruz Airport, Bombay', one of my poems translated into French. I was moved to tears.

It wasn't me who said the French don't read poetry, was it? Whoever did must be nuts.

PATTERNS OF DOMICILE

Shortly before the year ended, I got a letter from an English friend who lives in Herefordshire. She'd been kind to me during my jobless months after Oxford, letting me stay in the attic room of a huge house in London which she herself was occupying temporarily while its owners were away. She wasn't particularly well off at that time but she refused to let me pay for the room or the breakfasts she made me every day, a chore that neither I nor her two young sons made any lighter for her—they in a state of noisy insurrection at the table and I, believing myself to have been badly treated by another English friend, in speechless gloom.

She has been to Bombay several times—it was where I'd first met her and her husband—and she stays with us for a day or two on each visit. She's someone I miss and she writes to me every Christmas. 'I don't for a moment believe you haven't been over here once since 1983,' she writes this time, 'and I'm most offended you didn't let me know and come and stay.' The fact is, I haven't been to England since 1978.

Her response is typical of well-wishers who seem always to expect me to be in a place other than the one I'm in, and who deeply resent being told that I'm not in the place they expect me to be. In the eighteen years since I decided not to return to a job in London and be in Bombay, I've offended a number of people.

'What a waste!' exclaims one. 'With your brother in Air India you could get out of this place practically free! Every year! You really must hate travelling!'

Lady, I've been to more places in the world than you, and yes, I no longer travel for a lark.

'Do you mean to tell me,' says another, 'that you stay stuck in Bombay year after year? I just don't believe it.'

Well, sir, I'm not stuck.

Friends who returned to India after studying abroad have similar encounters; the experience is a common one. It would seem that once you've crossed the black waters you're never the same person. There's a special code of conduct for you. Its chief point is that you should leave the country as often as you can after you return.

Of course, in a way, you do come back a different person. You come back with a pendulum in your head. It never stops swinging between two points of reference—'here' and 'there'.

I first left India thirty-one years ago and a good part of those years has been spent in discussions and arguments—with Indians and non-Indians—about the pros and cons of 'here' and 'there'. I don't exaggerate. My choice of domicile hasn't affected the tenor of the discussions and they continue as before. So does the pendulum in my head. What do I say to friends much younger than me who have never crossed the black waters but who occasionally make fatuous remarks about the lands beyond them? According to the code I should say, 'Please find out for yourself,' and politely. Instead, I find myself bellowing, 'Go!' Soon after, I find I'm a referee, mentioned in their applications to universities abroad. I make and sign the references gloomily. 'Why do we do it?' I asked a fellow referee the other day, 'they'll never come back.'

They don't. And when they do, on the occasional vacation, their symptoms are distressing.

A weeps copiously in an unreserved compartment, unable to bear the inhuman conditions of a long-distance train journey. B worries that he hasn't lost every trace of his 'Indian' accent after two-and-a-half years abroad. C is happily married to an American and couldn't care less if she saw Bombay again or not.

My distress at these symptoms—only three of many—isn't only due to the fact that they remind me of mine and several of my friends' when we too were young, down here on a visit. It's also due to an attitude to India that the symptoms represent. We have heard, through V. S. Naipaul, of the successful emigrant who, on a visit to India, wept because he'd forgotten what poverty was. I've heard, through friends, of the wife of a foreigner with an important job here, who, when she first came to Bombay, wept continuously for a fortnight for reasons similar to the emigrant's. Both the amnesia of the first and the culture shock of the second are so familiar to me by now that I should be able to say something wise and comforting to both their types, a word of explanation, perhaps. Instead, I find myself tired of explaining. Instead, I find myself thinking, 'Get lost.'

That's certainly what I thought when Mrs Bhatt (let's call her that) one of my mother's acquaintances, on a visit to Bombay after a few years in the States, unleashed a tirade against fruitwallas. She couldn't understand why fruits weren't sold in plastic bags as they were in the supermarkets 'out there'. She couldn't understand how we could pick our fruits from open stalls. She was outraged at our 'dirty habits'—something she had instantly forgotten by just being 'there'.

Those very same stalls, and the fruits so elegantly arranged in them, will draw gasps of admiration and wonder from another kind of visitor—the foreigner for whom I'm a permanent fixture in Bombay, and who calls upon me to explain India's wonders and beauties and terrors. The season for this type of visitor is generally between November and February and, on an average, ten of them visit each season. They range from impressive academics, less impressive students interested in Indian writing, to friends of friends of friends. For them nothing, including one's mind, is to be in plastic wraps. To shut them out, to burrow under a bed sheet pretending terminal illness, would be a sign of inhospitality. And which foreigner ever heard of an inhospitable Indian? I'm almost one already. Their curiosity is all-consuming. Their questions probe my mind like flies do a rotting papaya. I feel drained. I stop explaining. At last, I feel, I'm seen exactly as I see myself—permanently 'here'. The pendulum stops swinging briefly.

OUT OF PLACE

Two men sit outside a laundry, each darning an item of clothing. The one on the left, with a moustache, works on a black lace shawl, the second on a grey pullover.

A straggly line of construction workers goes past them, all the workers young, some of them barely men. I know they are construction workers because their clothes and arms are powdered white and because a couple of them are wearing hard hats, the kind construction workers wear in countries where they have to wear them. Like helmets for those driving motor-powered two-wheelers.

Motor-powered two-wheelers come in different shapes and sizes. Not so much helmets. Helmet after helmet comes over the hump of the Ponte alla Carraia in Florence, and charges down it, two-wheeler lights blazing in the twilight: ranks of Myrmidons surging across the bridge to the heart of the city.

Must this stop? Do I want it to stop? I've been back ten days after a seven-week trip abroad and my eye finds nothing to anchor itself to. All's in flux. Parallel reels of film unspool in my head; get entangled with one another; at times jam.

That friend in Paris, an expatriate who hasn't been back for twenty-eight years, asks, 'Give me one good reason to visit the country again.' Do I really tell him, 'Well, there's me?'

I tell him, well, there's me. But do I also tell him, half-joking, half-desperate, that the Cowasjee Jehangir Hall has changed since the days of our childhood? That it has become Bombay's National Gallery of Modern Art?

I go to the gallery and see what's supposed to be contemporary German art on display. If this is what contemporary art is, forget it. If I mentioned this gallery to my friend, forget it. If this is what I've come to, forget it, please forget it, I can't connect. A glass of tea may help.

It was on the way to get that glass of tea in a place I know that I came across the two silent darners, the construction workers and . . .

I step into the laundry and am reassured. Rows of shirts lie on their backs like exhausted rowers in a scull-boat. In fact they're in a glass case. The scene's familiar, but briefly. Bodies in a glass case in a garden in Pompeii are untidier. They lie sprawled and twisted in the positions they assumed at the time of death. The Garden of Fugitives. It's no use. I hand in some of the clothes I wore abroad and turn away.

Here's that thin Frankenstein-type man who brings me bottles of gas when I call the gas house. He's very thin, very smiling. Reassuring to see him but if he sees me he'll ask for his Diwali hand-out and I'm not handing out anything to anyone right now. Right now, I'm taking. Sloping off past him I'm stopped by a woman I barely know. She tells me her uncle's gone missing. He's an artist.

Before I meet her, before the Frankenstein-type man, before the laundry and the dead shirts, I run into two women I do know. We stop in the street and find ourselves talking about art. Enough, enough, enough. Not art. I want, only want. Not art. I want that glass of tea.

Or paneer. Homely white slabs stare at me from another glass case. Some other day, you tempters, you deadly icebergs. I have to drop anchor first, in that glass of tea.

Approaching the lane of the place I know, I worry. What if it's gone? What if tea is no longer served in a glass but in thermocole? I turn into the waist-crunching entrance of a narrow lane and am dismayed. A jute curtain stretches from the top of a building to the lane; bits of mortar rattle down. A construction worker perches on a piece of scaffolding and looks upward like a kingfisher which has just swallowed a fish.

It's Genoa, one of its lanes in the old city, hung with clotheslines while hard-hatted workers tear the insides of buildings apart. And the place I know, which calls itself a canteen and names itself after a hill station is in front of me. There's normally a plate of fried fish at the entrance, the fish ready to take away. I ask for the fish. The man at the counter looks at me sadly and says it isn't ready.

What's there to be sad about? I think, as I step into the place and find somewhere to sit, at the same time panicking a bit. What if it's the wrong time for tea too?

I look at an ad for Pepsi stuck on a wall. It shows plates of idli and sambar. An ad on another wall, not a stick-me-up but a fresco in Italian russet, advertises Coke—'No pulp, no fruit'. That schooner I saw on the wall of a restaurant in Genoa, a painting in oils, what were its colours? From where I sit, I can look through the serving hatch into the kitchen. There's a fire as in a furnace. A man turning parathas, a man shaping glass in it, as I saw one do in Murano.

The glass of tea arrives. It's fluted, like glasses of tea normally are. I tell myself that it's made in Murano. A schooner appears on a wall. It stands on a dark blue sea. It's painted white and brown. It's come to take me home.

A GRAVE IN THE HILLS

Driving from Clermont-Ferrand to La Bourboule, my stepdaughter Katia spoke casually of fogs that suddenly blotted out the road. Making the fifty-kilometre trip every weekend, she had once been caught in a particularly nasty fog and had thought her end was near. Her mother, sitting next to her, sighed.

Six hours earlier I'd been sighing too, between trains in

Paris. I'd arrived from Frankfurt with more luggage than I could handle, and the straps of a brand new shoulder bag creaked ominously. (The straps of two others had snapped during earlier stages of the journey and there was no reason why this protracted game should stop.) I was on my way from Roissy to Gare de Lyon to catch a train for Clermont-Ferrand. At both stations and at Chatelet, where I changed trains, I had to carry my luggage a long way. 'Because I am neither hot nor cold but lukewarm,' I prayed to a particularly intimidating escalator at Chatelet, 'spew me out of this mouth, Lord. Me and all twenty-three kilos of my suitcases and all ten kilos of my hand luggage.' The weight had made the whole trip horrible. Now I just wanted to sleep.

'Let the fog descend,' I thought wearily as we drove into the mountains. 'Don't let me see my bags again.'

~

The burbling sound of 'La Bourboule' may more appropriately belong to a champagne rather than to a town, but it's where my wife Veronik grew up. Its name is derived from the Celtic god of water, Borvo, and its waters, rather than champagne, keep its citizens going. Situated in the Massif Central, geologically the oldest part of France, it belongs to the region of Auvergne, a rough and craggy country whose volcanoes fell quiet thousands of years ago, leaving behind a landmass pitted with lakes and craters. An ancient town called Besse is supposed to lie drowned in Lac Pavin, the deepest of Auvergne's crater lakes. Its waters are not to be disturbed. The legend is that if you throw stones into it, you'll kick up a fearful storm. Mountain storms are awesome and Pavin's cold circular eye invites them openly. It's the dead eye of Besse.

The tops of many of Auvergne's mountains are barren but not because their trees have been chopped down. The mountains themselves are hard and unyielding, their gift of streams their only concession to the hard-worked people of the land. It's a generous gift all the same. Auvergne is the birthplace of all of France's rivers.

There are supposed to be about three hundred volcanoes in Auvergne, some of them active when the Celts, the original inhabitants, practised their druidic rites in the hills. These included human sacrifice. Megaliths litter the hills but the sacrificial bones have turned to powder or been washed away. The hard land did not accept them.

Though the fires of the volcanoes finally retreated, they kept in touch with the surface. Auvergne is a kettle constantly on the boil. Water streams from its fissures, hot springs the Romans built their spas around. La Bourboule is one such spa, though developed relatively recently. Its waters heal, but not miraculously. A whole industry of doctors, medical attendants, hotels and children's homes has grown up around the 'season'— between May and September—when patients with chronic chest and skin problems come to the baths from all over France and elsewhere, to be cured. Pierre Quainon, Veronik's grandfather, had been a mason who had built many of the town's houses. Francois, her father, had been a small farmer keeping poultry and cows, but Adéle her mother, had risen to be an hotelier and the proprietress of a children's home. Her son Jean and his wife Claire successfully ran a hotel.

~

The hill people of India walk fast, their spines erect, their gait sure. The people of Auvergne don't. The young prefer their motorbikes and sports to walking and the old have grown old too soon. The women, in particular, age quickly. Dressed in traditional grey or black, they are a familiar sight on the steep roads, gripping their canes and walking with slow short steps. Neglected by the rest of France, unlike the rich South, Auvergne also got little attention from the Germans during the Occupation, though Vichy, the headquarters of the collaborationist Pétain government, is situated in the region.

During the Occupation, two of Adéle's tenants had been Jewish. She had been denounced by French collaborators and threatened. She got away with her life but in La Bourboule's large graveyard is a memorial to those who didn't—martyrs of the Resistance. I'd seen it on a previous visit, watching an unknown person being buried. This time, higher up in the hills, I hoped to find another grave.

~

The grey stone farmhouse we drove to was abandoned, its roof caved in. Most of its furniture had rotted or been picked clean by visitors. We saw it on our way to Picherande, a grey unpeopled slope which livens up only in winter, when the skiers come. Francois had given up his poultry and cows after he'd been injured in the First World War. A metal plate held his femur together. He could only walk with the help of two canes. His bones, according to Veronik, had slowly turned to powder. The owner of the house we saw had given up for another reason. His sons had moved to the city. It was a common story in the region. The land could not be tamed.

~

In the middle of October, it began raining suddenly. The tops of the mountains which dominate the western end of La Bourboule were submerged in cloud. Sudden storms are common to the region and the power of the few I've been caught in has been fearsome. The sandstorm over Aden which I saw from the deck of a ship, a dark plume of sand hanging over the yellowed city, a gritty hail forcing us to go below deck (See 'Sandstorm at Sea' on Page 103), or the convection storm in Bombay one November, when the clouds, ranged from end to end of the sky, came over us like hundreds of hooded serpents, didn't have the same effect. A mountain storm lays its hand on you suddenly, crashing out of a clear sky. It's best to be alone in the mountains then. A black cloud swiftly swirls up behind a peak, darkening the slopes, turning day into night. A few seconds after the eclipse, it explodes, making the valley thunder with echoes. Since it can do nothing against the mountains, storm and mountain become allies, a vast trap in which the drenched town quakes like a mouse. Sometimes there's no town at all, only the blackened landscape. It's then that one comes closest to insignificance, to a desire to be extinguished, to be nothing at all. It's then that the chilly winds under the cloud feel like the touch of death.

~

No storm broke on my way to Murat-Le Quaire, a village of 110 people that overlooks La Bourboule. More than a hundred years ago it was more important than La Bourboule but the development of the spa had drained it of its importance and its people. Adéle had been one of them. She had lived there for many years and her children had been born there, but forced to take up a seedy hotel in La Bourboule, she had built it up single-handedly, wrecking her health in the process and alienating her children.

I'd gone to Murat-Le Quaire to look for her grave. She had died four years ago, when Veronik had been in Bombay. Katia had found her dead on the floor of her room. Veronik had somehow managed to reach the church in La Bourboule in time for the funeral service. There, a cousin, in a moment of anger, had accused her of being responsible for Adéle's death. To have been absent in India rather than in another part of France had been her crime.

There was a small graveyard at the entrance of Murat-Le Quaire and though I spent some time there, I found no grave that bore Adéle's name. An old peasant on the road told me there was another graveyard by the church. It was larger. Among the many family vaults there, were a few marked Guillaume, the name I was looking for. Perhaps there was yet another graveyard. The owner of a store opposite the church said there wasn't and assured me that Adéle Guillaume was indeed buried opposite. She had been a much-respected person in the area. There was no question of it.

So I went back among the vaults and the gravestones, peering at every name and scrutinizing every photograph. Could that have been her when she was young? Had the photographs got mixed up? I got acquainted with the Jean-Jacques and the Marie-Claires, with the grandfathers and grandmothers of those who had left the village, with the other Guillaumes and with whole families that hadn't left. I did the rounds four times.

Back in La Bourboule I spoke to Jean. 'The grave's unmarked.'

'It's a scandal,' he muttered, looking dejected. Veronik gave a small scream.

'How many times have I told you,' Clare cried, setting out lunch, 'to attend to it?'

Lunch wasn't spoiled. The storm passed as quickly as it broke, as often happens in the mountains.

~

The lazy days of sunshine in La Bourboule, of eating at the stone table outside Veronik's house, the endives, the cèpe mushrooms gathered from a forest looking like clods of mud, of driving to abandoned farmhouses in search of furniture and of painting in the garden, were over.

Lulled into security, I spent three weeks with Veronik in Paris. I postponed leaving for Bombay three times.

When I finally decided to leave, immigration officers at the airport reminded me that though my visa was valid for three months, it was one which required me to hop in and out of the country; each stay was to be for ten days only. I'd forgotten about that.

I could have been in big trouble but escaped it. What trouble there was had to do with another shoulder bag Veronik had given me, its straps attached with foolproof plastic clips. I waved to her at the departure gate and turned a corner. The clips were far from foolproof. The bag went thump.

~

Thump goes the heart in its cage of bone, its straps attached to flesh. If they break when you're asleep and pitch you to the floor, as they did Adéle, it's probably a merciful act. Memory isn't that merciful; nor the weather around some graves.

'The heart of standing is you can fly'

BEING HUMAN

REPUBLIC OF VICTIMS

'Victims Arrive, Aid Leaves Mumbai' says the headline on a paper that's two years, ten months and fourteen days old. Below the headline is a photograph of a ten-year-old boy lying on a bed in one of the Mumbai's hospitals. The photograph shows him looking at the camera while he clutches a tiffinbox and a video game cassette. He has a bruise under his left eye. He doesn't smile.

The paper describes the boy as being one of the victims of the earthquake that hit Gujarat on Republic Day 2001, three days before the photograph was published. Others might prefer to call the boy one of the earthquake's casualties rather than one of its victims. 'Victim' carries a special charge, it speaks of a condition that can't be easily redeemed or is impossible to redeem. The boy was brought to Mumbai fast. By a private helicopter, the paper says, along with three others from the same village. The village was Bhachau, one of those near Bhuj that was almost totally destroyed.

The private helicopter, it turns out, had been hired by Nancybhai Ladha, a trustee of Nanavati Hospital which admitted the boy and the three others from Bhachau. For Mumbaikars it was a feel-good story, like some other stories of that time. The paper sums it up in another headline above photographs of two of the other casualties: 'Mumbai Rallies to Help its Neighbour'.

Feel-good feelings never last long—they're not meant to. Victims see to that. Who isn't overwhelmed by the force of conditions that are unredeemed, that seem irremediable, and by the lives and deaths of those who inhabit such conditions? I don't have to go back two years, ten months and fourteen days to recall such conditions. The present, this very moment, is crowded with them. All the same, I will go back.

On the same page as the photograph of the rescued boy is another story. It's by Vaibhav Purandare and is datelined Kothewadi, Ahmednagar. It goes: 'The residents of Kothewadi village, perched atop a tiny hill on the mostly barren landscape of Ahmednagar district, are shaken. Not due to an earthquake. For them, traumatizing tremors came on the night of 16 January, when a gang of twenty-five dacoits targeted every home in the village, assaulting the men, raping over ten women and subjecting many others, mostly women, to severe physical torture.

'In an incident that matched the barbarity of bloodshed in Bihar, the armed dacoits committed sexual assaults on women from 11 p.m. till 4 a.m., sparing neither a six-year-old nor a 70-year-old village grandmother. A bonfire was then made of the clothes of all the women and the burning garments flung on to their battered bodies, inflicting burns. In addition to this, the dacoits damaged wooden doors, smashed earthen pots and other storage stuff for money and jewellery, and even wrenched out a portion of a woman's ear to get hold of a precious earring.

'But the victims' woes were compounded with the apathy of the police. When some of the villagers had rushed to inform the police about the fateful incident, they were asked by the guardians of law to arrange for a vehicle, and if not that, at least for the expenditure of petrol . . .'

Back to the present, and to our shame, a continuous line of victims, a continuing kind of travel expense. Every day an afternoon paper gives me the number of people who died crossing the city's train tracks in the previous twenty-four hours. Today's tally comes to twelve. The paper also tells me that the number of those who've been killed while crossing the tracks since the beginning of the year is 3,315.

There are people who'll try and convince you, every day, that Mumbai is a city of survivors, that it has no victims. What do you think?

THE HEART OF STANDING IS

> Every part of a model aeroplane is important, in so far as no model will function without all its essential components. If any part, however, can be considered of more import than another, surely it is the wing. In view of this, it is surprising how little attention some aeromodellists pay to the design of this most fundamental accessory, especially in the matter of wing section.
>
> Lawrence H. Sparey and Charles A. Rippon in
> *The Model Aeroplane Manual*

A crow flies past me at eye level, travelling from right to left. It doesn't fly straight. It rises a little, then dips, and rises again as I've seen model aeroplanes do when they're flying well. It's the sort of action that concentrates the vision of anyone obsessed with flying model aeroplanes. We, men, women and children watch our models fly with bated breath, and when they make a perfect landing, again with a slight upward tilt of their bodies, a final lilt in their melodious passage through air, they take our breath away. Our spirits lift even as their small wheels touch the ground. Something we were responsible for, for making from scratch or for assembling from a kit, has made a perfect flight.

My obsession with model aeroplanes must have begun in Bombay—planes made of folded paper launched from balconies, darts flung across classrooms, the usual stuff. But it was in Poona that the obsession found room to thrive. My grandmother's bungalow, picturesquely named 'Hill Crest', was on the outskirts of the city, in the equally picturesquely named Salisbury Park. At the time I am speaking of, in the 1940s, Salisbury Park was a vast tract of land, almost treeless, except for the trees that grew in the gardens of the few private bungalows in the area. My brother and I never saw Salisbury Park green, we saw it at its most arid; I don't remember it ever raining in Poona.

That was because we almost inevitably went to Poona before the monsoons, during our long school vacations. Salisbury Park stood as though covered by coarse, brittle straw. Black rocks pushed their snouts through it, as if they were sniffing for rain. It was dry, but it was paradise for me.

On a hillock which bore a pir's tomb and a single tree—we called it One-Tree Hill—I could launch as many planes as I could get my hands on: small gliders with a lead weight in their noses bought from a shop in the city—you launched them with a catapult, they generally made a loop in the air before gliding to earth; a British-made rubber-powered plane bought from a shop in Bombay, a FROG with a number ... model after model of that plane barely rose before crashing to the ground; a balsa glider I made from a kit—it never balanced well whatever I did with it; and my favourites, the gliders made by the National Defence Academy in nearby Khadakwasla. Hand-launched from the hillock, they soared in unimagined currents of air, they flew beautifully and landed safely even on the rocks. You could adjust their wings, make them flat like those of a crow or V-shaped like those of a pigeon. All I know about the flight of birds I learned from those model aeroplanes.

So it doesn't surprise me that the flight of a crow or a pigeon or a seagull—which my kit-assembled craft resembled—takes me back to those days in Poona, to those early flying models, recreating, in fact, whole acres of childhood in an instant, transporting me from my present relatively static state to a time when things, however momentarily, leapt and soared and flew.

This happens, it happened a moment ago when the crow crossed my sight ... and I find myself asking. Is being still, being static, really as bad as it sounds? Hasn't too much happened in the past, too much sound and fury, too much pointless flying around, too much restless fantasy? What's wrong with trying to be still, with gathering what comes to you, with not going all out to get it?

A line from Bob Dylan's recent song 'Not Dark Yet' comes

as a disapproving answer. The song is about a frightening kind of stillness, of giving up, of waiting for death. Dylan sings, '*I was born here and I'll die here/ against my will. / I know it looks like I'm moving/but I'm standing still.*' And as though to confirm this menacing stasis, comes poet William Empson's line on event-induced paralysis. '*The heart of standing is you cannot fly.*'

No event I can think of accounts for my present paralysis. It doesn't look like I'm moving; I'm standing still.

The other day, going up a lane which leads to a fire temple, a freshly painted wall caught my eye. It was painted a rich, deep-yellow ochre, exactly matching the yellow ochres I used to make out of my mother's bottles of poster paint. I stood still for a minute. The paints are still there on the other side of the wall. There was laughter in the flat, sheets of drawing paper, Winsor & Newton paint brushes. A glider, its wings V-shaped, flew above me. I heard the whirring of a propeller and saw a kite perched on a pir's tomb. A crow preparing to land in a garden nearby let down its undercarriage.

Wings are of the greatest import, as the book said. Wing sections lie buried in our bones, where once upon a time they structured them. Nothing or no one may put those humpty dumpties together again. But stand still.

The heart of standing is you *can* fly.

PART OF AN EDUCATION

It was in the summer of 1963 that Oxford's dark immigrants came to the notice of the local population in an unconsciously communal act. Two of India's favourite playback singers were giving a concert in the Town Hall and every Indian and Pakistani immigrant in Oxfordshire seemed visibly and vocally to be there. The darkness of the audience was given further weight by its preference for dark winter suits, a combination that makes all coloured people look substantially more massive than they are. There must have been at least a thousand Indians and Pakistanis in quiet, vacation-deserted Oxford that day. People stared at them from their stopped cars.

I had lived through the summer of '63, my last summer vacation, and the following year on the fringe of Oxford's Jericho. Though subject to invasion like its Biblical namesake, the walls of this particular Jericho stand fast, thicken daily and are invisible.

My landlady had hesitated when I asked to be shown the room she had advertised. I had told her I was Indian and perhaps, as in other British cities and where Indian students find themselves looking for rooms, I would have been turned away—were it not for the fact that at Oxford, at least, I had means of finding out from the Delegacy of Lodgings whether the vacant room had 'just been taken'—the usual excuse—or not.

Not that this would have guaranteed me a room. No foreign student, coloured or otherwise, has a foolproof method of knowing what the grounds of his being refused a room are. A Canadian friend of mine had once had this verbal bouquet flung at him—that she, the landlady, had admitted him, a colonial after all, only because he had been white.

I had opportunities to leave Jericho's ugly fringe later but I stayed because it was cheap and I wanted to discover details about immigrant life there. My racial indeterminacy helped. It was possible for me to overhear and sometimes participate in anti-darkie talk at the bus-stop, the supermarket and the local, about a tenth of whose customers were Pakistanis.

I heard what Oxford's people said about immigrants, I know what the immigrant feels about his host. Neither party guessed how much in my own experience could neither contradict nor confirm one or the other attitude but cause me confusion and distress.

Grounds for this particular distress had opened a few hours after I left Bombay in 1957. A very young ship steward had refused a request for a glass of water from one of the ship's passengers with the remark, 'You're only an Indian'. The remark spread swiftly through the passengers and soon a dark, impotently-threatening crowd had gathered round the boy. I felt sorry for the boy at the time because he suffered so obviously from the effects of his impulsive remark and would, I was sure, suffer further under his superiors. In the seven years that have followed, the refused glass of water has become a sea of prohibitions. The immigrants resent it. Unfortunately, few of them have the confidence or the ability to state their case in the press.

But the case against the darkies of Jericho, a mixture of Arab, West Indian, Indian and Pakistani, is one that anyone can make with ease, both in the press and outside it.

One woman said she could tolerate anything but their spitting. Spitting released widely-felt but valid British fears of tuberculosis. Others objected to their methods of cooking: the slaughter of poultry in the basement, the after-smells of 'curry'. Most disregarded their clumsy attempts to break into English, pushing them into further difficulties of speech, and solitude. So much was said against them. No one said anything for them. Least of all the Indians at the University.

As set against about 2,000 Indian immigrants in Oxford, working in the Cowley car-works, restaurants, building sites and the bus services, there were sixty-six Indians at the University in the academic year 1963-1964. We were not a community, we did not club together, nor, unlike a previous generation, were we united by any great hope for the motherland. The unreality of our situation was made further unreal by the nature of what some of us read, so that the death of an Anglo-Saxon hero on a tenth-century battlefield could be made to appear more vivid than the slaughter of ill-equipped soldiers in Bomdila.

It was only when our British friends receded during the vacation that we stood exposed, somewhat alienated, to each other's gaze, lamenting over our pints of bitter that we were being ill served by our superiors, our government, and Oxford.

The myths about us were many. There is, for example, the myth that because most Indians have ready cash they are rolling in the stuff. This was true of the princely families Oxford once cultivated and the few 'royals' it still does, but misrepresents the average Indian student now. Since 1957, Indian students have been allowed a maximum quota of £650 for Oxford and Cambridge, £600 for other universities. In Oxford about two-thirds of this goes to the university, leaving the student with the prospect of spending more than six months in the year, his exciting vacs, on less than a pound a week, a third of what it would cost to rent a room in London—a trouble he tries to get out of by resorting to blackmarketeers, gambling, working in the vacations and skipping meals.

To many Indian students, the immigrant is a squalid reminder of conditions they have done little to alleviate in their homeland, a despoiler of the Indian image abroad and an embarrassment. They fail to realise that the social pressures the immigrant is subject to overlap with those on them and that the immigrant is in a position to be financially much better off than they can ever be as students.

Also, as far as the local population can see, there is no difference between them and the immigrants except, perhaps, of age. The Indian student is as likely as the next 'darkie' to have committed that mysterious theft in the supermarket. He is as suspect to the Law and will be stopped in the streets after midnight. The first person to be arrested in a canteen where a friend of mine worked was a newly-arrived Pakistani in his teens, who, she insists, could not have committed the theft he was accused of since he was not on the premises then.

Another girl at Oxford (a blind date and quite fearless) told me with blatant honesty that she would go out with anyone but Pakistanis. Pakistanis, in fact, have acquired a sexual notoriety once reserved for blacks. Though the Indian students I knew didn't feel responsible for their immigrant countrymen, most of them believed they had to pay for their presence.

Six months after Oxford, trying to maintain a certain independence to be able to write by taking temporary jobs where an arts degree is utterly useless, the pattern that emerges follows the fortunes of most immigrants here. On three occasions I affected a neutral accent over the telephone and was called for an interview promptly. I was then told in the politest way possible that either I did not ring at all, had come to the wrong place or had misunderstood the speaker. Personally, I would prefer a slap in the face to this mask of politeness no reaction of mine can dent. The mask, as thick as the climate of rejection itself, remains. It is in the midst of a new insecurity that the Indian or any dark immigrant walks—an insecurity made all the more bizarre by the more extreme sentiments heard in Hyde Park or in workers' pubs that we are either Communist-sponsored or have come all the way from our countries to make use of Britain's social services.

Desperately, one tries to keep oneself from sliding into the lunatic fringe of prejudice, to attribute one's joblessness to personal and not national factors. As desperately, one concludes that particular areas of anti-Indian feeling, far from never having existed at all, but forced into the open by public pressure, have hardened and that Indian students in the country, once expected to submit with awe to British institutions and personalities, are now expected to react to the new indifference of people here with the same bitter inarticulacy as their less literate countrymen. The irony of the Oxford Indian's denial of the immigrant and his final graduation into second-class citizenship of a country whose democratic institutions those of his own are supposed to be modelled on, could not be more complete.

An English friend of mine, living with a coloured family in his last year at Oxford, told me how the youngest girl in the family confessed one day how much she regretted being born black. In London, an Indian, but not recognisably so, my hand stops over the gap following Nationality on one of the many job forms I've filled in after Oxford. The temptation to put down one of the many European nationalities I've been mistaken for is very strong. After all, no one has asked for my passport, not yet. I write: Indian. The apology that follows this piece of information is, by now, predictable.

A BALANCING ACT

Have you ever wondered how totalitarian you are in your thoughts and how liberal in your actions? You must have. The sentences passed by the kangaroo courts in our heads don't generally match the sentences we speak.

I tell the kangaroo court in my head, 'That book should be burnt', or 'That film should be banned', or 'That person should be hanged'. I may even say so in public. We all say things in public on impulse. But we generally try to hold back the impulse, we soften the sentences passed in our heads by saying things like, 'I shouldn't bother with that book', or 'Don't see that film even if someone pays you to', or 'Ignore that person'.

It isn't always a question of not speaking our minds, though in some cases it might be. It's more a matter of not speaking the first thing that comes to mind. It's a matter of recognizing that the mind has a civilisation and a culture of its own however much it is influenced by the civilizations and cultures around it.

I use the word 'around' to imply both proximity and distance. Civilisations and cultures that affect our minds by their immediate proximity are different from those at a distance, both in time and space.

When we discover that we rely more on those distant

cultures and civilizations than on the immediately prevailing ones to shape the daily course of our thoughts and actions, a terrible conflict starts; terrible because the people in whom that conflict takes place have to walk a tightrope all their lives. Or they choose to fall on one side or the other of the tightrope.

Such persons may well be experts in the field of artificial intelligence, but with values so dependent on earlier cultures and civilisations that they can justify acts of sati which take place now. Or they may attempt to so cyberize themselves as to evolve various digital strategies by which they can hope to exorcise an old civilisation and culture from themselves altogether.

These aren't imaginary options. Many of us have met people who have chosen them. The first kind of person, the brilliant fundamentalist, can be found in important positions in many workplaces today. The second, the liberated cyberman, is fast crawling into such spaces too. My admiration for the tightrope artist who has forever to balance the claims of modernity against the claims of antiquity and the other way round too, grows, though I don't have a head for heights or a talent for balance.

Balance. What a dreary word. How much more entertaining the pratfall, the slide on a banana peel. When the fall hurts we try to get some sort of balance into our act. When that gets boring we're drawn to the fall. I seem to prefer it that way.

So while all you lovely tightrope artists inch your ways forward above me, I'll stick to the ground, if you don't mind. Defying gravity and pondering weighty matters aren't for me unless the weight is of the sort that concerned Sisyphus. Rolling a stone up a hill when it always rolls down once it gets to the top is a clownish act: Sisyphus is one of an ancient civilization's great clowns.

The kangaroo court in my head has passed a sentence which says, 'Death to all tyrants.' But what I write is, 'Bring on the clowns.'

THE WORST THING ABOUT BEING HUMAN

'Hypocrite reader! . . . You! . . . My twin! . . . My brother!'
from 'To The Reader' by Charles Baudelaire

The worst thing about being a human being is being a human being. 'I wish I was bird', as the railway clerk in Nissim Ezekiel's poem says. But if I were, the worst thing about being a bird would be being a bird.

Being a human being, being a bird, has a lot to do with language. We use language as a weapon, we use language as a shield. To use language to communicate, for communion, seems to require special skills. I've seen too many sparrows fighting during the day to think otherwise.

Their dawn jingle-jangle (or dawn song I'd say if I were feeling romantic) of apparent communication lasts no longer than the first grains of truth they see. There's plenty of bajri in that plate, you %*&!, stop squabbling, there's enough to go around. For God's sake, stop that racket.

They don't. Neither for God's sake nor mine. We don't. Neither for God's sake nor ours. Perhaps one of the worst things about being a human being is an inability to recognise what being human means.

Two teenagers stab an older man to death. We say it's human after all, he bought them for sex. Crowds of commuters pass a dying man in the street. That's inhuman, every reporter will cry. See what the beastly city's done to them? It's made them inhuman. And what about you, Mr Reporter? Rescued anyone lately?

Language as a weapon, language as a shield, language as a cliché. Here are some recently heard definitions which, in fact are as old as Hell. What's an intellectual? Someone who cares for ideas, not people. Who's gay? Everyone but me. This from someone who admits that he uses gay men for sex. Is photography an art? I don't think so, says the painter who bases his paintings on photographs.

Social conventions require that we don't go about wearing our hearts on our sleeves. People who do so are exhausting. Who hasn't been assaulted, at one social gathering or the other, by someone so emotionally messed up that he or she can only talk about his or her wounds? Convention says that kind of behaviour spoils the party, and convention, up to a point, is right. Such matters should be kept between friends, says convention. Wait for it, there's a new definition coming along, new but as old as Hell. What's a friend?

Friend is someone who will inevitably betray you. Well, perhaps not inevitably. Let's try again. Friend is someone who betrays you as much as you betray yourself.

I think if we recognised this we'd come a step closer to understanding what being human means. Social convention may require that you, as a casteist, contemptuously refer to another as being one; that you, as a thief, contemptuously call someone else by that name. But, when you, as a frequenter of brothels, join the chorus of voices that demand that they be abolished, you betray yourself totally. Who should you expect friendship from then, your favourite sex worker? Call her a slut and you don't know how much of a slut you are. If you do know, admit it, at least to yourself. It's a way of acknowledging you're human. Every human being who has the capacity to fantasise must know that every human being is a slut.

It's one of the great themes of literature, not to mention religion, that those who throw stones from a moral high ground do so blindly, that they are unaware that they are flesh and blood to the people they stone.

Christ's relationship with Mary Magdalene is no mere anecdote, it represents a bond. It represents, in its straightforward clasp, a sacred acceptance of the 'sluts' we are.

No, I don't believe in Adam and Eve, the Fall, or any theology that claims that human beings are basically sinful creatures, who can only be redeemed by the hand of God. It worked for Maradona in his infamous goal against England, but like so many millions, it doesn't work for me.

When you reach out to someone drowning, when you reach out to someone dying in the streets, when you reach out to your sluts dying of AIDS, it's your hands that do it, not God's.

All intellectuals are eggheads, concerned with ideas, not people. All gays sin against nature, they should be hanged. All modern art is phoney. Photography isn't an art form, my son takes better snapshots. Have it your way, Mr and Ms Cliché, but have you rescued anyone lately?

HUMANIST FIRES

Yesterday I met a committed humanist. I suppose committed humanists are committed, among other things, to see the positive side of being human. They generally have secular beliefs, and almost always regard religious beliefs as the chief perverters of human values. Some are atheists. But without necessarily being humanists, most of us see the positive side of being human. I'm human, I'm alive. That's positive enough for me. You're human, you're alive. Get out of my way.

Let thousands of positive-feeling human beings into train compartments or have them choking the city's streets on a working day and you quickly realise the positive side of not being human. You appreciate the practically empty compartment, the day of the deserted street. It's human to be human and most human beings are shits.

That, at least, is what a writer in Britain's *Evening Standard* concludes about one human being—V. S. Naipaul. The writer attacks Naipaul's ditching his Argentinean mistress for a Pakistani woman whom he has just married. 'A grand man and a great writer V. S. Naipaul,' the writer says, 'but human, all too human.'

There's surely something more to being human than sadly concluding we're human after all. Why do we find it necessary to assume that grand men and great writers like Naipaul aren't human in the first place? Why are they looked upon as gods, even by those who have no special use for God? Is it a human trait to regard our heroes as omniscient, infallible, even immortal? Perhaps it is but surely no thinking person can let it rest there. If it's human to adore blindly that's one side of being human that needs to be expunged from our systems. That side makes us move in herds, more stupefied and bovine than those poor creatures suffering from mad cow disease. It leads to the creation of Hitlers.

I have nothing against beasts. In fact, I quite like them and think I'm pretty beastly myself. But just as beasts can be beasts in the worst possible sense, so can humans be humans in the worst possible sense. Abandoning reason is one way by which a human being not only becomes human in the worst possible sense but also a beast in the worst possible sense. The conflicts in former Yugoslavia threw up many such beasts. We'll have several of our own before we go to the polls.

In order to have free and fair elections, it seems necessary to resort to foul words and dirty deeds. So the dovish Shimon Peres turns hawkish a month before Israel's elections, causing a rocket to slam into a refugee camp, killing more than a hundred humans and wounding at least a hundred more. Was it a human error or, as an Israeli general claimed, a calculated human decision? So we have our growing anti-Pakistan rhetoric, leading to more vile anti-Hindu and anti-Muslim campaigns. Someone's going to get badly hurt. It's only human after all, isn't it?

Humanism can be an enriching faith, extremely difficult to practise in all circumstances, but well worth the gains in human terms. It is built on caring, compassion, even love if possible. But it has problems explaining evil and its all-pervasive presence in human affairs. One of this century's most deeply committed humanists, E. M. Forster, advised, 'Kindness, kindness and still more kindness.' I know people who sincerely want to follow that advice and who even believe that they do.

But what they achieve in practice is cruelty, cruelty and still more cruelty.

Most of us are not good enough to be good humanists; our morals are too good for us. Or we fail to realise the nature of what seems to be ineradicable—the evil in us. I've seen it break out between the most loving and caring of couples and destroy them. If humankind cannot bear too much reality, perhaps it can't bear too much happiness either.

If that sounds terribly inhuman and pessimistic, I'd argue that a dose of pessimism helps set things right, restore human balance. If we believe in humanist values, we have to ask ourselves, at the end of the century, where humanism went wrong, why it so obviously failed. Because in the face of what has replaced it—religious fanaticism, terrorism, suicide bombers, religious assassinations and ethnic wars—I see nothing else to fall back on except a recharged humanism. Some deep and troubled soul-searching is called for. Because if we don't return from that exercise recharged with faith in our humanity, in humanism, the streets of our cities may soon be deserts. For reasons other than bank holidays and people staying in to watch cricket.

I remember Bombay during its curfews in the days before Independence. The men of the house didn't go to work or returned from work early. It was an anxious time for a child. The morning papers carried photographs of burning trains and trams on fire. One day we saw a tram burning in Princess Street. Huge flames had erupted around the driver and he was flapping his hands over them. It must have been a short circuit that caused the fire and I imagine the driver, though hurt, escaped. We didn't find out because the car we were in sped past the tram without stopping. We were in a hurry to get home. The city would soon grow dark and silent. Curfew was approaching.

I may have forgotten many things about my first seven years in Bombay but the image of the tram driver remains. He was dressed in khaki, a Muslim with a white beard and his hands flapped over the flames in futile attempts to put the fire out. The fire burned as in an urn, but was fiercer than any I'd seen in fire temples. It burned in the middle of the street like a sacred fire but there was nothing sacred about it. It was strong, human, the result of error. And a human being was trying to put it out in an ineffective way.

Humanism is both a fire and a fight, otherwise it's no good. An old man standing in the middle of a fire without being consumed by it is not my favourite image of humanism, but for the moment, for me, it'll do.

WHO ARE YOU CALLING MAD?

A woman cuts off her sleeping husband's penis and we wince. After the jokes and sniggers, the verdict. She is acquitted. We don't like it. Many men want the woman to be put away permanently. The judge ruled her temporarily insane, didn't he? She's under observation, isn't she? But who are we calling mad?

I don't hold the view that men alone have created a system through which they drive and call a woman mad. Women and children have contributed to that system too, often consciously. But for the moment, in the space of a short article, let's concentrate on non-mad mighty man's mighty mite.

During her trial, the woman's husband was shown to be brutal in his sexual demands and responsible for marital rape. Many men won't condone such behaviour in other men, even if they are guilty of it themselves. It's seen as an aberration, a departure from the accepted norm. But the brutality of much 'normal' behaviour, normal 'manly' behaviour, goes unnoticed.

The harm we do mothers, wives and daughters, any girl or woman for that matter, in the normal course of our relationships with them is something we rarely see. There's the perfectly normal process of fathering and raising children. In time, the process normally transforms the child-bearing woman into the middle-aged drudge into the heap of bones in a corner. Men initiate the process but are unwilling to or more frighteningly, unable to stop it. Should we be surprised that she picks up a weapon to end the process herself?

In a series of paintings which she exhibited in 1973, Nalini Malani showed women stripped, flayed and skinned like the carcasses of cattle. They weren't dead. In fact, some of the figures half rose to resist something outside the frames they were in; we were made to feel that that something was men. Those paintings came to my mind when I thought of the woman on trial. Art's not always there when you need it and it hasn't made me treat women any better, but it can remind us of things we've forgotten or buried deep within ourselves—in this case the intolerable position of women in a world of men. An acute loneliness is part of that position. It can soon turn chronic, a part of a woman's 'normal' condition which we turn away from*. If and when we do turn back, turn to look at

---

*Jussawalla wrote in a catalogue essay for Malani's show at Pundole Art Gallery, Mumbai, which ran from 2 to 12 Jan 1973: Nalini's bodies are all female. Put another way, Nalini presents us with the female as body and body alone, a male's-eye view which is further accentuated by the physical placement of the bodies; they are all seen from on top. In other words, the nature of the aggression, even when presented in terms of a claustrophobic room or an occluding wall, is ultimately male. These are women subject to a world made by man, the doer, the maker, the aggressor.

This in itself is not a new statement. What is new is that these women fight back. They will not watch and wait and endure with their large sad eyes as women have been shown to be doing ever since Amrita Sher-Gil. These bodies hardly have eyes to see—they fight with only a dim awareness of the nature of their aggressor, but they fight. A young painter has succeeded in breaking a monotonous and misleading stereotype in paintings of astonishing maturity and power. It is a remarkable achievement. (Space did not allow us to include this remarkable piece of writing. The other constraint was the way in which Jussawalla refers directly to paintings as he writes, which would help someone walking around the gallery but which would be difficult without illustrations.)

her again, we may be pained but we expect her to accept that condition.

When she doesn't, when the loneliness leads to neurosis or severe mental disorders, few of us can deal with it. Men are conditioned into believing that when a woman behaves 'oddly', she needs sex. This is one of the worst things a man can say about a woman. We rarely consider that she may not need it at all, at least from a particular man, or has chosen not to have it or has been having the wrong kind.

Celibacy or abstinence doesn't automatically lead to neurosis; its cause may lie elsewhere. But to believe that it does, to believe that a woman who shows signs of neurosis, especially if she is unmarried or single, is one who doesn't get as much sex as she needs, is one of our dumber inventions, designed to boost our egos, make us feel more important to women than we are, and make them subjects of whatever absurd fantasies we have about the healing power of our genitals.

Some women have learned to laugh at such fantasies. Others have denied them. Still others have mocked them in print, going so far as to savage the heterosexual act itself.

In her book *Intercourse*, the American writer Andrea Dworkin does just that, describing the act of intercourse in such ugly terms, terms that spell death rather than life for a woman, that for a man reading the book even castration comes to appear a more pleasant prospect than sex.

Dworkin's book upsets me and I don't accept its basic premise, that heterosexual intercourse, by its very nature, violates the woman. But at least it counters the smug male assumption that such intercourse, by its very nature, is what the 'sick' woman deprived of it needs to restore her to health. A woman subjected to such potent healing may not like it because she doesn't like the man. A wife who has grown to dislike her husband intensely may be repeatedly subjected to it because the man believes he must have as many children as he can, or thinks he's just being kind. When a woman can't get out of such a relationship, her body is slowly destroyed. Sometimes she destroys it herself.

Christina Stead's novel *The Man Who Loved Children* describes just such a woman, married to a man who has no obvious faults. In fact, he is shown to be likeable, manly in a non-macho kind of way, large-hearted and generous. As a 'normal' man he has 'normal' desires, including the perfectly healthy one of having as many children as he can. It's the wife who can't cope, whose health begins to deteriorate, who starts hating her children who, in turn, hate her and sometimes their father. He doesn't see the violence coming and it's one of the author's strengths that she makes us believe that good, optimistic men, like her protagonist, both hearty and hale, are incapable of seeing it come, just as they are incapable of seeing their wives' distress.

Acts of temporary insanity must be seen in the context of the permanent sanity that has brought them about. The permanent sanity of male societies, their sexual and social norms, have driven many women mad, and not just temporarily. It's this permanent sanity which has to be addressed and redressed if we are to redefine ourselves as men and woman and have a better future. In the meantime we will continue to put away the madwomen we ourselves have created, temporarily or for life.

UPROOTED

He stared at the typewriter and asked me if it was a computer. I said no, it was a typewriter and showed him a page of what it could do. He is the delivery boy of the vegetable stall on the corner and he had brought me some vegetables. He looked longingly at the typewriter. 'I was learning how to type. I went to four classes. Then I had to go away,' he said. 'Can you find me a job?'

His name is Mahesh and he comes from a small town north

of Allahabad, like his co-workers. He works twelve hours a day, delivering vegetables to anyone who lives in the area. And it's a vast area of high-rise buildings, the success of his errands almost entirely dependent on lifts. Some of his clients pay him a little extra for his trouble, others don't. A month on the job and he was looking for a new one.

'You could go to typing classes in the city,' I suggested foolishly, knowing full well that he wouldn't have the time or the money to attend them.

'Where are they?' he asked.

'I'll try and find out,' I replied, anxious to end the conversation.

At the door he turned and asked, 'If I go to these classes, will I get a job?'

'I'll try and find out,' I repeated, and shut the door behind him.

There's little one can do. At one time or the other, everyone in a job which is seen as being 'good' is approached by the unemployed and by those trapped in bad jobs to do something for them. 'Find me a job', or 'Find my nephew a job', or 'Get me a government job' are common remarks, reminding the employee of a desperation they once felt but are in no position to do anything about for those left out—the desperate others. From village to city, from city to other cities, migrants move, looking for jobs. When they land up at your doorstep you have nothing to offer.

And yet there are success stories. Ali, the friend of a friend, manages a shop in Saudi Arabia. Despite beatings, thefts and attempts on his life, his business is expanding. Eight years after leaving Mumbai, he has come back to get married. He told us grim stories of the Saudi system of justice, of the exclusion of Indians from much of Saudi society, of the strictness of Saudi law. Yet he approved of the strictness. He felt it was necessary for a society to function. It was a base for prosperity. He preferred it there to here. He had breathing problems in

Mumbai, he had a bad cough. He asked us to make telephone calls for him, and read addresses. Unlike Mahesh, he can't read or write.

Getting to know Ali, I realised how dependent the illiterate are on others. Letters to his family have to be written for him, letters have to be read. Street signs are no use to him, so explicit directions have to be given. Yet he has picked up Arabic and understands more English than most people around him realise. Polite and considerate, he will try not to make a fool of himself in front of others more educated than himself. He keeps his appointments and is punctual, unlike most of the educated people I know. And he's a success.

Ali's story is the story of most hard-working Indians, this time not in Britain, the United States or Australia, but in Saudi Arabia. Instead of going to typing classes in Mumbai (assuming he could) should Mahesh the delivery boy also try to emigrate? Friends I ask don't know why anyone should be bothered, there's nothing we can do anyway. But given the trap he's in, I suspect Mahesh will break out and go Ali's way.

BOYCOTT

This is about something we do from time to time to feel virtuous. We boycott someone or a country's goods or a particular occasion because we disagree with what the person or the goods or the occasion represent. The disagreement has to be strong, even violent, for a boycott to happen. Boycotting British goods during the Swadeshi movement meant not buying them; it also meant burning them in public.

We continue doing similar things to people we consider awkward. Less than two months ago Tikambai Sahu, a twenty-six-year-old mother of two, was stripped and beaten to death in a place called 'Vijaynagar slum' on the outskirts of Nagpur, punished for being a witch.

It's quite easy to appear virtuous; you go along with the herd. Students in England happily boycotted South African wine along with non-students since students didn't buy wine in the first place; we were into beer. Writers in a university town in the States happily stopped buying Gallo wines—there was a word-of-mouth boycott because the company was meant to be treating its workers badly—since there were other equally good Californian wines to choose from. Cool. Painless and cool.

Fasting can't be that painless. It's a form of boycott—avoiding food one likes. And I'm told 'the virtue of that kind of boycott lies in its pain'. I'd have thought women have enough pain to bear without adding to it by fasting, but no. I haven't yet met a woman who hasn't suddenly stopped eating her favourite food for reasons only she can understand. I'm sure the reasons have got to do with men but I'm not at all certain what those reasons are.

This behaviour, this withdrawal from favourite foods, is most conspicuous during the mango season. Women who love mangoes stop eating them, making a point of doing so in the presence of a man, generally a husband. Is such abstinence, frequently accompanied by a lowering of the eyes, a firm shaking of the head and a pursing of lips—especially when the man continues to entreat the woman to have her favourite fruit—a reversal of Eve's temptation in the original garden, man being tempter now and the woman grown wise enough to refuse?

Or is the refusing of mangoes akin to a vow, like 'Lord, see what I do. I give up my favourite food for him, for you. Make him behave better.'? I suspect it's that.

Quite pointless. The man will simply help himself to the woman's share of mangoes and continue to behave as abominably as before.

Caste wars, superstitious rituals, witch-hunts are extensions of such behaviour. They can't be joked about. For a person to be ostracised for a crime she doesn't know she has committed, to then be tried and killed for a crime which in fact, she hasn't committed is unforgiveable—the boycott of a person carried to its extreme. What happened to Tikambai Sahu is unforgiveable. She was suspected of having caused the death of a young girl in her neighbourhood through the practice of witchcraft. So, according to reporters Abhijit Sathe and Sravani Sarkar of *The Indian Express*, after she was declared guilty by a self-appointed panchayat: 'She was stripped, thrashed and paraded naked all over the locality all night by a group of drunks. She was finally left to die in the early hours of the morning. One of her eyes was crushed . . .

Finally, one of the women mustered up enough courage to cover her naked body with a saree . . .' By then Tikambai was dead.

The reporters add: 'Tikambai's is the seventh case of witch-hunting to have occurred in the Vijaynagar slum in the last three years.'

VISIBILITY ZERO

'September brings fantastic clouds,' the geography master said. We looked up in September and saw fantastic clouds. 'November is generally dry and clear,' he'd say. We saw that November was generally dry and clear. But that was many years ago. For the last ten years or so, a yellow-grey smog seeps into Bombay in November and doesn't lift till February. The city blurs in the sulphurous haze. Eyes smart, the horizon is blotted out.

It's been the same this year. I am lucky to see the sunrise, but after that the hills on the mainland are bleached, whole ranges of the Sahyadris gone into thick air. Last night, a narrow street close to where I live thundered with bombs. The blasts were continuous, a chain of explosions that went on for more than fifteen minutes. Smoke drifted across the neighbourhood, rising above its tallest buildings. A dog ran without stopping. The streetlights blurred. It's the wedding season, and marriages are rarely made with a clear view in sight.

Almost exactly a year ago, we stood on the rooftops and watched a blacker smoke drift across the city. For ten days we were abandoned to murderers, looters, rioters and arsonists. Then in March, the bomb blasts. Later in the year, the earthquake and the mass deaths of women and children on the tracks. Abandoned? Yes. Not only by the law but it would seem by God. Maharashtra had hardly seen a blacker year. We wanted it to end and end fast. If the devil had taken over, well, let the devil take it.

It'll take some time before we stop saying 'Happy New Year' to all and sundry this month, but there's no reason to believe it'll be a happy year, at least happier than last year. It may even be worse. His Satanic Majesty is a stayer, having been in the business for a very long time. He has the stamina of a long-distance runner and the persistence of a lodger who refuses to be evicted. Since he lodges mostly in our hearts, the problem would seem to begin and end there and often it does. When the heart stops. But in order to live, and live in the fullest and best sense of the word, we have to get him out before. How?

There's another problem with happy new years. The unhappiest year for a nation may be the happiest year in one's life. When we say 'It's been a good year' or 'It's been a bad year', most of us mean it personally. So despite the unhappy turn of events in the city and the nation as a whole and despite a nasty accident to my father, last year was a happy year for me. Yet why do I get this feeling—and I know others share this feeling—of being smothered by gloom? Why does the smog sometimes turn into a fog so black that no light is visible?

Between the winter solstice and the New Year there's the birth of Christ. I've seen the celebrations of about ten anniversaries of the event in the West and despite the occasional kindness of friends and the less occasional comfort of strangers, it's a miserable time to be there. The carcasses of bulls, sheep and pigs hung upside down in the shop windows, the forced and frantic joviality, the robotic mimicry of shopping and the sharp rise of road accidents depress and weigh people down. It's the season when there's the greatest number of suicides. One Christmas I met Waguih Ghali, an Egyptian Copt who wrote in English. He killed himself during another Christmas. Time may have conjoined the two Christmases in my memory when, perhaps, only one was involved. But that is my association with the season. Of death rather than birth. 'Where is the life we have lost in living?'

The answer to T. S. Eliot's question lies in religion but it may also lie in poetry. To become believers, to have faith, may be our only redemption but many of us are too full of doubts and anxieties to go that way. Even if we go that way partly, even when we fully realise what the religious life means, we backslide into the ditch of disbelief and remorse. Besides, wherever we look we see the ugly face of religion; the fratricidal monster and his progeny have set up house in so many hearts in this country and abroad. As fundamentalists raise their fists and their voices and the moderate clergy of all religions fall silent, we see the very fabric of organised religion come apart in front of our eyes. There is no shelter there, no source of light.

Art, in some quarters, is regarded as a substitute for religion but I find the idea false. Granted that there's often an obvious dividing line between the two, what really separates one from the other? Before our more secular times, most of the greatest art, and this includes folk art, has been religious, and religious music helps us understand ourselves and the nature of the world as few things can. Religion, even in or perhaps especially in a secular state, simply cannot be wished away, much as some people would like it to be, by a constitutional amendment or a law in the statute books. It has its place and purpose because His Satanic Majesty has. It exists because he does. Or does he?

In his book *The Heart of Religion*, the Buddhist teacher P. D. Mehta says he doesn't: 'There is no Evil One—no Diabolos or Satan or Ahriman or Mara—as a being or personal entity; nor is there any metaphysical principle of evil. However convenient a postulated entity or principle may be for talking purposes the real evil is in me, myself, in you yourself, in our own psyche.' He goes on to say that 'this evil, our impure state, is very much the concern of religion'.

It is also very much the concern of art. But art by itself, despite the music or the play or the painting that can produce in us a profoundly religious experience, cannot diminish that evil. Except perhaps temporarily. It requires religion to do that, to draw out the good in us over a period of time so that the good prevails and the good life begins. Art shifts our experience of ourselves and others onto unexpected planes, sometimes in a major way. It offers a shift of perspective, and, since this piece concerns blind spots, that shift may bring to light what we are normally unable to see. It's more a way of looking than a foundation on which we can base our lives. Yet artists will fight for a vision as though their very lives were at stake. In the deepest possible sense, that vision is the foundation of their lives.

In a Christmas letter to Pamela Hansford Johnson, Dylan Thomas, then nineteen years old, felt convinced that 'the very angle of man is necessarily inconducive to higher thoughts. Walking, as we do, at right angles to the earth, we are prevented from looking, as much as we should, at the legendary sky above us and the only-a-little-more-possible ground under us . . . Think how much wiser we would be if it were possible for us to change our angles of perspective as regularly as we change our vests: a certain period would be spent in propelling ourselves along on our backs, in order to see the sky properly and all the time; and another period in drifting belly-downwards through the air in order to see the earth. As it is, this perpetual right-angle of ours leads to a prejudiced vision. Probably that was the divine plan anyway . . .'

'To change our angles of perspective . . .' That is what Thomas' poetry tried to do and what all good poetry tries to do. We become bird, beast or insect for a while and how much wiser we are for it. Evil is temporarily diminished. Vision begins to reappear.

As I write, there's another wedding down the road. There's the sound of crackers and silver horse-drawn carriages inching over the exploded remains which lie like white rose petals in their path. The saris are splendid, their colours rich. It's a fabulous wedding but common enough.

But the other day, two uncommon things happened. As the sun rose, I found I could see right across to Uran on the mainland and beyond. The sky was barred with clouds but the Sahyadris were in full view, range after range. Starting from the left, gliding past the island of Elephanta, I could see the beginning of the ghats and the hill station of Matheran, then Uran, the flames of the refinery, the hills further south until they tapered away into the horizon. I could see the horizon and patches of red earth and green on the excavated hills as the sun shone on them through the barred clouds. The red was a golden red such as I'd never seen before. What shift of atmosphere, what god of freak weather brought me that day?

The second thing I saw was an ant carrying a grain of sugar across the kitchen table. The sugar sparkled like an ice cube in its mouth. It was half the ant's size. I imagined a man carrying a block of ice half his size, not in his mouth, but anyhow.

The strength of the ant produced a chink of light. The radiance of the day set the heart on fire, dispersing its smog. The devil and his gang were temporarily scattered. Sufficient unto the day is the evil thereof.

INCIDENT IN PARIS

'No, no, we saw nothing,' said the agitated woman. 'Absolutely nothing. Nothing.'

She was part of a group of middle-aged women who had earlier been talking angrily against the police. They were standing at a street corner, a little away from five or six police vans which had blocked off part of the street. Their old clothes spoke of housework, of meals awaiting them in kitchens. They hadn't assembled out of curiosity, unlike many in the street that day. They lived in the neighbourhood, which two men had sprayed with bullets the day before. Bullets were embedded in the walls of a Jewish restaurant behind the police vans. Behind its doors lay the unseen debris of an explosion. It was when one of the women had been asked if she'd seen anything that she'd taken fright. No, nothing. Absolutely nothing.

In a circle between the police vans and the restaurant, a well-dressed man was performing an extraordinary dance. A camera stuck to his eye, he pushed out one leg, then another, then gyrated forwards and backwards to get his angled shot of Jo Goldenberg, the restaurant's sign board. Policemen in plain clothes, dressed in suits which seemed identical to the man's—light grey, well-pressed—went about their business. Eyewitnesses say the killers had been well-dressed too.

La Rue des Rosiers, the scene of their adventure, has traditionally been the home of Jews in Paris. Some of its crumbling buildings still indicate what it must have been like as a ghetto. Not very straight, at a slight gradient, it narrows sharply at a point. Forty years ago in that street, predecessors of the French police so busy that day, also went about their duties zealously—rounding up Jews to deport them. If you want to kill a lot of Jews today, you don't have to be so circumspect. Get someone to block off the narrow point with a van, and enter from the wider side with friends, with machine guns.

On 9 August 1982, the killers weren't so ambitious. Though

their target was Jews, they had selected a restaurant which, though known for its Jewish delicacies, wasn't patronised by Jews only. Shortly after one o'clock in the afternoon, a man went out of the restaurant, leaving behind a metal box which erupted in a cloud of smoke. As though at a signal, two men appeared at the wider end of the street, walking casually and firing at everyone in sight with their machine pistols. One of them threw a grenade through an open window of the restaurant. After the explosion, they entered by its main door, firing continuously. Their work done, they retreated the way they came, still firing, towards a waiting car.

August is the month for holidays in France. Paris empties of Parisians and fills with tourists. If the killers had calculated on an international cast of victims, they weren't wrong. Of the six people killed, two were American. The twenty-two injured weren't all Jews and some of them weren't French. One of the persons killed was a sixty-five-year-old Moroccan who worked in the restaurant.

When the TV camera crews and photographers descended on the scene that day, the street turned against them. Journalists were pushed about and abused, called the real assassins. Why did the press daily report Israeli atrocities in Beirut? Why those photographs of blown-up civilians, why unremitting scenes of Israeli violence on television? The killers had taken revenge for what they thought was happening in Beirut. The feeling was that the French media had grossly misinformed them; that the French, traditionally anti-Semite, were simply continuing to be so by being anti-Israel, now in the guise of political legitimacy. No one doubted that the killers belonged to the Palestine Liberation Organization (PLO).

Two days later, in another district, a bomb went off on a window sill, seriously injuring a passer-by. At 5.30 that afternoon, while a memorial service of the victims of La Rue des Rosiers was going on in a synagogue, a car bomb devastated part of the Iraqi embassy, injuring five. The first was the work of Action Directe, French supporters of an extremist wing of the PLO, the second of an unknown Islamic group, protesting against the French sale of arms to Iraq.

During the next four weeks in Paris, more explosions killed or maimed. Different groups claimed to be behind them. On my last day there, there was an unsuccessful bomb attack on a Jewish school.

School is never far from a French person's thoughts. In a small town in central France, a young woman, rebelling against its memory, had said, 'A French student needs only three things now—the bac, drugs, and a mistress.' The first, a qualification required to get into university, is the culmination of ferociously competitive years in school, constrained by a rigid syllabus. New schools in small towns may occasionally be designed with schoolchildren in mind. In Paris, they look like old prisons. 'What the young French would like now is no authority. Anarchy for two or three years, without Presidents,' the same young woman had said. A joint of Lebanese hash passed from hand to hand. Her friends ordered cognac freely. I didn't think history had been kind enough to leave open the door of anarchy for them, so late in the century. The bar we were in was called 1900.

The paper napkins of Jo Goldenberg's restaurant carry the star of Bethlehem. The ceiling has bullet holes. I am sitting at the bar, drinking white wine, two days after the incident. A few days before, my stepdaughter had told me. 'The French never like to show their feelings. They try to keep a hard exterior.' The woman behind the bar tries to serve drinks normally, answer questions, but doesn't succeed in keeping a hard exterior. A few feet from her, a dark-haired man is being attended to by a group of people. He says nothing. The woman finally goes up to him and implores him to eat something, if only for the sake of his children. He is the son of the Moroccan who was killed.

'Begin-Sharon—*Assez de Sang!*' 'Enough blood', says the graffiti on the intestines of the Paris metro.

'Begin-Sharon, *Nous sommes avec vous.*' 'We are with you', chant the processionists, leaving the synagogue after the memorial service. They want Israel to smash Lebanon. They want to destroy the PLO in Paris. An eye for an eye.

At Jo Goldenberg's restaurant, the man sitting next to me, pretending to read a newspaper, is no ordinary customer, I think. He wears a shabby jacket but belongs to the better dressed, in grey suits, in the depths of the restaurant. A phone rings. The call is for him and he disappears up some stairs. After a while, I see him on the landing conferring with a man in a grey suit, watching everyone in the restaurant. I will see him again on another occasion.

It had to do with music. Not far from where I lived, a blind sitarist, accompanied by friends, used to go from restaurant to restaurant, drawing the most exquisite notes from his sitar. I thought he was an Indian but he turned out to be a Bangladeshi. I thought his circle was European, but its leader claimed he was not.

'I am from Kashmir,' he said loudly, when I went up to introduce myself and congratulate the sitarist. 'How is it you say you're from India and you don't speak Hindi?' I said I did, except that my mother tongue was Gujarati.

'You cannot be from India if you do not speak Hindi,' he shouted. The sitarist looked upset. The language the Kashmiri spoke sounded correct but stilted, the Hindi learnt by a foreigner. Why was the sitarist troubled? Had I stumbled onto something? Were his friends pocketing his earnings? Was he just a front for other, more political activities? Why did I hang on, pretending nothing was amiss? Why did I sit with them when they wanted me gone?

'You are not from India,' the Kashmiri shouted again. In a mirror, I saw the man in the shabby jacket observing us all.

North Africans live on La Rue des Rosiers too. Most French people call them Arabs. Near the narrow end of the street is a bar run by one of them. The poorer French go there to drink cheap African wine, the young to play pinball and meet their girlfriends. I used to go there a lot. If I ask myself why, as I used to then, why I was obsessed with the street, and why, at the same time I was dissatisfied when I went there, I find I have no answer, except one obscurely to do with expecting an act of revenge. After the incident a little further up, there always used to be someone posted at the door of the bar, keeping an eye on the street. When it was clear that the time for revenge had passed, I stopped going there.

The Memorial for Unknown Jewish Martyrs is a simple enclosure, quite close to the town hall, which, newly restored, shimmers in public splendour on La Rue de Rivoli. The memorial is tucked off the main street, invisible until you're in the depths of a lane.

Today, two days after the incident, everyone goes through a body check there. There are stalls which distribute pro-Israeli literature, there's a signature campaign to get the PLO out of Paris.

The memorial is packed. It's impossible to reach its gates because of the crowd. It's a hot evening, and though it's past eight, there's still a lot of light. An old stone building overlooks the memorial. It's a girls' school, three stories high, its windows barred. Three men have succeeded in climbing onto one of its high plinths. Hung with cameras, the wide straps of which crisscross their chests, they look like armed guards. They oversee the proceedings at the memorial.

The crowd swirls below them, restless. 'You can't be a Jew in France,' says a banner. 'It's our silence that killed,' says another.

The crowd parts. A young woman with a pinched face has been overcome by the heat. She staggers and is caught by her companions before she falls. She is lifted and carried to a place on the pavement directly below the photographers. They continue their watch, unflinching. She is unconscious, the blood drained from her face, her thin arms spread out.

'Too many of them.'

PEOPLE

CONVERSATION WITH AN INVISIBLE MAN

His face was in shadow. The darkness of his hut, lightened only by two improvised kerosene lamps—tiny bottles with wicks stuck in them—seemed physically to have got hold of him. The white of an eyeball or a line of teeth would occasionally flash out of the dark blur, and it was only because I had first met him outside the hut, late in the evening, that I could recollect his other features. Now he was retreating into the darkness, regaining that invisibility which Orwell has pointed out as characteristic of those who work with their hands. And yet, when I began talking to him, I had hoped his invisibility would lessen. When I entered his hut, I had genuinely wanted to see him.

In one sense, though, he had never been invisible. We knew of his existence. But there were so many of him. When we first moved into a tall block of flats in Bombay, the area around the block was relatively undeveloped. Then, from our eighteenth-floor window, we saw the other buildings rise and had our comfortable view of the workers—men, women and children laying slab upon slab, working till late in the night, relay after relay of them running like the ants that crawled down our kitchen wall into the garbage bin. Then, as more and more buildings began coming up, we saw their children in the streets, their clothes hanging loosely on them, standing and staring at bus queues, at people getting into taxis, or at those settling back in their larger cars. The tribals came, looking for jobs. Now they sat on the small grey stones left by the roadbuilders, mumbling to themselves and scratching their bellies. One, not having eaten for six days, slept in a pile of rubbish and woke up paralysed. The hospital my wife took him to would have nothing to do with him. Nor would the police. 'Too many of them,' was the comment. Too many of these invisible people.

How did they stand it? When the airconditioners came and pushed their snouts through the walls the workers had raised, while rain poured through their roofs and made their floors of carpet of slime, did they feel nothing? When the sleek, fat cars began sliding out of the towers they had built, did their fingers ever itch? Why were they so patient? Why didn't they organize themselves? It was time for me to be attacked, to have my lifestyle ridiculed. I decided to confront an invisible man.

His name was Shankaran and he shared his hut with Mohammed. They both came from Kerala. We spoke Hindi.

'I am a fitter,' Shankaran said. 'I get Rs 7 a day. I spend Rs 8 a day. Borrow here and there. Get into debt. Have to send money to my parents. I work from 6 to 1.30 and from 2.30 to 7. Sometimes I have to work from 6 to 2 so I get only a half-hour break. If I object, the contractor can ask me to leave. Nothing here is ours. They don't even give us medicine. If we cut ourselves, all we can apply on the wound is chalk. Some months ago, a UP-walla fell six floors down the lift shaft. He broke his back but he survived. It was the workers who paid his hospital bill, not the contractor. If someone falls and dies, the contractor is supposed to pay Rs 5,000 to the man's family. But he only does it if there's someone to speak up for the man.'

The two buildings he was working on loomed over the hut, twenty-three stories high, their topmost slabs lost in darkness.

'Now it's the monsoon. The wind blows hard on top. We have to go and work up in the air. We never know what can happen to us. We have to stand on planks, nine inches wide, ten kilograms in one hand, ten kilograms in the other. They don't provide us with lifts. If the rich work for ten minutes like this, they'd know what it was like. We have to go up and down twenty-three slabs, eight or nine times a day, carrying thirty kilograms each time.'

'Why do you find it difficult to organize yourselves? Is it because you're from different parts of India?'

'No, that's not the problem. People are afraid of the contractor. And if only three or four of us unite, what can we do? If the police come, who will run, who will stay? I can't say. I'll be hit. No one will look after me.'

'How old are you?'

'Twenty-eight.'

'That means for most of your life you have been a citizen of free India. In these twenty-five years of independence, what do you think the government has done for workers like you?'

'Nothing.'

'And for the peasants? They say the peasants in Uttar Pradesh are well off now. And the peasants in Tamil Nadu. Because of new techniques in farming.'

'I have been only in Kerala, Madras and Bombay. I don't know about UP. But the government has done nothing for the peasants in Kerala. Mine was a house of great trouble. I had to start working when I was seven. I worked for half an anna a day, then one anna. Now I earn Rs 7. In this time, how many burdens have I carried? My daily expenses are Rs 8, and I have a lifetime ahead of me . . . I used to work in a refinery in Madras. We had a strike. The workers starved during the strike but we held out for thirty days. Then they got the police from Kerala. They came with revolvers. Bullets are the tools of the government. They came from three gates. They used lathis. I had to go back. If there are twenty-five of us, the government brings fifty. The government doesn't help the poor. It doesn't understand that the poor must be pushed forward . . .

'Between 1965 and 1967, I worked in Thumba at the rocket station. We had to work on burning sands, put it on our heads. We were never given chappals. Even the UN people there didn't give us chappals. But we stayed on because they promised to make us permanent. While climbing the three-hundred-foot tower, we would feel, if not permanent today, then tomorrow. If not tomorrow, then the day after. But they didn't make us permanent. In 1966, they told one of my friends, 'You're not even literate so how can you be made permanent?' Dr K was the rocket station director. When I finally asked him why they didn't make us permanent, he asked the chowkidar to kick me out. I lost my job. The police came and evicted us from our homes.'

'But were they all like that at Thumba? Wasn't there a single big man who saw your problems?'

'Once Dr Bhabha came to visit us. I was sweeping the road in front of him. He stopped me and said it wasn't my job to do that. He said, "Stop this work. I too am an ordinary man like you."'

'Tell me frankly, don't you get angry when you see people like me living in the flats you've built?'

'We can't visit your flats. The gurkha chases us away.'

'Yes, but what do you want to do about it? Don't you think someone like me can do anything about it? I teach in a college. What do you think I should do to change the situation?'

'You should tell the students what the world is like. Your students will go into government service. If their mothers and fathers did nothing for us, they will. Of course, you have to teach them to pass, but in between you should tell them about us. If you don't do this now, they will never know. The children of the rich know nothing about us. When I go to the toilet outside, what a place I have to squat in—slime, long grass, anything can bite me. They have rooms to go to. Our children drink water that is mixed with oil. They drink milk. Even after your work you should teach these children. Tell them about us.'

'But in what way can the rich change the situation for you? Don't you think you have to unite and change it?'

'You must be earning Rs 1,000 a month.'

'No. Half that.'

'Then you can spare at least Rs 50 a month. You could help us with that.'

'But what's the use of that? There are five hundred of you here. Each of you would get ten paise a month.'

'If everyone living in a block of flats agreed to give, it would be different.'

'If there are seventy flats in a building and each gives Rs 50 rupees a month, you'd get Rs 3,500. Divide that by five hundred and each of you would get Rs 7 a month. Does that make a lot of difference?'

'It's something. We don't have to distribute the money. We can invest it or let it accumulate to build a house. You can build a house for Rs 18,000. We could do that.'

'But what kind of solution is that? What will make a rich man want to give you Rs 50 a month?'

'The rich must get an idea of what our conditions are like. If we had a club for the poor and three or four rich people also came to it, they would know how we live and suffer. Then everything they do, they'll do with their hearts.'

No, I wanted to insist. No, they wouldn't. I had expected a radical solution but what Shankaran was suggesting was nothing but charity. I had expected an attack on my lifestyle but by asking me to get to know more about his situation, Shankaran hadn't attacked it at all. If knowledge of appalling working conditions was all that was necessary for a revolutionary change of heart on the part of the rich, then the contractor would be the most revolutionary of people since he knew most about the working conditions that kept large numbers of people overworked, underfed and totally unable to assert their rights.

We had begun the conversation almost alone. Now the hut was filling with people. A small boy kept tugging at Shankaran's sleeve, wanting him to go outside but he continued talking to me, brushing my apologies aside, by saying his time was his own now. If their days belonged to the contractor, he said, their nights were their own. Some workers stood around listening.

Only an action of theirs which made complete nonsense of

our own acts of charity and condescension would make them visible to us, I thought outside. When I left the hut, I couldn't remember their faces.

TWO SISTERS

Seen from the road, the house shows no sign of life. A small jungle spills onto the pavement, shuts the front door from view. But inside there is continual life, an unflagging dance without music that draws everyone it touches into its ambit.

The landlord of the house walks in with some neighbours, talking loudly of load-bearing walls. The neighbours stop by a woman in a high-backed chair. She is frail, her hands clutching the armrests as though she were strapped to the seat of a plane about to take off. She turns to her neighbours and gives them her full attention. They are stilled, quickly made reverent.

A young woman comes in from the bank across the road to use the phone, as the one in the bank is out of order. She is received by the frail woman's sister as though she had come in from an exhausting journey. Several calls are made, the young woman insists on paying. Equally insistently, the payment is refused. It isn't a game. Courtesy comes as naturally to the sisters as the puzzled awe of their friends when they see lives that seem so appallingly vulnerable, and yet are not.

The sisters teach English and French privately. An Iranian ex-student, on a short stopover in Bombay, will make it a point of visiting them before flying out again. The families of another Iranian student—whom they looked after when his brother was murdered in the States—insists that they're part of the family now and that the sisters should live with them in Iran. The anthropologist Verrier Elwin used to make what he called 'a pilgrimage' to see them whenever he was in Bombay.

If they were robbed of their possessions, the thief, if he knew them, would revisit them only to meet them again. It's the effect they have. It's not, I think, the effect of artificial kindness or cultivated eccentricity—those are a different kind of magnet—but of a goodness they refuse to make seem important, mixed as it is with irreverence, a sense of fun.

This goodness hasn't come naturally, at least not to the woman I'm talking to—Hilla Vakeel, now seventy-seven—the one in the high-backed chair. In her polished turns of phrase lie imprisoned glints of malice, a long-repressed fury. Her laughter, her head cocked to one side, is often aimed into the air, as though seeking its echo from a witty devil hidden somewhere in the room. If she laughs in the direction of Dossan, her sister, older to her by three years, she gets an attention that speaks of years of a shared, possibly stifled life. There's no resentment. One of their friends speaks with horror of Dossan Vakeel's natural goodness, her utter lack of guile. 'She gives away all my property,' Hilla complains. Much-loved brooches inevitably 'repose on other bosoms'.

It is Dossan who keeps house, bringing a compulsive order to it in ways that continue to baffle her sister. Each morning, the clothes horse is draped to perfection. Every item of clothing in exactly the right order, each in its pre-ordained place, a masterpiece of tidiness inevitably destroyed in the process of putting on the clothes. Sometimes a blue-ribbon bow crowns the achievement of a Dossan Vakeel masterpiece. Their father used to say that if Dossan had a chance she'd put a blue ribbon on a broom. The blue ribbon appears to be a standing joke and when it gets to be too much for Dossan, she throws her face into her hands and laughs. Her perfectly-groomed silver hair isn't tied with a blue ribbon. Nor are the bundles of clippings of her sister's work which she has carefully laid out for me on a table in the next room. It's a room familiar to members of Nalanda, a group that came into being to promote Indian studies, and the meetings of which the sisters have hosted for twenty-four years. There are scores of bundles, masses of clippings—of reviews written for the Asiatic Society, articles, a weekly column written for the *Kaiser-i-Hind*.

Once, when Dossan Vakeel was studying music and had 'got as far as Beethoven' on the piano, an Englishman offered to take the piano away and tune it for her. Instead he stole it. That was in the late 1930s. The music stopped. But not her sister's admiration for the English. 'It was another Englishman,' she says quickly, as though still not able to believe that it could have been an Englishman who tricked Dossan, who 'ran all over Bombay to try and find the man.' She feels she 'shouldn't be saying it but she gets on very well with the English'.

Not so with her own community. She believes she's 'quite a strong Zoroastrian', but still holds her father's view that 'the servants in Hyderabad are more polite than the Bombay Parsi'. In the columns of the Parsi-owned *Kaiser-i-Hind*, she berated the average Parsi boy for being 'a hopeless prig', and the community as a whole for being 'artistically bankrupt', eternally gripped by gluttony.

The community was one part of her target. Generally speaking, it was the professionally solemn, whom the early years of the war must have made impossibly pompous too. So, on 14 June 1940, as a means of 'speeding up the war effort in Bombay' she recommends that its citizens drink, and encourage others to drink, heavily. 'I am informed that on every bottle of whisky that costs Rs 12, the local Government gets two and the Imperial Government about five. Which means that seven-twelfths of every sip of whisky is a gallant contribution to the Treasury and only five-twelfths a wretched pandering to one's own palate . . . every sip makes for Hitlerian defeat . . .'

'Hate brings health,' she says on another occasion. On yet another, she recommends that 'children should be taught the correct use of abuse in schools, and at an early age'. On 15 September 1940, appalled by the 'modern biscuit-box houses' which had come up along Bombay's Marine Drive and Churchgate Reclamation, she suggests that Britain might be 'persuaded to send out men who are training for the RAF and get them to treat every one of these architectural monstrosities as targets for practice ... after the residents had been evacuated'.

Such remarks went deeper than Miss Vakeel intended. One wounded reader wrote in to say that his one ambition in life was to ship her off to Dover to be placed on the cliffs 'opposite the gunner with the deadliest aim in the whole German army'. That was because she had once suggested that 'presidents at public meetings, especially those who insisted on standing on their legs for hours on end, should be electrocuted'.

'I once wondered if the columns were read,' she says. 'Now I wonder if they are misunderstood.' Her writing was read and won her admirers, among them Aubrey Menen, an old friend, who repeatedly urged her to write more. But she argued then that English was a foreign language and that she'd never be able to write in it as an English person.

Yet all the people she knew and met in her childhood were in 'the British mould'. The study of her grandfather, who was in the Railway Police, had great bookcases, deep leather armchairs, a family tree on the wall—'completely Victorian'. ('All Parsis are children of Victoria,' she says firmly.) Her mother died when she was six and with her father away in Baroda, working as a commissioning agent, the grandparents employed an English governess for the sisters. There was also a much-adored elder brother who plied the sisters with Dickens' novels instead of boxes of chocolates on their birthdays. They read English classics in the evenings. Often the brother would read to them; these were thrilling occasions. The slightest sign of inattention would make them unforgettable—he had a very short temper.

Clearly his influence on his sisters went deep. Hilla Vakeel is unable to stop talking about him, recalling those readings and those Sunday afternoons when they laughed so much: 'It's a wonder we didn't get appendicitis.' She misses him and people like him now, when, she feels, 'the sum total of personality has gone down. There's such an aridity of personality these days'.

She is cautious about her disappointments. 'Living in India today is a little disillusioning. You won't find good citizens.' Then, suddenly brightening:, 'But you'll find *The Good Citizen*'.

This is a slim book made up of weekly snippets of advice for children, which she wrote for *The Times of India* in 1949. It preaches, and I doubt, despite the praise bestowed upon it by the then Educational Inspector and Nehru, that it could have made a single child nobler, kinder or better behaved than he was naturally inclined to be. The writing has lost its sparkle. Sadly, it's as though the writer were saying: 'Now India is free and I'm an adult. I must put away childish things'. The party is over.

Still, it was a long party and one day in 1931, it went like this: prominent members of Bombay's high society are gathered in one of the halls of the Begum of Janjira's palace on Bombay's Ridge Road. Most of them are unwisely dressed, for though ruby earrings and emerald bracelets shoot gladdening sparks through the gathering, the churidars of the nawabs and rajas, the suits of the Englishmen, the silk saris of the Parsi women, cling to their wearers as though they were drowning, and intended to drown their wearers with them. It is, after all, 25 October, a Sunday, and perhaps the stream of constantly flowing water which is supposed to cool the hall, as in any respectable Mughal palace, even an imitation one like the Begum of Janjira's, isn't working as it should. Only the conversation, skilful, high-spirited, promises to freshen the evening and one of the persons responsible for it is Hilla Vakeel, who is also one of the women the occasion is in honour of. It's an At Home, organised by the Three Arts Circle. She is one of its honorary secretaries. The other woman being honoured is Miss P. Vimadalal, also an honorary secretary. They are friends, and their returning to their respective homes well past midnight, after previous meetings of the Three Arts Circle, has scandalised many.

Was it on this occasion or another that, escaping to the rose garden behind the palace with a few others and a glass of sherbet, Miss Vakeel raised her glass and said, 'I'm drinking to a free India,' and Mr Roy Hawkins, fresh out of England to work for the Oxford University Press, answered, 'May I join you?'

It isn't important. Perhaps what's important is to know that for almost ten years, from the late twenties to the late thirties, the Three Arts Circle met at the place every week to 'create and promote intellectual, artistic, active and higher interests and values'. So, in 1931, if you happened to be a member of the Circle and were alive and well on Saturday, 4 July, you could go to a meeting in honour of Mr Grant Anderson and his Repertory Company (from London) and hear 'songs by Miss Noreen Nagle, a charming mezzo and Mr Wright, a rich baritone, a Parsi quartet and a trio comprising of Miss Moore, Miss Gonet and Mr Ignatius'. And there were the special charms of Miss Iqbal, 'the famous Calcutta film star', on loan from the Shri Krishna Film Company to perform a Marwari dance.

Do you go? There are, after all, the talkies, and during that week they are showing *Romance* (with Greta Garbo) at the Rialto, and *Min and Bill* (with Marie Dressler and Wallace Beery) at the Capitol. And if you really want to see Grant Anderson's repertory company in 'various London successes' and Tagore's *Chitra*, you can always go to the Royal Opera House tomorrow. The Three Arts Circle disintegrated, but not before producing several issues of an attractive illustrated weekly (at two annas a copy)—which, for all its gloom over the decline of good manners and the frivolous young—was surprisingly forward-looking:

> 'The feminist revolution is at present in a process of realization ... The feminist movement is rapidly becoming an enormous, coherent and self-conscious force. Feminine opinion, becoming conscious of power tends, towards a more precise assertion of the rights and independence of women ...' (*Three Arts*, 26 September 1931).

Hilla Vakeel's first published piece appeared when she was seventeen. By the time the Three Arts Circle disbanded, she was a writer of some distinction. In 1938, when she was in her early thirties, she was asked to edit the first Indian journal for women, *Indian Home*. Though she had no editorial experience, she accepted. She was writing reviews and columns for other papers. She was working too hard. She felt horribly exploited. In 1939, her adored brother died of diabetes. She continued working for *Indian Home* a little longer. Then she had a breakdown.

It hit her suddenly. Leaving work one day, she felt frightened of the journey ahead. She felt she couldn't walk to the nearby station to take the train home. Somehow, she got to the station and sat down. A passing friend noticed her and took her home in a taxi. For almost forty years, apart from one attempt that made her severely ill again, she hasn't moved out of the house.

Gradually, her sister stopped going out too. And it's Dossan Vakeel's attempt to justify her decision that results in a small scene:

> Dossan Vakeel: It doesn't matter that we don't go out. The mountain comes to Mahomet.
>
> Hilla Vakeel (*to me*): It was a fright I had . . .
>
> DV: Hilla has brought such a lot to the house.
>
> HV (*sourly*): Such a lot of trouble.
>
> DV: We have such fun at home—thanks to Hilla. The mountain comes to Mahomet. We've had such good parties.
>
> HV: Lady Cynthia Asquith says in her autobiography that the most successful parties she had were those where she served only lemonade and biscuits.
>
> (*She gives her sister a hard look.*)
>
> DV: But dear, she was Lady Asquith!

It's a strangely riveting scene, happening in exactly the place where other scenes were acted out. In the early 1950s, Ebrahim

Alkazi ran a twice-weekly workshop for Nalanda, and remembering it with pride, Hilla Vakeel recalls the pandemonium, the laughter, the Japanese curtain which was used as a backdrop being swished around on its iron rail, the famous French mime who complimented her on succeeding in having what he most wanted—a theatre in his own home.

Other echoes and scenes come crowding in thick and fast: Pavlova's dying swan, seen from a box in a theatre in Bombay—'so magnificent, you could feel her feathers withering away'; Verrier Elwin's stupendous voice, echoing in a little municipal hall—'What a speaker! You had to be at his feet to learn English'; the voices of Aubrey Menen and John Rowdon as they took part in their dramatized version of each day's war bulletin on AIR . . . 'Society meant something then. It meant ideas, selectability, charm, graciousness. Not all this . . . boorishness'.

There have been great personal disappointments—gifts unused, voyages not begun. As a young woman, she wrote of herself as a 'tomb for the shattered glory of God's dreams', Of India today, she says, 'There'll always be people who justify humanity. But on the whole, it's a pretty messy situation.' One of her greatest disappointments is Nalanda. 'Almost twenty-five years of it and what have we achieved? We are trying to succeed where the prophets have failed to improve human consciousness. Dossan doesn't believe in setting the world right.'

'Do you?'

'I believe in trying. I really shouldn't be saying this, but I always want it said of me that I plucked out a thorn and planted a flower where I thought a flower would grow.'

She returns to her breakdown as though still puzzled by it. 'I have such a fright of distances.' The expression on her face is pinched, uncertain which way to go. It begins to clear. 'Aubrey Menen used to tell me that meant I didn't want to go to heaven.'

She tilts her head sideways and laughs.

THE GAMBLER

There was a time when gamblers were as common as cockroaches. Every joint family could boast of at least one. If you went two or three generations further back you could come up with a bagful. Whether you disapproved of gambling or not depended very much on your status. For the rich it was meant to be a pastime, for the poor an addiction. It was in the middle and lower middle classes that the two attitudes met, causing much pain and confusion.

'There,' it was pointed out in hushed tones, 'goes Mrs Boxwalla's daughter. She wrecked her life on cards. Who will marry her now?' 'There,' it was pointed out in somewhat other tones, 'goes Currimbhoy Jivanji. He's the greatest gambler of all, King of the Racecourse.'

An uncle of mine was a bookie, another uncle was into football pools. One of my grandfathers gambled and died reasonably well off; the other who didn't, died a pauper. Gamblers lurked in every corner of my childhood like question marks or cautionary tales. Gambling was supposed to be bad for us. We were not supposed to gamble. We didn't.

Where are they now, the card players, the sharpers, the big-time punters? Though there are stories of bookies so wealthy that they lie on beds of notes, gamblers, as we knew them even twenty years ago, seem to have disappeared. They rarely make news, leave alone good copy. Compared with the great gambling stories, even of the recent past—stories set on racecourses, in card rooms and casinos, involving characters who grew larger than life with each great gamble they took—today's stories of lottery winners and losers seem shabby and cheap.

For the buyer of lottery tickets is basically a gambler with a weak heart. Not for him the high-risk plunge, the rush of adrenalin when his number comes up, the madness of doubling and tripling the stakes when he should go home. Today's high-profile gamblers are Harshad Mehta and Nick Leeson, not old Mr Byramjee of the Turf Club and the boring old winners at Monte Carlo and the racecourse. The latter can be safely ignored.

Other addictions can't be, and as every compulsive gambler knows, gambling is an addiction. Alcohol, cocaine and smack have taken over the place where gambling once stood, invoking a mixture of pity and awe. If gamblers once killed for money and still do, drug-related killings have totally eclipsed them. Terrorist extortions have far exceeded theirs in scale and proved more deadly. In a world where, in the name of 'social cleansing', children are shot in the streets like rats, where investors are ruined overnight by the collapse of banks, where ethnic cleansing is more vicious and widespread than natural calamities, the old-fashioned gambler has become small fry, his addiction too trivial for social concern. Yet the addiction continues, the gambler suffers, the gambler goes on.

Dostoyevsky used to be a gambler and wrote a short novel on the theme, basing it on his obsession with roulette. The novel goes straight to the heart of gambling and the psychology of the gambler. Yet it is a sentence in his second wife Anna Grigoryevna's *Reminiscences* that provides the clearest clue as to why her husband and persons like him gamble. She writes: 'The change of scene, the journey, the repeated experience of tempestuous emotions, radically changed his mood.' In other words, gambling exhilarated rather than depressed him, it did him more good than harm. In other words, as John Berryman puts it, 'Life, friends, is boring/but we must not say so.' Gambling is a way of not saying so, of getting a thrill out of life which, by the simplest of means, a throw of the dice or a deal of cards, becomes simultaneously risky and competitive.

This doesn't prevent gamblers from going through bouts of self-hatred and scorn. Such bouts are a regular feature of most addicts' lives, whatever they may be addicted to. *The Gambler* may be seen as Dostoyevsky's way of trying to cure himself of his addiction since, despite its vivid descriptions of the excitement of gambling, it is, in a sense, a cautionary tale, addressed to himself: Gamble, win, have a system that will make you go on winning but in the process you will lose the woman who loves you, your friends, your self-respect. You will end up little more than a worm. That, in fact, is what happened to Dostoyevsky himself.

In the course of their addiction most gamblers develop a system which, despite evidence to the contrary, they believe is infallible. Dostoyevsky had one such system. In a letter to his sister-in-law he writes, 'Please don't think I am so pleased with myself for not losing that I am showing off when I say that I know the secret, of how not to lose but win. I really do know the secret; it is terribly silly and simple and consists of keeping one's head the whole time, whatever the state of the game, and not getting excited. That is all, and it makes losing simply impossible and winning a certainty.'

But if winning is a certainty in whatever game you play, then you're not gambling. *The Gambler* itself pours scorn on the system. Its greatest moments are passages in which gamblers lose their heads, throw all caution to the winds and plunge into a turbulence they don't know whether or not they'll survive. Like the stormy passages of a Beethoven sonata, they grip us just as the gambler is gripped by his madness, and lead us to the dark and terrible heart of gambling. There you come face to face with nothing less than Death. Anything less is not worth a gamble. The true gambler is one who abandons his system as one would a life raft in a savage sea. He abandons all hope and is convinced he'll win. His addiction drugs him into that state of contradiction.

It was in that state of contradiction that Nick Leeson probably made his last desperate bid to win back the money he lost. Or perhaps he was just working under orders. But I doubt he's suffering from any withdrawal symptoms now, his spell of 'gambling' was too brief for that, though it's said that even a brief spell can be addictive. Lose everything and the hope persists that with your last rupee you'll win everything back.

Gamblers are prepared to go beyond the last rupee, 'on a toboggan that goes faster and faster', driving them to pawnbrokers and moneylenders, making them mortgage their homes. This could be said of other addictions too, except that this particular toboggan run has no end. There's a limit to the amount you can drink or smoke or shoot into a vein before you kill yourself. There's no limit to what you can lose. The gambler naked, stripped of all he possesses, is no figment of the imagination but an everlasting icon—man humiliated and defeated in trying to be a man.

'I had got this, you see, at the risk of more than life,' says Dostoyevsky's protagonist on winning 1,700 gulden at the roulette table. 'I had dared to run the risk and now I was a man again!' Other addictions can be cured, the gambler's can't be. Or to put it another way, no medical treatments have been designed with him in mind, no pills can get him of it. He alone can cure himself of his addiction.

This makes the gambler unique amongst addicts and is perhaps one reason why he has remained a fascinating figure through the ages. He plays with chance, chance plays with him, but his destiny remains in his own hands. He is existential man, demanding a second chance though he may never be given one. Though his aim is to live, live and live in the greatest blaze of glory, he is the deathwish in person. For the gambler, alone in his pool of light, his every move watched by the squalidly normal, the game is always up.

THE LIBRARIAN AND THE LABYRINTH

Dr Bernard Anderson was once keeper of Hell. Hell was a cupboard. It stood in St. Xavier's College, Bombay, in the Fathers' Library, and it contained books the Church had forbidden its members to read. ('That's Hell,' said a priest, pointing out the cupboard). Dr Anderson was in his late teens, the eldest surviving son of a large family which his father could no longer support. He dropped out of college to look for a job. The Rector of the college advised him to look after the Fathers' Library for a small salary. That was about fifty years ago. Dr Anderson has since worked only for libraries and has been chief librarian of three—those of the Heras Institute, St. Xavier's College and the University of Bombay. He is frank about the fact that he didn't much care for books before. He insists he 'walked into the profession by accident'. And into Hell? Dr Anderson won't say. The holy fathers went there often—that was part of their job—how could they refute what was in the texts without reading them?—and presumably survived the shock.

It could of course be said that a man who has been so closely associated with the libraries of academic institutions has always been a keeper of Hell. In these regions, at exam time, is a low moaning, the sight of hundreds of crouched shapes moving their lips as though in unintelligible prayer, gnashing their teeth, gnawing through the wood of pencils and the plastic of ball-point pens, fighting back nausea, fainting. And perhaps Dr Anderson is being justly punished by whatever good angel looks after students by being put in a narrow cell, about five feet wide, where he now sits, between huge metal racks and windows that are barred, continually preyed on by research students, old insurance salesmen, and the occasional inquisitor like myself. He has a squeezed look, as befits his cell, his punishment.

According to a librarian who was once taught by him—Dr Anderson still lectures for the university's degree course in Library Science—this self-sought obscurity is typical of the man. He is 'unassuming to the point of self-effacement' . . . He is 'a just man . . . His students are totally dedicated to him . . . He has done more for librarianship than activist librarians . . . He has done the ordinary job of librarianship in an extraordinary way . . .' But he doesn't want to be noticed.

Yet, from this near-invisible position he has engineered visible changes. He dislikes petty restrictions and would like to conjure away those that remain with a wave of the hand, if possible. His concept of libraries is open-door, open-rack. Books on open racks, libraries free for all. Few people know that the University of Bombay's library is open to any citizen of Bombay. Dr Anderson believes that in the absence of a proper public library, it can serve as one—there is no membership fee. It has its regulars. An old historian uses it only for its collection of autobiographies and has gone through nearly 150. Dr Anderson believes most school and college libraries in the country are underutilized and that 'we have to open up their doors to the students' parents too'.

When he was deputy librarian, then chief librarian at the university, no one needed to open any doors to get to meet him. There weren't any doors. Perched on a slightly raised platform, as though on an apron stage, he would both be accessible to students and keep an eye on the library's greatest area of stress—the catalogues. Many didn't know how to use them and Dr Anderson had to move in swiftly to soothe the sorrowing and instruct the lost.

Not all librarians are so kind. Some are positively sadistic. For example, the man who was Director of the National Library in Buenos Aires between 1955 and 1973 takes an open delight in misleading and maddening the public. He writes, for example, of a circular chamber in a library which contains 'a great circular book whose spine is continuous and which follows the complete circle of the walls'. He writes of a country whose national poem consists of a single word (not God); of a book published in Bombay that contains an infinite number of pages so that a page once lost can never be found. The ex-librarian is the Argentinian writer Borges and his speculations on Time, Language, and the infinite magic of books distract me from my assignment. I begin wandering in his great labyrinths. Days and nights pass. I grow weak with wonder. I don't ever want to get out. Until a voice on the phone firmly reminds me that however valid Borges' concept of endless Time may be, my editor doesn't share it. I am to finish the assignment at once. I see a light with what looks like the university library in it. All I have to do is describe the building. Easy.

The library building is Dr Anderson's second home. Borges would say his first. He talks about it with a touch of pride. It's exactly a hundred years old. He calls it 'A Temple of Learning.' How many people know, for example, that embedded in the leaves and flowers on top of two pillars in the main lobby are the stony likenesses of Homer and Shakespeare? I look and see. They look like large dusty fruit, doomed to eternal pallor in the sunless lobby.

Then there's the clock tower—the one that represents old Bombay for most people. 'You must write about it.' But it is the most indescribable structure in the world. Those lumps and nodules when seen from afar, that crusted conical top, yield only one analogy: the long-faced carbuncular characters drawn by the cartoonist Don Martin for *MAD* magazine.

So I'm in a bad mood. So I took a wrong turning. That evening, I feverishly go through the notes Dr Anderson has made for a lecture on librarianship in the hope of finding a lead on the library. Nothing. That night, Borges tightens his grip. I begin to hallucinate. I see Dr Anderson and myself babbling bits of Borges at each other: 'Tlon!' 'Uqbar!' 'Ragnarok!' 'Undr!' Then:

Dr A (sadly): *A memory of unspeakable melancholy: at times I have travelled for many nights through corridors and long polished stairways without finding a single librarian.*

There's nothing for it but to surrender. Let Borges take over. The assignment be damned. 'It is necessary only to invent a book to believe that it exists,' says Borges.

The next day I invent *The Encyclopaedia of Metaphors*. It exists in a Himalayan library the name of which I mustn't disclose.

It's a living, breathing book in a script no one can decipher without the librarian's help. This book has recorded and continues to record the time and place of birth of a new metaphor, describes the span of its useful existence, and gives the time, place and cause of its death. Certain entries, like the one under 'Hell', do not throw much light:

'The time and place of its birth remain obscure, and the persistence of memory, misfortune, and bad hangovers have ensured it a durable life.'

The entry under 'Temple of Learning' is, however, a useful one. Its descriptive history takes in the Assyrian king Ashurbanipal's library of clay tablets in Nineveh; the libraries of Taxila and Benares; the library of Alexandria and its deliberate burning. Among its footnotes is a short one on the University of Bombay. It records its birth, with high hopes, a hundred years ago, its vestigial existence now. 'Pots of new money in the city, my dears,' adds the footnote, striking an unexpectedly merry note, 'Bugger new learning!'

So that was the way out. Borges was trying to help. I just had to ask. Now the clock tower looks threatened by the Stock Exchange building that looms grinning behind it and I feel protective. I hurry towards it, arming myself with Borges' descriptions of the library of Babel to use as a weapon, if necessary. That library is 'composed of an indefinite and perhaps infinite number of hexagonal galleries, with vast air shafts in between, surrounded by very low railings'. It is 'a sphere whose exact centre is any one of its hexagons and whose circumference is inaccessible'. The library is the Universe.

It's night and I'm back at the clock tower. A little alarmed, I notice its somewhat hexagonal shape, its low railings. I think of Dr Anderson's good work, of an old man with his autobiographies, of my becoming a member of the library soon. Its tower no longer looks like something out of MAD; it really isn't such a bad place after all. And *The Encyclopaedia of Metaphors*' tiny footnote registers a barely audible stir, which the watchman, ignorant of the nature of the miraculous volume he props his head against each night, will probably mistake for the sound of a fly settling to sleep, but which is really my sigh of relief.

THE MANY MURDERS OF DATTA SAMANT

In November 1981 we found ourselves locked out of the offices of the *Indian Express*. (I was on contract as Book Reviews Editor.) I forget what day it was, but by around 11.30 a.m. that day there was a sizeable crowd of journalists outside the main doors of Express Towers, Bombay. The management had taken us completely by surprise. We'd been told that there was a dangerous animal about, that its one aim in life was to terrorize workers, that it was being used by Mr A. R. Antulay, then chief minister of Maharashtra, to close down the *Indian Express*, Bombay. The paper hadn't been nice to Mr Antulay. It had exposed his involvement in a major scam. Dr Datta Samant, in the guise of a trade union leader, was the dangerous animal Mr Antulay was using to get the *Indian Express* by its throat.

If many of us didn't believe the story then, many more don't believe it now. And for those of us who had doubts about Dr Samant's style of functioning, the lockout did what he on his own may never have succeeded in doing: it pushed us into his camp. Between November 1981 and March 1982, the month when the offices of the *Indian Express* reopened, those who may have been natural enemies became committed comrades. Gate meetings, slogans, flag waving, speeches and gatherings at Oval Maidan, and a meeting with Dr Samant naturally followed. They saw us through a lot.

Long before he was assassinated, Dr Samant survived repeated attempts at character assassination. R. D. Goenka, the owner of the *Indian Express* and Arun Shourie, its editor, could not be expected to be kind to him during the days leading up to the lockout and after. What amazed and saddened me then, as it does now, is that some of my friends and colleagues also painted him purely black. If there was an arch villain in Mumbai in the early 1980s it was Datta Samant. Can the mill owners who hated his guts at that time be proud of themselves now? The strike was broken, labour was broken, its leader has been killed by hit men engaged by cowards. Is a millowner one of them? Is he reading this? Who is the villain now?

Sanctimonious editorials in *The Times of India* and the *Indian Express* can't disguise the fact that in many people's eyes the villain is still Dr Samant: those who live by the sword die by the sword, the editorials profess to say. In fact, what they say is an eye for an eye and a tooth for a tooth. Revenge, Thy Will Be Done.

It is awful to see that body, covered in a white sheet, being carted out of the coroner's court. It's worse reading sanctimonious editorials and listening to the smug, sometimes gloating comments of friends and strangers. He had it coming to him, they say. I'd say we all have it coming to us if this is how we justify his murder, and the many committed by us before.

He did use strong-arm tactics, he may have used violent means to gain his union's ends. But it says something terrible about our own inner violence, the coward and the hit man within us, when we say justice has been done, it had to happen this way.

'Rembrandt's goose is cooked.'

THE ARTS

LALITHA LAJMI AND THE FAMILY

The family is a unit which Indian painters are just beginning to see. Given the long history of that unit and the almost indissoluble bonds between its members even now, when the unit is under severe pressure and shows signs of breaking up, the painters' indifference to it amounts to a blindness which requires a preliminary diagnosis at least.

Indian poets and writers of fiction have written about grandfathers, grandmothers, mothers-in-law, and the lesser species that inhabit the cracks and crannies of a home—junior-in-laws, cousins, visiting uncles—each exerting its benevolent or pestilential influence over its own sub-division, its area of power, relegating the child to a neglected corner in which he will probably perish; a few will learn to observe.

Such work had no parallel in traditional Indian painting and whatever family portraits were commissioned over the last two hundred years or so were based on European academic models.

The beginnings of a change came suddenly and the advent of the camera in India (around 1850) had a lot to do with it. The photographic studios that sprang up all over the country drew both the rich and the not-so-rich into their interiors: make-shift Aladdin's caves which they needed no password to enter—to marvel at backdrops of moonlight, motorcars and roses, to turn their backs on them, to lean against an assortment of props to keep themselves steady, or to sit side by side on massive sofas, holding their breaths—all to pose for family photographs, those stiff reminders of a time when the camera rushed in to fill an ancient vacancy, a hole in the subcontinent's heart. In what seems to be an instant, the camera fulfilled a social need, a longing to be recorded, which Indian painters had turned away from for centuries.

We've had to wait a long time after that for the painter's intervention. It's only in the last ten years that the family has become the major theme of an entire show—most strikingly in the works of Nalini Malani and now, Lalitha Lajmi (Nilima Sheikh's narrative of a young daughter-in-law is another example, but not having seen her recent work, I can't say if the preoccupation continues).

Interestingly, in depicting inter-personal relationships within the family, both Malani and Lajmi rely on psychoanalytical insights—chiefly those related to an individual's sense of 'inner' and 'outer' space. It can hardly be an accident that Indian painters have begun taking such areas seriously in the same decade as psychoanalysis has begun to be—when the practice of psychoanalysis has taken firmer root in the country and its uses have begun to be more widely discussed. If the camera opened a door, psychoanalysis has turned the area behind it into a maze which is likely to fascinate more painters.

In the work on show, Lajmi relies on the studio photograph with that neglected, observing child as a recurring motif. In a painting of a family group, the chalky, sandy colours she uses cement her figures together into a firmly bonded wall. So oppressed are they, so lacking even an inner life, that their joint effect itself is oppressive. Lajmi's oil paintings make no attempt to attract the viewer, except through occasional items of architecture—fanlights, lintels and balustrades which she has always excelled in painting and which are once again shown in careful and loving detail. The watercolours, on the other hand, with the sepia tones of old family photographs, are painted to attract, and the eye easily delights in them.

Lajmi uses space disturbingly. Simple elements, like a slightly curving wall, a jutting table or a vast floor become interfaces of imprisonment, her characters trapped between the silence of their dead selves and the deadly presence of others. If the paintings are based on memories of a particular family, the memories have not been used to liberate the painter. It is as though Lajmi were determined to go on reliving those memories, moment by unfaked moment. The painter neither seeks atonement nor offers it to members of the family. It is partly the cruelty of her task that distances one from these works—a distance the painter wilfully seeks.

If the painter's intention were different it wouldn't be unfair to ask her what exactly wiped out these people and the exact nature of the family oppression each suffered from. After all, the pressures on an old grandmother are different from those on a little girl. But the paintings don't encourage such questions. 'Don't come too close,' the figures seem to be saying, 'we're hardly human.' What the paintings do say is that whatever the nature of the oppression, it was speech-destroying and formidable.

SOUZA: A BITTER PARTING

The exhibition catalogue says F N SOUZA. The gallery holding the exhibition is London's Gallery One. The catalogue also tells me when the exhibition took place: November-December 1962.

Which means I was at Oxford and had gone to London to see the show. I'd have gone anywhere to see a Souza show in the 1960s—within limits, of course. I mean, I didn't go to New York to see any of his shows there after he left London, his home for more than twenty years. I remember after he left—for good, he said—I felt deserted. I feel deserted now.

The catalogue shows Souza baring artificial fangs. They're painted on a strip of card which is held by the artist's mouth. The back of the catalogue shows the back of the artist's head, a painted arrow plunged deep into his neck. Both the photographs are black-and-white so the back of Souza's corduroy jacket on the back cover, a steep slope on which the result of the wound freely falls, is blotched with black blood.

The catalogue has a colour reproduction of a painting I've always loved—*Landscape with Planet*. It also has exquisite line drawings of the woman he was living with at that time. I must have met the couple a few years after the exhibition—in 1966 or '67 when I was living in London myself. Souza had had another show by then, of black paintings, canvas plastered (no other word comes to mind) with thick, black paint, with objects and figures dug into them with the same fierce, controlled energy that characterizes his best work. The person of Souza himself was associated with a fierce but uncontrolled energy. Stories of his rudeness and drunkenness did the rounds amongst the few expatriate painters I knew, so I expected to have a difficult time when I heard that he wanted to meet me.

What had made him curious about me, if I remember right, was an article in *The Hampstead and Highgate Post*, which was about Indians living in London. Souza and I were among them.

He turned out to be exceptionally mild. I suspect now that he longed for the company of 'artistically inclined' Indians and a chord was struck. We got on very well.

Years after I returned to Bombay he sent me letters from New York, mainly detailing his belief in Redmonism and The White Flag Revolution. Two of Redmonism's paradigms are, first, that 'Nature is the sole principle, the Creator of God and the Procreator of Man', and second, that 'the moral law is not binding to all men'. He wrote about himself and Redmonism to many people in Bombay. In the first two months of 1985 he wrote poems about Redmonism or poems with a Redmonist point of view, amateurish stuff which was published by Pundole Art Gallery to coincide with an exhibition of his paintings held there in March.

I hardly met him during his many visits to Bombay, though

two of his daughters stayed with us when they were in the city. But he met many painters and critics and, on a few occasions, wrote about them with characteristic savagery and scorn. Does this explain the near-indifference to his death, the mealy-mouthed praise? I'm shocked. He was more than a friend. Surely there's little doubt that he was one of our greatest painters.

When Eunice de Souza and I were collecting material for an anthology of prose for schools and colleges, we decided to publish something he'd written for *Encounter* in 1955 and which we found in *Words and Lines*, a collection of his prose pieces and drawings, published by Villiers, London, in 1959. The piece we chose was 'Nirvana of a Maggot', an account of a few months he spent in a nearly deserted Goan village. Apart from its vivid descriptions, written it would seem with the same passion with which he painted, is a passage on writing. After confessing to feeling ill-at-ease with words, to a sense of failing as a writer, he says:

> What I'd like to do first of all is to merely articulate freely and easily. I have never learnt grammar and I can't spell correctly. Yet I want to say something, to make just a sound, even a guttural sound or a grunt, an onomatopoeic sound emitted with a clearance of the throat. What I'd want to do is to suspend my vocal "cords" on the nib of my pen like a mouthful of food at the end of a fork; to throw my voice like a ventriloquist's, but over a page; to emit sounds with gummed backs like postage stamps which stick firmly on paper; to make the split point of my pen the sensitive needling of a seismograph, as I can easily do when I draw . . .

In spite of this feeling of incompetence, or perhaps because of it, Souza wrote well. And he wrote as he painted, a man with a mission. If we were fools who couldn't see, and he truly believed we were fools who refused to, it was his business to open our eyes. What Andrew Sinclair, notorious for his novel *The Breaking of Bumbo*, wrote in the Gallery One catalogue is true: 'Souza sees himself as a priest of paint. His job is to show God the flawed face of men; and men the beauty and wrath of God.'

Unfortunately, forty years after those words were published something else seems truer—something that Souza himself wrote in another piece that appeared in *Words and Lines*.

That book was re-issued in its original format by an Indian publisher recently. Hardly anyone in a city which buys, sells and talks art all the time and which has pretensions to be one of art's international capitals, seems to have been interested in buying the book since copies can be bought off one of the city's pavements at ten rupees each.

What Souza wrote in 'A Fragment of Autobiography', the piece I referred to, is:

> As for me, I was a rickety child with running nose and running ears, and scared of every adult and every other child. Better had I died. Would have saved me a lot of trouble. I would not have had to bear an artists' tormented soul, create art in a country that despises her artists and is ignorant of her heritage.

It's something I read with great bitterness now.

NAIPAUL'S FICTION AND REMBRANDT'S GOOSE

With V. S. Naipaul in town and a seminar on the visual arts going on at the same time, it seemed a good idea to ask some people what they thought about both Naipaul and art. The answers were surprising. Everyone I questioned said Naipaul was important and art was important. But not important enough for them to read Naipaul's books or see exhibitions of art.

In Naipaul's case there was a qualification. Yes, they would be interested to read what he had to say about India but weren't interested in reading his novels. This is an old obsession of ours. We so much want to know what people say about us that we forget other worlds exist. Why should a Trinidadian of Indian origin *have* to write about India? Naipaul chose to and then again he didn't choose to. Many of his novels, stories and the books he made of his journeys have nothing to do with India. As far as I know, Kenneth Ramchand, another West Indian of Indian origin, has not chosen to write about India at all.

Naipaul himself believes that the novel isn't a sustainable art form now and it's likely that fewer people will read them in the near future. We are well into the age of information, opinion and analysis where Naipaul's kind of fiction is seen as stressful, even 'high funda'. It tries the imagination and the imagination apparently is not to be tried in an age of factoids and news bytes. The house for Mr Biswas seemed like a permanent structure but it isn't.

Strangely, the reason that an experience of the visual arts isn't as valued as it used to be springs from the same perception—the perception of impermanence. It is now widely held in influential art circles that installations have superseded traditional methods of painting, carving, chiselling or working with clay. The canvas and the potter's wheel are defunct. Art of long-lasting value was created on them and art that lasts long is art that is exploited long. It becomes commercial. Or so the installation bands all over the world say, guerrilla installation bands—so fierce is their commitment. Let us make art out of rice pudding and chocolate cake and leave our work out in the rain. Rice pudding and chocolate cake dissolve in the rain. Everyone is happy. That didn't last long, did it? From now on, Art isn't meant to.

Seminars, however, do take long and long are the papers read out in them. Even as I write, thousands of words are pouring out of someone's mouth, words on the installations of X or the fissures of Y. These words will soon be printed in a book. The words will stay long after the art works they describe—the puddings, the cakes and the icing on the cakes—have disappeared. For the first time in history, words written about an impermanent art form seek a permanent place in their stead. Future generations will see what that art was like also temporarily—through fading photographs and deteriorating videotapes.

Come, art critics, dinner is served. Rembrandt's goose is cooked.

CANDOUR AND SECRECY

The area of Bhupen Khakhar's work which I originally wanted to explore wasn't its content. I merely wanted to look at the figures in his paintings more closely than professional art critics had done. That might have led me to questions of content, but I wasn't certain. I share Geeta Kapur's difficulty with trying to define what the content of Khakhar's work is (see her chapter on the painter in her book *Contemporary Indian Artists*). But I don't share her view that the figures he paints 'often turn out looking like cardboard puppets rather than flesh-and-blood characters'.

I don't see any of those figures as cardboard puppets. That's why I want to write about them in the first place. I am drawn to them, not merely to look at them but to look into them. Painted cardboard has its effective say at political rallies and in the theatre. To me, Khakhar's figures say something else.

I have to approach that something else in a roundabout way, for it's obscure and I'm not sure that in the end I'll be able to clarify it at all. Many poets have written poems on individual paintings, and one of my favourites is a poem by Thom Gunn on a painting by Caravaggio. The painting depicts Saul's conversion to Christ on the road to Damascus. After setting the scene and describing some of the elements of the painting, the poet says:

The painter saw what was, an alternate
Candour and secrecy inside the skin.

Gunn's lines help me say what I want to about Khakhar. Most of the painter's figures, however firm they appear to be, lack bones. There is skin, sometimes layers of it. It overlays a substance that may or may not be flesh. The figures don't openly tell us what they are made of, but at the same time, from inside their skins, from under their clothes, they tell us everything we need to know about them. And yet, we are never entirely sure. They never entirely trust us with themselves. All we can be sure of is that the painter has looked inside the skin of the person painted and has carefully compounded what he has seen into an inner biography of the person. In a Khakhar painting, individual figures often relate to one another as part of a long story the painting tells; while the individual figure itself tells the inside story of a lifetime.

Khakhar lives in Baroda and there is a painting on a wall of his house which I'd like to describe. I had gone to Baroda to see whatever work he had with him. Apart from the painting I'm going to describe, and two or three others, he had none. Practically everything he hadn't sold in India is now in England. I had to be content with seeing slides of his paintings, which is a poor way of seeing them. I shall try and write in some detail about the one painting I did see.

It is called *Man Sitting on Bed* and shows an impressive figure sitting on a bed, his legs dangling over the edge, the feet not touching the floor, his left arm, stretched out but folded at the elbow, casually resting on two rolled-up razais, his right arm at rest by his side. The face is uncommonly powerful, suggesting both serenity and strength, and my first response to the figure, based on memories of Khakhar's early use of Indian iconography, was that the pose was a parody of the Nataraj, the dance of Shiva. A foolish response? There is, apart from the calm strength of the face and the god-like span between the eyes, an outrageously pronounced fold in the figure's dhoti, concealing and at the same time comically drawing attention to a prime item of Shiva-worship. But . . . the point of the painting is not parody.

Something has happened inside the figure, under its skin. The awkward bulge on the back of its left arms isn't just a wrongly-placed muscle; it suggests an inner dislocation, a slipping of strength. The goitrous swelling under the left armpit is not a crudely-drawn deltoid; it is the product of an internal plague, an excess of the heart. And gradually, you begin to see that though the figure presents itself outwardly as strong, reposeful and radiant, there have been secret displacements inside it, demolitions, collapses, both major and minor but in either case, permanent—all marvellously suggested by the painter through his cunning shifting about of the living breathing stuff in a human body.

This isn't to suggest that the original Ranchodbhai whom I had the pleasure of meeting on this visit requires the urgent care of a doctor. But I do suggest that the uncanny transformation of his mundane weaknesses into an image of lasting strength is due to the care of a friend. It is so with practically every important figure Khakhar has painted—whether it is the elderly Shankerbhai Patel who is blind to or dreaming of or who has lost touch with the garden of sensual pleasure in *Portrait of Shri Shankerbhai V. Patel near Red Fort* (1971); the sensitive young man who would rather dream than fight in *Muktibahini Soldier* (1973); the thin-legged man in the vulcanising shop, the substance of whose chest (and high hopes too, presumably), appears to have collapsed around and below his waist—so ridiculously low is his centre of gravity—the umbrella less a support than a phallic joke (more of this later) in the painting *Vulcanising* (1978). Khakhar knows them all personally and he knows them well.

We will look more closely at some of Khakhar's recent paintings to see how he has developed this business of transforming his private knowledge of the persons he paints into social and psychological statements of growing power. On occasion, of monumental strength.

Looking at paintings in the form of slides isn't a good idea, as I said earlier, but the method has its surprises. There is a painting, *Man with Bouquet of Plastic Flowers* (1975) which has as its central figure a man holding just such a bouquet. He is flanked on his right and left by panels showing individuals of his class working in an office, relaxing on a swing, visiting someone who isn't well, one man watching his own reflection in a glass cabinet. The painting is the largest Khakhar has completed so far, 5'10" X 5'10", and I was told the size contributed greatly to its impact. In a slide of the whole painting, the central figure's eyes, like the mouth, appear mean and narrow. Then I was shown a detail of the face. The eyes are starkly open, the face grey, catatonic. It came as a shock. The man is mad. He hasn't been destroyed; but his way of surviving his environment is to have gone mad. His bouquet of plastic flowers makes sudden chilling sense. His look empties the panels he is flanked by of their mundane meanings and at the same time charges them with a more terrible one. It is the very separateness of individuals of a certain class, the non-communication between them, that has driven one of them mad. And to emphasize the man's inner choking, the perpetual taste of ashes behind the clamped mouth, Khakhar shows the joined middle of his shirt-front as an almost transparent sickly-white substance—to suggest that it is more part of the man, inside him, than of the shirt, a worm-like resurrection from the guts that has risen to throttle him, or even a damaged stem, grown sick and etiolated in the lightless case of his body, that can just about support the man's drying head, even as he clutches those small terrible artificial flowers.

That look of intolerable inner oppression is not new to Khakhar's work. It is there, as the painter Gulam Sheikh pointed out to me, on the face of the mother in *Mother and Father Going to Yatra* (1971). Only there it is controlled, well under the skin. In the recent paintings, like a long-bottled-up genie, it begins to jump out. And it does so chiefly through the eyes and the mouth.

Consider another strong painting, *Man Eating Jalebee* (1975). It shows a man in the right foreground doing just that, while behind him there is a sea, conversation, a departure. A detail of the face: the man is barely eating the jalebee. His eyes indicate he is not thinking of it at all, his teeth are gritted, he is going to have to force the sweet between them. And we are recalled to the sexual suggestiveness of the left hand on the table. Food in the place of sex? It would be a travesty to reduce any of the painting's meanings into something as crude as that. But we have seen that hand in a Khakhar painting before. It occurs in *Lewd Joke* (1974), with its two fish hanging behind the laughing boys, its masturbatory homosexual overtones.

This leads me to make a simple point about Khakhar's sexual imagery. It is never talked about. The aggressively sexual imagery of George Keyt, Souza and Laxma Goud has led us to our usual healthy excitements with the sensual side of our culture. Khakhar's has produced a long awkward silence.

This imagery has become more and more explicit. Compare the phallic joke of the gardener with the watering hose in *Goa: Church* (1972) with the exposed genitals of *Hatha Yogi* (1977) where even the animal skin the man is sitting on appears to flow towards the viewer, more slimy than furry, a product of the genitals themselves. If this is vulgar in the extreme, too crude for most tastes, consider that an artist can be forced into crudities because of that very good taste which politely ignored his earlier, much milder phallic jokes. And subverting polite taste is exactly what everyone has praised Khakhar for! Presumably this is a commendable act only if it is restricted to the hygienic contexts of social criticism and art history. Khakhar, the much-applauded clown, would appear to have had the last laugh. Our hypocrisy has been fathomless. He has barely touched it. We always thought he was making fun of the other lot—the bourgeoisie. The joke's been on us.

It appears to have been on the British too. Making full use of the more liberal climate in Britain during his two brief stays there, he has produced explicit sexual imagery that in some way challenges that very liberalism. I'm not sure if every British art critic and admirer of Khakhar's work expected the Indian to make quite so free with his cherished ideals—liberalism being one of the most cherished. *Man in Pub* (1979), with the man clutching a repulsive pair of gloves in front of his crotch, the very arrangement of his trousers on a chair in a narrative panel suggesting a sexual posture, is a painting about sexual frustration if ever there was one. For the man there is no enjoyment in any sexual act, even a solitary one. His expression is held-in, taut. And his thighs and hips are gripped by the sides of his jacket as though in an iron clamp.

I think I've said enough to suggest that Khakhar's figures are not puppet-like, not to be neglected as products of bad draughtsmanship, but of the essence in what he wants to say. I will not mimic the clichés of a class- or socially-oriented criticism of his work (Geeta Kapur's chapter, not surprisingly, is brilliantly free of these) which have emphasised the satirical, common-man qualities of his work with those of my own brand of criticism. Not certainly, 'man's essential loneliness', 'sexual alienation', 'existential anguish', etc. None of that, I hope. But it is very difficult to produce a generalisation that can sum up his content. If Khakhar's figures are lonely, and not all of them are, it is due to reasons specific to the individual painted—each individual's candour responding to the artist's, the artist's secrecy corresponding with what each individual wants kept secret.

Painting them then becomes an act of empathy. The painter enters their vulnerable selves to exploit their vulnerability; in doing so, he exposes that vulnerability to public gaze. And we, the public, find ourselves admiring and supporting it. It shames us into acknowledging our own. And so the painter makes the weak lastingly strong. By exposing his subjects' strong weaknesses to our feeble strengths, he makes them acquire a permanent place in our affections. That is why we are drawn to them, why, sometimes, we love them. Painting as an act of empathy occasionally becomes a transformed act of love.

There is one more characteristic of Khakhar's figures which I'd like to touch on since it leads naturally to my final point—that of considering the painter's religious or metaphysical beliefs—does he have any at all? Some of his important figures have a slightly upward tilt of the head—in the profiles of Shankerbhai V. Patel in the painting already mentioned, and of the man in the barber's chair in *Barber* (1974). Not in profile but staring at a point just above the viewer, there is the man in the foreground in *Factory Strike* (1972), the accountant on the phone in *I. V. Shah: Accountant* (1973), and most pronounced of all, the boy with the harmonium in *Royal Circus* (1974). The expression on their faces, specially on the accountant's (and there are faces without that upward tilt which have that expression too) suggest fatal wistfulness, an irretrievable loss. But does that loss belong to the skies? Is Paradise lost? Out there?

Considering all Khakhar's work so far, including a slide of the magnificent *Death in the Family* (1978) with its spirit floating obliquely above a house, I'd answer No. Neither popular Christianity with its mechanical projection of Heaven and Hell as out there; nor popular Hinduism, with its multiple gods, its cycles of birth and rebirth, appear to have led Khakhar to a basic religious or metaphysical belief. For Khakhar, the Hindu gods definitely came down to earth in colonial times and now exist as oleographs or cheap plaster casts in glass cabinets, looking like spoiled schoolboys (like the Shiva in *Glass Cabinet and Shiva* (1977), closer to the cakes he has painted elsewhere than to the skies. It is his friends, of the earth, who have risen and taken their place. It is Ranchodbhai who is Shiva. Even the spirit above the house in *Death in the Family* isn't evidence that Khakhar believes in an afterlife. To my mind, the spirit is simply heading towards the township with its vulcanising shop, fruit stall, its various businesses, towards further human affairs, away from the dust, straw and animal life on the right of the painting.

Sheikh was a little uneasy when I told him this. 'A painting should not be seen that way,' he said. Even when it is a narrative painting? Many of Khakhar's paintings tell stories. Their characters have a past and a destiny. The spirit-like form also has a destiny. In the face of the painter's many inventions, I can't resist inventing a destiny for the spirit. It will head towards the township, and without any fuss, stirring about as much dust as an ant would, will settle back into the life it has never left, as one of a bunch of bananas, a cycle tyre tube, or a leaf in a pot of tea.

This probably makes Khakhar appear to be less of a painter than an animator who makes films for children, and me, an idiot child in the audience. Since I think he is the best contemporary painter we have, it can do him no harm if I suggest that there is a kinship between the world of his painting and that of animated cartoons for children. For one thing, the worst things never happen in both. I think Khakhar's faith in the created world of his paintings is such that he believes it can do without death. Life never leaves it. It never can, it can only be transformed into another kind of life. If this is part of his fantasy, not his beliefs, I would argue that fantasy is central to his beliefs. That is why, despite humanistic elements in his work, he can't be called a humanist, or as Geeta Kapur suggests, a realist. A humanist can't allow himself to believe in a deathless world, since man is chiefly precious to him because he is mortal. And a realist can't be called that if, in his vision of existence, he doesn't allow for his own permanent extinction.

I don't know how Khakhar will develop. Perhaps, sooner or later, the worst things will happen in his paintings and he will surprise us with the manner in which he deals with them, but if I had to define him according to the evidence of his works so far, I'd call him a Master of Mischief, one who, along with the many venerable objects he has overturned, has succeeded in standing Plato on his head. If he has a belief, I think it is this: The world we inhabit and the world of ideal forms are both part of one world—this, the only one there is. And the ideal world is represented in his paintings. In other words—and it must appear that I am now trying to stand all previous criticism of Khakhar on its head, but I say it most tentatively—Khakhar is not basically concerned with attacking the injustice and hypocrisy of the world we live in through his paintings. He attacks the world because it is not like his paintings. If he lived in a world that was a good reproduction of the world of his paintings, he would be quite comfortable in it. That is not the stance of a satirist, a reformer or a social critic. But it is still a deeply subversive one. The art it results in, at its best, shakes many of the uplifting values we try to live by at their very root.

Are we to believe then, that if Khakhar's paintings represent an ideal version of the world we inhabit that he doesn't allow the figures in them (and by implication, us in our less perfect world) any alternatives to the bad situations they are sometimes in—of madness, fruitless work, unfulfilled sex? I think the answer is: no, he doesn't. This will dissatisfy many but it is an artist's answer and many artists before Khakhar have given it. The ugliness and evil of the world we inhabit can only be redeemed by beauty—however sinister and unacceptable that beauty may appear to us when it is first revealed. The artist's chief business, some would say his only one, is to assist in that redemption.

Khakhar is currently at work on the largest painting he has attempted so far. It is meant to be a companion to *Death in the Family* and is called *Marriage in the Family*. Like the former, it tells a story, using groups of figures to tell it, and some of the explicit elements I've pointed out are already there. After the show of slides at Sheikh's house, Khakhar worked on the painting late into the night. Next morning, to my surprise, I saw the detail he had worked on set alight by the sun. One of its rays had slipped through a chink in the curtains and hit a spot on the canvas exactly behind the detail and set it ablaze.

If, when I left Baroda, I thought the sun's ray was an exceptional gift of life and felt a lightness of heart, wasn't it because I had spent some time in the presence of work which, like the quirky shaft of sunlight, intrudes where it is most wanted—into that negative region of the self where nothing is visible, whose every thought is chill, every dream dead, the mind having fooled itself into giving darkness and death a pre-eminence they do not have? Khakhar's work answers such folly by cleverly showing that's just what it is.

MAKE MINE MOVIES

I remember there was this blood-red sky and a whale singing in it. The whale was spotted. I know: we had drawing books of Willy the Whale, the outlines to be filled in with paint. I remember the heron shedding a tear, one sole tear that hung from its eye till it distended, detached itself and splashed into the lake. The course of that tear changed the course of my life. Willy was dead.

The whale that sang for bird, sea, flower and tree had been harpooned, I think, and the heron was in mourning. So were the lake, the forest and the sky. Are these memories false? No one's been able to tell me. No one seems to have seen or heard of the film I saw, an animation film called *Make Mine Music*.

I remember my mother and her elder sister Freny in whose flat we were staying at that time. I remember the humiliation of trying to keep out of their sight, moving from room to room in that flat on Altamount Road, so that they would not see that I was crying. Shoulders hunched, head lowered, I had become the heron, grieving for its dead friend. I don't think I've ever felt such pain in my chest before or since. My heart was broken. I remember the two formidable women confronting each other:

'Did you say something? Why is he crying?'

'You must have said something. Why else would he cry?' Six-year-olds weren't supposed to cry, so the tears came slowly, squeezed out by a pressure of my chest which, after several bouts of pneumonia, was more like a tube than a chest. I couldn't bawl.

Exasperated at not being able to place the blame anywhere, neither on each other, nor the servants, nor the neighbours, they warily approached me one last time—children know when it's one last time; they have to say something, even if it means bursting into uncontrollable sobs that very moment; and I wasn't known to speak.

'Chullee rurtu thun.' The bird was crying, I said in reply to the question.

Now they were alarmed. Questions about my sanity, I imagine, whirled through the heads.

'Bird? Bird? Which bird are you talking about?!'

'Film nu.'

Hundreds, perhaps thousands of films later, I wonder if it was that scene with the heron in *Make Mine Music* that set the pattern of my responses to every film I see. Willy the Whale does sing again, from Heaven—that was the whale in the sky at the end of the film—and all creation is happy but I wasn't. Perhaps the ending seemed false to me. The moment of truth, for me, was in the heron's grief and in the suddenly shattering fact that loved and loving creatures do die, even in what we called cartoons then. I'd witnessed such deaths before. Bambi's mother dies but I barely remember the scene in the film. And nothing very bad happens in *Dumbo*. *The Wizard of Oz*, with its tin and lion men terrified me as did the forest fire in *The Jungle Book* (in colour). I still remember the fire, the whole screen a sheet of flame, but barely recall Mowgli. And Mowgli was Sabu, the very Sabu my parents were so proud of, the one Indian actor in Hollywood.

Such is the intensity of the moment of truth films provide that I try not to see them anymore, at least not in public. When I do, I become a six-year-old again—tears, terror and all. That's not a nice thing to have happen to you when you're in your fifties, so I've decided to stop. Even recalling a film's moments of truth can be distressing. Films devour me as a sponge devours plankton. At the end of its meal, I'm spat out of cinema halls, drained, a wreck. We had no 1.30 shows when I was a child but even to be expectorated at the end of the 3.30 show, the matinee, was to hit the pavements in the harsh light of day. The contrast between the wild prairies of the cinema hall and the streets of Bombay couldn't have been greater. It disoriented me, as it disoriented others, even further.

It's not as though I didn't try to do something about it. I did. I decided to contain my experience of films, control it, as it were, by putting it down on paper. On the pages of a ruled exercise book I drew further rules, vertical, making a box of, I think, four columns: Film, Director, Music, Photography. After every film I saw, I put down the names of those that fell under the appropriate category and in a space under Remarks, wrote what I thought about the film I'd seen.

In the beginning, what I thought was mostly what *The Times of India* critic thought, there was no one else in 1951. But I gradually came to have views of my own. I think the process steadied me a little, helped distance me from the sponge. Till the next time round.

We were a regular film-going family, in the sense that we saw films together about once a week, almost always on Sundays. After a generally silent drive to the cinema hall and the customary purchase of packets of wafers and chocolates, there'd be a far-from-pregnant pause. Once the film got going, my father would get involved in the action perhaps more than anyone else, punctuating the proceedings with whoops and cries. Suddenly, on occasion, he would rise from his seat in an attempt to ward off a sword, descending, let's say, from Basil Rathbone's hands on Errol Flynn's neck.

Since my mother was the strong, silent kind and my brother and I the weak, silent kind—what relatives pityingly called 'the quiet type'—my father would take it upon himself to comment briefly on the film after the show.

'Ghela ganda.' Silly nonsense, he would say after a disappointing Abbott and Costello or an improbable action adventure. Or he'd say, 'Soo fine acting' (what fine acting) of a star whose performance impressed him. Sometimes his comments had a more sinister purpose. Stated casually, almost in the air, while opening the door of his car, say, to drive us back home from the cinema, the comment would be directed to one or other member of his family, with the intention of making him or her think. 'What? Can there only be unhappiness in an artist's life? No happiness at all?' he said after we saw *Lust for Life* at the Metro.

This was meant for me, the artist, whose glum and acned mien tried him greatly those days. I was meant to respond. Needless to say, I didn't. After *Pather Panchali* at the Liberty, he said, 'You see what befell the family after she treated her mother-in-law that way?' This for my mother who he felt, quite wrongly, was mistreating his mother.

It was generally my father who decided on which Hindi films we should see. The films themselves would have been suggested to him by his patients, some of whom were film stars. In this way we saw, among others, *Barsaat*, *Baiju Bawra*, *Anarkali* and *Aan*. Meena Kumari had invited us to see her on the sets of *Anarkali*—a dungeon scene which we saw. But the Anarkali we went to see had been replaced by Bina Rai. My father couldn't believe his eyes. What had happened to one of his favourite patients? As for *Aan*, billed as India's first completely technicolour movie—it was a mishmash. The colour held but nothing else did. A mixture of Cadillacs and swordfights, good acting and bad, confused us so much that I never wanted to see a Hindi movie again. And the beginnings had been so propitious.

In those years, in the 1940s, there used to be a tradition,

now made irrelevant by video. At children's birthday parties, if the children were too many or too small, they wouldn't be taken to the cinema, the cinema would be taken to them. At one such party (or was it my navjote?), my father decided to show *Andaz*. The patients' waiting room, emptied of its sofas, became the darkened cinema hall and as the hired projector whirred and the hired screen came to life, scores of eyes, young and old, watched, enthralled.

It was some years after my first 'moment of truth' in cinema but in *Andaz* too they came thick and fast. Two I remember most vividly are Nargis in a state of shock after her father's death, spilling a glass of milk; and the moment Raj Kapoor swats Dilip Kumar over the head with a tennis racquet, sending him rolling down the stairs like a dazed fly. So that's how men fought over a beautiful woman. Great. I was growing up.

Did I spend my childhood only seeing sad films? No. But funny films had their problems too. If sad films led to uncontrollable tears, funny films led to uncontrollable piss—if I laughed too much I wet my pants. Several cinema seats in Bombay must have borne evidence of my affliction. But the one I remember most clearly was borne not by a seat but a carpet. It belonged to my best friend's mother and, at the moment of urinary epiphany, held about twenty children watching 8mm cartoons. (It must have been a party.) The evidence, mercifully, was attributed to the pet Australian terrier Trixie, though, as I left the flat surreptitiously, I heard ominous cries and exclamations. The servants were insisting that Trixie had been tied up near the kitchen, a considerable distance away from the carpet, right through the show. The cries came from my best friend's mother and his aunts. That was a narrow escape but at the Strand, watching Bob Hope in *Fancy Pants* (or was it *Paleface*?), I peed quite openly. There was an incredibly funny dialogue which involved gallstones and gold gallstones, so I just hitched up a side of my shorts and peed. I can still hear the hiss, amazed that an elder cousin sitting next to me didn't (or pretended not to), the effusion gradually settling around the shoes of the man sitting in front of me. If he'd been wearing sandals I'd have been thrashed.

It wasn't only with family that we saw films. Sunday morning (10.30) shows could be seen with friends; so it was that my best friend, whose mother's carpet I'd wetted, and I went to several. Avid readers of comics (his father ran New Book Co. and had stacks of them), we saw the first (black-and-white) versions of *Superman*, *Batman*, *Captain Marvel* and *Flash Gordon*, and unanimously felt they were trash. Once, at a morning show, we crept into a cinema hall to see a film which wasn't meant for the eyes of persons under twelve. It was Jean Cocteau's *Beauty and the Beast*. It scared the shit out of us. So did the gentleman who, leaning over to us from the row behind, asked us how old we were. 'Twelve,' we said, quaking. 'You don't look twelve,' he said and chuckled, the chuckle rippling through the whole row behind. We watched the rest of the film not just terrorised but mortified. We watched the comic hero films at the Capitol, *Beauty and the Beast* at the Empire and films I've forgotten at the Excelsior. These cinema halls are close to where I work now and together with the Metro, Eros and the Regal, formed an acre of my childhood. 3-D came and went with *Bwana Devil*, *House of Wax* and others. Cinemascope came and went with *The Robe*, *River of No Return* and others. The wide screen has come and will go. But the acre remains, only its magic's gone. I don't want to go back to it, to be six years old again. Though I'd like to tell my father, as someone in *Finnegans Wake* does: 'Carry me along, taddy, as you done through the toy fair.' But he can't.

Once we were teenagers we saw films on our own. *Rock Around The Clock* came to the Strand, the audience went wild, danced in the aisles and seats were broken. It was the end of a chapter. But it was at the Excelsior that a bird broke my heart.

THE SHOWGIRL AND THE BABY

When Robert Mitchum hoists Marilyn Monroe onto his shoulder at the end of *River of No Return*, he does what every man wants to do at least once in his lifetime: sweep a woman off her feet. Clark Gable does it more literally at the bottom of the great stairway in *Gone with the Wind*. He has Vivien Leigh floating like a feather across his arms. Both men make the hoist look effortless, but it's effortless only when it's in the head. In actual fact, sweeping a woman off her feet involves a knack, a certain swing of the body. In actual fact, very few men have done it; those who have belong to a very small club.

I must confess I belong to that club. I swept a woman off her feet in the West End in London. She was playing Alizon Eliot and me, Nicholas Devize. The play was Christopher Fry's *The Lady's Not for Burning*. She was supposed to be seventeen, but was, in fact, much older. I was just past eighteen. She was the first woman I swept off her feet. Louis, the director, showed me how to do it. It was like taking lessons from an expert swimming coach. One minute you're drowning, the next afloat. After the first heft, there were many others. The actress stopped being nervous. When I lifted her up before that first night audience and she felt as light as air, I felt I had become a man.

It didn't make me fall in love, though. She was supposed to be a blonde, but was, in fact, more of a brunette. The main character of the play, the witch who wasn't meant for burning, was supposed to be a brunette, but was more of a blonde. But what if the actress I held in my arms, however briefly during rehearsals, had been a blonde? She was pretty, sensitive and soft-spoken. She had a yielding, wistful air about her. In the play, I refer to 'the sunlit barley of her hair'—a perfect description of Marilyn's hair. What if she—the woman who had made me feel like a man by being so light in my arms—had had Marilyn's hair?

Probably nothing would have come of it. I loved Marilyn, I loved her hair. The actress and I liked each other too. But she had other plans. As for that bit about London and the West End, it was London and it was a stage in the West End but it was a small stage—part of a YMCA hall. I was part of their dramatic society. I was trying to get out of my shell.

The truth is, for reasons that have everything and nothing to do with this account, I had been a horrible prig in Bombay. What was perhaps more horrible to me at that time was that I was aware of it and could find no way out—except to try and get away to England, to get away, metaphorically speaking, to its fields of sunlit barley. Less than a year after I arrived in London, I had my bit of it on that stage. It was a minor conquest. And like many other things that happen to Bombay boys, it began with cinema.

Cinema is what we went to once a week, sometimes more often, and the cinema is what we normally took our classmates to on birthdays. At someone's birthday party, I remember about twelve of us sitting through *River of No Return* (in Bombay's Regal cinema, I think), squirming during that pleasantly unpleasant eternity of time between puberty and manhood at the lubriciously drenched Marilyn—the lucky river (in fact the studio tank) gets to drench her several times— only to emerge from the cinema after the show with nothing to offer our host but very embarrassed thanks. Marilyn had got at us in a way we didn't know how to express. I, at least, clung to dumbfounded innocence, to the wrong side of the gorge that separates the men from the boys. Beneath me raged turbulence.

The wide screen hit us with the same force that adolescence did. Both happened at around the same time. The 3-D *Bwana Devil* had come and gone and failed but we had seen the first Cinemascope movie, *The Robe* and been enthralled. We had seen Marilyn in the second, *How to Marry a Millionaire*, and here she was in another, *River of No Return*. Clearly, a new age was dawning. But the sun had really risen a little earlier, in the pre-Cinemascope days. It was a red sun, an evil sun, it was evil Marilyn in a red dress. And the film was *Niagara*.

Hoardings of that film, with a red, incandescent Marilyn lying across the entire width of the Niagara Falls, hung over Bombay for days, turning from gold to scarlet to crimson, depending on the light. I sneaked into the Regal (I think) to see it. I must have been around fourteen then and the film wasn't considered a suitable one for me to see. It wasn't. It had steamy love scenes, it was about adultery, it had two murders (one of them Marilyn's), and another death (Joseph Cotten going beautifully over the falls in a little boat). I came out of the cinema feeling like an adult.

Not every Marilyn movie has made me feel that way, but the sun that rose with *Niagara* lightened several of my days in the years to come. Seeing photographs of her, or a movie, inevitably brought about a subtle change. The day became the colour of her hair. She became a constant presence, like the day, even when not seen. When that sun finally went out, eight years later, I was back in Bombay. My brother gave me the news. It was on the front page of *The Times of India*, I think I can say quite truthfully that most of the city went into mourning.

After her death, the Marilyn industry swung into action and this year may see some well-synchronised swinging—a perfect chorus line of ghostly Marilyns. An ardent fan of hers, who used to live in Bombay but who now works in Toronto, says bookshops abroad are crammed with books on her, shelf after shelf of books. He claims there's nothing of hers he doesn't have—Marilyn plates, Marilyn cut-out dolls, Marilyn buttons—and when fellow fans offer him something they think is new, he finds he already has it. His latest acquisition is an eighteen-inch porcelain figurine of Marilyn as she was in *Gentlemen Prefer Blondes*, wearing her famous red dress and rhinestones. He has ordered another figurine of Marilyn as she is in that equally famous scene in *The Seven Year Itch*, when her skirt billows up and around her, exposing her shapely legs. There are hundreds if not thousands of Marilyn Fan Clubs all over the world. She continues to live in the eyes of millions of men.

The symbol of those eyes, as one of her photographers put it, was the camera, and Marilyn knew it. Someone else has said that her one lasting love affair was with the camera. If the camera hadn't existed, Marilyn wouldn't have. Just as surely as if oil paints hadn't existed, the Mona Lisa wouldn't have. We can't bring ourselves to think of an oils portrait of Marilyn any more than we can think of a photographic portrait of the Mona Lisa. Both represent their respective media fully.

Philippe Halsman, the photographer mentioned above, knew this. 'She would try to seduce the camera as if it were a human being,' he said. 'She knew the camera lens was not just a glass eye but a symbol for the eyes of millions of men; so the camera stimulated her strongly. Because she had a great talent for directing the entire impact of her personality at the lens, she was a remarkably gifted and exciting model.'

But there was one part of her anatomy that Halsman regretted the camera couldn't quite catch. It was the part Norman Mailer called 'that famous set of cheeks' and which Marilyn was hoping to bare on the back cover of *Playboy*. During the filming of *Love Happy*, Groucho Marx had told her, 'You have the prettiest ass in the business.' Halsman remarked that 'it seemed to wink at the onlooker . . . to capture that wink with a (still) camera is not that easy.'

The ass that winks, even when covered, can be seen on the screen. Off it, it had nothing to wink about. It had been degraded and violated by men who didn't care for her and whom she didn't care for either. If she destroyed man after man in her life, men who didn't even know her destroyed her in their talk—her eyes, her lips, her breasts, her ass. If we are to believe the latest reports, that ass was violated even on the night of her death, the night of 4-5 August.

What led her to that death—the barbiturates and the booze just before, her affairs with John and Robert Kennedy—has been much discussed. So have the absence of a father in her life and the presence of the many substitute fathers she almost invariably turned against. Her hatred was reciprocated. Director after director came to loathe this increasingly uncharming creature who turned up late, was rude to those on the sets, and forgot even the simplest lines, incurring take after take (a scene with Tony Curtis in *Some Like It Hot* required forty-seven takes). Tempers rose and so did costs. Could her phenomenal amnesia have been inherited, a legacy of the mental illnesses that destroyed two of her grandparents and her mother? Her husbands doubted her sanity, her last husband, Arthur Miller, was almost driven to the brink himself in the course of their four-and-a-half-year marriage, Marilyn's longest. But there are no signs of that illness in any of the photographs of hers that we've seen. We've seen terrible pictures of Rita Hayworth during her mental collapse and of Elizabeth Taylor during her days of alcohol and breakdown. But no photographs I've seen of Marilyn approach anywhere near the haggard faces in those pictures. Even the photograph of her shortly after her first miscarriage in 1957 shows her smiling from the (hospital?) bed. It must have cost her a good deal to do that, even as an actress. She desperately wanted children.

I've noticed children are drawn to photographs and movies of Marilyn; they watch transfixed. I wouldn't be surprised if a five-year-old started a Marilyn fan club, Marilyn would probably have made a very loving mother. But there's one photograph no child should see, not, at least, until it knows deep in its heart that Marilyn had been a very beautiful woman. It's the photograph of Marilyn's face after her autopsy. It is grey, sagging, puffy. The pathologists' tools have done their work thoroughly. On that once lovely face, they've drawn the indelible conclusion of suicide. And left it at that.

We now know it is more likely to be a case of murder.

Marilyn, in her last days, had become meat for a mincing machine. Its teeth ground away in her nightmares but in fact it was a real machine, close at hand, preparing to swallow her up. It consisted of the Mafia, one of whose bosses she had slept with; the President of the United States and his Attorney-General brother, both of whom she had slept with; and the FBI, the chief of whom no one wanted to sleep with but occasionally had to. Each had taken bits of her heart until there was practically nothing left. Now it is time to get her head. It is got with barbiturates, deliberately given by someone else, not Marilyn, according to a report. Now it is time to get her ass, that sweet winking ass that delighted so many men. This is going to be its last degradation.

According to the report, to ensure that Marilyn died, a contra-indicated drug had to be administered. The clash of the two drugs in her system—the first was pentobarbital—was bound to kill her. But to ensure that no trace of the drug remained in her intestines, it had to be given another way—up the rectum. So they shoved a suppository of that drug into her. She had, so far, been unconscious. And slowly, as the night passed, she would die.

If this is too sordid to believe, one doesn't have to believe it. I only half-believe it myself. Perhaps, as some people say, the only death left to invent is to prove that Robert Kennedy wasn't murdered but committed suicide. But if we invent the death of our stars it's because we invent the lives too. I didn't invent the role I played on that stage in London. I did my manly bit of woman-lifting on it and it went to my head. Now I have one more woman I have to sweep off her feet, one last bit of lifting to do—the corpse of Cordelia.

It's extraordinary to learn that Marilyn played Cordelia in a studio production for the Strasbergs, her drama coaches. To the desperate end, Lear cannot believe that Cordelia is dead, though, in his heart of hearts, he knows she is. That's what many of us feel about Marilyn too. We carry her in our arms as

Lear does Cordelia and howl at the universe. Justice wasn't done! There is no Justice! If she was murdered, we may believe that some sort of justice may still be done if her murderers are found, but I doubt it. Lear killed the man who killed his daughter. It hardly matters if we kill the men who killed Marilyn—daughter to some, mother to others, bitch goddess to millions. I can never think of her as a goddess, bitch or of any other kind. 'Look at that face,' Laurence Olivier is supposed to have said of her on the sets of *The Prince and the Showgirl*. 'She could be five years old!' A baby girl, not a goddess. And everyone's baby's gone.

'Words are far from dead'

MEDIA

THE JOYS OF XEROX

A sheaf of Xeroxes sent by poet Darius Cooper from San Diego, California, reminds me that it's so easy to lose touch. Writers stop writing to one another or emigrate and you suddenly realise that it's ten years since you last heard from X or twenty since you got news of Y. One of the Xeroxes I was sent was of the cover of a special issue of *The Massachusetts Review* which concentrated on South Asian expatriate writing and art. It listed a few writers I knew and many I didn't know. My heart leapt. It was good to learn that Indian writing was alive and well wherever the writers had settled. But where have some of them settled? I've really lost touch.

Lawrence Bantleman, for instance. *Graffiti*, his first book of poems, published in 1962 when he was nineteen (by P. Lal, Writers Workshop), signalled the arrival of a subtle new talent and was instantly noticed. Moving from Calcutta, where he was based, to New Delhi, he edited the literary section of the journal *The Century*, published three more books of poems and then vanished into Canada. Vanished, I say, though we did keep up a fitful correspondence before he stopped it altogether. From the Writers Workshop catalogue I notice that Lal has also published one of his plays, *The Award* (1974). But even if I were to get in touch with him through Lal, the nature of his journey has been such that it has taken him very far away and I'm afraid we may have little in common now.

Is that important? No. What's important is to realise that beneath the tip of visible writers is the mass of invisible ones. Some of them deserve to be read, or re-read as the case may be. I'm sure Bantleman is one such writer. As is Victor Anant whose novel *The Revolving Man*, published in London in the 1950s, took on the issue of racism when most of us were being naïve about it. Whatever became of Anant, you may ask. But if there's ever going to be a detailed map of Indian writing after Independence, he must feature on it.

Closer home is Kewlian Sio and I'm glad to say that I do know where he is though we hardly meet. His stories, published in the quarterly *Quest* immediately attracted attention and his first collection *A Small World*, singled him out as a warm, sympathetic and sensitive storyteller. Sio continues to write stories and poems unnoticed as, I believe, he would prefer to be, but there's another kind of invisibility he wouldn't have wished on himself. If we haven't read his first collection or his latest, *Dragons* (both published by Lal), it's not out of his choice or ours. Those authors who don't disappear via immigration like Sio, our book trade makes disappear via poor distribution. I'm in no position to single out Lal for this state of affairs though it's quite fashionable to do so. As a publisher, I find I've had to confine the sales of books I've published largely to Bombay. To get the situation to change I'd require resources of imagination and cunning which I regret I lack at the moment (they'll come back, they'll come back). There's a whole attitude to books and writers that needs changing; publishers are only part of that attitude.

The change could begin in a small way by using the humble Xerox. Nissim Ezekiel used to cyclostyle his new poems and pass them around among friends before they were collected in a book. When the books went out of print, as they all did, one by one, he had to Xerox them and pass copies around. I believe a Xeroxing programme would resurrect many long-buried, forgotten books. If nothing else, it would help younger writers get a more detailed picture of the literary terrain than the one that exists now, dominated as it is by only the canonical writers. Not that they're much better off. All Ezekiel's poems except his most recent ones, are available in *Collected*

Poems (Oxford University Press), but where would you go if you wanted to pick up A. K. Ramanujan's *Relations*? Or *Comrade Kirillov* by Raja Rao? Don't come to me though I have copies of both. But if you do, I'll ask you to get them Xeroxed.

Start your own home publishing programme by Xeroxing a favourite book of yours which is out of print and which you'd like others to read. Sell it at cost to a friend, at a profit to those who aren't friends and at twice the price to an enemy. If you're averse to such practices, get the book Xeroxed anyway and exchange the Xerox for a Xerox of some other out-of-print book you covet but which doesn't belong to you. Of course if you covet all the volumes of the fifteenth edition of the *Encyclopaedia Britannica* and have only an early Kahlil Gibran to offer in exchange, the deal may not work. But I'm serious. Good books have to be kept in print and Xeroxing them is one way of doing it.

THE NEW INDIA, THE NEW MEDIA AND LITERATURE

I'm grateful to the PEN All-India Centre for giving me the opportunity to speak on a subject which has troubled me for some time. How much time it is difficult to say, but it seems to me that while critical discussions on the quality of our media or the quality of our literature have been going on for a very long time, little has been said about their relationship, both during the crucial colonial period when it was formed and now, when the relationship—like virtually everything else—seems to be in a mess. I believe something good can come out of the mess. Otherwise there'd be no good reason for giving this talk. I'd merely be adding my voice to the general chorus of doom which, like the pandemonium of our traffic and the shrill irregularities of our telephones, has become a regular feature of our lives. We have heard it too often and it has gone on for too long. 'No one reads books any more'; 'Cinema has produced greater art than literature—and in a shorter time'; 'Words have lost their meaning—in fact, they're dead' are some of the lines of the chorus. It would seem that in their battle for our attention, even before the conflicting claims of our media and our literature have been clearly heard, literature has conceded defeat.

And yet—to begin with the press—our editors have never shown so much interest in writers and writing as they seem to be doing now. Who would have thought, even five years ago, that an upmarket glossy like *Gentleman* would risk carrying a nineteen-page literary section every month? Or than an afternoon paper like *Mid-Day* would have two pages of reviews and interviews with writers every week? Or that a popular Bombay tabloid (*The Daily*) would run an apparently inexhaustible series on Indian writers? (It has now dealt with more than thirty.) Or that another upmarket glossy (*Bombay*), not known for its literary interests, would be so generous as to pay writers of fiction Rs 2,000 for a 2,000-word story?

And who would have thought, ten years ago, that journalism would become such an attractive profession for so many young people? That it would make them write imaginatively and that, unlike a previous generation of journalists, they wouldn't consider the writing of poetry, novels or plays a frivolous distraction? I know for a fact that a few have completed manuscripts of their own and the literary ambitions of others aren't scoffed at.

Other media have been concerned with literature too. There have been several documentary films on our writers and while records of poetry aren't in sight, poets' voices have been taped and shelved—for posthumous airing, perhaps, or other deathly occasions like the presentation of awards to those whose books have been out of print for several years. A library of video cassettes of poets reading their own work is being built up at Vagartha, Bharat Bhavan, Bhopal. (The films are being made by Dilip Chitre.) All would seem to be well. Are there any real grounds for anxiety?

There are, but some of the anxiety may be due to an ongoing crisis—very much a twentieth-century one—which has nothing to do with the current state of our literature. It has rather to do with the spread of mass culture and the difficulty of living with it. It's easy to point to its most debased elements and say that's all there is to it. Much more difficult is the task of reconciling our belief in the freedom of choice with our objection to what most people decide to choose. In terms of television programmes, it could justifiably be argued that there's very little to choose from. But it's possible to fight for and get better programmes. This has certainly happened in many of the countries which have had television longer than us. There too, especially in England, initial objections to television—like it would lead to the death of conversation, interfere with children's reading, etc.—have grown more controversial. It's just that with the growth of responsibly produced, informative and entertaining programmes, television has developed a stronger validity and the objections are being dealt with in a new context.

This kind of qualitative development, by no means a linear one, is a characteristic of the newer mass media, and if we oppose this development, we must be clear whether we believe that the media are in themselves pernicious, or whether, despite our democratic beliefs, we don't like to see them grow too fast and on too wide a scale. Why, for example, does the unprecedented video boom make us uneasy? Is it because it happened too fast? Do we really feel it has a harmful effect on children? In the midst of change, we might be unable to find the answers. But the change is evident and we might study the evidence with profit.

In a recent article, 'Looking Sideways' in *Express Magazine*, 29 July 1984, the critic Meenakshi Mukherjee sees an unfortunate change in our attitude towards literature. She sees a fresh neglect of local writing, whether written in the Indian languages or in English. The media are obsessed with prize-winning books and what foreign critics have to say about them. The rest are given a sideways look.

Well, any Indian who wins an international award is news and there'd be something wrong if our media ignored it. But Mukherjee is quite right. Betting on the international prize winner has become a national obsession. No one gave us a prize for organising the Asiad—we ourselves did, but we did win the World Cup in cricket. Rushdie did win the Booker award and Chandrasekhar did get the Nobel. All this is news and cause for celebration. But should it affect us at all if, say, no Indian writer got the Nobel before the century was out? Should anyone be made to feel that because of that fact, apart from Tagore, we've had a century of mediocre writers?

We've been dependent on praise from abroad for so long and so much has been written about that dependence, that there might seem to be no good reason for bringing up the subject again. My reason for doing so is that in the context of the new India, getting an international award itself has acquired a new meaning. Not for the person who gets the award—the cake is getting bigger, richer, and someone has to get a piece of it—but for the new elite, the buyers of international goods, the readers of the very magazines referred to earlier—the magazines themselves encouraging an international lifestyle and form of consumerism that goes with international status. You don't have to read between the lines. The message to the reader is loud and clear. If your status is to be judged by your Toyota, your Sony VCR and the designer clothes your children wear, the status of our intelligentsia is to be judged by the number of Nobels, Bookers, Magsaysays and so on that they may win.

It would be a great mistake to think that this equation of status with international goods and prizes and the new consumerist mentality is restricted to the thin upper crust of the Westernised urban elite. If that was the case ten years ago, it certainly isn't so now. In a recent article ('Morality and the new elite') in *The Times of India*, Praful Bidwai defines the new ethical principle our elite live by as 'acquisitive individualistic hedonism'. It has some of the features mentioned before, and he estimates that it affects a fifth of our population—about 100 to 150 million people—or about as many as live in a medium-sized West European country. This elite he characterized as consisting of 'industrialists, urban and rural businessmen, professionals, traders, agency men, rich and middle farmers, rural entrepreneurs and sections of the self-employed intermediate classes'. More importantly, Bidwai brings out the peculiarly Indian features in the development of this new hedonism which, according to him, make it unique. He argues that the Indian elite is marked by a much higher level of consumption than was its Western counterpart and that this has led to a callous indifference to problems of poverty and an unprecedented moral chaos. Also, acquisitive hedonism has grown too fast, with little to check it, quite unlike the situation in Western countries during their early capitalist stage.

What the checks were isn't strictly relevant to my subject, but it requires no great imagination to see that with the absence of checks, a lack of authoritative alternatives to our press, our television and our cinema, our literary culture reflects some of the worst features of our society. As I see it, it's a society characterized by mindless chauvinism, obscurantism, and critical chaos. And its chief casualty, as I shall show later, is the Indian language writer.

Chauvinism, obscurantism and chaos are subjects which the press has examined with some authority and insight, but it has hardly been concerned with their literary manifestations, it has scarcely been interested in following literary movements, and it has never regarded the promotion of sound literary values as one of its responsibilities.

This peculiar neglect of literature, which often goes with an open hostility to it, has been such a consistent feature of our press and has gone on for such a long time that I'm surprised no detailed study of the phenomenon exists. If it did, it might have thrown light on the peculiarly modernising role of the writer in a traditional society like India, helped us see why the press, by and large, has opposed such a modernizing, and traced the conflict to its historical roots.

When the American architect Frank Lloyd Wright dismissed his fellow architect Le Corbusier as 'a journalist', he was expressing an artist's derision, familiar to a great many artists in the West, and which Western journalists have learned to react to in kind. Wright's snobbery may have been echoed by some artists here, and the early days of Fleet Street too—when writers were badly exploited by their journalist editors—have their Indian parallels, but the rift between the press and the writer here was primarily caused by very different, very unique factors.

I see a few vaguely, but two stand out. First, the growth of a national English press in India took place in the absence of a national English literature. In virtually every sense, the national press in that language preceded a national literature—a feature we may share with other countries which have been colonized, but the reverse of which is true of the colonising country. (The relationship between the regional press and regional literatures may provide a fascinating contrast, but it's too complicated a subject to go into here.) In other words, the national English press in India came into being quite independently of its national English literature. Right from the start it proved it could do without literature. Its object was news and political views. That policy has persisted to this day.

The second factor that led it to neglect literature, or at least take a strongly biased view of it, was, to my mind, the growth of nationalism. This period in our history coincided with a number of modernist movements in all fields of art in the Western European countries and England. By virtue of their association with these countries, all modernist ideas came to be seen as the decadent products of oppressing imperialist nations. As the struggle for freedom intensified here, the freedom Western artists won for themselves through bold, innovative, experimentalist approaches to their art were seen as enslaving irrelevances for our own. In terms of literature, the nature of the freedom struggle itself, with its Gandhian emphasis on non-violence, pastoralism, and highly pietistic attitudes to human relationships, demanded writing that was anything but modernist. The press became a leader of the opposition and came down heavily on writing which didn't promote the national cause. It chose not to understand such writing because it believed there was nothing to understand in it. In fact, it became thoroughly philistine. Its prejudices have lasted to this day.

I began by saying that there is a new breed of magazines and newspapers which is less philistine, but which, with its emphasis on international status and glittering prizes, is really directed to the new elite. If the earlier, more philistine elite jumped at the word surrealism as though it had been informed of a vile, evil-smelling species of rat, the new elite will jump at the word intellectual, and for more or less the same reason. What is common to the two elites is that they're profoundly anti-intellectual.

Both are opposed to adventures of the mind, both are against innovation and daring in the world of ideas. If innovation and daring are essential to a thriving literary culture, we are still very far from having one. On the contrary, there are signs that our literary thinking is getting more and more bogged down in traditionalist and revivalist values. Far from building on our Western heritage of ideas, we seem anxious to get rid of them once and for all, even as we acquire more and more of the West's material products. The result may well be a literary intelligentsia totally divorced from the reality of modern India. Those of us who are obsessed with our glorious literary past are unlikely to have anything to say about our arms build-up, our nuclear programme or the technocrats who may one day rule us. Nothing would suit the government better than writers who live in the past.

Earlier, I mentioned the lack of authoritative alternatives to our media and now, when I have to define those alternatives which are not authoritative, at least not yet, I confess they are hard to find. One of the reasons is that the most positive developments against the values of our new elite are happening in no one place. If our academic institutions and universities were alternatives to much of the crude thinking that went on in our business houses and political institutions even ten years ago, I'm afraid that is no longer the case now. For a variety of reasons, the authority of our universities has been seriously eroded.

Another reason the alternatives are hard to spot is that the people who represent them are often involved in the new media themselves. It's an observable fact that many of those who belonged to the radical Left ten years ago now work for the very newspapers and magazines they despised. While their objections to the bourgeois press may continue in theory, in practice they have all but broken down. But I'm not primarily thinking of that phenomenon. I'm thinking of the positive uses independent, socially concerned individuals and groups are putting the new media to. What's exciting about this development in the last few years is that dissent isn't expressed through the press alone. The audio-visual narrative, once the exclusive province of advertising, has been seriously used to cover issues of housing, communal riots and dowry deaths. Young filmmakers are seriously involved in making documentaries on important social issues. Most hearteningly, independent groups of video filmmakers have spring up recently, engaged in the same task. It isn't likely that they will change the viewing habits of our elite and the kind of fodder they demand. But it's possible that an alternative consciousness will spread among those who both need an alternative and see it of great importance to establish one.

That, at least, is the hope, and I think it's important that Indian writers share that hope and support those individuals and groups who haven't broken away from cinema, television and video as from an alien triple-headed monster, but who see them as vitally important in helping to spread an alternative consciousness of ourselves and the world to the distorted one so prevalent today.

The distortions come from the top and, as I indicated earlier, in the field of literature they have affected Indian language writers badly. The obsession with international recognition and status has bred its opposite, an obsession to be recognised only by one's peer group, one's own caste or one's own region. Because his books aren't available in an international language; because, unlike the Indian painter or Indian musician, his work has to be translated into a language like English in order to reach an international audience, out goes the value of English translations, out go Western democratic values themselves. In come the old ones of caste, hierarchical divisions and our glorious literary heritage. That, as far as I understand, is what nativism amounts to, a subject to which the journal *New Quest* (May-June 1984) devotes a whole issue ('The concept of Nativism', 'Nativism in Modern Kannada Fiction', 'Nativism in Modern Marathi Drama' and so on). In it, the novelist Bhalchandra Nemade, a powerful and influential force in Marathi writing today, defines Nativism in Hindu revivalist terms and says that 'it tends to be lyrical rather than rational, traditional rather than modernist, and has past rather than future connotations'. That he finds very positive.

Of interest also is the following passage:

> A most serious trend ... is the way some of our writers strive to become 'national' and even 'international' by getting their work translated into English. This has become a spurious means of building literary reputations. It is time we realized

the fact that beyond our own 'language groups' all that we do smacks of mediocrity. Like the sadhus camping on the Ram Leela ground in Delhi in G. V. Desani's *All About H. Haterr* (sic), our writers and politicians seem to carry the name boards: 'All-India Sadhu' and 'International Sadhu' and so on. Likewise, Chairman Mao Tse Tung's remark in 1955 that Jawaharlal Nehru does not seem to know that India is a part of Asia and not of the West was a plea for nativism in the post-colonial Asian countries. We have fostered a kind of internationalism which is profitable only to the West. It is a kind of internationalism which recognizes a Kissinger, a Walesa or a Golding, but not Gandhi and Premchand and Karanth.

Perhaps Nativism's distrust of the rational prevents its proponents from thinking rationally. Nemade would like the West to recognise Premchand and Karanth but wouldn't like their works to be translated into English. (Nor, presumably into Chinese or Japanese, both very far from the writers' 'language group' and to which, he feels, their work should forever be confined).

Earlier in the article, he decries a society's isolationist tendencies which may develop into racist arrogance and self-centredness. He gives Ancient Greece and Egypt as examples of such societies, doomed, because of their isolationism, to extinction. I fear the qualities of racist arrogance, self-centredness and isolationism are very much there in Nemade's concept of Nativism. If they don't doom the country to extinction, they may well doom the growth of a vital, imaginative and critical literature. Words are far from dead. In the best of literature they free imprisoned visions and make us see whole societies and situations afresh. The state of our own society may never have seemed so awful as it does now.

Let it not be said in the future that by failing to find alternatives to the mindless internationalism of our new elite and the regressive parochialism of our writers, we allowed it to become too awful for words.

RADIO DAYS

One of the headlines in *The Times of India* in front of me reads, 'Hams hand out succour in times of trouble in sea and on land'. I read it again, 'Hams hand out . . .' I have visions of dozens of pink hams bobbing up and down in the sea, stretching out helping hands to those in distress. Did a sub have one too many last night? Did he see pink elephants too? Beginning to read the story I discover it's about radio hams—those amateur radio operators who have antennae permanently attached to their heads like creatures from outer space and who never leave their wireless sets alone for a minute. The story is about the public service they do; they are sometimes the first to pick up SOS messages and arrange for help. There's also a private side to their passion, the conversations they have with one another, which the story doesn't touch. Hams are like Freemasons or Rosicrucians, members of an exclusive club; each has its own language and secret code of conduct. Sometimes I wish I belonged to that club though the thought of being called a ham ever after isn't exactly appealing. Radio has entertained and comforted me perhaps more than any other medium and I wish I could do it justice.

So what glued our ears to our sets in the 1950s? Not just the gum of the *Binaca Hit Parade*, but three serials—*Leslie Charteris' The Saint*, *Superman* and *Dan Dare*. I don't remember much about *The Saint*, but every episode of *Superman* swept in on a wave of music—Wagner's 'Ride of the Valkyries'. And in case we were likely to forget, every episode of *Dan Dare* was ushered in with this portentous trumpet blast: 'The makers of Horlicks present *Dan Dare*, pilot of the future'. The serials didn't do much for Wagner or Horlicks, at least in our household, but my consumption of comics soared.

The stories we read in the comics and the ones we heard on the radio weren't complementary but each fed the other until our obsession with our heroes was fuelled to fever pitch.

Missing an episode plunged us into gloom. Not being able to hear one, because of static, was worse. And it was a brand-new Philips set, lovingly encased in teak by Manilal, my mother's carpenter, that paid the price for such interference first.

Not being able to hear a word of a *Superman* episode because of static, I gave its glass panel a shove. It split neatly in two. Both mother and carpenter were speechless. At that unfortunate moment, *Superman* came to life with a tremendous roar. The volume was on full. The noise seemed to unlock Manilal's, mother's and, by now, my father's tongues simultaneously. It was Babel, it was hell. Once again, I couldn't make out a word that was said or perhaps I've chosen to forget each and every one of them.

In London, I discovered the scope of the radio play. Professional actors used their voices over a wide and marvellous range, while sound effects, not just the odd seagull crying, freed the imagination to build up its own landscapes, seascapes and interiors. The BBC actively encouraged the writing of radio plays—it still does—and it was for the BBC that Samuel Beckett wrote one of his finest, *All That Fall*. It's a favourite of mine and I've probably read its script more often than any other single text.

It has a large—physically large—character called Mrs Rooney, who talks to herself and to those who chance upon her on a lonely Irish road, along which she labours on her way to pick up her blind husband who is due to arrive by train at the local station. In the short space of about forty minutes, the script covers whole areas of life, death, violence and loneliness which would normally be the province of full-length plays or novels. It's the perfect radio play.

In fact, I doubt if it could ever be transferred to the stage without losing a great deal of its mood and atmosphere. For example, at one stage in the play, a rattletrap of a car comes chugging down the road towards Mrs Rooney and stops by her. Mrs Rooney is lifted into the car with great difficulty. Car proceeds on its journey and runs over a hen. Mrs Rooney's own squawks and ruminations on life—'this dust will not settle in our time'—punctuate the journey, which, in Mrs Rooney's mind at least is a very long, very painful, very dusty one. I can't see that state of mind, that journey, being presented on stage.

All India Radio has also gone a long, dusty way but with neither oasis nor end of journey in sight. It's quite simply lost in a desert of our own making. Shortly after Independence, we had the facilities to grow into a nation for which radio would be the most useful and entertaining means of communication. Even now we are reminded from time to time that there are more transistor radios per person in India than TV sets. Some villages have none of the latter at all. But we botched it. For many of us, radio as a medium has simply gone off the air. Is it too much to hope that there will soon be a daring and imaginative policy by which we can tune into it again, knobs and all? Or should we spend the rest of our days as hams, picking up distress calls from sea and land, and from those who realise that their best radio days are gone?

DEATH OF A JOURNALIST

A body lying face down, the thick soles of the boots, a bloodied notebook . . . they were the first images we saw.

We were later told that the body found somewhere in East Timor was that of thirty-year-old Dutch journalist Sander Thoenes. Someone who knew him wondered why he had gone to the area where he'd been found, an area known to be dangerous. From what he knew of the journalist, the person felt his going to such a place was 'out of character.' He conjectured that Thoenes might have been on the trail of an important story.

Thoenes hadn't died of a heart attack or some other natural cause. The marks on his body and the bloodied notebook indicated that he's been killed.

We weren't shown the bodies of those who were killed when NATO bombed a television station in Belgrade. The victims were members of the staff, linked, through their work, to journalism. (I think one of them was a newscaster). Nor were we shown the bodies of the Chinese journalists who were killed when NATO accidentally bombed the Chinese embassy, again in Belgrade. But the anger and sorrow I felt on seeing Thoenes' mutilated body matched what I felt when I heard of the earlier deaths. I know other journalists experienced the same feeling on the three occasions I've mentioned, not just in this country but in whichever country they got the news.

On such occasions it doesn't matter whether the journalist killed belongs to one's own camp, to a camp one sympathises with, or even to the enemy camp. The death of someone in one's own profession, whatever side he or she has been on, is felt to be the death of 'one of us.'

There have been, are and will be, vermin journalists: spies responsible for sending other journalists to their deaths (macabre dispatches—some, in all probability, yet to come to light), defamers posing as seekers of truth; personal-score settlers; cheque-book scum, their egos as inflated as the sums they're paid and the stories they tell; editors whose lifestyles are paid for by amounts meant for their staff and contributors . . . in short, those who defile journalism by their presence in the profession, a profession built on the trust of readers who expect, from those who practice it, nothing less than honesty.

I will also admit that I have less than brotherly feelings towards journalists of a kind less monstrous than those I've just mentioned but who are monstrous enough—apathetic subs, production teams which ritually junk the visual matter sent to them (photographs, paintings etc. some of them rare) once they're through with the matter, and journalists who head departments without having a head of their own. Their influence in an office can be deadly.

All the same, professions make for ties few outside the professions can understand. Should some of the monsters or mini-monsters I've mentioned be killed in the line of duty, I'd feel bad, just as other journalists would. But would I feel bad if they'd been killed after abandoning that line of duty at mortal or great cost to others while still professing to be journalists? I hope not. It's also a journalist's duty not to let the bonds of a profession overpower his or her decisions, the rational taking of sides. It's part of one's duty to stop feeling that a profession makes him or her a member of a club that mustn't be attacked or that we are all members of the same club even when some of the club has become a pigsty.

Among the journalists who've been killed, whether by accident or by design in their line of duty, I continue to think of Dhiren Bhagat, Alan Twigg, Sanjoy Ghose, the cartoonist Irfan and now Sander Thoenes. If something similar happens to journalists who've been irrevocably corrupted, I'll try not to think about them. The profession of journalism has to do with lines made not only of words, with not only by-lines. It also has to do with lines of duty, lines of fire and the lines we ourselves have to draw between the good, the bad, and the damned amongst ourselves.

THE FOLDS OF AN ORIGAMI LOTUS

This is being written in the open, on a page in a notebook. I'm using a pencil to write it. You'll read it on another page, hopefully in the form it finally takes. Unless a virus intercepts what I've written and makes it say whatever it wants it to say.

On such occasions, readers who complain that what I write makes little sense to them will find that what I've written makes no sense at all. On such occasions, it doesn't make sense even to me. That's bad news, especially if you believe, as I do, that writing is an attempt to make sense of a world which, without the writing and our trying to read it, makes very little sense in the first place.

But is it art? I hear this again and again. Is journalism art? This from writers who should know better.

No journalist admits to trying to create a work of art when he's working on his copy, but the copy can turn out to be a work of art all the same. Several people consider John Hersey's long report on Hiroshima to be a work of art, and I agree.

Also, when I find myself going back to the work of journalists I'm more familiar with—Sham Lal, Dom Moraes, Dhiren Bhagat, Sudhir Sonalkar, Ivan Fera and P. Sainath, to mention just six—it's not because of the information they provide me in the first place (a journalist's primary objective), nor because of their views which I may disagree with, but because of their art.

This is also true of the journalistic work of those who don't see themselves primarily as journalists. Among them are Claude Alvares, Hartman de Souza and Cyrus Mistry. What draws me to what I consider the best of their journalism is its art.

This is heresy to both journalists and artists. The younger journalists have fewer problems with the world 'art' than older journalists do. Many in the profession still consider art to be the province of those who waste a lot of time playing around with words and forms when a straight jab to the chin, written as one, does the job better.

Worse still, art, in the eyes of such journalists, is the province of the undisciplined, the queer and the demented—categories strictly excluded from the province of journalism, one presumes.

Any good boxer should be able to tell an art-hating journalist that an effective straight jab is acquired, it doesn't come naturally, and even when it does, has been worked on. When good, very good, it's art.

A teacher of origami could tell him the same thing about a lotus. It's all in the folds, practice, getting them right.

A book tells me that origami is treated as an art in Japan and that 'the simple, folded object is considered to be superior to that which is cut or glued'. So, 'out of respect for the tree spirit that gave its life to make the paper' you make a work of art. It's the paper you write on, the paper you read. Journalism is like poetry, like origami, whether you like it or not. It's got art. Some of my writer friends refuse to see that.

I could have used the page I'm writing on to make a stork, a swan or a lotus. It would have pleased both journalist and artist camps. They wouldn't have felt obliged to read what I've written. But I chose to write. I'm bad at origami, a little better at writing (I hope). In one sense they're one and the same. Without cutting the paper I think I'm making a lotus. But it could be I've got the folds wrong and created a frog.

'I'm getting on in English.'

LANGUAGE

RAINBOW OF LANGUAGES

Petrol burns. It also leaves colourful patches on the streets. The taxi driver I'm talking to right now complains that there are colourful patches under his car. I agree but I want to move on. He too agrees and moves on.

On the way to my destination he apologises for not having stopped for me. I'd had to run a few steps to tell him 'Stop! Stop!' He calls me 'Chacha'. In the space of a few minutes, driving with assurance, he goes through a rainbow of languages. Urdu, Gujarati, Marathi, I'm his for the asking.

But he doesn't ask. He doesn't ask me where I am from, not expecting my knee-jerk reply, 'From where you picked me up.' That usually provokes another knee-jerk, 'But what is your native place?'

When I answer the drivers who ask, they tend to be doubtful. One aggressively said I was lying, insisting that I had to be a foreigner. It led to a row.

But the driver this time, aglow in his rainbow of languages, is different: I discover I've left my wallet at home. When I tell him that, he shifts gear into the further reaches of the spectrum. Tamil, then Konkani and English. 'What difference does it make, sir?' he asks. 'You can pay me any time.'

I test him. Did he know my name? He didn't. Then how did he trust me? 'Kabhi milenge,' he says. We'll meet some time.

I get him to double back to where I live, pick up my wallet, and pay him off at my destination. I wonder, 'Who was it who spoke that rainbow of languages?'

The answer, I think, lies in the past, in the late 1930s or early 1940s. With the English-language-empire on its way out, a patchwork of languages, sometimes well spoken, sometimes not, rainbowed the streets with its petrol.

Few people seem to understand it doesn't take a generation to lose or win a language. It can take anything between a couple of days to a couple of years. A Hindi-speaking child, pushed into a Mandarin-speaking culture at the age of three, will soon talk Mandarin, not Hindi. Satellite television presents us, in the form of British soaps, young Asians who don't 'talk Asian'.

I don't ask the taxi driver where he is from but I think he's a Tamilian who has been living in Bombay for a long time. How long? I'd say about forty years. Perhaps he was born in Bombay. In which case, it's likely that he can speak Tamil but not read it. In which case, even if he can read it, he has little or no access to his favourite writers.

One of the tragedies of intercity immigration in India is that, by and large, when you leave your 'native place' behind, you leave your 'native literature' behind. Avid readers of Marathi writing, whether timepass or not, become pale ghosts of themselves in Calcutta and New Delhi, if posted in those cities for even a couple of years: I know post-graduate students in Bombay who, away from Karnataka for more than two years, have told me almost in tears that they have lost access to writing in their 'native language'.

The mandals for various regional groups in the city aren't usually concerned with such problems. They are places for social chit-chat, social functions, the occasional game of carom.

'What do you read?' I ask my taxi driver hesitantly. 'What is your native language?'

'I am Indian, sir,' he says. 'I speak all Indian languages since I meet all Indian people. Who has time for reading, sir? I speak, I don't read.'

I pay him off, another illusion gone. His eyes shine like marbles. He is on some sort of drug.

'Which country you are from?' he asks.

GETTING ON IN ENGLISH

Mahesh Elkunchwar, known for his Marathi plays and their Hindi translations, has had a play of his translated into English. Called *Atmakatha* in Marathi, it was recently performed in Delhi under the title *Autobiography*. A report in the literary section of *The Hindu* doesn't say how the audience reacted to the play but Elkunchwar's own reaction to it is refreshingly open.

'We have to reassess our meaning of the phrase English theatre,' he is reported to have said. 'Why are Indians against English theatre in India? Any theatre that is good theatre is valid regardless of the language. English is an Indian language and if good work is being done in the language it should be appreciated.'

The implications of English being an Indian language could be debated for hours. Some Hindi writers who are particularly dismissive of work being done in English in this country couldn't have liked Elkunchwar's remark one bit, but Elkunchwar has never been afraid of speaking his mind and what he said about English is one more example of this.

I myself hold no special brief for writing in English. The writing's good, bad or indifferent and that's all there is to it. It perpetually falls into the trap of not meeting the standards it sets for itself and there's still a lot of bad work being published. But Elkunchwar's remarks reflect a trend, a realisation that there can be a fruitful crossing over from Indian-language territory into the territory of writing in English. Other writers have grasped this too. Vilas Sarang and Damodar Prabhu, both predominantly Marathi writers, are writing their latest novels in English.

I don't really know how important a sign of the times changing the language of one's creative work is. It may not be very important. It's just that it comes naturally to some of us. Sometimes we speak two or three languages in the day and probably more than half-understand one or two more. But to write in a language different from the one you're used to writing in is a different matter altogether. My Gujarati comes fairly naturally to me but I would have to make a huge effort to write, say, a play in it now. For the moment I'm getting on in English.

Getting on in English was the title of a standard textbook for language classes at an intermediary level at the International Language Centre in London where I taught for almost five years. It was written by John Haycraft who was head of the centre and it was basically about an Englishman who was trying to get people interested in an invention of his—an inflatable umbrella. Classes consisted of people from Europe. They ranged from waiters and au pair girls to young executives trying to smarten up their English to students from the Middle East.

No South Asians took English-language classes though it was clear that many in London could afford them and could do with them. Unlike other Asians, Europeans and Africans who have had to learn English as a foreign language, we have never felt we had to. We being the elite (as Elkunchwar says, 'English is an Indian language') who can speak and write it reasonably fluently. I believe this has been a disastrous assumption.

How disastrous I was to learn for myself when, on returning from London in 1970, I devised a course similar to Haycraft's for first-year college students whose English was poor and for a small school in Colaba whose students mostly came from working-class families. Many school and college teachers felt such courses were necessary not only to build up the confidence of 'vernacular' students as they are still called, but more importantly to help them pass their English exams, which a large number of them regularly failed. The students were in a tragic situation, entirely the result of a skewed educational system and our complacent attitude to English. I think my courses helped. But given the moribund system, no place could be found for them on a regular basis. Which made them next to worthless.

The other day, the ex-principal of the school, visiting a neighbour, dropped in to see me. 'Yes, yes, the courses had definitely helped,' he said, his eyes lighting up. 'But who cares for such things anymore?'

Yes, I'm getting on in English. Back to class one, lesson one.

BEING THERE: ASPECTS OF AN INDIAN CRISIS

One never knows when the blow may fall, says Graham Greene's sad narrator in *The Third Man* and of course he is right. Since History is full of nasty surprises, the writer, like everyone else, will do no more than fall flat on his face several times in his life if he's lucky, or get censored or killed if he's not.

A historical date makes its mark suddenly, a hole in a once-clean target, and stays with us till we die. 15 August 1947 is one such date in India. So also is 25 June 1975, when the Emergency was declared.

Suddenness is History's trapdoor, through which we fall— armchair critics along with our armchairs, bombed civilians, those dispossessed of their homelands, those sifting through garbage for food, those dragged out of their homes at midnight, our cups, saucers, pets, everything through that same trapdoor— to certain oblivion—unless there is someone who doesn't flinch from seeing what happened and sets it down.

The resilience of individual writers has helped them survive the worst shocks of history, and there's nothing so bad about the situation in India that will silence its writers permanently. But if Indians who write in English don't normally consider it important to produce novels of social history or write poetry which fully confronts the social and political realities of their time, despite their real admiration for such work from other countries, there must be a reason—perhaps several reasons—and I think it's important to examine them. Some of us, certainly, are going through a crisis which is making us question the validity of our work and our usefulness as agents of social change. Now, more than ever before, we are unsure of ourselves as witnesses. Far from helping to change the course of history, we find we are its bullied victims. It's as though History is telling the writer, as the Englishman in Victor Anant's novel *The Revolving Man* tells the protagonist, 'Spin, you Hindu bastard. Spin!' And the bastard goes on spinning.

The expectation the Indian writer has had of himself since Independence has been the expectation of writers in some Commonwealth countries, not all, and some of the phrases I use, like 'agent of social change', may sound absurdly inappropriate to, say, an Australian or Canadian writer. But I believe that no Indian writer can avoid taking a moral stand on the many social evils in his country, especially when, in view of the obvious poverty and distress there, it's a social privilege to be able to write, or travel abroad and pontificate, as I am doing.

So, when I speak of the crisis some Indian writers are going through, I imply that it's as much a moral crisis as an artistic one. It is intimately connected with what we thought we would write shortly after Independence—as also with our readers' expectations of what we should write—and what we find ourselves writing or not writing now. So the writers I have in mind are those who have experienced the two disturbances of jailbreak and re-imprisonment: the exhilaration of being free to write as we chose, of being able to overturn British norms of language and literature (even decency) and the oppression, forty years later, of finding ourselves strapped, rather like forks choked with spaghetti. Our ends may appear to be dipped in blood—the prescribed blood of others that is meant to baptize the 'real' writers of this century—but in fact it's the usual ketchup. We just haven't dared enough.

I could have chosen a less cosy simile, but it seems an appropriate one to apply to those of us who have chosen to stay on in 'the soiled and cluttered kitchens of the mind'—to lift a phrase from an old poem of mine—with our gaze turned away from the great public events on the sub-continent—events that are affecting at least as many million lives as the last global war did.

Why do Indian novels and verses have so little to say about those events? Why don't we do more than we have? What's the problem?

The problems of Indians who write in English are boring to themselves and to others and I suspect they've activated many unsuccessfully stifled yawns at ACLALS conferences too. But since the problems, like the English language itself, refuse to go away, we return to them again and again. Indian writers have done so obsessively, and it is characteristic of our approach to our problems that we blame the English language for a lot of them. In fact, our attitude to English is one of the major aspects of the crisis I referred to earlier.

So, in his poem, 'Rough Passage', R. Parthasarathy writes of his 'tongue in English chains' and of speaking 'a tired language'. Meena Alexander speaks of being 'exiled by a dead script' in an eponymous essay; Arvind Krishna Mehrotra, in his essay, 'The Emperor has no Clothes', shows the language to be honeycombed with traps for the unwary writer; Keki Daruwalla sees the language he uses as an exasperating mistress in his poem 'The Mistress'. And English language and literature are subjects of attack in my poem 'Missing Person', in which the colonizer himself joins in the attack, asking his creature to get back to his (own) language.

Getting back to one's language, returning to one's native land, are familiar refrains in colonial and post-colonial writing and every writer haunted by them has had to lay the ghosts in his own way. Speaking for myself, when, in 1970, after many years abroad, I returned to my native land, I had no native language to return to—there are no poets and novelists in the Indian dialect (Parsi Gujarati) I speak, though it is freely used in adapted versions of foreign plays; it's very much a spoken dialect, full of literary potential, but regrettably unexplored. So I've remained an English-language writer, affected by works in English produced in whatever country the language is spoken and written and by works translated into English. Oddly enough, I didn't realize how precarious that made my position until three years ago and it was the Hindi novelist Nirmal Verma who helped me see it.

Having spent many years of his life in Prague, Verma was very much the cosmopolitan author on an extended return ticket until he went back to India in 1968, and in an essay, 'Returning to One's Country' (translated by Meenakshi Mukherjee), he speaks of the anguish of being home and not being home, of being 'a native stranger who has come back—an alien Indian who is suspect everywhere, most so to himself'.

When I met him three years ago he held the Nirala Chair for Literature in Bhopal—a city in India's Hindi-speaking belt—and he offended me a little by saying that I couldn't possibly have any idea of the kind of young Hindi writer who came to him with his work and what his problems were. I replied with some heat that I didn't see why he should be any different from young writers in Bombay and why his problems should be so very different either. Verma came back with great vehemence. 'They are different because they write and talk only in Hindi,' he said. 'They don't know a word of English.'

Since then I've thought a lot about the young writer in Bhopal and am appalled by what he must think of me. Not having access to a vast body of international literature—Hindi being poor in translations from other literature—he can't but resent my privilege. Or he may choose to ignore me, taking the narrow view that the experience of any literature outside Hindi is not worth having. We would have two different views of history and we would not be able to argue which was more falsifying—my Eng Lit view or his. But I hope we'd share at least one thing—an anxiety not to falsify, to witness authentically, to truthsay, because we are aware of what falsified history did in Germany and is doing in Soviet Russia and South Africa. We'd share the hope that the only way to be a responsible writer was to be true to oneself and what one saw; that we were responsible to those who came after us—to bear witness to what the official lie or the censor or Time was always trying to wipe out. If we agreed on that, then we might find our strategies with two languages—whether we were writing poetry or prose—not very different. We might find both our languages—his Hindi, my English—in their currently accepted forms in daily commerce, wholly inadequate to fill out the poetic and fictional worlds of our witnessing. We would then have to chip away at the language, or pummel it, or pare away at its outer shell to get at its kernel and draw out its life-giving essence. We would have to make it new, create new forms with it, make it nourishing.

That this has been the ambition of some novelists writing in England during the last fifteen years, is clear from works like Angus Wilson's *As if By Magic*, Anthony Burgess' *Earthly Powers*, Rushdie's *Midnight's Children* and V. S. Naipaul's *Guerrillas* and *A Bend in the River*, their writers very much historical witnesses.

I'm glad to know that Patrick Swinden in *The English Novel of History and Society, 1940-1980* (Macmillan, 1984) thinks that because of works like these, it's no longer necessary to be defensive about the English novel, as was the fashion in the 1960s, and glad that writers from Commonwealth countries other than England are contributing so much to its importance. However, our Commonwealth brothers don't seem to be in any hurry to get easily assimilated nor do some of their critics want them to be. So Rushdie, in order to stress that he hasn't written an 'English' novel, will link it to oral storytelling in India, while a sympathetic critic, John Thieme, will emphasize its dilatory Scheherazadian element. (I haven't read Amitav Ghosh's *The Circle of Reason*, but he told Mayuri Chawla in an interview in *Society* magazine, that he has based the three parts of his novel on the musical raga.)

Of other Indian novelists, S. C. Harrex has said that Mulk Raj Anand 'has Indianised literary and political models derived from the West, and westernised traditional values'; Vineypalkaur Kirpal has said that both in *Kanthapura* and in *The Serpent and The Rope*, Raja Rao has tried to tell 'a breathless, endless tale in the manner of the *Mahabharata*' and Vijay Mishra says that R. K. Narayan uses the dialectics of maya in *The Guide*.

Yes, we're not too pleased to be fitted into any of Eng Lit's formal categories, and try hard to reject its formative influence.

In an interview with Peter Nazareth, published in 1978, I said that 'if you break away from that structure [of Eng Lit] completely, if you attempt to completely smash this structure of English culture or Eng Lit, a very fundamental personal disintegration takes place too. I have not found the alternatives. I can only suggest that by smashing this structure, you go through a process of terrible disintegration. What follows I'm not sure'.

Nine years after the interview I'm more certain. I'm certain that while 'Missing Person' is about such a disintegration, my own personal disintegration has neither been very fundamental nor terrible. I have not changed. And 'Change' was the cry we rallied around at Independence. Change was what we thought would come over us when we overthrew the British norms of language and literature I spoke about earlier. But they have proved tougher than we thought; some of us have become the new colonials, and our expectation of ourselves has been false.

I hope it's clear to you now that the crisis I've been attempting to describe all along is a crisis of identity. We have so far touched on two causes for it and they have both to do with distrust. I mentioned Nirmal Verma's distrust of himself as an observer when he returned to India, but it's a familiar enough malaise among writers who have never left India too. And then there's a distrust of the English language and English literature. But what if you begin to distrust your whole being, distrust your modernity and everything that's made you modern? Can you write anything at all then when it was the very force of modernism that compelled you to write a certain kind of literature in the first place?

In a justly celebrated paper, 'The Search for Identity: A Kannada Writer's Viewpoint' the Kannada novelist U. R. Ananthamurthy deals with precisely these questions. He describes an Indian writers' seminar which was disturbed almost literally by a stone. The writers, gathered in a North Indian city, were discussing very much what we are in Singapore: 'Why is the Western mode of thought and writing the model for us? Why are we unoriginal in our treatment of form and content in the novel, drama and poetry? While Indian dance and music are uniquely Indian, why does contemporary Indian literature take its bearings from the literature of the West? Are we really a nation of mimics, victims of English education, which has conditioned the faculties of our perception so much that we fail to respond freshly to the immediate situation in India?'

A painter who was present then told a story which impressed Ananthamurthy deeply. He said that during his wanderings through villages in the North, he came across a hut in which he saw a stone. It was decorated with red powder and flowers, which meant it was an object of worship. He asked the owner of the hut—a peasant—if the stone could be brought outside the hut since he wanted to photograph it. The stone was brought outside and the photograph taken. The painter then realized that he might have polluted the stone by shifting its position, and apologized to the peasant. The peasant said it didn't matter. He'd just fetch another stone and anoint it with the powder. So, the painter said, any piece of stone on which the peasant put the powder became God for him. The objective and subjective were one in such a person. He belonged to the illiterate Indian mass—70 per cent of the population. Western education had alienated those at the seminar from him and those like him. If they didn't understand the structure and mode of his thinking, they couldn't become true Indian writers.

The painter's argument shook Ananthamurthy as I said and though he was later nagged by a doubt that 'the authentic Indian peasant . . . was also an imported cult figure of Western radicals reacting against their materialist civilization', his self-doubt, common to 'educated Indian writers of [his] generation', nagged him more. The peasant continued to bother him.

The poor peasant, the trapped young writer in Bhopal, the contracted tribal breaking stones on a city street—they aren't figments of an Indian writer's imagination but indelibly part of his consciousness. Blanking them out can only be momentary. He doesn't have to go far in India to see them or people like them. So Nirmal Verma, on returning to his native land, steps out of the brief embrace of a cinema hall in his essay 'Returning to One's Country' and is appalled at the obscenity he was subjected to—a commercial which showed 'smooth-faced healthy children being fed cornflakes by their smiling mother'—nothing he'd get too worked up about if he were in London—but in India he can't reconcile the children he sees on the screen with the children outside it—'wilted faces under a merciless sun'. It's the context which makes the commercial obscene; there's a wide gap between the streets and the screen—just as there is a wide gap between me and the peasant, the young writer and the tribal.

Development used to mean bridging the gap, of creating a more modern, more just society and until a few years ago very few of our nationbuilders doubted that the way to bring such a society about was by spreading literacy, education and the benefits of science throughout the country. The die-hard capitalist and the Naxalite differed in their methods but their goal was the same—to create a modern developed state, totally free of India's crippling anachronisms.

Now the word development itself has begun to stink and a few anxious people in the Third World are seriously beginning to question whether some of the old ways were that anachronistic after all.

In India, for example, millions of lives have been marginalized by the construction of dams, hydro-electric projects and the hydro-politics behind them. The marginalization of the Indian writer—whether writing in the Indian languages or English—is indeed petty when compared to it. Its reach is ferocious and devastating. But when the tribal sees his land gone, taken by the Damodar Valley Corporation or DVC, does he simply take to the bottle and slink away? Yes, he does, but he also sings. He speaks out:

> Which company came to my land to open a 'karkhana'?
> It awakened its name in the rivers and the ponds calling itself the DVC
> It throws earth, dug by a machine, into the river.
>
> It has cut the mountain and made a bridge. The water runs beneath.
> Roads are coming, they are giving us electricity, having opened the 'karkhana'.
> The praja all question them. They ask to what this name belongs.
> When evening falls they give paper notes as pay. Where will I keep these paper notes?
> They melt away in the water.
> In every house there is a well which gives water to grow brinjal and cabbage. Every house is bounded by a wall which makes it look like a palace.
> This Santhal tongue of ours has been destroyed in the district. You came and made this bloody burning ghat, calling yourself the DVC.

The song is by an unknown Santhal from West Bengal and it appears in an essay by an Indian social scientist, Shiv Visvanathan, who argues, as the blurb of the essay says, 'that the crisis of survival—from survival of the poor to the survival of the human race—is not a result of a failure of the modern project of development, of modernization, of science and technology, but a consequence of their very success'.

In the essay itself he states that 'the tragedy of modernization in the Third World is doubly violent. It has sprung not only from the violence of the West through colonialism and science but also from the modernist impulse of our elites, internalized without a clue to its doubts or its genealogy'. If this is correct, then it has serious repercussions for the modernist impulse in literature, and is the greatest threat to the modern writer's identity. Such a truth, if it is the truth, can pierce his heart, the heart of language and nail his tongue to his palate permanently. Its scope has room for Ananthamurthy's self-doubt and mine but also puts us in our place. Where did we modern Indian writers think we were going when we so little questioned our modernity?

Well, as another poet said, 'I learn by going where I have to go' and I have come to Singapore fully knowing that I've travelled this far, not on the wings of a modernist impulse—though without that impulse I wouldn't have got this far—but on those of a modern aircraft. Nor, despite my doubts about development have I come here to argue that I'd have preferred to travel by bullock cart because I suddenly prefer the good old ways. I don't. But the scientist's words help me see that I'm part of an elite—an international elite—with many Third World writers in it—that has too easily taken its modernizing role for granted. Caught up in the convention of a conference to make ourselves heard, we may or may not listen to one another. But we're fairly certain who won't listen to us back home. Who are we writing for there?

Edwin Thumboo told Peter Nazareth in an interview that the historical perspective is important to Singaporeans because, owing to the rapid modernization of the city—an international city—they are in danger of losing their historical hinterland. That is also true of those who live in Bombay as I do. But it's possible that the historical perspective way not come in the form in which Thumboo and I expect it. It may not come in the shape of a grand novel or poetic epic. It may come—as it already has—in a series of speak-outs—like the song of the Santhal and, in English, the poems of Dilip Chitre, Keki Daruwalla, Kamala Das, Nissim Ezekiel, Jayanta Mahapatra, Arvind Krishna Mehrotra and Gieve Patel, which deal with historical events like the Bangladesh War, the Emergency or the Bhopal disaster, or deal with local and family history.

Speaking out, saying it, is how India's bhakti poets set about their work, trying to change social consciousness, singing to the lower castes that God was in their hearts, not in Brahminic temples. Now, when it's essential to get back our sense of the sacredness of things—of land, river, tree, even the peasant's stone—it may be that these poets will help us—showing us that a linear view of history and development—even literary development—was not modern at all but against life itself and contained the seeds of its own destruction.

I implied in my opening remarks that the word 'witness' is not very satisfactory when applied to writers. But there's one in which it applies perfectly—and that is, of 'being there'. It was Whitman's position in an open society, as it is also the position of those writers who live in oppressive regimes, in states of special fear or on the margins of history.

That sense of 'being there', in works of fiction and poetry, is never finally dependent on where the writer is physically situated. The Sunderbans of *Midnight's Children* are no less real for the writer's never having visited them. (I consider the chapter on them to be one of the richest in the book.) That sense is finally dependent on the quality of the writer's imagination and the strength of his talent.

'Literature is not in the business of copyrighting certain themes for certain groups', says Rushdie in 'The Indian Writer in England'. 'And as for risk: the real risks of any artist are taken in the work, in pushing the work to the limits of what is possible, in the attempt to increase the sum of what is possible to think. Books become good when they go to this edge and risk falling over it—when they endanger the artist by reason of what he has, or has not, artistically dared.'

And, in his Nobel lecture, Czeslaw Milosz speaks of the poet's double role. 'He is the one who flies above the earth and looks at it from above but at the same time sees it in every detail.' The near and the far. And though he says, 'distance is sometimes impossible', and soaring above earth's good and evil seems 'a moral treason', yet, 'in a precarious balance of opposites, a certain equilibrium can be achieved thanks to a distance introduced by the flow of the time. "To see" means not only to have before one's eyes. It may mean also to preserve in memory. "To see and to describe" may also mean to reconstruct in imagination. A distance achieved thanks to the mystery of time must not change events, landscapes, human figures into a tangle of shadows growing paler and paler. On the contrary, it can show them in full light, so that every event, every date becomes expressive and persists as an eternal reminder of human depravity and human greatness. Those who are alive receive a mandate from those who are silent forever. They can fulfil their duties only by trying to reconstruct precisely things as they were and by wresting the past from fictions and legends.'

There are a score of sub-Rushdies in the making in India, I was told by Dhiren Bhagat, a young writer, just before I left Bombay. There may well be half a dozen sub-Miloszs too. If their solutions to the problems of distance and authenticity are so inspiring, it may be a hopeful sign. But a lot of the time, considering what needs to be done in India, we are perilously close to agreeing with Milosz that 'all art proves to be nothing compared to action' and too readily accept his anguish.

He confesses that, as someone 'who wrote a certain number of poems out of the contradictions engendered by an earth polluted by the crime of the genocide', as a pained historical witness, he 'would have preferred to have been able to resolve the contradiction while leaving the poems unwritten'.

'Our hearts hear ancient music'

POETRY

PREFACE TO *3 POETS*:
MELANIE SILGARDO, RAUL D'GAMA ROSE, SANTAN RODRIGUES

The poet is the most conspiratorial of artists. No other artist is privileged to enter another person's mind so invisibly. Poems need nothing but themselves to make themselves felt; no musical instrument, no wall to hang on, no stage or screen. They do without publishers for years, as novels can't. Spoken or read, they require merely our confidence to receive them.

I believe this is part of the unique pleasure poetry gives us: this simplicity of access, this unencumbered transmitting of one mind's experience to another. A mind that thrills to a single poem, has for a moment at least, severed itself from the commonplace with no help other than what it itself has brought to our commonest mode of communication: a sequence of words. And with no more fuss than opening a book, looking at a typed or handwritten copy or merely listening.

It is perhaps for this reason that neither readers of poetry nor poets are unduly discouraged when the expected intermediary between them fails to materialise. I mean the publisher. 'Poetry doesn't sell', 'We have no one who can tell us whether this manuscript is worth publishing or not'. We have heard it before and are not impressed. We simply restrengthen the traditional link between poet and reader and listener: the direct, the conspiratorial link.

If there were no readers of literature, the poet would be the first to find one. Indian poets have never had to go that far, nor are they ever likely to, but the extent to which they have relied on themselves to find their readers has gone unremarked. In the last fifteen years, considering this activity in English alone, I can immediately think of the following: Nissim Ezekiel's cyclostyled batches of his own poems (including *Hymns in Darkness*) and his publishing Gieve Patel's first book, *Poems*, in 1965. Arvind Krishna Mehrotra's cyclostyled copies of his *Bharatmata* (1966) and his publishing other poets in his magazines, *ezra* and *damn you*; the books of poems published by P. Lal; the books published by Pritish Nandy; Dilip Chitre's printed copies of his *Ambulance Ride* (1972). Santan Rodrigues' cyclostyled copies of his *I Exist* (1973); K. D. Katrak's and Gauri Deshpande's first publishing of *Jejuri* by Arun Kolatkar in their *Opinion Literary Quarterly* (1974); and the books published by Clearing House (1976), run by Arun Kolatkar, Arvind Krishna Mehrotra, Gieve Patel and myself.

I may have left several other instances out, but not intentionally. My intention is really to show that the phenomenon of poets publishing themselves and other poets is not a secondary feature of Indian publishing, but the chief one. We are not and never have been the poor cousins of big publishers. We have been the only means by which poetry has been kept alive while the big publishers slept.

The three poets in this volume are, I believe, the youngest group to attempt this. They are correct not to wait in line for older poets to discover them. Readers of their published work and those who have heard them read their poems have done that already. We may realize, however dimly, that it is the hard work of the poets and the existing conspiracy that has found us out. We would be correct in anticipating a great deal of pleasure from this volume.

Those new to the work may also be new to poetry. They are part of the new ground that is broken; in this way new readers will continue to be found. Welcome to the conspiracy.

SMALL BEGINNINGS

'It's not true that poetry doesn't sell,' said Veronik. 'On TV5, someone with a big publisher in France said that it doesn't sell like fiction, in one or two years, but can go on selling for maybe fifteen.'

True, I thought, having had to keep two small presses going for some time. Now, twenty-seven years after the first books published by Clearing House and fifteen after the first published by XAL-Praxis (Praxis in short) the number of copies brought out by those presses and which sold—a few titles went out of print more than ten years ago—come to around 11,000. Only two of the books were plays: Gieve Patel's *Mister Behram* and Cyrus Mistry's *Doongaji House*. The rest were books of poetry.

When Clearing House began publishing in 1976, there were a few small presses in the country, the most notable being P. Lal's Writers Workshop. It was eighteen years old then. It began with P. Lal's decision to publish himself. Seven others joined him to form a group. In Lal's own words:

> Apart from Deb Kumar Das ... there were seven others. I possess an aging brittle sheet of letter paper—'Lovely Bond', Made in Sweden, circa 1958—with all the ringleaders' names elegantly printed in saffron and their addresses in black, in a semi-circle on the left to suggest the curving leaf of the Writers Workshop logo: Sasthibrata Chakravarti (this was before he renounced his family name and inheritance and started freelancing for his bread-and-brata); Anita Desai (her story 'Grandmother' opens the first issue of the Writers Workshop bi-monthly of creative writing *The Miscellany* in 1960); William Hull (whose transcreations of the Latin poet appeared as one of the first batch of six Writers Workshop publications *The Catullus of Williams Hull*; P. Lal (listed as Secretary); Jai Ratan (whose first book, one of the six, was a collection of stories, *The Angry Goddess*); Pradip Sen (a volume of poems, *And Then the Sun*); and Kewlian Sio (short stories, *A Small World*).

A small beginning. Fifty-five years and more than 3,000 titles later, is Writers Workshop still a small press?

I don't think it is. Nor is Carcanet Press, one of Britain's most respected publishers of poetry. It too began small. As far as I remember, in the early 1960s, *Carcanet* was the name of a journal, it wasn't a publisher. The journal was brought out jointly by students of Oxford and Cambridge. There was some correspondence between Ajit Singh (then Cambridge, now Associated Capsules) and me (then Oxford, now another kind of capsule) about bringing out an Indian number. With me now is the *Carcanet* issue of Winter 1966, edited by Farrukh Dhondy and Diane Troy, and designed by Fershid Bharucha (now a publisher himself, of comic books and comic-book art in Paris). Adi Katrak and I have some poems in it.

That's the way it was, getting published in little magazines, getting published by small presses. Over many years the poetry sold. That's the way it still is.

READINGS WITH PARROTS AND ANGELS

The voices of those of us who speak English in India aren't the voices which are heard in the poems we write. I put it as bluntly as that.

Every poet has at least two voices: a literary voice, and the one in which he normally speaks. That makes good social sense. Dylan Thomas had few friends towards the end of his life but he would have had fewer had he tried to talk to them in the way he declaimed his poems.

The eighteenth-century poet Oliver Goldsmith was a bad talker—so much so that his contemporary, the actor David Garrick, wrote him a cruel epitaph: 'Here lies Nolly Goldsmith, for shortness call'd Noll / Who wrote like an angel, but talked like poor Poll.'

Many of the poets I know talk like poor polls, poor parrots; some of them write like angels.

My point is about disjuncture, and I make it because I haven't seen it made before. It may seem like an academic point but I think it has some implications for practising poets.

Whether we've been through a course of Eng Lit or not, all that we know about what poetry was, is and should be, has come to us from certain 'givens'. All the givens have been debated and some overturned, even if temporarily.

For example, no poet I know subscribes to Wordsworth's theory that 'Poetry is the spontaneous overflow of powerful feelings: it takes its origin from emotion recollected in tranquility'. Yet, generations of students and readers of poetry grew up believing that was true.

Similarly, very few poets I know subscribe to Eliot's idea of the impersonality of the poet, with its claim that 'poetry is not the expression of personality but an escape from personality'. Yet, I once believed it to be true.

Both the statements have no colonial connotations. They can be debated without referring to any of the colonial realities in which the statements were made because those realities are excluded from the statements. They aren't value-free statements but are language-free in what they say; I mean they don't apply to English alone. In other words, when Wordsworth and Eliot try to define poetry, I take their definition to apply to poetry in any language. Some people may regard this as a mistake but I myself don't find it difficult to apply their statements to all the translated poetry I know, whether the original poems were in Tamil, Greek or Hebrew. It just so happens that I no longer find their statements valid.

A given may come to us whole but may manifest itself in a peculiarly broken form. This is what happens in India when the given has to do with the English language.

Many of us try to write poetry which is colloquial in its thrust, which tries to follow the patterns and nuances of everyday speech. This is a strand in modern British and American (particularly American) poetry which continues to this day though there are poets who are strongly opposed to it.

The colloquial strain is there for anyone to hear in the poems of Whitman, Sandburg, Auden, Larkin, Plath and Sexton. In India it's there in the poems of Ezekiel, Ramanujan, Kamala Das, Eunice de Souza, Imtiaz Dharker and Mukta Sambrani. The legitimacy for this colloquial direction in poetry came from abroad, from poets like Whitman, Eliot and Pound who lived in societies which were fully English-speaking, unlike ours. Whitman could use an illiterate soldier's way of speaking in *Leaves of Grass* if he wanted to. Eliot could use working-class slang in 'Sweeney Agonistes' when he wanted to. We only have our own colloquial middle-class uses of English as currency and sometimes not even those.

If you go to a poetry reading you will sometimes find that those who speak a baffling, even incorrect kind of English will read poems, their poems, which are perfectly intelligible, even acceptably colloquial, though the English of the poems clearly isn't the English they speak. What does the word 'colloquial' mean then, if it doesn't mean the kind of English the poet normally speaks? How does one explain the poet's performance?

What's at work here is an overcoming of disjuncture—the kind of disjuncture between the spoken word and the written word that Whitman and Sandburg never had to contend with and never foresaw since it happened and is happening in the colonies. I sometimes find it useful to see India as a continuing colony, her ear forever cocked to the voices of masters who live abroad. It easily explains why her filmmakers both mimic and aggrandise Hollywood, why her pop stars sing in American accents, (though British pop stars do the same) and why we think we know everything there is to know about English just because we acquired it from a people who once ruled us and for whom it was a native language.

I find it much more difficult to explain why, despite the disjuncture and faults in the English we're nurtured in, many of us talk like parrots but write like angels.

POEMS AFTER AYODHYA

The Times of India has received a number of poems since 6 December. They range from passionate pleas for sanity to carefully crafted laments for Bombay. Many newspapers and magazines must have received similar poems recently. The question is should editors publish all of them or any of them on the grounds that they are 'sincere', 'heartfelt' etc. responses to a national catastrophe? If readers' letters on the same subject are allowed, why not readers' poems?

A simple answer would be that just as not every letter to the editor is published, not every 'poem' need be either. Another answer, which will doubtless sound snobbish and which is prefigured by my enclosing the word 'poem' in inverted commas, is that while every reader can be expected to write a letter, not every reader can write a poem. In moments of great passion or anguish or love, we all believe we can. Under the pressure of a certain kind of emotion, we resort to writing poems; otherwise we believe poetry stinks. Under that pressure it's almost impossible to believe that poetry is not the 'spontaneous overflow of powerful feeling', as the Romantic poet said.

Sad as the situation after Ayodhya is, it's also sad that such spontaneous overflows from readers don't generally make for poetry. Sad because the reader also wants to do his bit, wants to stand up and be counted among those who are against the fascist forces in the country; but editors, while saying 'Yes' to his spirit, say 'No' to his effort.

The reader won't be made any happier if he's informed that most editors in the country claim they 'don't know anything about poetry'. (Several editors I've met have made this claim.) The reader himself may be part of a public which believes that poetry and politics don't mix; in other words, that there can't be any such thing as political poetry. (I've met several readers and they've all told me this.) Then how does the reader describe his or her poem on the destruction of a mosque?

If it isn't political, if poems on 'the burning of Bombay' aren't political, what are they? It would be a different matter if the fires had been caused by a rain of meteorites but we know they were not. Where there's a human hand, there's politics. Some believe that every act of writing is a political act. We know that 'the hand that signed the paper felled a city'.

The words are Dylan Thomas's and while their meaning is clear, they don't imply that poets *must* write about their fallen cities. I think that's exactly what the Gujarati poet Sitanshu Yashashchandra meant when, at a multilingual kavi sammelan held in Bombay recently, he objected to the demand that poets must necessarily voice their response to the city's riots. The voice of a poet may have its very roots in historical violence that has become personalised. The roots can go deep as in the case of the Israeli poet Yehuda Amichai, so that even a love poem of his gets circumscribed and threatened by war, just as his country is; or they can be shallow, as in the case of the British poet Adrian Mitchell whose posterish anti-war poems were so popular in the 1960s.

But neither should be expected to write 'poems of the moment', as some of the organisers of the sammelan (and the public) expected their poets to. Significantly, the writer of the report on the sammelan which appeared in *The Independent* questioned Yashashchandra's stance. She said it 'poses a relevant question: if the poet does not raise his voice in times of crises, does it not indicate an evasive refusal to comment?'

The writer, who is a teacher of English literature at a Bombay college, seems to have forgotten one of the lessons literature teaches us. That is, that while literature doesn't disallow the spontaneous poem, every important poem on a national crisis such as the one we are going through has been written some time after the event. If it takes time to piece together the happenings of the last few weeks in the mind, it may take a longer time to piece them together in a poem. Many poets have an innate sense of history and that sense has taught them that violence, at least, wasn't born yesterday.

For a poet to refuse to take a populist, sloganeering stand on a political issue is not necessarily an evasive action. The place where that action takes the poet may be the one place where his next poem comes from—and the poem may be on the very issue he supposedly 'evaded'. To express public solidarity with fellow artists is one thing, to write a poem another.

The state of the country is not a workshop that makes poems happen. If some people believe it is, then let them also understand that the state of the nation is indivisible in time; that it can't make poetry happen at one time and not at another; that it always makes poetry happen; and hence, since poetry is so dependent on the state of the nation, that poetry is always political.

I mean 'political' in the broadest possible sense, but that's a dirty word at the best of times. It seems that it's only at the worst of times, such as the ones we're told we're going through now, that the word becomes legitimate. More than legitimate, it becomes the very bedrock of poetry, the kind that at other times, everyone, including teachers of literature, caution us not to write.

SHUT UP, MEMORY

Strange things happen in the head. It's a circus where memory plays tricks. The snout of a steam engine enters through the right temple like a neatly flattened bullet and emerges through the left as part of a ship. Behind the driver's cabin, instead of the rest of the engine, is a deep stern, rudder and propeller attached. Both sides of the thing are perfect; perfect but mismatched. That's memory for you as you stumble through the dark wood Dante made memorable in the middle of the road of your life. And you thought you were on the right track.

It's others who point it out to you. 'Jussawalla, you've

goofed again. Call it what you will, but it is not, repeat not, a steam engine.'

'How dare you?' you fight back. 'How dare you suggest I get steam engines wrong? I remember them perfectly. They were part of my childhood.'

'We suggest you're approaching your second,' they say. 'We suggest you look closely and see.'

I look closely and see: yes, I've got it wrong.

Sometimes an unease of the mind, a safety catch in memory itself, saves you before you're found out. I quoted the first line of a sonnet by Keats: *'Bright star, would I were steadfast as thou art'*, fully believing that the sonnet ended with the line *'Till love and fame to nothingness do sink'*. I said as much in an article. 'Check,' something told me. I checked. The last line of the Keats sonnet is *'And so live ever—or else swoon to death'*. And the first line of the sonnet whose last line I got wrong is 'When I have fears that I may cease to be' followed by 'Before my pen has glean'd my teeming brain . . .'

My brain gets teemier, steamier by the minute. This is no burnt-out case addressing you. It's a firepot, a stew, a red-chilli broth, one of its most potent ingredients, memory.

What on earth possessed Nabokov to call his autobiography *Speak, Memory*? He, arch-remembrancer, must have known that it speaks all the time, that sometimes it just won't stop. Memory? If you're the real thing talking to me again, I'd say, Shut up. I've heard enough.

The trap is age. The trap is if, after a certain age, you get memory to shut its trap—how that's possible I have no idea, but it should be possible through yoga, gymnastics or the silent art of Zen—you risk shutting down yourself. This is true of all writers but particularly true of poets, I think. Odd how it's almost universally held that you write your best poetry when you're young. Odder still that those who hold this belief should include many young poets who think they're burning the candle at both ends when they don't know the first thing about striking a match. Fire in the mind, fire in the belly. At the centre of those fires, memory, losing shape like a charred dummy, but never fully turning into ash. Until, almost inevitably, very near the end.

The loss of memory is unexpected, frightening. The old are reduced to tears of helplessness by their inability to remember: the young are doomed to remember. Poets, young, middle-aged and old, by virtue of their calling, are fated to make of memory something substantial, even if it turns out wrong. All this in the face of a fact that most people are aware of: memory is almost never good for your health.

Confronted with someone who looks the picture of misery, we unthinkingly tend to advise her: 'Get out of it. Cheer up. Remember the good times.' Dante (once again) knew better. He wrote (quite memorably again), 'There is no greater sorrow than to recall a time of happiness in misery'.

Then why recall happiness? Why remember? We're quite right in asking memory to shut up but we forget that time will do it for us anyway. It will punch memory with great holes, like bullets do targets at a shooting range, or bubbles of air do cheese. Sooner than we think, memory will be a universe of black holes. From which no light can emerge.

It's scary and I'm scared.

Speak, memory, speak.

'Why hide the fact?'

AUTOBIOGRAPHICAL

A DESTINATION OF THE HEART

Like Salman Rushdie, I was delivered to Bombay by Dr Shirodkar. I can't say I've appreciated that fact. All the same, being born seven years before Salman had one clear advantage. For those seven years, he couldn't tread on my turf. After those years, we went to the same school, lived on the same street and finally he wrote my novel, *Midnight's Children*. Everyone born in the 1940s wanted to write *Midnight's Children*. Only he went and did it.

I was often ill. Pneumonia dogged me from year one. For me, the predominant Bombay colours during the years before Independence were pale blue, pale yellow and the whites of my father's doctor's suit and nurses' uniforms. I lived in his clinic, not because of my ill-health, but because we had no other place. That had its advantages too. In the clinic I saw Congress leaders come and go. A broken Yusuf Meherally was handed over to my father after the allopaths had done their bit. My father couldn't save him. I remember his body being carried through the clinic corridors, the nurses' heads bowed. For a while, because of the presence of Congress leaders in the clinic—they had a fondness for enemas—the place was under police surveillance. Can I possibly remember the violence that followed the Quit India call at Gowalia Tank (now August Kranti Maidan)? I think I can. The clinic was on Cumballa Hill (now August Kranti Marg). Unknown to Dr Shirodkar, whose clinic was quite close to my father's, he had not only delivered me to Bombay but to a momentous bit of its history.

I really wish he hadn't. Or couldn't I have waited till that fateful stroke of midnight when everything was over? As it happens, I was delivered to a violent time. I remember photographs of suburban trains set on fire, my father having to visit us before curfew (my parents lived separately for a while), talk of war and one day soon after I'd turned four, the sound of three tremendous explosions. The *Fort Stikine*, exploding at Ballard Pier, sent shockwaves to Cumballa Hill. Curtain rods fell from their sockets, a door latch got twisted. A tall tree of smoke rose behind Malabar Hill. The grown-ups said Japan had attacked.

These images are part of my poem, 'A Letter for Bombay', and similar images occur in a sequence of poems, 'Missing Person'. When people point out the violence of some of my images, perhaps it's because they spring from a violent time. Still, we had our American films (even if they reached Bombay two years after their Hollywood release), American chewing gum and thanks to Mr Phirozeshah Taraporevala's New Book Company (he was my best friend's father), an endless supply of American and British comics. There were morning shows of *Batman*, *Superman*, *Captain Marvel* and *Flash Gordon* at the Capitol cinema and there was Superman, *The Saint* and *Dan Dare* on the air.

All that changed in the 1950s when Morarji Desai became chief minister. He launched programmes of fearful and numbing austerity, and the import of 'foreign culture' in the form of comics and even books was banned. From a violent and occasionally happy city, Bombay became a dull city, for me the dullest in the world. I disliked school (not the school's fault perhaps) though I liked many of its teachers; Bombay's institutes of higher learning looked like dumps and were spoken about as if they really were. There was little to do in the evenings, nothing to read. I felt trapped by my family. I had to go.

I spent about eleven years abroad. People asked me why I came back. Why?

When even in 1970, more and more people were beginning to realise that they could only survive in Bombay, not live in it. And why do I stay? When all its old problems have got magnified and when its poverty clings to you, drags you down, immobilises you as only this country's poverty can. Perhaps there's an answer in 'A Letter for Bombay'.

In the poem I speak of wandering like a medieval apothecary abroad and in a 'pouch wriggling against my ribs, carry a quintessence of you (Bombay), not wholly without potency'. The pouch wriggling against my ribs is my cockeyed way of referring to my heart.

And another poem, this time by R. S. Thomas, 'Here'. Why is he where he is, why does he stay there, he wonders in the poem, and ends: 'It is too late to start/For destinations not of the heart./I must stay here with my hurt.'

Bombay, for me, is or has become a destination of the heart. I must stay here with my hurt.

A LIFE PRESUMED LOST

(On his mother, Mehera Jussawalla)

Whenever I recall the flat in Bombay where I lived for a few years before I left for London, I hear music. My brother Firdausi is playing a Mozart minuet on the piano; or the radiogram is playing an aria sung by Beniamino Gigli; or Firdausi is belting out his version of the aria under a shower, or, on a Sunday, my father is listening to qawwalis.

I never saw my mother listening attentively to any of the music being played in the flat. My memory of her at that time, when she was in her forties, is of a woman who never set aside time for herself, supervising our servants, busy in the kitchen, making sure everything in the flat was in the right place, attending to phone calls. But I also recall her pleasure when I used to choose whichever records she asked for from a dark brown box. That was in another flat, my aunt Freny Antia's on

Altamont Road, where my mother and I stayed when she and my father separated.

The separation lasted for more than two years, and after we returned to my father's nature cure clinic where we used to live before the separation, she involved herself wholeheartedly in helping him run it. I don't remember listening to much music then. Though my mother said she loved Juthika Roy's voice, I never saw her play any of the Juthika Roy records which she had bought. In 1951, we moved to a flat on Warden Road.

I said my mother never appeared to listen to music attentively, but clearly she did. As she moved around the flat, straightening a cushion here or aligning a chair with the edge of a table there, if she knew Firdausi or I were within earshot, she might say something startling about a piece of music she may have heard a day or two earlier, or one that was playing on the radiogram at that moment.

I recall three such occasions. One day she told me that whenever she heard 'Humoreske', she felt like crying. (This was Dvorak's 'Humoreske', played on the violin by Fritz Kreisler.) 'I'm a misunderstood woman,' she told me vehemently on another occasion. 'What they're saying is right.' (She was referring to The Animal's version of 'Don't Let Me Be Misunderstood' which was playing at that time.) And once, when she was in her late fifties, she said with grim finality, 'I'll never fall in love again.' Those were the words of a song sung by Dionne Warwick, which we intermittently heard on the radio in 1970.

I choose these three recollections from among many because, to me, they represent three aspects of mother: One, she was an emotional, hypersensitive woman, often having to suppress her feelings after real or imaginary slights. The hurts would flow in tears later. Two, she was misunderstood. Her open-heartedness, her vulnerability, and her desire to help others with all her heart often clashed with her outspokenness and temper, leaving old friends and relatives wounded and new acquaintances wary. Three, she was a passionate woman and fell in love more than once in her life. She loved my father but after they married his responses to her were often cold and hurtful. He idolised his mother and worshipped work.

She had a gift for painting—a great sense of colour—but didn't develop it, choosing instead to devote herself to father, her sons, and making the Warden Road flat look beautiful. As she grew older and friends dropped away, she felt neglected, though Firdausi, who stayed with our parents, was an affectionate son, cheerfully drawing her out of her depressions, and ensuring she got the best possible treatment during her declining years. When she died in 2006, ninety-four years old, there were very few people at her funeral. To outsiders and those who didn't know her, hers would seem to be a typical case—of a woman discarded, a life presumed lost. But it wasn't like that. Not exactly.

Mehera, my mother, was born in the home of the Jalnawallas in Jalna on 26 April 1912. Her mother Aimai was a Jalnawalla before she married Kaikhushru Mehta, a businessman from Surat. Mother spent her childhood in Jalna with her two brothers and three sisters. She rarely spoke about Jalna, which was in the Nizam's state of Hyderabad when she lived there, except to say that though she was regarded as an odd child, she was her father's favourite; that she remembers dozens of men eating at a huge dining table; and that the piles of discarded mango stones during the mango seasons looked like mountains.

The Jalnawallas were very wealthy. An ancestor of theirs, living in Bharuch, accompanied a British garrison to Jalna and became a successful merchant there. He changed his name from Hamawalla to Jalnawalla. That was in the early 1800s. Wikipedia also tells me: 'By the end of the (19)30s, the Jalnawallas owned 64,000 acres of land, 17 cotton ginning and pressing factories and more than 300 houses and bungalows'.

But by the end of the 1930s, Aimai Mehta and her family

were no longer in Jalna. They had moved to Bombay and later to Poona in the early 1920s for reasons that aren't clear. The wealth of the Jalnawallas didn't follow them; they were left to shift for themselves.

Aimai's husband was absent a lot of the time, away on business or with his mistress in Bombay. Her daughters found husbands of their own and according to talk in the family, that was something she encouraged. By 1930, her eldest son Dinshah had established a nature cure clinic and soon became one of Gandhiji's favoured doctors, supervising his fasts.

It was when Tagore visited Gandhiji in Yerawada jail—on the outskirts of Poona then—in September 1932, trying to persuade him to break a 'fast unto death', that mother's fortunes changed. Her brother Dinshah's partner Gool Pocha— they weren't married then—felt that mother's restless, imaginative personality needed a change from the life she led in Poona. She felt mother would flourish in Santiniketan and told Tagore so. The next year mother went to Santiniketan.

She was a student at Kala Bhavan and her chief teacher was Nandalal Bose. I see her, along with Nandalal's other students, painting on the walls of the ground floor of the old library building, Nandalal drawing bold outlines which the students filled in with tempera. A line of dancing Santhals and decorative floral motives were part of the fresco. I see her, sometimes dressed in a sari, sometimes in a blouse and slacks, picking up the fallen shefali flowers in her path, walking down an avenue of sal trees with a friend or running towards a mango orchard. She also danced.

She played the Ace-Princess of Spades in the first performance of Tagore's *Tasher Desh* (*Card Country*), a wild satirical play he had just written. (Quashiq Mukherjee, director of the Bengali film *Gandu*, is thinking of making a film based on the play. He describes it as 'Tagore on an acid trip.')

It dealt with rebellion and freedom, subjects close to mother's heart, and when I wondered how she could play her part in

Bengali, and that too in front of a Calcutta audience which was known to be nothing if not critical, Firdausi told me. It seems she had picked up Bengali—enough to be able to burst into it when she got very angry. When Firdausi would ask her why she spoke to him in a language he couldn't understand, she'd reply that we never understood what she said anyway whichever language she spoke in. So she might as well speak in Bengali.

She was twenty-one years old, sometimes regarded as a 'foreign' beauty, and was made to stay with a Dutch couple because of her 'foreign' ways. The western clothes she occasionally wore set her apart and she avoided the ritual of touching Tagore's feet.

She had her male admirers. An eighteen-year-old Khushwant Singh was among them. 'I had also befriended a Parsi girl, Meher', he writes in his autobiography *Truth, Love and a Little Malice*, 'who often dropped in to listen and chat with me. The monk [Khushwant's room-mate] never spoke to her, but no sooner would she leave than he would ask me if I had made any progress. "Have you held her hand? Kissed her?" He was disappointed at my failures.'

But the admirer who disturbed her most was Krishna Kripalani. They probably fell in love. He may even have been the chief reason she left Santiniketan. She once told me that she feared losing her family if she married him.

But most of the time she told her sons and nieces that she had to leave Santiniketan because Dinshah had run out of funds to support her. Back in Poona, she missed Santiniketan and sold what jewellery she had to pay her own way there. But it wasn't enough.

My father Jehangir, who assisted Dinshah in his clinic, used to meet mother there and after a brief courtship they married in October 1935. A year later they were in Newcastle Upon Tyne, not on a belated honeymoon, but because father wanted to break away from Dinshah's clinic and start a practice of his own. He'd got himself admitted to the Davidson College of

Natural Therapeutics; a loan from one of the Wadia charities helped him get there. Mother, determined not to be left behind, was helped by the Tatas.

In 1936, though the worst of the depression years in Britain were over, Newcastle and the areas around it, particularly Tyneside, were still badly affected. Millions were unemployed and food was still rationed. Mother recalled days with little to eat, poor heating, poor lighting, she and my father shivering in their digs, staring at the lone poached egg on their plates. But they were liked in the college and did well. Mother qualified as a masseuse and assisted Dr Davidson for a while. Father was reported to have done so well that the Wadias refused to take their money back.

Mother's new dream was to help father set up an independent practice in Bombay and she did this in her wholehearted way, but with many interruptions. Problems, mostly to do with each other's families—his uncritical devotion to his mother, for instance, her excessive admiration of Dinshah—became obstacles, leading to frequent ruptures and rows. She felt she was wronged by my father and his mother. She put up a fight. By the time I was born in 1940, she wanted justice.

She expected more love from me than I could give. After Firdausi was born in 1944, he provided that. In 1957, immediately after I left for London, she developed a lump on her breast which some surgeons thought should be removed immediately. Greatly distressed, but drawing on her belief in alternative systems of medicine perhaps, she went to the Christian Science sessions organized by Jer Master. Over time the lump dissolved.

This may have been another turning point in mother's life because on the two occasions I came back from England to see her, I saw that she had set aside a part of her evenings to pray. When she visited me in England, twice, I didn't see her pray. But in Bombay I saw her pray silently, her eyes often open, looking into the distance as she told her beads. Her prayer books, some of which she passed on to me, weren't Zoroastrian. *Morning and Evening Thoughts*, *Little Book of Prayers* and *Prayer for All Times* were written by Christians.

But she wasn't strictly a Christian or strictly anything else. She was critical of those who, in her eyes, removed themselves from life only to pray and meditate. She grew less enamoured of her brother-turned-guru Dinshah (Dadaji), but cared deeply for his wife Gool and their children. She said her prayers but believed in action, in helping people in practical ways.

She was like father in this but more emotional. She helped her servants and their children with gifts of food and money, sometimes secretly. She helped her married woman servants open their own bank accounts. She tried to help solve my wife Veronik's problems, her relatives' problems, so doggedly sometimes that they thought her interfering. It was 'in her nature', as we say. She worried. And she worried more about the well-being of others than her own.

All the same, she needed interests that took her out of her flat. She learned how to sew like a professional under the needle-eye of Ms Hyam, well-known for being a perfectionist. She passed on this skill to her niece Zareen Engineer (now Mistry). She employed a thin sad woman called Emily to sew for her and she sold their products for charity.

She got back to painting in 1966 when she joined Jyotindra Roy's School of Batik Painting. She respected Professor Roy (as she called him) to the point of idolizing him, a throwback, perhaps, to the time she spent in Santiniketan, studying under teachers she respected.

She got to know Kamila Tyabji who persuaded her to be part of her Women's India Trust. There she helped, again giving all of herself, in the making of jams, bedspreads and tablecloths. But it didn't last. Kamila appreciated her work and her personality and was genuinely sorry when she left.

She had her share of illnesses, once being hospitalized for

exhaustion during her eighties. It turned out that she had, of all things, acute anaemia. Anaemia! When she herself fed others so well and meticulously prepared meals for father according to his difficult dietary instructions. (Firdausi tells me that this was during a time when father was in hospital too. She had decided to stop eating normally until he returned home.)

Sushilkumar Shinde thought fit to praise her in public. As guest of honour at the function when father was given the Dhanvantari Award (in 1989), he singled out mother in the audience and said the doctor could never have been as successful as he was without his wife's help. It was a politician's gesture but he was right.

Father died in 1997, mother in 2006. Her last two years, when she was generally confined to her bed, were hard, particularly for Firdausi. He got day and night nurses to care for her. Her grand-niece Anahita deVitre and niece Zareen, her oldest friend Homai Irani and Homai's closest friend Perin and another friend Rani Shah were regular visitors. Veronik and I would visit with prepared meals to supplement those Firdausi provided. She needed us to talk about cheerful subjects but I wasn't good at that.

She once told Firdausi that the time she spent in Santiniketan was the happiest in her life. There's a small painting from that time of a woman in a white sari running across a bare field. I think that woman is meant to be mother but I can't find the painting.

In her autograph book, the young Khushwant has painted her holding a sitar, the instrument he was trying to master. In the same book, on its last page, Krishna Kripalani has written, 'May no obscure mind ever judge an innocence so wild and wondrous'. I believe my parents did manage to love each other again as they got older. Mother learned to control herself when provoked and to hold her peace. She may even have withdrawn too far into herself, refusing to speak her mind for fear of being misunderstood.

She set me free in many ways, primarily by allowing me to be myself, even when I behaved in ways that hurt her badly. I loved her but, like father, couldn't show it.

She couldn't understand why some broken relationships were never restored. When her father-in-law Merwanji—whom his wife and sons had separated from as long ago as 1914—was dying in a hospital in Bombay, he refused to drink water from the hands of anyone but mother. He had visited her in Bombay, shabbily dressed, almost a pauper. After recovering from her shock—father had never mentioned him to her—she took him in and fed him. She might have done so permanently if, I presume, objections from his family hadn't prevailed.

Mother also longed to make peace with those who had wounded her. Father's mother, the brave, independent woman who caused her so much distress in the early years of her marriage, recognized this when she had to be nursed through her final illness in the Warden Road flat. 'Finally,' she told mother, 'there was only you. You were the constant woman.'

Those mother helped and who helped her in turn sometimes return to haunt me. One of them is Saku, a servant who worked for her for more than thirty years. Less than two years after mother died, she appeared to me in a dream. Looking at my notes, I write:

Mother is lying on the bed in Veronik's room, 'haggard, crippled, unable to raise herself'. I stand outside the door. It's closed and I'm horrified. A vision of Saku appears, 'smooth-skinned, sensuous and serene, quiet, noble in her bearing, as though she is mother's angel and knows more than I do. No rancour in her look, just 'I've been through it, I know it. Rest.'

A PLACE IN THE SUN

(On his father, Dr Jehangir Jussawalla)

On 29 July 1993, I bought two pairs of pathanis at English Shoes, Lahore, and casually asked the salesman—a middle-aged man—if he knew anything about a house in Temple Street where the Jussawallas once lived. He looked at me with wide-open eyes. 'The Jussawallas? They were very well-known. The house must still be there.'

It may have been, it may still be, but I never found it. I found Temple Street but no one I asked could direct me to a house where a family called the Jussawallas had once lived. My father had told me that there was a house in Temple Street, Lahore, where he had spent part of his childhood. He couldn't remember the number of the house; no one, to this day, can tell me. He, his mother and his three brothers left that house in 1914 and settled in Poona.

My first unsuccessful steps out of English Shoes, Lahore to find an ancestral house are linked to other, hopefully more successful steps to find my father, his years before I was born, the events that led him to be a doctor, to choose Nature Cure as his practice and to build up that practice at his clinic in Bombay. The practice thrived and his Natural Therapy Clinic, started at Petit House, Gowalia Tank on 15 February 1938 and continued the following year onwards at Sunama House, Cumballa Hill, drew a wide range of patients: Congress party leaders, film stars, sportspersons, business magnates, industrialists, a police commissioner or two, but mostly middle-class professionals and housewives whose health had suffered. There were those who wanted to put on or lose weight, those who believed in the comfort of enemas and bowel-washes; those who needed to be given special kinds of massage for muscular and joint pains; those whom other systems of medicine—not just allopathy—had rejected; and those very damaged people who simply came to my father for moral and emotional guidance. He believed in treating the whole patient, with diet and nutrition as the base for his practice. He believed, as he said in his acceptance speech when he was given the Dhanvantari Award in 1989, not in normal health, but absolute, positive health.

Every patient of his that I've met has told me that, as a masseur, he had wonderful hands. But, like every ambitious doctor, he knew he needed more than his hands to succeed; he needed assistants. At the height of the clinic's success, between the late 1950s and early 1970s, he had twenty-five assistants, women and men. In the months before his crippling fall in 1993, he had none.

He also needed machines. To the delight of my brother Firdausi and myself, the clinic, where we spent part of our childhood, had many: space-age contraptions that sent out infrared and ultraviolet rays with a faint buzz; steam-bath and radiant-heat cabinets, on which patients' heads rested, sometimes goggle-eyed, as though they'd been decapitated; a sitz bath; a needle bath; a python-like hose that ejected water with great force—we weren't allowed to touch it—in other words, the tempting jet bath; and glassy, tubed contraptions—again, flying-saucer furniture—for bowel washes. Like Dr Dinshah K. Mehta's Nature Cure Clinic and Sanatorium at 6, Todiwalla Road, Poona, where my father first learned the basics of Nature Cure, his Natural Therapy Clinic was a one-stop shop. You bought the treatment you wanted, or, as was more likely, depending on the doctor's diagnosis, you were ordered to buy something else.

My father, whom I'll call Jehangir from this point on, didn't seriously consider becoming a doctor until he was in his twenties. As a schoolboy, he cycled, swam, played the violin and studied normally. But a class master noticed he kept too much to himself. He was advised to become a scout, which he reluctantly did.

He liked being a scout. The scout movement inspired him,

and after passing a scoutmaster exam when he was fifteen, was made assistant scoutmaster of the Second Poona Parsi Troop.

His eyesight was bad, he began wearing glasses, and fearing physical weakness, took to what was already something of a craze among young Parsis in the 1920s—physical culture. This was basically a course of physical exercises which sometimes involved pumping iron, sometimes not. Sometimes it involved muscle control as at Mehta's physiculture centre where nude men, covered in special paint, struck dramatic poses for minutes, without moving or showing even a flicker of expression: statue-posing.

Despite being part of Mehta's physical culture group for a while (in December 1928), Jehangir never told me if he statue-posed. But what's clear from his diary is that in 1927, when he was twenty, after some training at a Southern Command centre, he was a physical training instructor at Deccan College. A few months before he turned twenty, he found he didn't need glasses.

This was directly due to the letters he exchanged with Dr Bernarr Macfadden, the American 'father of physical culture' and the course of eye exercises he was sent. He saw his restored eyesight not as a miracle but as proof. The seed of 'natural healing' was planted.

Two years later, Mehta started his Nature Cure Clinic 'with a tap of cold water and a galvanized tub', as his biographer Sundri P. Vaswani says. In those two years, despite an exciting trip abroad as one of the scoutmasters who led the Scouts of the Bombay Presidency to a world jamboree in Liverpool, Jehangir's mental and physical health collapsed. He fell in love with a girl cousin, a doomed affair that preyed on his mind. In 1928, two bad attacks of influenza weakened his heart. When Mehta's clinic opened in 1929, Jehangir, who had trained under him at his physiculture centre, was one of its first patients. 'October 31, 1929', his diary entry read. 'Treatment of fasting, milk diet, exercises under Dinshaw (sic) Mehta in Poona.'

It was a decision that was to change his life in more ways than one. Deeply impressed by Mehta's personality and principles, he began to take Nature Cure seriously. In February 1931, he joined the clinic as a helper. The next year he was put in charge of the Bombay branch of the clinic, at Wassiamal Building, Grant Road. This was the beginning of an on-off relationship. He was asked to manage the Poona clinic in 1934, then the Bombay clinic again in 1935. There was never enough money; payments from the main clinic were erratic. In terrible turmoil, on 1 April 1935, Jehangir resigned. Mehta is reported to have wept at the news.

Six months later, Jehangir married Mehta's sister Mehera whom he'd met in Poona but got to know better during a panther shoot in Sinhgad. Surprisingly, he took charge of the Grant Road clinic in Bombay again. Mehera helped. They lived in Dadar.

But the old problem of payments recurred. Jehangir's need to break away, to make it on his own, intensified. Exactly a year after they got married, they left Bombay to study at the Davidson College of Natural Therapeutics, Newcastle Upon Tyne, he for a triple-barrelled ND, DO, DC (Doctor of Naturopathy, Doctor of Osteopathy, Doctor of Chiropractic), she for a diploma in massage. Part of his expenses was covered by Wadia Charities, hers by the Tatas and Jehangir's mother Aimai.

Jehangir was devoted to Aimai. There's little doubt that without her courage and strength of character, she couldn't have raised her four young sons on her own. After they left Lahore in 1914, she was, in every sense of the term, a single mother, having abandoned her husband Merwanji to his reckless, spendthrift ways.

Jehangir was a dedicated vegetarian; he wrote books, pamphlets and articles on the subject and firmly believed, despite scepticism in his family, that being a vegetarian was necessary for one's spiritual growth. I remember him having chicken when we lived at the clinic. That went, sometime in the 1950s, I think. A little later went eggs.

Cooking for Jehangir, with his strict dietary compartments—no potatoes with rice, no fried food—was a thankless task, especially since he showed no appreciation for the meals Mehera made for him, in the beginning with the help of a cook, later on her own.

I don't remember any lunches with Jehangir when we lived at the clinic. He was always so busy he probably skipped them or ate on his own when he was relatively free of his patients. Dinner came from the clinic's kitchen, a little different for the family, I imagine, from what the in-patients got.

But after we moved to a flat not far from the clinic, at Warden Road, in a building constructed by Jehangir's elder brother Savak—finally a place of her own for Mehera, who longed for it—there was no question of lunches with or for Jehangir. A home-cooked dabba was impossible since he usually left by 6 in the morning, sometimes by 5.30. So he had lunch by himself at his clinic. The lunches were sparse: nuts, dates, dahi or lassi, sometimes cornflakes and milk and always, during the mango season, mangoes and milk. Milk was an essential part of his diet. He never stopped talking about the wholesomeness of milk or the benefits of a milk diet.

The milk diets fattened his underweight patients. They didn't fatten his skinny sons. In 1993, when surgeons cut open his flesh after he fell at his clinic, to pin together a femur which had shattered, they were amazed his bones were so strong. He was eighty-six then. 'Milk!' was the bulb that went off simultaneously above Firdausi's and my head. 'They're strong because of the milk!'

But milk also weakened his credentials in the eyes of sceptics and pill-swallowers, some of them relatives. They were used to stronger stuff. Jehangir didn't touch tea, coffee, wine or spirits—his was a strict Brahminical regime. That, and his 'natural' treatments, endeared him to some Congress leaders.

Morarji Desai, whose fasts he sometimes supervised, was a good patient but difficult to like. Jehangir admired Jawaharlal Nehru despite being roundly scolded by him once on account of Morarji. 'You're playing fast and loose with the CM's life! You're starving him!' Nehru shouted on the grounds of a house in Juhu where Morarji was temporarily staying. Jehangir tried to explain that fasting wasn't starving but that wasn't necessary. Morarji arrived on the scene, his face glowing. He had gone for a brisk walk. Nehru relented.

Jehangir was scolded by Gandhiji too who sent for him occasionally when he was fasting. 'Jussawalla, I don't like this,' he said more than once. 'Your clinic is for the rich. It should serve the poor.' And when Jehangir was preparing to leave for New York, to attend the golden jubilee conference of the American Naturopathic Association to which he had been invited, Gandhiji 'wrote back in his typical Gujarati on a post card: "By going you are not helping India. Stay here and serve",' Jehangir had reminisced in an interview with Hiren Bose, *The Indian Post*, 9 October 1989 (shortly after the news that he'd been awarded the Dhanvantari).

I can still recall the desolation I felt when the TWA plane, with Jehangir in it, lifted off the runway at Santa Cruz airport and disappeared into the grey monsoon skies. He was away for two months.

During that time the clinic suffered. So did Mehera whose efforts at beautifying the clinic, her only home at that time, weren't always appreciated. She had an artist's eye, she had spent some time in Santiniketan, and rather than be a masseuse in Jehangir's clinic, for which she had been trained, she was its decorator and housekeeper.

She transformed the clinic's waiting room from a dowdy box lined with photographs to an art gallery, hung with handpainted Amrita Sher-Gils, done not by the artist herself, but by an itinerant artist who, in her compassionate way, she tried to help. I can recall several living faces under those Sher-Gils—

Meena Kumari's, Bapsy Sabavala's, a grinning Tenzing Norgay's after his conquest of Everest. But what I recall with the greatest pleasure are the screams of patients. We had a small dog who would allow those in the waiting room to pet him before biting them.

Jehangir was on several committees, including the Health Panel of the Planning Commission but he wasn't an ideal committee man. For one thing, he didn't like leaving his clinic for a minute unless it was for house calls. Meetings in New Delhi and Calcutta sometimes left him agitated for days. On one occasion, during a session of the working committee of indigenous systems, he was surprised that the scholarly Dr Narasimha Rao refused to consider Nature Cure as an indigenous system of medicine. Rao was right. Strictly speaking, Nature Cure as a drugless method of healing, began in Europe in the eighteenth century, developed in various ways in the next century, and hit America at the century's end. It was eagerly promoted there by John H. Kellogg, Macfadden and Benedict Lust. India, with its many medical systems, was ready for one more. India was Nature Cure's logical next step.

Jehangir has said so in his book *The Key to Nature Cure*. At the same time, he had to believe that Nature Cure came from our rishis.

Fad, humbug, quackery: Nature Cure and Jehangir's practice have been called worse things in their time. The point is drugless systems of healing worked for him, and obviously for many of his patients. They worked for Mehera who, in 1957, was suspected of having a cancer; in her case the cure was Christian Science. They worked for Firdausi who was narrowly saved from an operation on one of his kidneys by Jehangir's intervention. They worked for my wife Veronik whose jaundice went with the daily supply of paan and a powder Jehangir secretly obtained and delivered. And when I see the spa at Veronik's hometown La Bourboule, with its scores of cubicles for hydrotherapeutic treatments and baths and its wonderful ambience, I'm reminded of the clinic and of how unrecognized systems of healing work.

They didn't exactly work for me. Though I'm grateful to the mochi who put me into a deep curative sleep—I don't think I've woken up fully—by chanting over me when I was bitten by a scorpion in Poona when I was two, I'm also grateful to the antibiotics which, because of Mehera's insistence, got me through bronchopneumonia when I was eight. It was Jehangir himself who told me, much later in my life, that they'd given me up.

In an interview with Ujwala Samarth in *Debonair*, Jehangir had said, 'We had one Universal Health Institute, on Lamington Road, where I was the honorary director. There were ayurveds, homoeopaths and allopaths, all working together. First the patients went through thorough examination. Then we would discuss the case, and if I said, "Look here, this is a case I can't treat," the homoeopath would say, "No, I will be able to do it." And he would treat the patient. We worked together, all of us. But that lasted only for a year.'

I've said Jehangir never had lunch with us after we moved to Warden Road but that isn't strictly true. He did on Sundays. But very soon after lunch he'd leave to teach a group of blind students physiotherapy. He did this at the Victoria Memorial School for the Blind where he'd been made an honorary director in 1952. It was an activity very close to his heart. He was proud of those students who went on to become professional masseurs and greatly distressed when the physiotherapy department closed. He spent his Sunday afternoons writing, then. And taking sun baths.

One of my most vivid memories of Jehangir is of him sitting on the west-facing balcony outside his bedroom, bare-chested, his skin glowing in the sun. He seemed resigned, his eyes closed, moving his body almost imperceptibly, basking in the sun, content with its healing.

He used to write at the clinic, he used to write at home. He wrote for many of the journals of his time, including *The Illustrated Weekly of India*, *Eve's Weekly* and *Kaiser-e-Hind*. Between 1949, when he brought out his first pamphlet *The Message of Nature Cure to Suffering Humanity* to 1994, when he brought out his last book *Nature's Materia Medica*, he published more than thirty books and pamphlets, many for Jasu Shah's Vegetarian Society to which he was committed.

In 1994, when he was the sole medical worker in his clinic, still accepting very difficult cases for treatment and preparing to write three more volumes, one on teaching blind students physiotherapy, he had a second fall. It broke his right thighbone. He never fully recovered from the operations that followed and, after a mild stroke, died on the morning of 5 December 1997. He was ninety years old.

Despite occasionally asserting that he'd never die, did he feel his age? The answer is: Yes. In an unpublished note he gave me when he was eighty, he wrote:

> 'Looking back from the high watchtower of old age on the past years of my life and all the complications of my paths, they seem to wind themselves sometimes on the brink of an abyss; but they lead against all expectation to the glorious heights of vocation and finally attain them, and I have every reason to praise the tender and wise ruling of providence, the more so as the paths which according to human ideas seemed to be sad and leading to death, showed to me and numberless others the opening to new life.'

BLACK MOON RISING

It's 9.45 a.m., polling day. A helicopter has been flying low, its nose pointed downwards, as though it were about to rake Colaba's voters and polling stations with rockets. What mission could it be on? Does it have infrared sensors to spot false identity cards? Can it freeze potential boothcapturers in their tracks? 'Those whiners that keep crashing into the flat in flames', I once wrote, thinking of the danger of low-flying helicopters. This one glides past the twentieth floor of a thirty-storey building by the sea. This won't do, I mutter to myself. It's worse than a loose cannon. Which madman could have sent it?

Ships—mostly tankers and cargo vessels—are peacefully at anchor. A line of fishing trawlers slowly moves south. From the fishing village nearby, clusters of people move south too. They are dressed in their polling-day best.

It's been like this at every election. The smell of joggers early in the morning gives way, today, to the scent of aftershave, expensive perfumes, ultra-sweet attar and flowers in the hair. The chlorine tang of bleach wafts off a kurta. Starched shirts, crisp saris, the occasional bit of jewellery—Bombay's upper and middle classes put on their election day uniform, and strut to their polling stations. Strut or march. One doesn't walk to a polling station, dear. It just isn't done. It's our day for showing off.

It's also our day for smiling at strangers. Election Day in a free and democratic society—how free, how democratic are questions I'll avoid for the moment—bestows on its members a certain complicity, empowers them with a secret they carry with themselves to the ballot box. The smiles exchanged between strangers and neighbours are coded with a simple message. We've made it this far, we've come through once again.

Consider some other parts of the country, like Bihar, and no, we haven't come through at all. Get frustrated. Consider villages abandoned to the politics of caste, poverty and terror and feel shame. Consider how we condone the politics of murder and revenge in role models like Phoolan Devi and act surprised that we've often elected a bunch of criminals to govern us. I feel a surge of anger. Should I tear up my ballot paper in protest?

There's predictable confusion in the corridors of the polling station. A couple is in tears because their names are not on the rolls. An election officer tenderly dabs the lower crescent of the nail on my left forefinger with indelible ink. This time she makes a mess of it. Instead of making a clean black dot, the ink spills, leaving behind it a tail like that of a comet or the handle of a ladle. But the dot's still there. I'm elated. The feeling will return, off and on, for the two months or so it takes for the dot to rise and disappear over the rim of my nail. I'll make sure, for weeks, that everyone notices that forefinger, especially those who haven't voted and who, for those weeks, will be burying their hands in pockets or behind the folds of saris. Next day I'm in another corridor, another place also by the sea. My father is being wheeled into an operating theatre for the fourth time. The tide is coming in. The rocks look ragged and rough.

A ward boy in hospital green comes dancing down the corridor, tossing a bunch of keys from hand to hand. He looks happy and confident as though he had just led his team to victory in a cricket match, as though he didn't have a care in the world.

My brother displays a plastic bag which contains the contraption they took out of my father's fractured thigh. He shakes the bag against the light; its contents rattle and gleam. The tide is in, the sun is going down, my father is still unconscious.

I look at the dot on my finger, a black moon rising.

SHIKAST I:
WHEN EARTH ROSE UP TO GET ME

When you faced the road and turned round to watch them dump fresh loads of earth, you couldn't see for the dust. When you turned towards the road again, you saw a line of lorries go by, their weighty cargoes of stone and rubble unable to stop their juddering and rattling.

One day, through the dust, I saw the shape of a cow galloping towards me. As it got nearer I saw that it was a cow galloping straight at me. I was walking a puppy, about eight months old. The cow snorted and lunged at the puppy. I picked the puppy up. The cow lunged at me holding the puppy. I put the puppy down. This time cow made contact.

Huge head tries to grind tiny puppy into ground. Puppy yelps. I scoop puppy up and run. Cow follows. If I zig, cow zigs. If I zag, cow zags.

'Don't panic!' a friend shouted from a distance, his legs spread like Wyatt Earp's, his hands by his holsters. Except that the chump had no guns, bullets or holsters on him. I panicked.

But a minute later came a skilful sidestep, the left horn of the cow grazing my sleeve; and I thought I was getting there. I saw a fruitful career in Spain ahead of me. I also heard heavy panting. A bhaiya, his eyes wild, sprang to restrain the cow, but it deflected off him onto the main road.

'What happened?' I asked, for the first time noticing that the owners of the cigarette stalls and the bania shop around us, along with several pedestrians, were grinning instead of applauding. I gave them a sour look and heard the bhaiya's answer: 'Uska baccha mar gaya.'

Its baby died. Just now. You see? I watched the cow running down Cuffe Parade. The bhaiya ran in pursuit.

I saw what the bhaiya meant and I didn't see. Maddened by grief, was the cow so deranged that it saw every little four-legged creature as its own lost baby? Or did rage make it want to kill every little four-legged creature because its own had just died?

I've often thought of the cow-puppy incident which took place during our first year in Cuffe Parade. Twenty-five years later I still don't know what drove the cow mad but given the evidence those years have provided, I'd say it was rage.

Grief, intense grief—and rage, wild rage—co-exist, except perhaps in a few saintly people. They are a deadly mix, tending to ignite without reason, without a thought to time, place or occasion. Why should all of you be so happy and I so miserable? they shout together. Together they make a woman swear revenge on her in-laws for the death of her daughters, though the in-laws may have had nothing to do with their deaths. They voice our incapacity to endure the fact that just as we and the living things precious to us came into life, we and those same living things must leave it. They are our cry for life. They are our breaking, our shattering, our defeat, our shikast.

Cuffe Parade is supposed to be a posh and genteel neighbourhood and those of us who live in it usually turn away from its other side. We haven't been particularly moved by the deaths of construction workers or domestic servants, crushed under lorries or falling from heights. Nor have we responded much to fires which have razed large areas of zopadpattis on either side of the complex. But terrible things have happened within each building. Where do the children play?

Some never will. They have fallen to their deaths, been run over by their own school bus, died in road accidents. Grief and rage abound in the neighbourhood as in any other. They fill each window as bees fill a honeycomb. At night every single window seems lit as though for a carnival, each high-rise a cascade of silver and gold sequins. At times it's magic, at times, not. One bad night I wrote a line: 'Every lit window a cry for help.'

But it's at ground level that help is most sought and perhaps most given. A friend of mine once called Colaba, close to Cuffe Parade, 'the anus of the world'. Both he and I have seen worse anuses. Honolulu, despite the small houses crawling up its hillsides, is supposed to be a gigantic Cuffe Parade, filthy rich. But its one low-life area is as scary as it can get. People don't look at you there, they stare daggers. From every bar stool and table, that look of daggers. Anyway, I'm frequently at ground level and ground level to me often means Colaba, the streets and lanes of which I like to wander in. In search of?

Well, nothing, really. We're just a night-pack of ghosts out there, some hunting, some being hunted, some begging, some mainlining, some hustling, clumps of street kids in the shadows, bent over cigarette foil, chasing.

Slumming, my cynical friends and enemies say. It's called slumming. Well, cynical friends and enemies, don't you remember the Robert Frost poem 'To Earthward'? It begins: *Love at the lips was touch/As sweet as I could bear . . .*

In the course of the poem, the poet regrets the inevitable dilution of early love's extremes of joy and pain, and ends: *When stiff and sore and scarred/I take away my hand/From leaning on it hard/In grass and sand,/The hurt is not enough:/ I long for weight and strength/To feel the earth as rough/To all my length.*

The hurt is not enough, domestic hurt is not enough, the pain in the windows—somebody else's pain—is never enough. That's why we go to the anuses of the world and into the entrails beyond them. We seek an underworld—Colaba is my pale bourgeois version of it—where we may, with luck, come across our alter egos: the murderer, the thief, the conman, the hooker, the sex offender, the person who almost committed the perfect suicide.

Suicide is a curious business—it's so easy to do and yet not do—and an editorial in *The Times of India*, on the Supreme Court's decision to overturn a previous ruling which decriminalized attempted suicide, adds a curious twist to it; it mentions something called 'chronic suicide'. I'd have thought all suicides are chronic—like the chronic cold, they won't go away—but what the term apparently defines is those who persist in drug abuse or alcohol abuse over a long period of time. Well, we've plenty of those in our neighbourhood.

Why try to hide the fact and where hide it?

You can't brush dirt under dirt no more than you can brush earth under earth. The earth, under your feet, under the pavement, has its claims and demands. It claims attention, it demands you be hurt and hurt again, if only to acknowledge how much you've been responsible for hurting other people. If you ignore these claims and demands for too long a time, if your life's just dreaming without responsibility, you may not stumble, may not fall, but be sure the earth will rise up to get you.

I'm a dreamer, always have been, and generally dream without responsibility. One night when I was happy, having gone from bar to bar through the entrails of Colaba, having decided that that was one way to escape the burden and boredom of responsibility, of numbing the pain of not handling it, I found I had difficulty walking. I'd got off a bus quite close to where I lived and discovered, to my stupefaction, that I couldn't walk.

I thought a meal would fix me up so I managed to sway, don't know how, into the nearest beer bar and had one. It was a spicy curry and rice. The spice, instead of damping the alcohol, worked on it like a drug. Soon I was out of the bar, shot out like a cork, I was dreaming, I was flying, I was moving faster and faster over heaps of small stones, I was going home . . . when I felt the taste of steel in my mouth. My head rang as though hit by a bell. The taste of steel was my blood. It filled my mouth. It began blotching my kurta.

SHIKAST 2:
TAKE ME IN THE SKY OF YOUR HANDS

Before her eyes was the violent blue sky—nothing else. For an endless moment she looked into it. Like a great overpowering sound, it destroyed everything in her mind, paralysed her. Someone once had said to her that the sky hides the night behind it, shelters the person beneath from the horror that lies above. Unblinking, she fixed the solid emptiness, and the anguish began to move in her. At any moment the rip can occur, the edges fly back, and the great maw will be revealed.

Paul Bowles, *The Sheltering Sky*

> *Blue world, O blue, blue world!*
> *Even to die into this blueness would be no pain.*
>
> Sergei Esenin, 'Confession of a Hooligan'

A clump of grey teeth had split my lip open. I couldn't have fallen. Earth had risen up to get me. I lay on the stones for a while, my head spinning, until firm hands pulled me up. It was the waiter who had served me at the beer bar and who had noticed my flight. He propelled me homewards. I found I could walk. I left him at a street corner.

My lip was beginning to swell and my kurta was splattered with bloodstains. Chowkidars stared, liftmen averted their gaze.

The wife was surprisingly calm. She cleaned me up patiently, not saying a word, then advanced on me with a bottle of almost pure alcohol. 'Surely no more of that,' I tried to joke feebly. Then the jabs of alcohol-soaked cotton wool began. I didn't scream but I wasn't brave. The healing spirit took over my wife completely. The jabs got more vigorous and frequent. Her eyes had grown steely and narrow.

'So this is how you spend your evenings.' Jab. 'This is how you turn up at the door.' Jab. 'Did you see the way you crossed the road?' Jab, jab, jab. I couldn't bite my lip because it had been bitten through anyway. I still didn't scream.

By morning my head had stopped ringing, but my lip looked as though there were a table-tennis ball behind it. I knew a friend who had fallen headlong down some stairs in circumstances similar to mine. He could have been killed. So could I have been. We had both seen stars and got away with it.

Once and only once did I see stars that made me weep. As children, we cup our palms over our eyes and see stars like specks of dust, moving. If we keep our palms there long enough we get the impression that we are moving out of our bodies into the stars. But the experience I'm thinking of happened when I was no longer a child. I was eighteen, lying on my back in a park in London, and looking at the stars. I had hardly spoken to anyone for weeks, hadn't eaten much, was suffering from delusions of grandeur. In short, I was either heading for a breakdown or was in the process of going through one. When something incredible happened.

I knew such joy as I have never known since. I felt such an understanding of things as has never come my way again. Everything, but everything, made sense. Every little bit of the chaotic world I was in and the terrifying sky above fell into place. I felt lifted into the stars. I felt such peace and joy, such incredible happiness that I cried for it to stop. Was this my one and only mystical experience? Was it the peace that passeth understanding? I'll never know. I only know I feel bereft, abandoned, I ache for that experience again, more and more certain that I will not get it because I thrash around in a state of disbelief and bafflement and the light no longer shines on me.

This is no dark night of the soul. It is defeat, despair, a state of sin. The Angel of Light has turned into an Angel of Darkness and God can't be bothered with me anymore.

It's hell, this damnation of perpetual defeat, this never-ending shikast. John Donne, poet and Dean of St Paul's, London, expresses the anguish of every abandoned believer— and I am not a believer—when he asks why God provides for 'every weed and worm and ant and spider and toad and viper' and no light shines on him. It's the old cry of why should all of you be so happy and I so miserable? It's the old-time religion again, this continuous shattering and falling apart, this ever-new shikast. Listen:

> 'What Tophet is not Paradise, what Brimstone is not Amber, what gnashing is not a comfort, what gnawing of the worm is not a tickling, what torment is not a marriage bed compared to this damnation, to be secluded eternally, eternally, eternally, from the sight of God?'

It's harsh, this sound of a broken man coming from a broken body. But is there something else to defeat? Is 'the only true body ... a broken body' as the thinker Norman O. Brown says? And 'Accept loss forever. To lose one's soul, Satori, when the ego is broken, is not victory, but final defeat, the becoming like nothing.'

That's the terror, the becoming like nothing, the terror of the abyss. It's the 'giant maw' in Paul Bowles' protagonist's consciousness, not a sky of comfort but a mix of blood and shit, a flying carpet of cockroaches that gets into mouth, ears, nostrils, vagina and anus. Before the light of the pure blue sky is the sky of pestilence, disease and death. Locusts fall from it, and sand and hail. The tree of life is upside down, its roots in a messy heaven, things that normally scrabble and crawl fall from it—scorpions, snakes and rats. Woodlice fall from it, pigeons fall from it, their mites infecting and choking our lungs.

The day after the nuclear test at Pokhran, I entered my flat to find table lamps toppled to the ground, paintings off the walls, the living room flooded. Pokhran had nothing to do with it, of course, but a giant hand had hit the flat in my absence, an unexpected thunderstorm. Another time, shortly after the monsoon, we watched a convection storm come in from the east. The entire sky became one slowly approaching hood, projecting hundreds of snake-mouths. When the hood went over our heads and the air became sulphurous, we weren't afraid, but we saw a sky that came with a warning. Look what I can be and do. I have the upper hand, always.

Between the clear blue sky and us, the sky of pestilence, disease and death. Beyond the clear blue sky a black hole—from which no light can emerge, not even God's. Scared witless, should I bury my head in sand? If ostriches have lost their ability to fly, so have I. Will I ever fly again?

One night I have a dream in which I see myself lying in a tub of water. The water is covered from end to end of the tub with what look like cornflakes but are, in fact, flakes of shit; odourless flakes of shit. Strangely I feel neither fear nor disgust. Just a sense of helpless despair.

Help comes from an unexpected source, the dream of a patient dying of AIDS. In the dream he is haunted by a spectre mantled with terrifying scales. The spectre haunts him for several days, an obvious Angel of Darkness. One day he has an insight. If Satan could come disguised as an Angel of Light, why couldn't God come disguised as an Angel of Darkness? 'I know that to really love God, I have to love Him when his face is averted,' says the AIDS patient to his analyst (in *Dreaming with an AIDS Patient* by Robert Bosnak). 'When He comes to me in apparent darkness, I wouldn't truly love Him if I only wanted His light. With this insight something has changed about the spectre. I begin to see light. The light is coming from behind the scaly mantle. He is opening up the mantle and I see eyes, thousands of eyes looking at me. I know that these are the eyes of Shekina, the female aspect of God dwelling in the world. The light is magnificent, and I feel seen. I feel totally seen. And I feel love.'

So the flakes of shit in my dream are not really shit, they are the eyes of God. The Angel of Darkness that haunts me, gives me so much pain, is really the Angel of Light. The giant maw behind the blue sky is filled with eyes, with stars, even though their light hasn't reached me. I must continue to love even if I see only darkness.

Before Peyton Loftis jumps to her death in William Styron's *Lie Down in Darkness* she has a vision of birds, many of which have lost the ability to fly—ostriches, emus and the like. 'I turn in the room and see them come across the tiles, dimly prancing, fluffing up their wings, I think: my poor flightless birds, have you suffered without soaring on this earth? Come then and fly. And they move on past me through the darkening sands, awkward and gentle, rustling their features. Come then and fly. And so it happens: treading past to touch my boiling skin—one whisper of feathers is all—and I see them go—oh my Christ!—one by one ascending, my flightless birds through the suffocating night, toward paradise.'

There are hands which are skies. My soul's deep in shit. Through the suffocating night, take me in the sky of your hands.

'Shakespeare was a Bengali'

JOKES APART

PORTRAIT OF A LADY

'Fine time you have come. Six o'clock for you is eight. If six persons die in accident you will write in *Debonair* eight? Talk inside only, not on my doorstep. Go away. It's too late to talk now.

'Again you knock? Have you no shame? Talk inside only, I say and again you say Sorry? My Monacos have become like blotting papers and you will eat? Go away. I'm very upset.

'Once more you knock? If goondas stoned your taxi, blame Fernandes. Blame Antulay, blame Bhosle, blame BEST, blame Shiv Sena, blame mill workers—fine blamers you journalists have become. Justice Lentins you think you all are, making big judgements in style.

'You blame the Law because it is too slow. Yes, it is too slow. Then if the common citizen takes the Law into her own hands, you blame the citizens. Again you answer back? You won't blame the citizens. You're sure?

'All right, come in. Let's see if you blame me or not. All, all will blame me.

'This way. You like chocolate cake also? Big eyes you are making at my chocolate cake. It's not for you. It's for a pig. This way. Now shut the door. Bolt it. Bolt it!

'So you've come at last. Two whole hours I waited. All this I made for you. Going downstairs, going to market, going to kitchen there, here, to and fro. I have no servant. My body is too big for shopping. Now I won't budge. If your hand is cut, use vodka. Help yourself. I won't budge.

'I started feeling low long before my husband died. I used to just sit. Then they found diabetes, then arthritis. "Shera," he used to say, "this is tragic indeed. But the universe of tragedy must be confronted on your feet." "Go Jerry m'n," I used to reply. "Let the Cheeno make just one pair of shoes for me, then I will stand on my feet." Such nice turns of phrase he used to have. Such jokes we would make. But he was too delicate. Modern life is like a rusty nail. It enters your flesh, here and there, and we use Dettol, we use iodine, we take tetanus injections. We manage. But it went through his lungs.

'I come from a strong family. My father was like Dumbo. My uncle was Ardeshir pehelwan of Peshawar fame. When my grandmother got angry, she broke up her bed like a biscuit. But he came from poor stock. Too much curry makes the blood thin. He was bold, mind you. He used to have long hair before it was fashion. His nose was just like Hedy Lamarr's. Samson and Delilah, the Bandraboys would call us. "You are my Samson," he told me on his last day in hospital. "You must complete what I couldn't." Such work he did with the Bandraboys. One proud mother said on Founders' Day, "Mrs D'Lima, let me tell you your husband is a miracle worker. He has turned our little pigs into Oliviers."

'And now I have this dirty pig on my hands. I thought of killing him just as they kill a pig. Have you seen how they kill a pig? I saw every Christmas. Khachack! Then blood like Flora Fountain. I saw. Jerry's family accepted me. Not like my brother and sister. And some Parsi friends.

'Show me your sudra and kusti. You don't wear? Good sign. I will show you my sudra and kusti. Murre re, with blood you turn white, now you turn red? What sort of man has your editor sent me? But your paper is full of naked ladies! My policy is no sudra, no kusti, no bra. So much weight on ladies' hearts, why should they bear more?

'Don't misunderstand, please. I am being frank because of other ladies also. All men think they can have us for nothing. Your *Debonair*—it doesn't use ladies for nothing?

'I told my son, "Roy, I can't bear this suffering any more. I want to kill the pig!" I put up with him after Jerry died because we had no money and he used to bring such nice things from abroad. That Black Label you are having, that vodka—he still brings. As though it can heal each and every wound. So some young girls come to see me. Roy's friends from Elphinstone. They heard my story and they said it's every woman's story when she has no means of her own, she has to depend on a man. They said they would contact *Manushi*. *Manushi* would print my story. But before anything could happen, the pig got wind of it. He moves in high places, he must have heard from one of his daughter's friends that I was going to talk. So he plays Good Samaritan. He contracts your editor and says in his sweet-sweet voice, "Mr Dharker, if you want a story on the housing problem, I know someone who'll make good copy. It's a very sad case and she'll talk. In fact, she won't stop talking." I heard him on the phone. I heard him. If I'd had strength then, I would have picked up a knife and killed him on the spot. But my blood sugar had dropped. I just kept sitting. Then sitting-sitting I said to myself, "This pig is also a spider. He has caught you and Roy in his web. Soon he will eat you up like a fly and throw Roy out in the streets. You have to act."

'So here we are, talking about my housing problem. What new thing will you write? The supports you can see with your own eyes, no? The cracked walls you can see, no? Fifteen years you take the landlord to court, no repair. Fifteen years you fight for tenancy rights, no result. That's why he steps in. To soften my heart. He thinks it is Mafco mutton?

'And why he wants to soften me up? So he thinks I will let this place be his also. Fight the landlord with me, he thinks, and my heart will melt. And let him bring strange ladies here! Am I his wife to put up with this? Do I live in posh areas like his wife? "No," I told him, "this is my and Roy's home. You are turning it into a brothel. Leave us alone." But he is a pig and never listens. An unclean animal. After today, he will leave us alone.

'His name is Noshir, Captain Noshir. Big pilot in Air India. High-flier. Scoundrel. Napoleon he thinks he is in his pilot's suit. Our conqueror. He will come here straight from airport. At ten he will be here. You will witness.

'He will let himself in and see the cake and brandy. That he must have after every flight—my chocolate cake and his brandy. He will have it, thinking of his new girlfriend, I suppose.

'He may think: She will come at eleven. I will take her to Taj, to Oberoi. We will go dancing. Thinking such thoughts he will get sharp pain in his bowels. He will feel nausea, his head will spin. Only then will I budge. He will not die, but while he is suffering I will ask him sweetly, "Why you are acting like this, Noshir? Too much brandy? What lights going on off on off? You think you are in Studio 29? You think you are with Homai? No, this is Shera. This is my and Roy's home. Sign this paper. Promise to leave us alone or I won't give you enema. I will let you suffer until Homai comes. She is a nurse. Let her give you enema." Let the poison work slowly. Let Homai see when she comes. You will witness.

'You don't want? Go then. You are free to go. Call the police. I will be arrested and you will be hero. You want to be hero, then go.

'When you will print my story? What are you saying, not on housing? It is every lady's story. Every lady will read it. Put this picture on cover. Why only pictures of naked ladies? It is portrait of me by EOS Studio when I got engaged.

'You're not going. I see you want to witness. No? Name of poison? Why should I tell you name of poison when you don't want to tell my story? You are not feeling giddy, you are only high. Such a small pinch I put for you. I take small pinches every day—in tea, in cakes, in soda. It is only like opium. You won't die.

'All right, promise to tell my story and I will tell you the name. Now promise one more thing. Have respect for me when you write. Treat me like a lady. You swear? Swear on God.

'Fine. Now sit down and wait. I will tell you the name of the poison.'

THE NONE O'CLOCK NEWS

This was a column written for The Sunday Observer *in response to the millennium madness that had gripped the press. Jussawalla created a series of deadpan reports from the year 2099. Some seem like they might come true in the very near future.*
Editor

29 AUGUST 2099

Another Bombay First

With the completion of the 56,0000th flyover last Thursday, Mumbai becomes the first city in the world to use only flyovers for its transport. Its last link with a usable ground-level road, once called Linking, now stands severed.

Some readers may remember that Mumbai's ground-level roads became unsuitable for traffic after they were occupied by refugees from countries which belonged to the former European Union—victims of expansionist Scotland's greed. After defeating France in 2047, Scotland went on to annex most of Europe, including Greece, Malta, Cyprus and the newly independent nation of Corsica.

While most of Mumbai's citizens have left the city to the refugees from Europe, its pavement- and slum-dwellers have been relocated in dormitory-dirigibles far above the city. These are permanently moored to the sea-bed.

Like its other flyovers, Mumbai's 56,000th will be given a special touch when it's opened today by American President Harold Loosefeather.

It will be for the exclusive use of turbojet-tricycle riders, in other words, UN observers, Scottish nationalists on holiday, and the occasional Parsi pedestrian.

Saucy Saucer

Rakabi-II, India's indigenous space saucer, which sucked up a shamiana and its VVIPs as it passed above them during Bhubaneswar's fifth aerospace show earlier this year, has flown past Mars.

Ground control reports that the spacecraft's wobbling trajectory indicates that outbursts of space rage involving the spacecraft's crew and its accidental passengers are in progress.

Space officials say that given the circumstances this is normal behaviour and there is no cause for worry.

12 SEPTEMBER 2099

Mother of all Parliaments

Parliament's new house, the Mummy Sabha, opened yesterday to rapturous applause from its members. The all-mother session was fully attended. Speaker Sangama Das, mother of fourteen, said that with the opening of the house, England had lost the right to call herself the mother of parliaments. In one bold stroke, India had become both the cradle of democracy and the mother of parliaments.

When Indo-Scot bard Vinay McNeigh pointed out to the Speaker that her metaphors were mixed and that after the Scottish invasion of 2047 both England and her parliament had ceased to exist, the Speaker shot back, 'You don't exist.'

The house was adjourned amidst scenes of pandemonium.

Teenage Terrorists Give the Slip

Eighteen-year-old terrorists Bipin and Omar have escaped from the capital's Tihar jail. The duo, sentenced to a year's rigorous meditation for hijacking an army helicopter and strewing Rajpath with banana peels during this year's Republic Day parade, has vowed to target Mumbai's flyovers next.

Those dismayed by the development include several army personnel who suffered severe falls during the marchpast and this paper's chief photographer Ashutosh Gokhale who was struck unconscious by a sliding horse which later grew very fond of him.

The UN's permanent representative in India, Maisie Albright, herself a victim of banana-peel terrorism, has urged the government to re-apprehend the culprits without delay.

Happy Days Are Here Again

With the passing of the Happy Days Bill, the voting age for Indian citizens rises dramatically from fifty to sixty-one. This is expected to reduce the average number of times an Indian citizen has to go to the polls in his lifetime. The number is expected to go down from the current figure of 550 to 322. S. K. Lohia (115), who has voted in all the 512 general elections held in this country since 2004, was too weak to comment on the change.

19 SEPTEMBER 2099

A Farewell to Arms

India's installation artist Teesta daBeesta has sued Aerospace Australia for accidentally shipping her artificial arms to Sydney as part of her installation.

The arms, which Ms daBeesta had temporarily set aside on the aerospaceline's counter at Mumbai's Mahanirvan spaceport, were apparently dispatched to Sydney along with parts of the installation by an over-zealous loader.

Surprised to find them on the luggage belt instead of on herself at Sydney spaceport, Ms daBeesta pleaded with the authorities to return her arms to her but to no avail. The authorities told her that since the arms had been shipped as part of her installation they could not be regarded as personal property.

The installation was re-assembled as 'Reindeer' instead of the planned 'Dinner Plate' with Ms daBeesta's arms serving as antlers. It won no prize at the Biennale to which the artist had been invited but has been bought by the Sydney Anti-Poachers' Club to serve as a warning to poachers.

An official at the Australian High Commission hinted that Ms daBeesta was unlikely to get her arms back.

Again

Escapee banana-peel terrorists Bipin and Omar have struck their first blow in Mumbai as feared.

Ms Maisie Albright's turbojet tricycle skidded on Flyover 4001 as she tried to negotiate a bend. Banana peels were found near the site of the accident. Ms Albright has urged the government to re-apprehend the duo without delay.

26 SEPTEMBER 2099

Going Ape in Cleveland

Apes were found to have occupied every seat in a cinema in Cleveland, Ohio, after frantic citizens alerted the police. The apes had broken out of Cleveland's Primate Language-Teaching Facility (PLTF) next door to the cinema during a special screening of the twentieth-century classic *Titanic*. Leader of the breakaway apes, Gloria Swanson, named after a star of the silent-movie era, admitted from her jail cell later that she wanted to prove to herself and her fellow students that even apes could understand what humans said to each other in *Titanic*. She went on to praise the PLTF's efforts in teaching her species language skills required to understand what humans said to each other in the movies.

She stated, however, that her experience of *Titanic* confirmed her preference for silent movies in which no one could hear humans speak.

Aspi and the Dolphin

Aspi Godrej-Lamborghini had a narrow escape in Mumbai yesterday when he was carried out to sea on an immersion platform during the Ganesh Utsav ceremonies. On arriving at the Tata Theatre helipad in South Mumbai where he had gone to see *Brouhaha*, a musical laser-show based on *King Lear*, he was put onto an automated immersion belt instead of being conveyed to the private capsule which takes him to his permanently reserved seat in the theatre.

A naval helicopter picked Mr Godrej-Lamborghini up from the immersion platform before he was ejected from it. A stickler for punctuality and courteous almost to a fault, the much-loved scion of the Godrej-Lamborghini clan insisted on riding to the theatre on the back of one of the chopper's Dolphin torpedoes instead of inconveniencing the navy further. Though there were many casualties, he arrived at his seat on time.

They Laughed their Heads Off

The trials of the 101 members of Mumbai's Girgaum Laughter Club and their leader, twenty-year-old Nitin Shah, have ended. Arrested for inappropriate laughter during a ride on Kolkata's ancient metro where only prayers or a pious silence are allowed, the sentences on them were passed and carried out at dawn yesterday.

They were beheaded.

3 OCTOBER 2099

No Laughing Matter

Descendants of some of the twentieth century's funniest novelists were physically attacked at the Eighth International Seminar on High Art now being held at the Kellogg Laughter Detox Facility (KLDF) in Omaha, Nebraska.

The KLDF, which treats an average of 50,000 patients a year for laughter dependency, is also a detention centre for the descendants of novelists who tried to subvert the high moral ethos of the US during the last century, now widely regarded as the worst century of the millennium with some of the worst cases of laughter dependency in human history.

When detainee Burt Vonnegut, great-great-grandson of novelist Kurt Vonnegut, asked yesterday's panel of speakers why he should have to pay for his forefather's sins, he was asked to read the Bible. When he refused, a copy was pushed into his hands.

This led to a violent altercation between the seminarists and the detainees until the lunch bell sounded. The detainees were then physically removed from their seats for being improperly dressed in jeans and T-shirts, a fashion of the last century. The regulation dress for seminars on high art is the toga.

GM Leaf Goes Wild

The Government of India is threatening to sue multinational giant Cabbage&King for producing a genetically modified lettuce leaf which is running rampant in Haryana. The new strain of leaf, Cariappa2, runs faster and further than its predecessor, Cariappa1, making farming the lettuce almost impossible. Inmates of the Czech refugee camp on the outskirts of Chandigarh have been known to chase the leaf cross-country but to no avail. Malnourished as they are, some of the refugees cross the limits of exhaustion in their pursuit, and have to be carried back to their camp in UN helicopters.

UN spokesperson for refugees, Freny Pithawalla, claimed that the new lettuce leaf was a drain on the UN's precious fuel supplies. She chided the Cabbage&King management for calling the leaf a runaway success.

Bananas Off

Fruit rights activists have called for a worldwide ban on banana-peel jokes. A spokesperson of the Mumbai branch of Peelings Have Feelings said that the group was particularly incensed by reports of the activities of banana-peel terrorists Omar and Bipin, which have appeared in this paper. Mumbai's banana vendors have called for an indefinite strike as a result.

10 OCTOBER 2099

Dead Men Rising

The hydraulic stilts supporting the Lodi tombs in the nation's capital are behaving ominously, according to Supernatural Agency Chairperson, Henrietta Lamb. At a press conference held at Tomb No 4 yesterday, Ms Lamb said that the stilts that had proved so effective in raising the tombs during Delhi's annual floods were once again behaving strangely. She spoke of the incident in 2066 when Tomb No 3's stilts had lowered it into the floods instead of raising it higher, thus causing it to be washed away. She reminded those present that this happened in the year when Indian culture was nearly washed away too, with Scottish troops poised to invade the country. She felt the odd behaviour of the stilts this year was also an omen. They were doing as they pleased, sometimes raising tombs to the maximum height (50 metres) at great speed in perfectly dry weather.

A tomb rose during the press conference too. This correspondent jumped off in time but cannot vouch for the others. Nor does he care. Rescue operations are unfortunately in progress.

Nobel for Literature: Not Worth a Yodel

The decision to award this year's Nobel Prize for literature to Corsican balladeer Enrico Graverno has led to nation-wide protests in Switzerland.

Since the prize went oral in 2069, with weightage being given to the sung rather than the written word, it was felt that this year's award should have rightfully gone to 103-year-old Swiss yodeller Franz (Frank) Lustiger, one of the last of his line.

When asked for his reaction, Indo-Scot bard Vinay McNeigh recited one of the best lines of the last century: 'You are in queue, please wait.'

17 OCTOBER 2099

Minister Streamlines Shuttle

The magnetic levitation (maglev) point-to-point shuttles now operating in the metros are in for a big change.

With a view to reducing costs, Minister for Railways Joydeep Bose has made it mandatory for all such shuttles to be hand-powered. They are to switch to the push-get-on-get-off-push mode of transportation from 6 a.m. tomorrow.

Called PGGP, this move requires commuters to push the shuttle until it reaches a decent speed, get on while it's moving, get off when it loses momentum and push again, and so on until they reach their destinations. Mr Bose says, 'The shuttle's frictionless magnetic tracks will make the going easy.'

Fresh tickets will be issued every day to commuters unable to board or reboard shuttles during their journeys.

Gland Finale

A concert is Munich had to be cancelled when members of the audience found their lymphatic glands swelling while they were listening to flute segments from Ravel's Introduction and Allegro for Harp, Strings, Flute and Clarinet, a piece that was to round off the Gunter Grass Zestfest in honour of the German author who won the Nobel Prize hundred years ago.

The swellings caused by the flute, later diagnosed as pitch-provoked glandular tumescence (PPGT), were painful and could have been fatal had conductor Al Horowitz not heard the cries and moans of the audience and stopped the performance. Observers could not help but remark on the coincidence between the swellings caused by the high pitch of the flute and the devastation caused by Oscar, hero of Grass's *The Tin Drum*, who could shatter glass by raising the pitch of his voice.

Flautist Elizabeth von Tromp is absconding.

Newsflash

Elizabeth von Tromp has been captured and sent to the moon.

31 OCTOBER 2099
Hazardous Books

In-Your-Face books have been banned with immediate effect. Explaining the ban yesterday, Minister for Health Sushma Reddy said that mounting injuries suffered by the public had compelled her to demand a ban.

The international craze for In-Your-Face books with their innovative use of artefacts and objects that literally flew off the page had prompted millions of Indians to buy them, resulting in injuries, sometimes severe, to various parts of the body, particularly to the face. The protective headgear required to read the books safely was unavailable in India since there is a ban on importing items made from genetically modified tea leaves and human fat.

Reddy admitted that the ghastly incident involving Bollywood star Tahira Tafat had influenced her decision to ban the books. It will be remembered that Ms Tafat had had two of her front teeth forcibly removed by a pair of pliers that had sprung out of last year's Booker winner *Hold Your Breath*. She had been unable to pursue her career in Bollywood thereafter.

Dassera Mix-up

The administrative tower in the capital's Ramayana theme park was burnt down yesterday by tourists from Rajasthan who mistook it for an effigy of Ravana. The futuristic tower, a long-standing landmark in the city and internationally recognized as a masterwork of architects Bhatia, Batliboi and Taj has been reduced to ashes.

Theme park CEO Kailash Singhvi stated, however, that the real effigy of Ravana would be left standing till Dassera next year to save costs.

Stealthy Mustard Fields

Fields of genetically modified mustard are moving towards Chandigarh at a stealthy pace. It seems the fields move only at night and cover about twenty-five metres at a stretch. GM experts are perplexed but Chandigarh residents are not unduly alarmed. Said housewife Kuldeep Gaur, 'Sarson da saag at my doorstep? What can be better?'

14 NOVEMBER 2099

Spacestation 5 Comes Alive

Government scientists on a regular flight to the moon had a narrow escape on Thursday when hundreds of stampeding bison crossed their path. The stampede occurred on state-owned Spacestation 5, when the space-suited bison leapt off the station instead of boarding the knackershuttle which was to carry them to Slaughterhouse Kookrekook, India's top foreign-exchange earner in space. A government spokesperson said that animals carried by Indian knackershuttles were well taken care of. Unlike those carried by knackershuttles of rival nations, they were soothed during their journey with music and herbal teas. He said that preliminary reports on Thursday's incident indicated that the bison stampeded when they heard the strains of a twentieth-century rock band, the Rolling Stones, instead of Tehmina Vakil's Buddhist chants which they were meant to hear. He claimed that the incident had embarrassed the Indian government and did not rule out sabotage.

Vatican Revamp

The Pope has ordered all priests in the Vatican to register for a six-week re-education programme since he has discovered that most of them are Buddhists.

28 NOVEMBER 2099

Musicians Hit Ceiling in Mumbai

Twelve harpists got stuck to the ceiling of the Jamshed Bhabha Theatre in Mumbai during a centenary-year concert yesterday. Preliminary investigations indicate that an inebriated technician pressed a switch which activated a magnet concealed in the ceiling, used with telling effect in the oratorio Elijah which was staged the previous evening. A rapt audience literally saw Elijah rise and disappear through the roof.

The metal-clad harpists, part of the Italian group Sinfonia Metallica, had just begun the second movement of Vimla Mirchandani's Concerto for Harps, Harmonium and Harmonica when the mishap occurred.

The harpists, along with their instruments, stayed fixed to the ceiling for more than thirty minutes before firemen could rescue them.

Camels Rescued in France

The caravan of camels which fell into France's largest underground cave a week ago has finally been located. A crack team of camel drivers from Dubai had to be specially flown in to entice the beasts back to terra firma. All 101 camels have been accounted for.

However, the 202 tourists who fell into the cave with the camels are refusing to surface, despite threats by the French authorities to gas them with a high-smelling cheese. The tourists, all British, claim that anywhere underground is better than life on the surface, especially in Britain. They demand underground asylum.

Population Threat in Britain

Britain's population will outstrip that of India in the first decade of the next century, warn population experts. The baby boom, triggered off by the birth of a fourth child to Tony Blair, a British prime minister and his wife, in the year 2000, shows no sign of abating.

Millions of British citizens who want to leave the country cannot because of the harsh immigration laws in the other countries of the Scottish Empire.

'It's a nightmare,' says Quincy Bhatt, ninety-nine, who has been living in Harrow with his eighteen siblings for seventy-five years. 'How I long for India now.'

19 DECEMBER 2099

PGGP Passenger Woes

Two months after Minster for Railways Joydeep Bose inaugurated his streamlined version of maglev point-to-point shuttles in the metros, a shuttle arrived at Safdarjung station in the capital without any passengers. Passengers claim that the push-get-on-get-off-push (PGGP) mode of transport failed when the shuttle unaccountably picked up speed between the Defence Colony and the Hauz Khas stations. The passengers who had dismounted to push it got left behind. Though they gave chase, they could not catch up with the shuttle.

The railways have refused to refund the price of the unused tickets but have issued fresh tickets for tomorrow.

DISCOVERIES OF INDIA; REVIEWS OF IMAGINARY BOOKS

The Mahabharata: Translated by U. M. Desai and the Sony Mule; Oxbridge University Press; Rs 500.

Reviewed by S. K. Padmanaja

This is the first translation of a world classic done by a word processor. We should all be proud that an Indian epic was chosen for this singular honour.

In May 1982, Masuru Ibuka, president of Sony, Japan, invited two of our top computer scientists, Dr L. P. Radhakrishnan and Dr U. M. Desai, to programme the original Mahabharata for his company's experimental word processor—the XQ-4—now marketed as the Mule. This word processor had been designed to translate and simultaneously convert the translation into a series of video games. Since the project was top secret, the word processor had been set up in Ibuka's own home.

Mission accomplished. Eighteen games, each representing the eighteen days of the Mahabharata war, are now on the US market. India has culturalised New York. While long queues wait to see *Gandhi*, gangs of youths, calling themselves either the Kurus or the Pandavas, fight it out on the streets. The book is a by-product of the games.

I am not competent to judge the accuracy of the translation but it takes longer to read than the comic.

The book does not mention Dr Radhakrishnan as co-author though, as I said earlier, he was invited to be part of the programme. Overanxious to please, as many of our scientists are, he began work on it before he was properly briefed. Unfortunately, the buttons he began punching in Ibuka's home were not those of the experimental word processor but of an experimental food processor. As Dr Desai points out, he was on his third hamburger when he noticed his colleague was missing and has dedicated this volume to his memory.

Assorted Peelings: Anjalie Eapen; New Scholars Inc; Rs 25
Reviewed by Sheela Bose

This is the third edition of a worthless book. First published in 1968, it consists of two essays. The first is a study of Shakespeare's food habits. Little is known about them but that doesn't prevent Dr Eapen from flinging her profuse peelings—and how little assorted they are—into our face. Her astonishing conclusion, based on the flimsiest evidence and much tendentious reasoning, is that he ate his food raw. Fond of fruit as he was, he was fonder of fruit bats. Puck in *A Midsummer Night's Dream* is a manifestation of the fruit bat (*Pteropus giganteus*) liberally found in the hills around Bombay during the time Shakespeare wrote. This leads her to conclude in her second and even more tendentious essay that Shakespeare wasn't an Englishman at all but a gifted tribal from those very hills.

Wiser counsels cannot deter the likes of Dr Eapen. Her reputation is secure. She has been called 'our finest Shakespearean scholar' in these very columns (see *Debonair*, July 1982) by a foolish writer who uses her idiocies to buttress his own. No, Dr Eapen, Puck is not a manifestation of *Pteropus giganteus* but of *Desmodus rotundus* which flock in the jungles of Bengal. I have no desire to argue with a person of her calibre but it should be self-evident to all thinking Indians that Shakespeare was a Bengali.

My Discovery of India: Edna Worple; The Ostrich Press, Rs 730
Reviewed by Lt Gen K. P. Rao (retd)

The author was already sixty when she decided to see India. Leaving her husband to look after the sheep at their farm in Queensland and driving a battered but sturdy Land Rover, she headed west. Mrs Worple had not left her farm before. She had not been to any big city. She had not even seen the sea.

Her first encounter with the sea, just off Perth, is described with some warmth. It did not deter her. Rescued by lifeguards, the Land Rover finally salvaged, she soon found a passage for herself and her vehicle on board a Greek cargo vessel bound for India. A dreadful storm turned the ship upside down, causing its crew to perish. But the author, strapped to her seat in the Land Rover which, in turn, was trapped down in the hold, managed to survive for twelve ghastly upside-down days before the ship was finally sighted and towed as it was to our shores.

Mrs Worple refused medical aid on being discovered and instead set off at a fast lick across our country, travelling from the southernmost tip to the north.

Though her prose is that of an unlettered person and her attitude often childlike, it is refreshing to read a foreigner who hasn't come to India to do dirt on the country but genuinely to discover it. She speaks with enthusiasm of our highways, our electronics industry and our transport systems; she even finds our cities clean.

There is a lesson in this for all of us, particularly our youngsters who, too prone to the pleasures of our cities, miserably lose the will to travel and discover India for themselves. India is in her villages, said Mahatma Gandhi and Mrs Worple's description of her stay in one of them should make us hold our heads high even as we gird our loins for the tasks ahead.

One minor bit of criticism though. Mrs Worple is niggardly with place names and though her descriptions of our mountains and jungles are eminently readable, we wish we knew where they were. Her village she calls Toyota but where is it? From her description of its inhabitants, presumably in Sikkim. And surely the 'Chigoku Sanchi range' she crosses in the middle of her journey is a misprint. The publishers should have checked.

NO REPLY

We have erred in subscribing to your magazine *Gay Pony*. We thought it had to do with horses. Some of our inmates are greatly distressed. Kindly cancel our subscription.

Cecily D'Costa
Secretary
Bandra Old People's Home
Mumbai

Dear Husband,
    Your letter did arrive. Apparently the postal service on your island is better than you thought. It's a bit of a bother. I'll have to ask the suitors to be on their best behaviour. Right now, Fido is sniffing a pair of your socks so he should be able to recognise you.
    Expect you on the 4th.
    Penelope.

Despite our request to cancel our subscription, you have sent us a fresh issue of your magazine. Kindly cancel our subscription and do not send us any more issues.
    Cecily D'Costa

To the Director,
National Museum of Antiquities, Cairo

Dear Mr Badawi,
    You have sent us an extremely old lady instead of the mummy we expected. She says her name is Tehmina al-Fayad. She claims to have fallen asleep in your museum and has no idea of what happened to her until she woke up in ours. Owing to the gullibility of some of our staff

she had already been on display for a few hours before she woke up. You may imagine the consequences.

We have preserved the crate in which you so carefully packed her and we can arrange to crate her back but please do send us the mummy we require.

C. V. Rahimtoolah
Director,
Central Museum of Antiquities
Hyderabad

We must once again ask you to stop sending us fresh issues of your magazine. They've had a deleterious effect on the morals of our inmates, some of whom are very old. We have admitted our mistake in taking out a subscription. How many times must we do so before you stop?
 In God's name, stop.
 DO NOT SEND US ANY MORE ISSUES!
 Cecily D'Costa

WE DO NOT WANT YOUR MAGAZINE. DO YOU HEAR? WE DO NOT WANT IT WE DO NOT WANT IT WE DO NOT WANT IT WE DO NOT WANT IT WE DO NOT WANT IT!!!!
 Cecily D'Costa

Dear Dad,
 Thanks for leaving me alone. The generals are so proud of me. I think they're going to get me to try the Chakravyuha tomorrow. Wish me luck.
 Love,
 Abhimanyu

ACKNOWLEDGEMENTS

Grateful thanks to the many editors who accepted or commissioned the work included in this book.

I dedicate my part in it to my wife Veronik; to Yogi Aggarwal, who ran Associated News Features and for whom I wrote for many years; to Darryl D'Monte and to the late Eliane D'souza, a Frenchwoman and close friend of Veronik's who provided me with space in her flat to use as my day-time study when it was necessary.

I am deeply grateful to Jerry Pinto, without whose enthusiasm, editorial judgement and hard work this book wouldn't have been possible.

ADIL JUSSAWALLA

SOURCES

EDITOR'S NOTE:

The pieces here were written in the main, for specific newspapers and magazines. However, there was a period of time when Adil Jussawalla wrote a column for Associated News Features that was syndicated in several newspapers across the country. These included *Deccan Herald*, *Lokmat Times*, *The Afternoon Despatch & Courier*, *Newstime* and the *Maharashtra Herald*. The newspapers carried the pieces on different days, depending on when they carried their review sections or their literary pages. We have retained the date on the clipping that we used in order to facilitate any further research. We have also appended the acronym ANF to that source so as to make things clearer.

ANF = Associated News Features
TOI = *Times of India*
STOI = *Sunday Times of India*
ADC = *Afternoon Despatch & Courier*
IWI = *The Illustrated Weekly of India*
DH = *Deccan Herald*

WRITERS

Six Authors in Search of a Reader: *Express Magazine*, 19 July 1981

Introduction to *Fair Tree of the Void* by Vilas Sarang: *Fair Tree of the Void*, (New Delhi: Penguin Books India, 1990)

Salman and the Sea of Paper: *India Today*, 28 February 1994

The Civilized Malcontent: *Debonair*, late 1979 or early 1980

Aubrey Menen: A Space of His Own: *Debonair*, July 1991

Notes Towards a Portrait of Nissim Ezekiel: *The Sunday Observer*, 12 December 1999

With Daya Pawar in Paris: ADC, 4 October 1996, ANF

Remembering Raman: DH, 1 August 1993, ANF

Remembering Sudhir: ADC, 7 April 1995

WRITING

The Joy of Sensuous Writing: *Fantasy*, Annual 1993
What's this? A New Two-nation Theory?: ADC, 16 August 1997, ANF
Between Vikram and the Vacuum: DH, 21 March 1993, ANF
The Ant in Publishing: ADC, 24 March 1995, ANF
Who Reads Us?: *Gentleman*, June 1997
The Book Should Be the Thing: *Indian Review of Books*, October 1992

READING

C is for Comics: DH, 14 March 1993, ANF
Library Memories: DH, 24 January 1993, ANF
Who Is My Neighbour?: 'The Sunday Review' of STOI, date uncertain, 1993 from internal evidence
Who Needs Novels?: *Debonair*, December 1988

AT HOME

A Glass Too Many: *The Daily*, 31 March 1996
Maps for a Mortal Moon: *Sunday Herald*, 1 February 2004
In Praise of Straggling: *The Sunday Observer*, 12 November 2000
The Cuffe Link: STOI, 2 August 1992
A Stranger in the Village: *The Daily*, 21 July 1996
Dead Man with Butterfly: *The Daily*, 3 Oct 1996
Show Me the Way to go Home: *The Daily*, 15 September 1996
Starting from Scratch: *The Sunday Herald*, 14 December 2003

TRAVELLING

Sandstorm at Sea: *The Daily*, 14 July 1996
Geography Lessons: *Jetwings*, Issue 7
Memories of a Book Fair: ADC, 13 March 1992, ANF
Letter from Venice: 5 November 2000, dated from an original typescript
Let Sleeping Passports Lie: *The Daily Sunday*, 14 April 1996
On Fire: *The Sunday Observer*, 4 November 2000
Toni Morrison, Paris and Me: *Lokmat Times*, 31 October 1993, ANF
Patterns of Domicile: *Debonair*, February 1988
Out of Place: *Gentleman*, February 2001
A Grave in the Hills: *Debonair*, November 1987

BEING HUMAN

Republic of Victims: *Sunday Herald*, 23 November 2003. ANF

The Heart of Standing Is: *Gentleman*, February 1998

Part of an Education: Unpublished work, written in 1965

A Balancing Act: *Newstime*, 30 July 2000

The Worst Thing About Being Human: *Maharashtra Herald*, 14 July 1996 ANF

Humanist Fires: *The Daily*, 21 April 1996

Who Are You Calling Mad?: 'The Sunday Review' of the STOI, 6 February 1994

Uprooted: Date uncertain, ANF

Boycott: *The Sunday Observer*, 20 August 2000

Visibility Zero: STOI, 2 January 1994

Incident in Paris: *Debonair*, April 1984

PEOPLE

Conversation with an Invisible Man: *The Times Weekly*, 13 August 1972

Two Sisters: *The Sunday Standard Magazine*, 31 August 1980

The Gambler: STOI, 16 April 1995

The Librarian and the Labyrinth: *The Sunday Standard Magazine*, 5 October 1980

The Many Murders of Datta Samant: *The Daily*, 19 January 1997

THE ARTS

Lalitha Lajmi and the Family: catalogue essay written for the artist's show 'The Family' at Gallery Chemould, Mumbai, Jan-Feb 1986

Souza: DH, 13 April 2002, ANF

Naipaul's Fiction and Rembrandt's Goose: *Sunday Herald*, 1 Febnruary 1998, ANF

Candour and Secrecy: *Debonair*, pp 62 to 67 and 75, date not stated. Issue when price rose to Rs 4.50 from Rs 3.50

Make Mine Movies: *Filmfare*, June 1994

The Showgirl and the Baby: IWI, June 20-26, 1992

MEDIA

The Joys of Xerox: ADC, 30 August 1991, ANF

The New India, the New Media and Literature: The text of the Sixth

Sophia Wadia P.E.N. Literary Fund Lecture, delivered on 10 December 1984

Radio Days: *Deccan Herald*, 18 September 1994, ANF

Death of a Journalist: *Deccan Herald*, 3 October 1999, ANF

The Folds of an Origami Lotus: ADC, 6 June 1999, ANF

LANGUAGE

Rainbow of Languages: *The Daily*, 28 April 1996

Getting on in English: ADC, 24 May 1996, ANF

Being There: Aspects of an Indian Crisis: *The Bombay Literary Review*; A Journal of the Department of English University of Bombay, 1989; later published in almostisland.com, Monsoon 2010 issue. Originally a paper presented at ACLAS, Singapore, 1986.

POETRY

Preface to *3 Poets*: Silgardo, d'Gama Rose, Rodrigues: *3 Poets*, New Ground, 1978, Bombay

Small Beginnings: *Sunday Herald*, 30 March 2003, ANF

Readings with Parrots and Angels: *Sunday Observer*, 15 August 1999

Poems after Ayodhya: ADC, 12 February 1993, ANF

Shut Up, Memory: *Gentleman*, May 1997

AUTOBIOGRAPHICAL

A Destination of the Heart: TOI, August 15, 1997, written for 'India at 50', special series

A Life Presumed Lost: *Parsiana*, 21 April 2012

A Place in the Sun: *Parsiana*, 7 November 2007

Black Moon Rising: *The Daily*, 12 May 1996

When Earth Rose Up To Get Me: *Gentleman*, May 1996

Take Me in the Sky of Your Hands: *Gentleman*, June 1996

JOKES APART

Portrait of a Lady: *Debonair*, December 1982

The None O'Clock News: Selection from *The Sunday Observer*, 1999 end to January 2000

Discoveries of India: *Debonair*, June 1983

No Reply: *Gentleman*, August 2001